MARY SHELLEY

FRANKENSTEIN

OR

THE MODERN PROMETHEUS

EDITED WITH AN INTRODUCTION
AND NOTES BY MAURICE HINDLE

PENGUIN BOOKS

PENGUIN BOOKS

Published by the Penguin Group
Penguin Books Ltd, 27 Wrights Lane, London W8 5TZ, England
Penguin Putnam Inc., 375 Hudson Street, New York, New York 10014, USA
Penguin Books Australia Ltd, Ringwood, Victoria, Australia
Penguin Books Canada Ltd, 10 Alcorn Avenue, Toronto, Ontario, Canada M4V 3B2
Penguin Books India (P) Ltd, 11, Community Centre, Panchsheel Park, New Delhi – 110 017, India
Penguin Books (NZ) Ltd, Private Bag 102902, NSMC, Auckland, New Zealand
Penguin Books (South Africa) (Pty) Ltd, 5 Watkins Street, Denver Ext 4, Johannesburg 2094, South Africa

Penguin Books Ltd, Registered Offices: Harmondsworth, Middlesex, England

First published 1818
First published in Penguin Classics 1985
This edition published 1992
25

Introduction and notes copyright © Maurice Hindle 1985, 1992
All rights reserved

The facsimile of the title page of the 1818 edition on page 1 is reproduced
by kind permission of the British Library

The moral right of the editor has been asserted

Set in 10/12 Monophoto Baskerville
Printed in England by Clays Ltd, St Ives plc

Except in the United States of America, this book is sold subject
to the condition that it shall not, by way of trade or otherwise, be lent,
re-sold, hired out, or otherwise circulated without the publisher's
prior consent in any form of binding or cover other than that in
which it is published and without a similar condition including this
condition being imposed on the subsequent purchaser

HAZLEHEAD ACADEMY

PENGUIN  CLASSICS

FRANKENSTEIN

MARY SHELLEY was born in London in 1797, daughter of William Godwin and Mary Wollstonecraft, famous radical writers of the day. Mary's mother died tragically ten days after the birth. Under Godwin's conscientious and expert tuition, Mary's was an intellectually stimulating childhood though she was emotionally undernourished. In 1814 she met and soon fell in love with the then unknown Percy Bysshe Shelley, and in July they eloped to the Continent. In 1816, after Shelley's first wife Harriet committed suicide, Mary and Percy married. Of the four children she bore Shelley, only Percy Florence survived. They lived in Italy from 1818 until 1822, when Shelley drowned, following the capsize of his boat *Ariel* in a storm. Mary returned with Percy Florence to London, where she continued to live as a professional writer until her death in 1851.

The idea for *Frankenstein* came to Mary Shelley during a summer sojourn in 1816 with her husband on the shores of Lake Geneva, where Lord Byron was also staying. She was stimulated to begin her unique tale after Byron suggested a ghost story competition. Byron himself produced 'A Fragment', which later inspired his physician John Polidori to write 'The Vampyre: A Tale'. Mary completed her story back in England and it was published as *Frankenstein, or, The Modern Prometheus* in 1818. Among her other novels she wrote *The Last Man*, a dystopic story set in the twenty-first century (1826), *Perkin Warbeck* (1830), *Lodore* (1835) and *Falkner* (1837). As well as contributing many stories and essays to publications such as the *Keepsake* and the *Westminster Review*, she contributed many biographical essays for Lardner's *Cabinet Cyclopaedia* (1835, 1838–9). Her other books include the first collected edition of P. B. Shelley's *Poetical Works* (1839) and a book based on the Continental travels she undertook with her son Percy Florence and his friends, *Rambles in Germany and Italy* (1844). Mary Shelley died in London on 1 February 1851.

MAURICE HINDLE was born at Great Barr, in the old county of Warwickshire, England. He studied at the universities of Keele,

Durham and Essex, gaining a Ph.D. in Literature from Essex in 1989. He currently teaches for the Open University. As well as producing editions of *Frankenstein*, *Caleb Williams* and *Dracula* for Penguin Classics, he has edited Godwin's last two novels *Cloudesley* (1830) and *Deloraine* (1833) for Pickering and Chatto's *Collected Novels and Memoirs of William Godwin* (1992). He is currently working on the life and writings of the early nineteenth-century chemist and poet Humphry Davy.

CONTENTS

INTRODUCTION

There is something at work in my soul, which I do not understand.
(Captain Walton, in *Frankenstein*)

As a cautionary tale warning of the dangers that can be cast into society by a presuming experimental science, *Frankenstein* is without equal. Mary Shelley's cleverly inspired theme of an uncontrollable creature wreaking vengeful destruction upon the heads of his monomaniacal scientific Creator and his world is sustained in a way that makes the book a powerfully unique presence in English literature. Much of the book's power came from being conceived, worked out and partially written while the author was living in the awesome surroundings of the French Alps in the exhilarating and challenging company of Romantic poets Lord Byron and Percy Bysshe Shelley. Its arrival was also helped along by Mary's desire to make her mark as a writer; she succeeded, but at the cost of making her hero–villain and his unnamed Creation (the two have been mythically woven into one by the modern popular mind) more famous than herself.

She set out in her story to 'speak to the mysterious fears of our nature and awaken thrilling horror'. Notwithstanding her youth and inexperience, the novel that resulted, based on her dream of 'the pale student of unhallowed arts kneeling beside the thing he had put together' (Author's Introduction, p. 9), has become the most enduring 'ghost story' of all time, if not (in Northrop Frye's words) 'a precursor of the existential thriller'. When the book first appeared in 1818 reviews were unfavourable, but Sir Walter Scott wrote that '. . . the author seems to us to disclose uncommon powers of poetic imagination . . . It is no slight merit in our eyes, that the tale, though wild in incident, is written in plain and forcible English, without exhibiting that mixture of hyperbolic Germanisms with which tales of wonder are usually told ... Upon the whole, the work impresses us with a high idea of the author's original genius and happy power of expression.'* The Tory *Quarterly Review*, on the other hand, declared that the novel 'inculcates no lesson of conduct, manners, or morality ... it fatigues the feelings without interesting the understanding; it gratuitously harasses the heart, and only adds to the store, already too great, of painful sensation ... the reader [is left] after a struggle between laughter and loathing, in doubt whether the head or the heart of the author be the most diseased'.† Such venomous comment came, not because the book failed to inculcate a lesson of 'conduct, manners, or morality' – its moral lesson that pride must have its fall should be obvious to the most indifferent reader – but because *Frankenstein*'s anonymous publication was 'respectfully inscribed' to William Godwin, Mary Shelley's father and infamous philosophical radical of the anarchist Left. In fact, most reviewers assumed the work's author to be Percy Shelley, Mary's husband, since to the world he was Godwin's best-known literary disciple. But *Frankenstein* is far from being a straightforward celebration of 'Godwinian rational principles'. Implicit in the novel's moral, if not overtly political, message are the questions: What kinds of action can be defended as reasonable? What are we to make of the discrepancy between the 'mad' scientist's reason, and the 'Godwinian' reason exercised by his 'hideous progeny'? Such philosophical subtleties were lost on most critics, who preferred to see in *Frankenstein*, as Mrs Piozzi did, nothing more than 'a wild and hideous tale'.

At any rate, *Frankenstein* became an immediate bestseller. When the second edition appeared in 1823, reviewers were quite thrown to find that the author had been a woman. *Blackwood's* exclaimed: 'For a man it was excellent, but for a woman it was wonderful.'‡ Even Lord Byron, not noted for his great admiration of intellect in *young* women (he made an exception in Mary Shelley's case), told his publisher John Murray: 'Methinks it is a wonderful work for a girl of nineteen – *not* nineteen, indeed, at that time.' Mary

---

* *Blackwood's Edinburgh Magazine*, March 1818.
† *Quarterly Review*, March 1818.
‡ *Blackwood's Edinburgh Magazine*, March 1823.

Shelley herself in her 1831 Author's Introduction repeats the question 'so very frequently asked' before attempting to answer it: 'How I, then a young girl, came to think of and to dilate upon so very hideous an idea?' The answer she gives is more detailed and candid in its way than one probably has a right to expect from an author. Yet it still tells us little about the young Mary Shelley herself. For one critic it is the *fact* of her youth that supplies the clue to *Frankenstein*'s power. Muriel Spark, in her study of the author, *Mary Shelley* (Constable, London, 1988), says of the novel that 'perhaps the wonder of it exists, not despite Mary's youth, but because of it. *Frankenstein* is Mary Shelley's best novel, because at that early age she was not well acquainted with her own mind.'

Because of her youth at the time of her writing *Frankenstein*, some 'admirers' of Mary Shelley have somehow managed to praise her work only by presenting her talent as a fortuitous refraction of the 'genius' possessed by her then virtually unknown love-partner and companion, Percy Shelley. We shall see later that in more ways than one, there is indeed much of Percy Shelley 'in' *Frankenstein*. The book remains, however, the product of Mary Shelley's own intuitive genius, even if biographical, literary and philosophical factors influencing her outlook were left indelibly 'fixed' in the story. It was her astonishing ability to synthesize these factors into a vital whole that makes the achievement so remarkable. To one of these factors, the biographical, we now turn.

MARY SHELLEY'S LIFE UP TO THE WRITING OF *FRANKENSTEIN*

Mary Shelley was born on 30 August 1797 at 29 The Polygon, in London's Somers Town district, near what is now Euston. Both of her parents were famous radicals of the day. Mary Wollstonecraft, her mother, was a pioneer feminist writer who had made her name with *A Vindication of the Rights of Woman* (1792), despised by the public at large for the attention it drew to women's second-class status in society and admired for the same reasons by the radical intelligentsia of the day. William Godwin, Mary Shelley's father, was an ex-Dissenting minister turned atheist who had leapt from obscurity to fame with his celebrated attack on 'positive institution', *Enquiry Concerning Political Justice* (1793). So influential were Godwin's political and moral ideas for a period that the essayist William Hazlitt was to comment later that 'he blazed as a sun in the firmament of reputation; no one was more talked of, more looked up to, more sought after, and wherever liberty, truth, justice was the theme, his name was not far off'.* Both Godwin and Wollstonecraft had been heavily influenced by the ideals of the French Revolution and were part of that small radical group centred on Joseph Johnson's publishing house (it included such people as Blake and Thomas Paine) known as the 'English Jacobins'. Mary Shelley, the offspring of a famous (some thought infamous) union, would later remark: 'It is not singular that, as the daughter of two persons of distinguished literary celebrity, I should very early in life have thought of writing.'

After seeming to fly in the face of their own views on marriage as 'a system of fraud' sustaining 'the most odious selfishness' (Godwin), Mary Shelley's parents married. Mary Wollstonecraft was pregnant and Godwin wished to protect her happiness, 'which I have no right to injure' since otherwise nothing 'could have induced me to submit to an institution which I wish to see abolished'.† But the partnership in which both fiercely individualistic members seemed to have found an unexpected happiness was short-lived, for, a little over five months after they married, Mary Wollstonecraft died of puerperal poisoning contracted following the birth of their daughter, Mary. Godwin, at the height of his powers, reputation and happiness, was utterly bereft. The trials of birth and death so central to *Frankenstein* were to become living torments for nearly half of Mary Shelley's life too, with the early deaths of three of her four children and the losses of Percy Shelley and Byron compounding successive agonies into a feeling of unendurable isolation, which only the nurture and thought of her one surviving son, Percy Florence, would relieve.

---

* 'William Godwin', in William Hazlitt, *The Spirit of the Age*, ed. E. D. Mackerness (Collins, London, 1969), pp. 35–6.

† C. Kegan Paul, *William Godwin: His Friends and Contemporaries* (1876). Vol. 1. p. 240.

Though Godwin was never to recover the zest for life he had found in the company of Mary Wollstonecraft, he nevertheless felt that a substitute mother should be found for 'the poor children', since he himself was 'totally unfitted to educate them'. He was openly frank about the 'scepticism which perhaps sometimes leads me right in matters of speculation [but] is torment to me when I would attempt to direct the infant mind. I am the most unfit person for this office; she was the best qualified in the world.' As with most men who claim 'unfitness to direct the infant mind', he felt an urgent concern about providing life proposals and solutions in the *abstract*, but shrank from getting too involved in the tiring and emotionally challenging (as well as hazardous) occupations of child rearing at close quarters.

Two years later, at the age of forty-five, the philosopher–novelist decided to marry his next-door neighbour, Mrs Mary Jane Clairmont, who, we are told, boldly wooed the famous man with the words, 'Is it possible that I behold the immortal Godwin?' She and one of her two daughters, Jane, were to be the bane of Mary Shelley's life for many years. Mary had never known a mother and she would not find a caring or thinking one in the new Mrs Godwin. But from the start, Mary was made aware of being the unique progeny of extraordinarily gifted and famous parents. To her father she became exceptionally attached, and this feeling remained throughout her life even though (as we shall see later) she had decidedly reserved views on revolutionary, or even 'liberal', politics. In letters to friends she talked of 'my excessive and romantic attachment to my father' and said that 'Until I met Shelley I could justly say that he [Godwin] was my God ... I remember many childish instances of the excess of attachment I bore him.' Unfortunately, as she also mentioned, her father was nearly always emotionally cool and distant. Even so, he had high expectations of her, as she quickly learnt: 'To be something great and good was the precept given me by my Father,' she wrote in her Journal: 'Shelley reiterated it.'

If the emotional side of her rearing was neglected, intellectual stimulus for what her father considered her 'considerable talent' was not wanting. She grew up, and remained, a bookish person believing that 'we are sent here to educate ourselves, and that self-denial, and disappointment, and self-control, are a part of our education'. It seems likely that such a 'self-controlling' outlook was to a large degree the necessary product of her father's rigorous, Calvinist-influenced philosophy; that, and a life which became replete with 'disappointments' and 'self-denials'. Although declining in popularity as the new century grew less and less enamoured of Godwin's brand of rational philosophy, his house was yet visited by some of the most famous writers and artists of the day. Mary Godwin would have listened keenly to her father's conversations with such people as William Hazlitt, Samuel Taylor Coleridge, Humphry Davy and Charles Lamb, whose *Tales from Shakespeare* was published by the Godwins' small publishing house, run from their new home in Skinner Street, near Holborn. It is told that when Mary and Jane hid behind a sofa to hear the poet Coleridge recite his *Rime of the Ancient Mariner* (a poem that greatly influenced Mary's *Frankenstein* story), and Mrs Godwin threatened to pack them off to bed, Coleridge intervened, pleading that they be allowed to stay and listen. Godwin practised to the best of his ability his famous 'benevolence' with Mary, but her upbringing, though successful in terms of intellectual growth, was for the most part a peculiarly detached affair. Mrs Godwin seems to have added her own brand of distant caring, for Mary wrote at the age of seventeen: 'I detest Mrs G. She plagues my father out of his life.'

It must have been with great joy then that she experienced the relief of some extended periods away from Skinner Street and its pressures. The opportunity for true companionship and freedom from her bookish existence and 'distant' family came when an admirer of Godwin's, a wealthy merchant called William Baxter, invited Mary for a long stay with his family at their home near Dundee, in Scotland. She made her first great friend here in young Isabel Baxter and it was the place where, as she says in *Frankenstein*'s Introduction, she discovered an 'aerie of freedom ... the pleasant region where unheeded I could commune with the creatures of my fancy'. In a letter to Mr Baxter, Godwin gives us a good idea of Mary's character: 'I am anxious,' he begins, 'that she should be brought up ... like a philosopher, even like a cynic. It will add greatly to the strength and worth of her character. I should also observe that she has no love of dissipation, and will be perfectly satisfied with your woods and your mountains.' But Mr Baxter should be warned of her tendency to 'formation of castles in the air: I wish, too, that she should be *excited* to industry. She has occasionally greater perseverance, but occasionally, too, she shows a great need to be aroused . . .' In another letter, Godwin contrasted Mary with her 'indolent' step-sister, Fanny Imlay (the offspring of a liaison Mary Wollstonecraft had with Gilbert Imlay before meeting Godwin), by describing the former as 'singularly bold, somewhat imperious, and active of mind. Her desire of knowledge is great, and her perseverance in everything she undertakes almost invincible. My own daughter is, I believe, very pretty . . .'*

When Mary returned to the Godwin household in 1814 she came face to face with the man who, after her father, was to exercise the greatest influence over the rest of her life – Percy Bysshe Shelley. Shelley, a hot-headed but eloquent Romantic of nineteen, had attached himself to Godwin as a disciple, often visiting Skinner Street with his young wife Harriet. His ardent hatred of tyranny and his idealistic political notions had caused him to be drawn as though by a magnet towards Godwin's *Political Justice*, and thence to the ageing philosopher's own house. The half-forgotten philosophical radical must have more than welcomed the attentions of the young man who considered him 'a luminary too dazzling for the darkness which surrounds him';† for, as well as helping to reactivate the philosopher's flagging ego with his 'reverence and admiration', this well-born youth's sincere wish to follow Godwinian principles of property-sharing meant that he would be more than ready to donate much of his forthcoming baronet's fortune to the ever-needy Godwin. The boundless generosity of 'the heir by entail to an estate of £6,000 per an' (as he announced himself in his initial letter to Godwin) was to be tried severely in future years, for though Godwin demanded and accepted much money from Shelley, he could never accept the fact of his daughter's elopement with a married man and their

---

* For both letters, see Spark, *Mary Shelley*, pp. 14–17.
† Kegan Paul, *William Godwin*, Vol. 11, pp. 213–14.

life as 'vagabond' exiles on the Continent. But that is what happened.

In May 1814 Percy dined at Skinner Street to discuss money matters with Godwin. The blooming but poised intellectual young woman of sixteen that Mary Godwin had become attracted him from the first.* By the end of June, Percy was a daily visitor to the Godwin house, with Harriet his wife virtually abandoned (she later committed suicide). On their frequent walks to Mary Wollstonecraft's graveside at St Pancras Churchyard, Mary and Percy, sometimes accompanied at a distance by Jane Clairmont, began to declare their love for each other. Shelley's 'child of love and light' was to have a profoundly tranquillizing influence on his volatile existence. There is no doubt that he was awed by her unusual combination of qualities – sharp intellect, intuition, generosity, strength of determination – awe that developed into an abiding love, as the following extract from the lines dedicating his poem *The Revolt of Islam* 'To Mary Wollstonecraft Shelley' (they married in December 1816) shows:

> So now my summer task is ended, Mary,
> And I return to thee, mine own heart's home;
> As to his Queen some Victor Knight of Faery,
> Earning bright spoils for her enchanted dome . . .

On 28 July 1814 Mary and Percy eloped to the Continent. With them went Jane, now styling herself 'Claire' Clairmont. Though Claire only came along for the adventure, Mary and Percy had been forced to escape from a Godwin outraged by his daughter's amorous entanglement. The following year was later to be described by Mary as 'acting a novel, being an incarnate romance'. But the Continental 'adventure' was a miserable affair. Though Mary turned this to useful literary account in her *History of a Six Weeks' Tour Through a Part of France, Switzerland, Germany and Holland* (1817), the threesome found little enjoyment as they

---

* For what appears to be a 'pen portrait' of herself at this time, see Appendix A, Vol. One, 77.17–21, where Frankenstein describes Elizabeth on his return from Ingolstadt University.

wandered from European town to town, friendless and with little money. Moreover, Mary found the presence of Claire virtually intolerable. Towards her middle age she wrote: 'Now, I would not go to Paradise with her for a companion – she poisoned my life when young . . . she has still the faculty of making me more uncomfortable than any human being.' At the end of the summer they returned to England, Mary and Percy taking up lodgings which Shelley hardly lived in, pursued as he was by creditors (his father having withheld his allowance), and Mary estranged from her own family. In February 1815 Mary's first child was born prematurely, dying a few days later, unnamed. It was the first of many deaths that were to cast a dark shadow over her existence. Some days after the baby died, Mary wrote in her Journal: 'Dream that my little baby came to life again; that it had only been cold, and that we rubbed it before the fire, and it lived.' There are uncanny echoes of resemblance here to the dream-inspired Frankenstein Creature, who also 'came to life' from the dead. In August Mary and Percy moved to Bishops Gate, Windsor, where in January 1816 their son William was born. He was to survive for a further three and a half years.

Just under a year later, in May 1816, Mary, Percy and Claire set out on their second Continental trip, this time with William. They headed for Geneva, settling there at Campagne Chapuis, a cottage on the shores of Lac Léman and adjacent to the rather grander Villa Diodati, where Lord Byron, having quitted England for good, had also decided to set up house. We get a good indication of Mary's state of mind at this period from a letter she wrote early in her Alpine sojourn: 'You know that we have just escaped from the gloom of Winter and London; and coming to this delightful spot during this divine weather, I feel as happy as a new fledged bird, and hardly care what twig I fly to, so that I may try out my new-found wings.' During the fine days of early June, the Diodati and Chapuis house-parties spent much time together, in the evenings sailing on the lake, 'which is delightful', Mary reported, 'whether we glide over a glassy surface or are speeded along by a stormy wind'. But the fine weather did not hold. Mary Shelley's *Frankenstein* Introduction tells us that it eventually 'proved a wet, ungenial summer, and incessant rain often confined us for days to the house'. It was during one of these 'confinements' spent, as had become customary, talking late into the night at Byron's villa, that all the elements came together in the mind that was to produce *Frankenstein*. The group, consisting of Mary, Percy, Byron, Claire and Polidori (Byron's personal physician), had been reading German ghost stories in French translation when Byron suddenly announced: 'We will each write a ghost story.' All agreed. Percy started a tale about his early life, which apparently soon fizzled out. Byron began a story about a vampire,* which Polidori later developed and published.† Only Mary and Claire could not think of anything.

Inspiration did not come easily to Mary: 'I thought and pondered – vainly. I felt that blank incapability of invention which is the greatest misery of authorship, when dull Nothing replies to our anxious invocations. "Have you thought of a story?" I was asked each morning, and each morning I was forced to reply with a mortifying negative.' But revelation was at hand. Among the topics of conversation during those nights following Byron's proposal, one in particular seems to have caught her imagination. The ever-reticent Mary recalls that one of the 'many and long conversations between Lord Byron and Shelley, to which I was a devout but nearly silent listener', turned upon the 'nature of the principle of life, and whether there was any probability of its ever being discovered and communicated'. Polidori's diary entry for 15 June – 'Shelley and I had a conversation about principles – whether man was to be thought merely an instrument' – is further evidence that thoughts concerning the mysterious powers animating life were prominent in the minds of the Diodati and Chapuis residents that summer. In her Author's Introduction Mary Shelley says that talk of Dr Erasmus Darwin's experiments and 'galvanism' led to speculations that 'the component parts of a creature might be manufactured, brought together and endued with vital warmth'. With such thoughts in her mind Mary went to bed, but 'When I placed my head on my pillow, I did not sleep, nor could I be said to think. My imagination,

---

* Printed here as Appendix B.
† For a discussion of this and an account of Polidori's life see Appendix C.

unbidden, possessed and guided me, gifting the successive images that arose in my mind with a vividness far beyond the usual bounds of reverie.' That summer's intense intellectual excitements now arrived at a historic climax as young Mary Godwin witnessed the fruition of her own mental labours in a scene that showed a gruesome congruity with her efforts:

> I saw – with shut eyes, but acute mental vision – I saw the pale student of unhallowed arts kneeling beside the thing he had put together. I saw the hideous phantasm of a man stretched out, and then, on the working of some powerful engine, show signs of life, and stir with an uneasy, half-vital motion [Author's Introduction, p. 9].

She then goes on to utter words (cast, be it noted, in a religious vein, *contra* Shelley and Godwin) to the effect that we, ever alert to the thermonuclear threat that we have brought on ourselves cannot help but see as shockingly prophetic, if not prescient: 'Frightful must it be; for supremely frightful would be the effect of any human endeavour to mock the stupendous mechanism of the Creator of the world.'

Towards the end of this essay I shall comment further upon the 'presumptions' of science and its dominantly masculinist promoters. For now it should merely be noted that in Mary Shelley's vision she proposed that the success of her scientist-hero in animating a corpse

> would terrify the artist; he would rush away from his odious handywork, horror-stricken. He would hope that, left to itself, the slight spark of life which he had communicated would fade; that this thing which had received such imperfect animation would subside into dead matter; and he might sleep in the belief that the silence of the grave would quench forever the transient existence of the hideous corpse which he had looked upon as the cradle of life. He sleeps; but he is awakened; he opens his eyes; behold, the horrid thing stands at his bedside, opening his curtains and looking on him with yellow, watery, but speculative eyes [Author's Introduction, p. 9].

'With speculative eyes': the Creature wants to *know*, just as we want to know, where he has come from and why he is here. Mary did not know, but was so terrified that she 'wished to exchange the ghastly image of my fancy for the realities around'. This she did and opened her eyes, but 'I could not so easily get rid of my hideous phantom'. According to her description in the Author's Introduction, she did not immediately connect the horrific 'waking dream' with her need to invent a ghost story – evidence, if any were needed, that this subject-matter was entirely new, different from the outworn stock-in-trade themes and imagery in 'Gothic' novels of the time. But suddenly, 'Swift as light and as cheering was the idea that broke in upon me. "I have found it! What terrified me will terrify others; and I need only describe the spectre which had haunted my midnight pillow." On the morrow I announced that I had *thought of a story*. I began that day with the words, "It was on a dreary night of November," making only a transcript of the grim terrors of my waking dream.'

The full text of this first sentence of the original story starts Chapter V, Volume One of the edition printed here: 'It was on a dreary night of November, that I beheld the accomplishment of my toils.' Percy Shelley was delighted that Mary had started to put together a story of promise and, as she wrote on, encouraged her to develop it to novel-length. This she did, and except for the Preface, and the additions and stylistic modifications to the text made by Percy, the book that was finished in May 1817 after they had returned to England, and finally published less than a year later in January 1818, was all of her own making. Indeed, in an 1817 pre-publication review of *Frankenstein* (which actually appeared only posthumously in 1832) Percy Shelley himself expressed wonder and bafflement concerning the book's conception, feelings which there is no reason to suppose were anything other than genuine and candid:

> [*Frankenstein* is] one of the most original and complete productions of the day. We debate with ourselves in wonder, as we read it, what could have been the series of thoughts – what could have been the peculiar experiences that awakened them – which conduced, in the author's mind, to the astonishing combinations of motives

and incidents, and the startling catastrophe which compose this tale.*

THEMES, SOURCES AND INFLUENCES IN *FRANKENSTEIN*

A reliable measure of the general mood from which *Frankenstein* emerged in that 'ungenial' Swiss summer of 1816 is provided, not by Mary Shelley, but by Lord Byron, in a letter he wrote to a friend six months later: 'I was half mad . . . between metaphysics, mountains, lakes, love unextinguishable, thoughts unalterable and the nightmare of my own delinquencies.' Polidori, another witness to this heightened mood, confided to his diary in the midst of it that the whole company 'talked, till the ladies' brains whizzed with giddiness, about idealism'. There seems little doubt that, as P. D. Fleck has asserted, Mary Shelley's *Frankenstein* expresses 'her view of the idealism that whizzed giddily about her head' that summer and also that it is a novel which 'contains in an imaginative form her criticism of [Percy] Shelley'.† The Romantic idealism of Shelley and his 'overreaching' heroes was, like all idealisms, based on a faith in man's, or more correctly, *men's* 'divine' or creative powers. It is Mary Shelley's critique of where such highly *abstracted* creative powers can lead when put in a 'realizing' scientific context and then driven along by 'lofty ambition' and 'high destiny' (p. 204) that we see in the pages of *Frankenstein*.

A number of passages in the book seem to reveal Percy Shelley as the initial model for its ultra-ambitious hero, quite apart from the fact that Victor, Frankenstein's first name, was the name Shelley took for himself a number of times in boyhood and later. Captain Walton, the novel's narrator and himself cast as an overreacher voyaging out for the glory of discovering 'the wondrous power which attracts the needle' and the 'undiscovered solitudes' of new countries, finds Frankenstein to be a 'divine wanderer' whose 'eyes have generally an expression of wildness, and even madness (pp. 14, 13, 28, 25). But as with Shelley's other, more sub-

* P. B. Shelley, 'On *Frankenstein*', *Athenaeum*, 10 November 1832.

† P. D. Fleck, 'Mary Shelley's notes to Shelley's poems and *Frankenstein*'. *Studies in Romanticism*, VI, 4 (1967).

lime side, 'no one can feel more deeply than he does the beauties of nature. The starry sky, the sea, and every sight afforded by these wonderful regions, seems . . . to have the power of elevating his soul from earth' (p. 28). We know well from Mary's (and others') descriptions of her life with Percy that 'such a man has a double existence: he may suffer misery and be overwhelmed by disappointments, yet when he has retired into himself, he will be like a celestial spirit that has a halo around him, within whose circle no grief or folly ventures' (p. 28). A technique habitually employed by Percy for creating this halo was one shared by Frankenstein: 'I lay at the bottom of the boat, and as I gazed on the cloudless blue sky, I seemed to drink in a tranquillity to which I had long been a stranger' (p. 150).

It is curious that in a letter Percy wrote to Mary Shelley during their time in Italy (he was often 'away from home' during their eight years' partnership) he referred to *Frankenstein* as 'fruits of my absence', for, as Christopher Small has pointed out, he did more than urge Mary on in her writing of the book (answering that 'need to be aroused' claimed for her by Godwin), 'He provided the subject.'* Yes; the 'subject' in terms of Percy Shelley's characteristic 'passion for reforming the world', and the 'subject' of his 'mad enthusiasm', science (in particular, chemistry) – both are brought together in the person of Frankenstein, or the 'Shelleyan Idea', as Christopher Small puts it. If we are never given a physical description of Frankenstein (apart from his 'wild eyes'), his whole presentation as Shelleyan Idea clearly comes through, if not through the pen of Mary Shelley herself, then more directly by the insertions and changes made by Shelley and adopted by the author. (Some of these, the longest dealing with 'scientific' and 'political' sequences, are indicated in Appendix A.) It is the forcefulness of this Shelleyan Idea in Frankenstein that probably led to Shelley's disclaimer on Mary's behalf in the Preface: 'The opinions which naturally spring from the character and situation of the hero are by no means to be conceived as existing always in my own conviction . . .'

---

* Christopher Small, *Ariel Like a Harpy: Shelley, Mary and Frankenstein* (Gollancz, London, 1972), p. 101.

Shelley's friend Thomas Jefferson Hogg says that in his youth Percy bought and experimented with chemical apparatus and materials and read 'treatises on magic and witchcraft, as well as those more modern ones detailing the miracles of electricity and galvanism'.* He further recalls that at Oxford, Shelley

> proceeded, with much eagerness and enthusiasm, to show me the various instruments, especially the electrical apparatus; turning round the handle very rapidly, so that the fierce, crackling sparks flew forth; and presently standing on the stool with glass feet, he begged me to work the machine until he was filled with the fluid [i.e. electricity, Ed.], so that his long, wild locks bristled and stood on end. Afterwards he charged a powerful battery of several large jars; labouring with vast energy and discoursing with increasing vehemence of the marvellous powers of electricity, of thunder and lightning; describing an electrical kite that he had made at home, and projecting another and an enormous one, or rather a combination of many kites, that would draw down from the sky an immense volume of electricity, the whole ammunition of a mighty thunderstorm; and this being directed to some point would there produce the most stupendous results.†

It is almost as if Shelley were providing film-makers of the future with that 'thunder and sparks' image of electrical reanimation of the Creature which has become so standard a feature of Frankenstein films. His interest in such things never waned, science in particular attracting what we might call his 'alchemical spirit'. In his visionary *Queen Mab* we are told that 'Happiness/And Science dawn, though late, upon the earth ...'‡ But the same poem reveals another interest which will tend to become a dark obsession, one that Mary is well aware of: 'How wonderful is Death ... the gloomy Power/Whose reign is in the tainted Sepulchres ...'§ For Mary, this atmosphere of gloomy fascination was reinforced

---

* Thomas Jefferson Hogg, *The Life of Shelley* (London, 1858), I, p. 33.
† Ibid., pp. 70–71.
‡ P. B. Shelley, *Queen Mab* 8, ll. 230–31.
§ ibid., I, ll. 1–10.

as she transcribed the third Canto of Byron's *Childe Harold* for him in July 1816. But if Byron's production had this effect, Shelley's *Alastor, or The Spirit of Solitude* presents us with a theme remarkably similar to that of *Frankenstein*, and we can be sure that the latter's composition was influenced by it. The heroes of Shelley's poems (as with Lord Byron's) are often hardly distinguishable from their creator, so that in *Alastor* we meet a youthful poet who 'drinks deep of the fountains of knowledge, and is still insatiate'. He is gripped, as was Shelley, by the idea that the 'principle of life' is somehow to be found by probing into what he considers the chief 'mystery of nature' – death and decay. He addresses his beloved Mother Nature, saying:

> ... I have watched
> Thy shadow, and the darkness of thy steps,
> And my heart ever gazes on the depth
> Of thy deep mysteries. I have made my bed
> In charnels and on coffins, where black Death
> Keeps record of the trophies won from thee;
> Hoping to still these obstinate questionings
> Of thee and thine, by forcing some lone ghost,
> Thy messenger, to render up the tale
> Of what we are.

When we go on to read

> In lone and silent hours,
> When night makes a weird sound of its own stillness,
> Like an inspired and desperate alchymist
> Staking his very life on some dark hope,
> Have I mixed awful talk and asking looks
> With my most innocent love ... *

we can be sure that a good part of Frankenstein's ambitious persona has its origin here. Mary Shelley has Frankenstein say, in

* P. B. Shelley, *Alastor*, ll. 20–34. This poem was published a few months before *Frankenstein* was started.

his more 'scientific' vein, that 'To examine the causes of life, we must first have recourse to death' (p. 50). He thus determines to 'observe the natural decay and corruption of the human body'; but 'to examine the cause and progress of this decay' he is 'forced to spend days and nights in vaults and charnel-houses' (p. 50). Of course, the 'lone ghost' produced by Frankenstein's meddlesome researches and experiments turns out in the end to be a rather unwelcome 'messenger', a visible reminder of his own 'enthusiastic madness'. Mary Shelley was not alone in having doubts about what she called Percy's 'abstract imagination', for the writer Hazlitt thought of his poetry as 'a record of fond conjectures, a confused embodying of vague abstractions – a fever of the soul, thirsting and craving after what it cannot have, indulging its love of power and novelty . . .'*

It seems highly likely that the epistolary form of *Frankenstein*, which adds so much to its stark drama, was adopted by Mary Shelley through her reading of the originator of that novelistic form, Samuel Richardson. In 1815 she had read his seven-volume *Clarissa Harlowe* (1748) and in 1816 she read the 'latter part' of it again, as well as two other novels, *Pamela* (1741) and *Sir Charles Grandison* (1754). Another favourite writer of Mary's was Madame de Genlis, whose *Nouveaux Contes moraux et nouvelles historiques* (1802) she was reading on the evening following her momentous visit with Percy Shelley to the Mer de Glace in Chamonix Valley, in July 1816. One of the dramatic sketches in the book is 'Pygmalion et Galatée, ou La Statue animée depuis vingt-quatre heures', which Burton Pollin assumes to have stimulated Mary Shelley's 'inspirational nightmare'.† As well as being a story in which the figure that Pygmalion has sculpted is animated into life, the pure and ingenuous Galatea learns (as Frankenstein's Creature is later to learn), about the shocking realities of slavery, tyranny, extremes of poverty and wealth, and deception.‡

---

* William Hazlitt, 'Review of Shelley's *Posthumous Poems*', *Edinburgh Review*, July 1824.

† Burton R. Pollin, 'Philosophical and literary sources of *Frankenstein*', *Comparative Literature*, XVII, 2 (1966), p. 100.

‡ibid., p. 101.

It follows, from Mary's having read 'La Statue animée', that we need look no further than the novel's sub-title – *The Modern Prometheus* – to discover *Frankenstein*'s main theme: the aspiration of modern masculinist scientists to be technically creative divinities. Who was Prometheus? There are two versions of the Prometheus story, which Mary Shelley manages to combine into one. The first and most famous is that in which the Prometheus of Greek mythology, a rebellious Titan, steals fire from Olympus in order to succour and save humankind. It was these two aspects of the story – his revolt against the gods, against 'destiny', and his desire to be the benefactor and saviour of humanity – that drew both Byron and Percy Shelley, but especially the latter, to the Promethean legend. Mary, Percy and Byron had all read Aeschylus's *Prometheus Bound*, and in 1816 Byron wrote his own *Prometheus*. But Shelley took the story to heart in a monumental way, developing to a fine pitch the Romantic notion of himself and his heroes as suffering champions of humanity. In *Prometheus Unbound* and other poems he was to elaborate this essentially religious feeling of election to saviourhood into his own version of socialist aspiration. But it was not this element of her lover's missionary zeal that called forth the novelistic response of *Frankenstein*. The later, Roman, elaboration of the Promethean legend rendered by Ovid (whose *Metamorphoses* she had been reading in 1815), has Prometheus as *plasticator*, a figure who *creates and manipulates* men into life, rather than 'saves' them:

> Whether with particles of heavenly fire,
> The God of Nature did his soul inspire;
> Or earth, but new divided from the sky,
> And, pliant, still retain'd th'ethereal energy:
> Which wise Prometheus temper'd into paste,
> And, mix't with living streams, the godlike image caste . . .
> From such rude principles our form began;
> And earth was metamorphosed into man.*

---

* Ovid, *Metamorphoses*, trans. Dryden, quoted in Pollin, 'Philosophical and literary sources of *Frankenstein*'.

Rather than take up Ovid's 'ethereal energy' speculation, Mary Shelley chose to focus on the 'particles of heavenly fire' aspect, the means whereby Prometheus quickened his clay images into life. As we know, the 'real' means by which she imagined life could be bestowed on an assembled corpse in her book was through the 'galvanizing' use of electricity. Humphry Davy, an early scientist and radical, was a famous chemist whom Percy Shelley admired, as he did the poet–botanist Erasmus Darwin, and who had been a visitor to the Godwin household in Mary's childhood. It was books by Davy, his *Elements of Chemical Philosophy* (1812) and an earlier publication, *A Discourse, Introductory to a Course of Lectures on Chemistry* (1802), that Mary was reading in October and November of 1816. The tone and content of some of Davy's views will repay attention, as they embody much the same message that Frankenstein was so entranced by in the momentous 'panegyric on chemistry' delivered by Professor Waldman at Ingolstadt University. Davy claims that 'science has done much for man, but it is capable of doing still more'.* More specifically Waldman feels that 'chemistry is that branch of natural philosophy in which the greatest improvements have been and may be made' (p. 48). When he claims that the modern masters of science have acquired 'unlimited powers', Frankenstein's whole being is numbed as if by sudden religious conversion:

> . . . soon my mind was filled with one thought, one conception, one purpose. So much has been done, exclaimed the soul of Frankenstein, – more, far more, will I achieve; treading in the steps already marked, I will pioneer a new way, explore unknown powers, and unfold to the world the deepest mysteries of creation [p. 47].

Familiar rhetoric to watchers of Frankenstein films today, but quite new in Mary Shelley's day. The voice of the 'real' scientist, Humphry Davy, is not far behind (or rather, in front) in its enthusiasm:

* Humphry Davy, *A Discourse, Introductory to a Course of Lectures on Chemistry* (1802), p. 17.

Science has ... bestowed upon [man] powers which may be called almost creative; which have enabled him to change and modify the beings surrounding him, and by his experiments to interrogate nature with power, not simply as a scholar, passive and seeking only to understand her operations, but rather as a master, active with his own instruments ... who would not be ambitious of becoming acquainted with the most profound secrets of nature; of ascertaining her hidden operations; and of exhibiting to man that system of knowledge which relates so intimately to their own physical and moral constitution?*

From the evidence of *Frankenstein*, of course, we know that Mary Shelley was not ambitious in that way, for one, and in fact sought to warn the world away from those dangers inherent in the type of attitude Davy was espousing.

It was, then, the Promethean 'maker', 'artist', 'shaper' of men in a scientist–hero guise that interested Mary Shelley, and which should preoccupy us; for is it not the modern experience of feeling manipulated by forces larger than ourselves (which are nevertheless humanly managed) – Big Science, technology, the 'machinery' of State, international business empires, the mass media, and so on – that links the lay person's predicament with that of Frankenstein's Creature, he who has been put together from dead human parts and then infused with 'a spark of being', without having any say in the form or purpose of his own genesis? As the product (Mary Shelley was living in the 'new age' of capitalist production) of a Proud Creator, the Creature is not unlike Adam in Milton's *Paradise Lost*, who reproaches God with his handiwork:

> Did I request thee, Maker, from my clay
> To mould me Man, did I solicit thee
> From darkness to promote me . . .?†

* ibid., p. 16.
† John Milton, *Paradise Lost* 10, ll. 743–5.

These lines of supplication, the epigraph to the 1818 edition of *Frankenstein*, are a major clue to the atmosphere of the book, just as Milton's re-working of the Biblical 'Fall' story is a felt presence and underlying reference throughout it. Mary Shelley had grown up in a house where Milton was required and revered reading, had read *Paradise Lost* and *Paradise Regained* twice during 1815 and 1816, and Byron's Villa Diodati, where the 'half mad' talk of the Geneva summer sowed the seed of her story, was a house where she knew Milton had actually once stayed. It is perhaps not surprising that a woman of Mary Shelley's intuitive capacities, living in a rapidly changing society, should call on Milton for guidance and inspiration, for he was a man who had himself lived through a historical period of enormous religious, political and existential turbulence and written an epic poem in response to it.

In using the Promethean motif for her novel, she had virtually declared herself to be dealing with a problem that had an enormously long and deep provenance in the West, stretching back to fifth century BC Greece. But the Miltonian scheme of God–man estrangement reaches back nearly as far, to the beginnings of Christianity. As long ago as the third century, the Manichaean Adam, like those of Milton and Mary Shelley, had uttered a wail of recrimination at discovering his own 'creatural' mortality:

> Then Adam cried and lamented: terribly he raised his voice like a roaring lion, tore his dress, smote his breast and spoke: 'Woe, woe unto the shaper of my body, unto those who fettered my soul, and unto the rebels that enslaved me,'*

When Frankenstein's Creature, baffled by his own existence, asks: 'My person was hideous and my stature gigantic. What did this mean? Who was I? What was I? Whence did I come? What was my destination?' (p. 125) he is unable to find an answer. Not only this, but even the plight of Milton's Satan seems mild compared

---

* Theodor bar Konai, *Liber Scholiorum* XI, tr. A. Yohannan, in A. V. W. Jackson, *Researches in Manichaeism* (New York, 1932). Quoted in Hans Jonas, *The Gnostic Religion* (Beacon Press, Boston, 1959), p. 87.

to his, for 'Satan had his companions, fellow-devils, to admire and encourage him; but I am solitary and abhorred' (p. 127). For the second-century Valentinian gnostic, a psycho-spiritual 'escape route' was available: 'What liberates is the knowledge of who we were, what we became; where we were, whereinto we have been thrown; whereto we speed, wherefrom we are redeemed; what birth is, and what rebirth.'* 'He who possesses the Gnosis, knows whence he is come and where he is going.'† This route to the Unknown Father of Light is not there for the utterly rejected and unnamed Creature of Frankenstein: in fact, through reading Frankenstein's Journal, which he has pocketed after quitting his Creator's house, he discovers that the 'disgusting circumstances' of his 'accursed origin' (p. 126) reveal more of a Father of Darkness at work. All he really knows of any consequence to his future is that 'I am malicious because I am miserable' (p. 140). The formulation Mary Shelley has given the Creature to utter is not gratuitous, however, but derives from two other sources – Rousseau and, in particular, Godwin, to whom *Frankenstein* was dedicated.

Mary Shelley had read Rousseau's *Confessions* (1782), but perused *Émile* (1762) and the *Nouvelle Héloïse* (1761) several times between 1815 and 1817. It was Rousseau who had secularized the idea of an unfallen state of innocence, that which Frankenstein's Creature supposedly enjoys before becoming corrupted by the evil ways of society and its people. The idea was then taken up in England in a slightly different form by William Godwin in his *Political Justice*. He believed that 'positive institutions' like government, the law and marriage tended to insinuate despotic practices into people's lives, but that a new system, based on 'universal benevolence', could create a just and virtuous society. Where would this 'virtue' come from? He insisted it would naturally emerge from the exercise of reason and free will, as developed in an 'enlightened' society. Such an enlightened society

---

* Clement of Alexandria, *The Excerpta ex Theodoto*, ed. and tr. R. P. Casey (1934). Quoted in Jonas, p. 45.

† *Gospel of Truth*, ed. and tr. Malinine, Puech and Quispel (1956). Quoted in Jonas, p. 89.

would have shed the superstitions of religion, the despotisms of government and the property fetishes attached to marriage and inheritance, for all these tended towards the establishment of selfishness, division and malevolence. Godwin, contradicting the seventeenth-century Hobbesian view of human nature as essentially 'self-interested', held that virtue and happiness could only spring from *socially* considered and constituted aims: 'the true solitaire cannot be considered as a moral being ... His conduct is vicious, because it has a tendency to render him miserable.' If this is true, then it is no wonder that the most solitary of 'solitaires', Frankenstein's Creature, abandoned by his Creator and rejected by the society around him, considers himself (echoing the Satan of *Paradise Lost*) 'the fallen angel' become 'a malignant devil ... I am alone' (p. 213). Like 'son', like 'father': it has been Frankenstein's gross error to decide with idealistic pride that *he alone* can put the world to rights through scientific experiment and the pursuit of knowledge: by 'building in' this disenfranchisement of the 'others' and the contributions and needs they bring to living reality, the Creature's subsequent isolation becomes a foregone conclusion, for, as the Creature tells Frankenstein, 'you, my creator, detest and spurn me, thy creature, to whom thou art bound by ties only dissoluble by the annihilation of one of us' (p. 96). In a passage which reveals Godwin's own Enlightenment insight into the dangers of putting the 'abstracted' pursuit of knowledge before collective responsibility and happiness, he makes his own prophetic contribution to a matter that is more urgent today than ever before: 'knowledge, and the enlargement of intellect, are poor, when unmixed with sentiments of benevolence and sympathy ... and science and abstraction will soon become cold, unless they derive new attractions from ideas of society.'*

Seven central chapters of *Frankenstein* are given over to the plight of Frankenstein's Creature. He tells the story of his outcast existence to his Creator following their encounter on the Mer de Glace. It is ironic that the Creature's narrative, so vital to the moral underpinning of the whole work, has been ignored in the

* William Godwin, *Enquiry Concerning Political Justice*, (Penguin, 1985), p. 300.

numerous theatrical and filmic re-workings of the story. Like the Godwinian philosophy which fell from favour so quickly after receiving feverish applause from the radical community, the moral–political argument of Mary's story has simply been left out, unwanted by an audience which prefers the more frightening (and 'simpler') grunts of a threatening monster. But the Creature's explanation of himself and his doings is a key demonstration of Godwinian social–psychological theory and in turn derives from the influential philosopher John Locke, another *Frankenstein* source to whom I shall refer more fully below. At the end of his tale the Creature tells the person he considers his 'natural lord and king' (p. 96) that 'My vices are the children of a forced solitude that I abhor; and my virtues will necessarily arise when I live in communion with an equal' (p. 142). He repeatedly asks for 'justice' in this Godwinian sense: 'Do your duty towards me, and I will do mine towards you and the rest of mankind' (p. 96). In a fit of compassion, Frankenstein promises to make the Creature a female companion, but then destroys this new creation, convinced that 'a race of devils would be propagated upon the earth' (p. 160). The Creature avenges this betrayal, murdering both Frankenstein's best friend Clerval and his new wife, Elizabeth; the rest involves Frankenstein's mad pursuit of the Creature across icy wastes, where they both eventually meet their deaths.

Besides using Godwinian ideas in her story, Mary Shelley very carefully applied the psychological sensationalist notions developed by John Locke which had been taken up with such zeal by French *philosophes* of the eighteenth century like Diderot and Condillac. Condillac was the most extreme exponent of sensationalism, while another materialist *philosophe*, La Mettrie, proposed in *L'Homme machine* (1748) 'a machine which can no longer be regarded as impossible, especially in the hands of a new Prometheus'.* During

---

* Quoted by Mario Praz in his Introductory Essay to *Three Gothic Novels* (Penguin, 1968), p. 29. It is interesting to note that the term 'modern Prometheus' was in use long before *Frankenstein* appeared. As early as 1709 Lord Shaftesbury (whom Mary Shelley did not read until 1825) talked of 'our modern Prometheus's the *Mountebanks*', and in the late eighteenth century the philosopher Immanuel Kant dubbed pioneer scientist of electricity Benjamin Franklin 'the new Prometheus'.

the year she was working on *Frankenstein* Mary Shelley devoted much of her reading time to Locke's *Essay Concerning Human Understanding* (1690). From November 1816 to January 1817 she imbibed Locke's *tabula rasa* theory of knowledge and applied it to the way the Creature attained to a 'knowing' personhood. The Creature plays out the Lockean theory to perfection by gaining all his ideas from sensation or reflection, seeking or avoiding the causes of sensation according to whether they produce pleasure or pain. The Creature explains:

> It is with considerable difficulty that I remember the original era of my being; all the events of that period appear confused and indistinct. A strange multiplicity of sensations seized me, and I saw, felt, heard, and smelt at the same time; and it was, indeed, a long time before I learned to distinguish between the operations of my various senses. By degrees, I remember, a stronger light pressed upon my nerves, so that I was obliged to shut my eyes [p. 99].

But when he gets used to light (a 'sensation' we shall have more to say about shortly) he finds he can 'perceive objects in their right forms' (p. 100). In the last words of the Creature, spoken to Captain Walton at the end of the book, we find ample evidence of the author's use of sensationalism: 'I shall no longer see the sun or stars or feel the winds play on my cheeks. Light, feeling, and sense will pass away' (p. 214). Cleverly (some might think not so cleverly), Mary Shelley manipulates the plot to her Lockean view by having the Creature learn the language, history, ideas and morals of the world by eavesdropping upon the fortuitously placed De Lacey household and reading *Paradise Lost*, Plutarch's *Lives* and the *Sorrows of Werter*, other fortuitous finds. He learns, along with the Arab girl Safie (possibly named after the Sophie of Rousseau's *Émile*), of 'the division of property, of immense wealth and squalid poverty; of rank, descent and noble blood' (p. 116). Such learning makes him reflect on his own position in, or rather outside, society. When he puts his new 'class-consciousness' to the test by declaring himself to the blind De Lacey, one's hopes for the Creature are raised, only to be interrupted and then dashed as the horrified eyes of Felix, Safie and Agatha (recalling the Agatha of Lewis's *The Monk*?) 'light' upon him. Ironically, it is the sensation of light and sight which at first so delights the Creature that now turns him into a vengeful murderer, for 'from that moment I declared ever-lasting war against the species, and more than all, against him who had formed me and sent me forth to this insupportable misery' (p. 132). Had Felix and his friends been able simply to *listen* to the Creature with understanding, without being overcome by his appearance, then we would not have had the *Frankenstein* Mary Shelley actually wrote.

Is Mary Shelley then asking us to think more carefully about a society which values appearance above a 'seeing' that should take into account the Other's feelings and needs? At any rate, if 'appearance' was to become a complex moral problem to negotiate in a society habitually unconcerned with 'seeing' the wants, needs and aspirations of other people, it, and especially the medium by which it reaches us, *light*, was nevertheless all-important to the Romantics of Mary Shelley's time, including herself. It is reputed that, on his death-bed, the English land- and sea-scape painter J. M. W. Turner declared: 'The sun is god.' The preoccupation with light did not end with Romantic painters and poets either, for Humphry Davy's approach to chemistry and life was based upon beliefs concerned with light and heat, as his famous paper, 'An Essay on Heat, Light, and the Combination of Light' makes clear. According to David Knight in the *Dictionary of Scientific Biography*, Davy believed that 'light within and without us is the source of perception, thought and happiness'. He also suggested that '*electricity might be condensed light*, given off at the poles as auroras' (my italics), which not only explains why, at the beginning of *Frankenstein*, Captain Walton aspires to visit the North Pole where he believes 'the sun is for ever visible' (p. 13), but once again provokes the thought that perhaps some yearning kinship exists between the gnostic poet-mythologists of antiquity and those of Mary Shelley's epoch.* In both periods, light was an exalted

---

* The American scholar Paul Cantor has made a similar observation: 'The parallels between authentic Gnostic and Romantic myths are often so striking that one is tempted to assume direct influence.' Paul A. Cantor, *Creature and Creator: Myth-making and English Romanticism* (CUP, 1984), p. x.

term denoting Divinity, for the gnostics an 'Unknown God', for the Romantics a presence 'known' through Nature; with the 'divine spark' of gnosis being the spiritual equivalent to the 'animating principle' which gave Frankenstein's Creature his 'light of being' via galvanic electricity. In a Journal entry made in February 1822, five months before her beloved Percy drowned at sea, Mary Shelley vowed that she would 'fearlessly descend into the remotest caverns of my own mind, carry the torch of self-knowledge into its dimmest recesses; but too happy if I dislodge any evil spirit or enshrine a new deity in some hitherto uninhabited nook'.

The remaining principal literary sources for and influences on *Frankenstein* should be mentioned. Coleridge's *Ancient Mariner*, to which Captain Walton attributes his 'passionate enthusiasm for . . . the dangerous mysteries of ocean' (p. 19), is alluded to throughout the novel. Like the Mariner, Walton sets out for 'the land of mist and snow', but assures his sister Margaret that he 'shall kill no albatross' (p. 19): this task is reserved for Frankenstein, since it is he who has the deadly weight of guilt hanging round his neck. The whole purpose of Frankenstein's narrative is of course to dissuade Walton from pursuing a 'fatal' course that will assuredly bring him his own burdensome albatross: he hopes that Walton will 'deduce an apt moral from my tale' (p. 29), and tells him, 'Learn my miseries and do not seek to increase your own' (p. 203). A stanza from Coleridge's poem, one that is said to have caused Percy Shelley to faint in terror, is quoted by Frankenstein as he wanders in a nightmarish daze following his Creature's 'birth'. He feels

> Like one, that on a lonesome road
> Doth walk in fear and dread,
> And having once turned round walks on,
> And turns no more his head;
> Because he knows, a frightful fiend
> Doth close behind him tread (p. 58).

This episode establishes the grim and relentless theme of pursuit between Creator and Creature that occupies the rest of the book. It seems plain that this pursuit theme was influenced very heavily by Mary Shelley's reading (for at least the third time) in 1816 of her father's famous *Caleb Williams* (1794). Percy Shelley was the first to notice the influence. In his posthumous review of *Frankenstein* he wrote: 'The encounter and argument between Frankenstein and the Being on the sea of ice, almost approaches, in effect, to the expostulations of Caleb Williams with Falkland. It reminds us indeed, somewhat of the style and character of that admirable writer, to whom the author has dedicated his [*sic*] work, and whose productions he seems to have studied.' Frankenstein does indeed seem to embody the characteristics of many of Godwin's sinful heroes. Caleb Williams himself claims that 'My offense had merely been a mistaken thirst for knowledge'; while his antagonist–pursuer Falkland suffers 'an impatience of imagined dishonour', an 'eminently mischievous' fault that leads him from pure motives of love into destructive hate.

Does one not detect here some very basic novelistic pattern, one that begins with another book which produced, as with *Frankenstein*, a mythical character – Cervantes' *Don Quixote* (1604)? Both Don Quixote and Frankenstein start out with the noble intention of helping their fellow-creatures, but their aspirations are doomed by their pursuit of a 'single vision', one that takes them further and further away from satisfying the moderate needs of the community, and nearer and nearer to a personally tragic denouement. This theme of a hero lured into existential danger by the abstract torment of 'metaphysical desire' is one brilliantly formulated and treated by René Girard in his *Deceit, Desire and the Novel*.* It will come as no surprise to learn that *Don Quixote* was one of the books Mary Shelley was reading during the composition of *Frankenstein*. Walter Scott noticed in his review of the book that '*Frankenstein* is a novel upon the same plan with *St Leon*', Godwin's 'alchemical' novel, whose hero, a man of Faustian ambitions, makes a pact in which he takes the curse of immortality in

* René Girard, *Deceit, Desire and the Novel* (Johns Hopkins University Press, 1976).

exchange for the Philosopher's Stone and the Elixir of Life. He discovers, predictably, that he has doomed himself to a life of eternal solitude.

Charles Brockden Brown was a writer much affected by William Godwin's ideas, and whose *Wieland, or The Transformation* (1798), read in 1815 by Mary Shelley, seems to have influenced the form of *Frankenstein*. In the novel, Carwin, a ventriloquist whose ambitions and 'monsterish' appearance make him a kind of composite Frankenstein–Creature character, exercises his talent to such an extent that it produces frightening consequences. Wieland believes that the 'voice of God' Carwin has 'thrown' commands and authorizes him to commit murder – which he does repeatedly, until Carwin's conscience compels him to cure Wieland hypnotically with his 'voice': 'Shake off this phrenzy, and ascend into the rational and human. Be lunatic no longer,' he commands. In Frankensteinian vein, he is led to the reflection: 'had I not rashly set in motion a machine, over whose progress I had no control and which experience has shown me was infinite in power?' Mary Shelley almost certainly used another of Brown's ideas from his *Arthur Mervyn* (1799) – a virulent epidemic – as the central idea for her futuristic and monumental novel *The Last Man* (1826).

It would be appropriate to pause at this point, in what can easily become a 'hunt the source for *Frankenstein*' game, and consider (adapting an observation of Christopher Small's) that Mary Shelley never borrowed any *specific* elements for her story from the many authors she had read, but, rather, was ready to accept what her imagination offered her, influenced, as it must have been, by her literary experiences.

SCIENCE, POLITICS AND THE 'FRANKENSTEIN IDEA'

Frankenstein – Gothic novel or science-fiction story? There is little doubt that Gothic tales had an important impact on Mary Shelley's sensibility, just as they did on Percy's. Quite apart from the Gothic-influenced novels of her own father and those of Brockden Brown, we know from her Journal that between 1814 and 1816 she read Mrs Radcliffe's *The Italian* (1797) and *The Mysteries of*

Udolpho (1794), M. G. Lewis's *The Monk* (1796) and his *Romantic Tales* ('Monk' Lewis also visited the Shelley–Byron group in August 1816), two of the Rev. Charles Maturin's novels, and William Beckford's *Vathek* (1786), to mention only the more famous Gothic storytellers she looked at. It seems clear that one 'authority' at least, the author of *Vathek*, itself a Gothic 'classic', would have been reluctant to admit *Frankenstein* into the ranks of the genre, even though it borrowed somewhat from the theme of his own book, 'insatiable curiosity'. Beckford wrote on the fly-leaf to his copy of Mary Shelley's novel, 'This is, perhaps, the foulest toadstool that has yet sprung up, from the reeking dunghill of the present times.' This repugnance of Beckford's for *Frankenstein* obviously relates to Mary Shelley's unadorned style of realistic description, something that produced a new and far more loathsome horror than the type of Gothic horror effects Beckford had been used to. But his appalled reaction also lends us a clue in our research for a definition of *Frankenstein*'s literary type: whereas Beckford's villain–hero (Vathek) has an 'insolent desire to penetrate the secrets of heaven', Shelley's protagonist possesses 'a fervent longing to penetrate the secrets of *nature*' (p. 39 – my italics).

In the traditional Gothic tale the supernatural element remains intact and is the means by which the violator of accepted rules is punished, usually being consigned to 'eternal damnation', as in Maturin's *Melmoth the Wanderer*. But with *Frankenstein*, the all-embracing 'Nature' that eighteenth-century Europe had so much revered gets disturbed and plundered. The 'New Promethean' is no mere schemer or plotter of intrigues urged on by the promises held out by forbidden lusts and powers (as in Lewis's *The Monk*, for instance). It is Frankenstein's desire 'to penetrate the secrets of nature' (the sexual metaphor is no accident, as we shall see presently) through the appliance of the new masculinist-made god, Science, so that he can achieve his long-held desire to 'banish disease from the human frame, and render man invulnerable to any but a violent death' (p. 40), that so sets him apart from his hero–villain forebears. In *Frankenstein* the old God who for Newton had been the author and controller of Nature now falls silent in the overbearing presence of glory-seeking 'Victor' (so aptly, though ironically, named). He spells out in terms that have not dated since 1818 (rather the opposite) the attractions that belief in and commitment to the new deity can bring: 'None but those who have experienced them can conceive of the enticements of science. In other studies you go as far as others have gone before you, and there is nothing more to know; but in a scientific pursuit there is continual food for discovery and wonder' (p. 49).

But if science goes on, even after the trail-blazing efforts of Frankenstein are cut short (on his death-bed he makes the almost unbelievable comment, 'I have myself been blasted in these hopes, yet another may succeed'), Victor, by the joint control of Gothic-tale convention and the hand of Mary Shelley, must owe his demise to *some* almighty force – what shall it be? It is, simply, the trap of human guilt, so deeply embedded yet ever-sprung for self-punishing action in the Judaeo-Christian spirit – but with the comfort of the Divine Protector removed. This guilt is doubly burdensome for Frankenstein, for, since renouncing his soul and the 'Father of Heaven' (after, a little like Luther and his devils, 'grappling with a palpable enemy') in the pursuit of 'one thought, one conception, one purpose', he becomes a 'father' himself; but his child becomes his 'sin', a rejected fleshly being. Thus he is physically trapped by a self-imposed patriarchy-within-a-patriarchy, he being the primary victim. If, as Mario Praz has claimed, 'an anxiety with no possibility of escape is the main theme of the Gothic tales',* then *Frankenstein* certainly qualifies for the genre, since both antagonists in the book are 'inescapably' doomed to pursue each other to the death: Frankenstein in order to expiate the guilt arising out of his presumptuous 'act of creation', the Creature to avenge his absolute rejection by all. In the end, of course, the fates of both Creator and Creature become more and more intertwined, their identities merging as they approach death: hence the so-called *Doppelgänger* motif of the story. One is perhaps inclined eventually to agree with Muriel Spark that *Frankenstein* is the 'first of a new and hybrid fictional species, in which

---

* Mario Praz, in his Introductory Essay to *Three Gothic Novels*, p. 20.

the influential currents of two minds – Godwin representing the scientific empiricism of the eighteenth century, and Coleridge, the nineteenth century's imaginative reaction – meet.'*

That the Creature is nameless, and denied any kind of individuality or recognition because he is a product of and belongs wholly to his Creator, signifies to one interpreter of *Frankenstein*, Franco Moretti, that the story is one born of 'the fear of bourgeois civilization'.† Moretti's ingenious Marxist analysis sees Frankenstein as a 'disfigured wretch', symbol of the emerging industrial proletariat of the early nineteenth century. 'Between Frankenstein and the monster,' he says, 'there is an ambivalent, dialectical relationship, the same as that which, according to Marx, connects capital with wage-labour.' Be that as it may, it was not long after *Frankenstein* first appeared that Mary Shelley's Creation was being appropriated ('by the appropriators', Moretti would no doubt say) by Tory radicals enthusiastically seizing upon the 'godless monster' theme as a propaganda tool against the atheistic and revolutionary tendencies of the time. *Fraser's Magazine* of November 1830 said: 'A State without a religion is like a human body without a soul, or rather like an unnatural body of the species of the Frankenstein monster, without a pure and vivifying principle.' The use of the 'monster' metaphor for political ends became frequent in the 1830s, when the demands for democratic reform in England intensified. But conservatives had been using 'monster' imagery to warn of the dangers of reform since the French Revolution of 1789 and its aftermath, the Terror. Edmund Burke had been one of the first to use such imagery, denouncing, in his *Reflections on the Revolution in France* (1790), armed insurrection as a pernicious monster set free by experimenters and reformers.‡

---

* Spark, *Mary Shelley*, pp. 153, 159.

† Franco Moretti, *Signs Taken for Wonders* (Verso Editions and NLB, London, 1983), p. 83.

‡ My source for this discussion of the use of 'monster imagery' in politics is Lee Sterrenburg's thought-provoking essay, 'Mary Shelley's monster: politics and psyche in *Frankenstein*', in George Levine and U. C. Knoepflmacher (eds.), *The Endurance of Frankenstein* (University of California Press, Berkeley, 1982).

During their systematic efforts to understand the Revolution and its outcome in Napoleonic despotism, Mary and Percy Shelley read not only the works of radicals like Thomas Paine, Mary Wollstonecraft and William Godwin, but also conservatives and anti-Jacobins, among them Burke and Abbé Barruel. They would have read Burke's *Reflections* and imbibed the melodramatic shape and tone of his narrative, extremely effective in an age of 'sensationalism'. To give an example that in its florid imagery startlingly recalls that of the semi-paranoid antique gnostics, Burke warns that military democracy is a 'species of political monster, which has always ended by devouring those who have produced it'. Burke's Gothic sense of a 'radical intrinsic' spirit of evil at work in society could well be describing the emergence of Frankenstein's Creature when he goes on to say that, during the French Revolution,

> vice assumes a new body. The spirit transmigrates; and, far from losing its principle of life by the change of its appearance, it is renovated in its new organs with the fresh vigour of a juvenile activity. It walks abroad; it continues its ravages . . .*

Mary Shelley's parents, Mary Wollstonecraft and William Godwin, were notorious targets for political attack in which monster imagery was employed. Between 1796 and 1802, when the conservative reaction against him was at its height, Godwin was depicted as an odious and terrifying devil, bent on the destruction of society by attempting to reform it using 'godless' principles. Burke described Godwin's opinions as 'pure defecated atheism . . . the brood of that putrid carcase the French Revolution'. It appears entirely consistent, of course, that the Gothic-minded Burke, who saw a 'monster' behind every threat to the status quo, also wrote in his *Philosophical Enquiry* (1757): 'Whatever is fitted in any sort to excite the ideas of pain, that is to say, whatever is in any sort terrible . . . is a source of the sublime.' Horace Walpole, 'originator' of the Gothic-novel format (*The Castle of Otranto*,

---

* Quoted in Sterrenburg, 'Mary Shelley's monster', p. 154.

1764), must then have found something 'sublime' in Godwin's work, for he considered him to be 'one of the greatest monsters exhibited by history', while the leader in anti-Godwin/Wollstone-craft loathing, the *Anti-Jacobin Review*, execrated their disciples as 'the spawn of the monster'. Finally, Thomas de Quincey recalled in 1837 that 'most people felt of Mr Godwin with the same alienation and horror as of a ghoul, or a bloodless vampire, or the monster created by Frankenstein'. Though the 'monster tag' began slipping away from Godwin as his fame receded, it did not disappear, but began to be applied to those collective forces gathering to challenge the dominance of the upper classes in Parliament – the working class. From the time of *Frankenstein*'s publication in 1818, when Regency England faced 'the most widespread, persistent and dangerous disturbances, short of actual revolution and civil war, England has known in modern times',* the 'Frankenstein Monster' image was appropriated repeatedly to signal the threat 'revolting mobs' posed to an increasingly affluent bourgeois class. The image was commonly projected during the 1830s, a period of revolutionary scares and agitation for political reform. It resurfaced in 1848–9 when the Chartist movement was at its height, was evoked again in the late 1860s as some of the working class became enfranchised, and the 1880s saw a revived use of the monster metaphor in a political cartoon depicting 'The Irish Frankenstein', a giant ape-like figure (no accidental usage this, given the contemporary disgust with 'atheistical' evolu-tionary theory) threatening the Irish Nationalist leader Charles Parnell with a knife. Exploiting the master–slave reversal theme of Shelley's novel, Tenniel the cartoonist has the cringing figure of Parnell gasp out: 'The hateful and blood-stained Monster . . . yet was it not my Master to the very extent that it was my Creature? . . . Had I not breathed about my own spirit?'†

If 'Frankenstein's Monster' was so readily pounced on and used by Manichaean-minded conservative commentators, are we

* Frank Darvall, *Popular Disturbances and Public Order in Regency England* (Oxford University Press, London, 1934), p. 306.

† The cartoon is reproduced in Chris Baldick's *In Frankenstein's Shadow: Myth, Monstrosity, and Nineteenth-century Writing* (Clarendon Press, Oxford, 1987).

to suppose that Mary Shelley was herself a 'reactionary'? Things are by no means that simple, as *Frankenstein*, in many ways an enigmatic book, bears witness. Part of the answer to that enigma may be contained in the following extract from her Journal:

> Some have a passion for reforming the world; others do not cling to particular opinions. That my parents and Shelley were of the former class, makes me respect it. I respect such when joined to real disinterestedness, toleration and a clear understanding ... I earnestly desire the good and enlightenment of my fellow creatures ... but I am not for violent extremes, which duly bring on an injurious reaction. I have never written a word in disfavour of liberalism ... But since I had lost Shelley I have no wish to ally myself to the Radicals – they are full of repulsion to me – violent without any sense of Justice – selfish in the extreme – talking without knowledge – rude, envious and insolent – I wish to have nothing to do with them.

As well as perceiving the dangers of abstract idealism, Mary Shelley had in her own life been stung by the deaths of many close to her, so it is not surprising that she saw the possession of domestic happiness and good friends as something to be cherished above all else. Her moderate and peaceful ambitions are announced in *The Last Man*, when the autobiographical Verney says: '"This", I thought, "is Power! Not to be strong of limb, hard of heart, ferocious and daring; but kind, compassionate and soft."'

In his important book *Fathering the Unthinkable*, ex-nuclear physicist and science historian Brian Easlea detects in *Frankenstein* 'Mary Shelley's indictment of masculine ambition' and an exposure of 'the compulsive character of masculine science'.* This would indeed seem consonant with the Mary Shelley/Verney statement about 'power' quoted above. Easlea focuses much of his attention upon the sexual and parenting metaphors used by 'probing' scientists from the natural philosophers of the sixteenth

---

* Brian Easlea, *Fathering the Unthinkable: Masculinity, Scientists and the Nuclear Arms Race* (Pluto Press, London, 1983), pp. 28, 35.

century to the nuclear scientists of the present. He notes that Francis Bacon, the 'Patriarck of Experimental Philosophy', called on his fellow men to inaugurate with him 'the truly masculine birth of time', so as to achieve 'the domination of man over the universe'.* Easlea's point that such a universe was and overwhelmingly still is seen as a 'resisting female' who must be 'aggressively penetrated' and 'conquered' can hardly be denied. He quotes science historian Carolyn Merchant's description of how, from Bacon's time onward, 'official' attitudes towards Nature altered: 'The constraints against penetration associated with the earth-mother image were transformed into sanctions for denudation. After the Scientific Revolution *Natura* no longer complains that her garments of modesty are being torn by the wrongful thrusts of man.'† Humphry Davy, the Romantic New Scientist figure already encountered here, seemed rather excited at Chemistry's prospects, for: 'The skirt only of the veil which conceals these mysterious and sublime processes has been lifted up and the grand view is as yet unknown.'‡

Mary Shelley demonstrates her intuitive grasp that Frankenstein's presumptuous act of creating life marks an incestuous violation of what Easlea calls 'the mother nature his seventeenth-century predecessors declared dead and buried', in the scene where the Modern Prometheus's attempts to sleep after he has fled from the hideous Creature he has created become 'disturbed by the wildest dreams. I thought I saw Elizabeth, in the bloom of health, walking in the streets of Ingolstadt. Delighted and surprised, I embraced her, but as I imprinted the first kiss on her lips, they became livid with the hue of death; her features appeared to change, and I thought that I held the corpse of my dead mother in my arms . . .' (p. 57).

This startling image is perhaps an appropriate point at which to close, for it seems to contain the essence of a warning that we ignore today at our peril. The 'incestuous' violation of life on this

---

* Quoted in ibid., p. 19.
† ibid., p. 22.
‡ ibid., p. 28.

planet has reached epidemic proportions, and much of the blame for this state of affairs must be laid at the feet of those who find an endless thrill of excitement in scientifically 'penetrating' the 'secrets of nature', taking little or no responsible account of the damaging implications 'theory' might have for 'practice'. Too often it seems the lure of power, profit and a so-called 'security' of nations obscures any elements of 'real disinterestedness, toleration and a clear understanding' that may have been present at the beginning of a theoretical scientist's practical researches. We should perhaps hope that the 'sexy' lure of scientific penetration need not have the cold kiss of death waiting behind it. A nuclear-weapons-infested globe readily poised to destroy itself does all too easily seem like a threatening fulfilment of Mary Shelley's pro-phetic 'Frankenstein Idea'. But alternatives exist. The author of *Frankenstein* would surely have echoed the words of her Enlightenment-minded father William Godwin: 'Real knowledge is benevolent, not cruel and retaliating.'*

MAURICE HINDLE
London, 1991

* Godwin, *Enquiry Concerning Political Justice*, p. 405.

NOTE ON THE TEXT

The first edition of *Frankenstein* was published anonymously in 1818 by the London printers Lackington, Hughes, Harding, Mavor and Jones, and was in three volumes. A two-volume reprint of the first edition was issued in 1823, this time bearing Mary Shelley's name. The single volume third edition appeared as No. 9 in Colburn and Bentley's 'Standard Novel' series in 1831. The text printed here is based upon this third edition and contains all of Mary Shelley's final revisions.

Although preserving continuous pagination, I have felt it important to indicate the three-volume divisions of the original 1818 edition and employ its chapter numberings. This helps us to notice the Chinese box structure of the narrative-worlds-within-worlds of the book: first we hear from Captain Walton, then Frankenstein tells his tale, until, at the pivotal core of the novel in Volume Two, the Creature recounts his own moving story.

Since Mary Shelley made a large number of revisions in 1831 and it is valuable for readers to be able to compare the 1831 and 1818 editions, I have provided a collation between these in Appendix A, showing the major textual variants. Some of these are of great interest and call for some detailed comment.

In the first edition copy of her novel that she gave to Mrs Thomas in 1823 (now housed in the Pierpont Morgan Library of New York) Shelley made a number of autograph corrections, additions and marginal notes. At the end of Volume One, Chapter II, she writes, 'If there were ever to be another edition of this book, I should re-write these two first chapters. The incidents are tame and ill arranged – the language sometimes childish. – They are unworthy of the rest of the narration.' For the 1831 edition she not only rewrote these 'two first chapters', but also divided the original Chapter I into what becomes the new Chapters I and II, the old Chapter II now becoming Chapter III. The changes made for the two new chapters involved more than stylistic improvements, however, contrary to her claim in the 1831 Introduction that she had 'changed no portion of the story nor introduced any new ideas or circumstances.' (Nevertheless her assertion that the 'core and substance' of the story had been untouched by the changes is a substantially accurate one.)

The removal of some of the 'tame and ill arranged' incidents had (what I consider to be) the unfortunate effect of eliminating a certain amount of 'scientific' language from the text. In the Thomas copy Mary Shelley had noted the textual contradiction of Victor saying 'our family was not scientifical', when a few lines later he records how his father explained the principles of electricity to him and demonstrated them with a 'small electrical machine' he had built. She removes the difficulty by having 'a man of great research in natural philosophy' impart the scientific information instead of Alphonse Frankenstein. This may well have been the same 'gentleman' who in the first edition had provoked 'utmost wonder' in Victor with his 'experiments on an air pump'. (For the 1818 'scientific' passages see Appendix A, 38.35–37, 39.8–35, 40.8–12, 40.27–41) Joseph Wright's famous 1768 painting of 'An experiment on a bird in the Air Pump' illustrates the widespread popularity of such demonstrations at the time. At the same time that she cancelled the passage including Alphonse Frankenstein's explanation of electricity to his son, Mary Shelley also removed the crucial denomination of this energy source as a 'fluid'. In doing so, she perhaps made it harder for future readers to identify with the speculative nature of this period of scientific endeavour, in which the 'vital fluid' was regarded by such people as Humphry Davy and S. T. Coleridge as a magical element animating all living things.

In the 1818 edition Elizabeth had been Victor's cousin, daughter of his father's sister. In 1831, though the term 'cousin' continues to be used as a form of endearment between them, Elizabeth Lavenza is no longer biologically related to Victor but is made the orphaned daughter of a Milanese nobleman lost in war, whose German wife had died giving birth to her. (Godwin, to whom Mary had become very close in his old age at this time, also deployed the ever-remembered family loss of Mary Wollstonecraft in the plots of his novels *Cloudesley* [1830] and *Deloraine*

[1833].) The aim here could well have been an 'early Victorian' attempt to shake off the suggestion of incest, which in earlier days had been a more acceptable theme, both for Mary and especially for the irreverent Percy Shelley. (See her novella *Mathilda* and Percy Shelley's verse drama *The Cenci* – both written in 1819.) Certainly we find the descriptions of Elizabeth in 1831 more angelic and generalized than those of 1818, when they are so obviously modelled on Mary's own physical features and character. (See Appendix A, 32.24–38.4 and 77.17–21.)

But if there is an attempt to tone down the identification of Elizabeth with Mary's 'former self', there is, in the 1831 descriptions of Victor, a nostalgic striving to evoke the presence of her beloved Percy. As well as Walton's delineation on page 28, lines 17–29, such nostalgia for past happiness is further evidenced by Mary Shelley's changing the destination of Victor and Elizabeth's honeymoon journey from Cologny – Byron's residence in the summer of 1816 – to Lake Como. It was on the shores of Lake Como where Mary and Percy had initially searched for a home together after their arrival in Italy in the spring of 1818. The deep and lasting effect of Percy's death on Mary Shelley left its imprint on the novel in other ways. Although 'fate' plays a causative role in the original plot of *Frankenstein* (the 'fatal impulse' of insatiable curiosity afflicting Godwin's Caleb Williams also plagues his literary descendant Victor Frankenstein), the 1831 edition registers her much stronger belief that Providence governs human action. (To her Journal in 1827 she confides how 'The power of Destiny I feel every day pressing more and more on me . . .') This emerges in the newly written passages describing Victor's feelings as he beholds the Alps at Chamonix. (See 91.4–92.21, 93.1–12 and 93.18–23.) The 'maternal nature' that had once provided the author with less ambivalent feelings towards the memory of her own mother is now perceived by Mary's Victor as 'a power mighty as Omnipotence' operating 'through the silent working of immutable laws'. This reveals a less settled, if not negative, attitude towards Nature, one that seems to draw on the feeling of impersonal monstrosity behind it, which pervades Percy Shelley's poem 'Mont Blanc'. Mary makes Victor's anguish even more poignant in 1831 by having him leave behind the family he had travelled with in 1818. He now Romantically communes with his 'mighty friends' the vast Alpine mountains, companions whose 'glorious presence-chamber of imperial Nature' grants him a temporary respite from society's demands.

This new injection of Romantic wildness into the text is felt in other places. For instance, the passages in which Professor Waldman's chemistry lecture provides the 'spark' igniting young Frankenstein's monomaniacal ambition to 'pioneer a new way' ('my mind was filled with one thought, one conception, one purpose', he says: see 47.13–14), is not in the 1818 text. Similarly, though the moral that an obsessive mission to create something without thought for its uncertain consequences is implicit in the 1818 text (Victor hopes that the gratification of Walton's wishes 'may not be a serpent to sting you, as mine has been' and also threatens to 'extinguish the spark which I so negligently bestowed' on his Creature), in 1831, the point is made much more explicitly. In 1818 Victor, having heard of Walton's ambitious plan to reach the North Pole, merely hopes that the telling of his story to Walton 'may enlarge your faculties and understanding'. But in 1831 the parallels of Walton's mission to his own disastrous over-reaching experiments are much more powerfully stressed: 'Unhappy man! Do you share my madness? Have you drunk also of the intoxicating draught?' Victor now hopes that the Captain 'may deduce an apt moral from my tale', a moral that Mary Shelley makes Walton recall in 1831 when writing to his sister about the perils he and his ship's crew face, immobilized in an Arctic (rather than Alpine) sea of ice: '. . . it is terrible to reflect that the lives of all these men are endangered through me,' Walton considers in 1831. 'If we are lost, my mad schemes are the cause.'

Although in her 1831 edition, Mary retained the novel's dedication to her father, the removal or toning down of Godwinian didacticism in certain passages of the 1818 text seem to indicate that she was much less enamoured of Godwin's radicalism in her thirties than she had been as a teenager. Thus Frankenstein's account of the education given to him and his brothers by his 'advanced' parents may have been perceived by Mary in 1831 as a remnant of a past 'childish' attachment to her father's radical precepts. (See Appendix A, 32.24–38.4 and 38.26.) Certainly, she was right to modify the passage in which Elizabeth, visiting the condemned Justine to offer her comfort in her final hours, abruptly (and thus somewhat comically) launches into a Godwinian diatribe against 'executioners, their hands yet reeking with the blood of innocence'. (Appendix A, 84.32–37.)

On the other hand, certain Godwinian notions fundamental to the moral fabric of the novel are allowed to stand, such as the Creature's argument to Victor: 'My vices are the children of a forced solitude that I abhor, and my virtues will necessarily arise when I live in communion with an equal.' (Volume Two, Chapter IX, p. 142.) (A discussion of the influence Godwin's writings had upon *Frankenstein* is to be found in my book of that title in the Penguin Critical Studies series.) Shelley also allowed Elizabeth's championing of Swiss republican institutions in her letter to Victor to remain in the 1831 edition. (See Volume One, Chapter VI, p. 63.) This may have been out of regard for the memory of her dead husband, who wrote the passage.

As well as altering double quotation marks to single throughout the text, I have occasionally lightened *Frankenstein*'s heavy punctuation. Nineteenth-century place names have been retained: the only one that has altered significantly is *Mayence*, now known by its German name of Mainz (p. 150).

SUGGESTED FURTHER READING

The number of studies of Mary Shelley and *Frankenstein* has increased dramatically in recent years. The selection I have made below includes works which should prove helpful both to newcomers to Mary Shelley and to those who want to explore in more depth the relations between her novel, the history out of which it emerged, and the issues it raises about the complex politics of human desire and action in 'modern times'. A good deal of literary criticism is now concerned to challenge our assumptions about gender and power relations in literature and society, and, as a result, some refreshingly progressive readings of English literature have emerged. All the references given are listed in date order of the edition I have consulted.

BIOGRAPHY

Richard Church, *Mary Shelley*, Howe, London, 1928.

R. Glynn Grylls, *Mary Shelley: A Biography*, Oxford University Press, 1938.

William A. Walling, *Mary Shelley*, Twayne, New York, 1972.

Richard Holmes, *Shelley: the Pursuit*, Quartet Books, London, 1976.

Jane Dunn, *Moon in Eclipse: A Life of Mary Shelley*, Weidenfeld and Nicolson, London, 1978.

Betty T. Bennet (ed.), *The Letters of Mary Wollstonecraft Shelley*, Johns Hopkins University Press, Baltimore, 1980, 1983, 1988.

Paula R. Feldman and Diana Scott-Kilvert (eds.), *The Journals of Mary Shelley*, Oxford University Press, 1987.

Muriel Spark, *Mary Shelley*, Constable, London, 1988.

William St Clair, *The Godwins and the Shelleys: The biography of a family*, Faber and Faber, London and Boston, 1989.

Emily W. Sunstein, *Mary Shelley: Romance and Reality*, Johns Hopkins University Press, Baltimore, 1991.

BOOKS AND ESSAYS ABOUT *FRANKENSTEIN*

Percy Bysshe Shelley, 'On "Frankenstein"', *The Athenaeum*, 10 November, 1832, p. 730.

Milton Millhauser, 'The Noble Savage in *Frankenstein*', *Notes and Queries*, 190, 1946, pp. 248–50.

M. A. Goldberg, 'Moral and Myth in Mrs Shelley's *Frankenstein*', *Keats-Shelley Journal*, 8, 1959, pp. 27–38.

Burton R. Pollin, 'Philosophical and Literary Sources of *Frankenstein*', *Comparative Literature*, XVII, 2, Spring, 1965, pp. 97–108.

Harold Bloom, '*Frankenstein*, or the New Prometheus', *Partisan Review*, 32, 1965, pp. 611–18.

P. D. Fleck, 'Mary Shelley's Notes to Shelley's Poems and *Frankenstein*', *Studies in Romanticism*, VI, 4, 1967, pp. 226–54.

Masao Miyoshi, *The Divided Self: A Perspective on the Literature of the Victorians*, New York University Press, 1969, pp. 79–89.

Robert M. Philmus, 'Frankenstein; or, Faust's Promethean Rebellion Against Nature', in *Into the Unknown: The Evolution of Science Fiction from Francis Godwin to H. G. Wells*, University of California Press, Berkeley, 1970, pp. 82–90.

Robert Kiely, 'Frankenstein', in *The Romantic Novel in England*, Harvard University Press, 1972, pp. 155–73.

Christopher Small, *Ariel Like a Harpy: Shelley, Mary, and Frankenstein*, Gollancz, London, 1972.

Samuel Holmes Vasbinder, *Scientific Attitudes in Mary Shelley's 'Frankenstein'*, UMI Research Press, Ann Arbor, Michigan, 1976.

Gay Clifford, '*Caleb Williams* and *Frankenstein*: First-Person Narratives and "Things as They Are"', *Genre*, 10, Winter, 1977, pp. 601–17.

Sylvia Bowerbank, 'The Social Order *vs.* the Wretch: Mary Shelley's Contradictory-Mindedness in *Frankenstein*', *English Literary History*, vol. 46, no. 3, 1979, pp. 418–31.

David Ketterer, *Frankenstein's Creation: The Book, the Monster, and Human Reality*, ELS Monograph Series, no. 16, University of Victoria, British Columbia, 1979.

Sandra M. Gilbert and Susan Gubar, *The Madwoman in the Attic*, Yale University Press, New Haven, 1979.

Katherine R. Powers, *The Influence of William Godwin on the Novels of Mary Shelley*, Arno Press, New York, 1980.

Rosemary Jackson, *Fantasy: The Literature of Subversion*, Methuen, London, 1981, pp. 99–104.

George Levine and U. C. Knoepflmacher (eds.), *The Endurance of Frankenstein: Essays on Mary Shelley's Novel*, University of California Press, Berkeley, 1982.

Lee Sterrenburg, 'Mary Shelley's Monster: Politics and Psyche in *Frankenstein*', in Levine and Knoepflmacher, op. cit., pp. 143–71.

Paul O'Flinn, 'Production and Reproduction: The Case of *Frankenstein*', *Literature and History*, Autumn, 1983, pp. 194–213.

Franco Moretti, 'Dialectic of Fear', in *Signs Taken as Wonders*, Verso Editions and NLB, London, 1983, pp. 83–108.

Paul Cantor, 'The Nightmare of Romantic Idealism', in *Creature and Creator: Myth-making and English Romanticism*, Cambridge University Press, 1984, pp. 103–32.

Mary L. Poovey, ' "My Hideous Progeny": The Lady and the Monster', in *The Proper Lady and the Woman Writer: Ideology as Style in the Works of Mary Wollstonecraft, Mary Shelley, and Jane Austen*, University of Chicago Press, 1984.

Richard Freeborn, 'Frankenstein's Last Journey', *Oxford Slavonic Papers*, New Series, vol. xviii, 1985, pp. 102–19.

Lester D. Friedman, 'Sporting with Life: *Frankenstein* and the Responsibility of Medical Research', *Medical Heritage*, vol. I, no. 3, May/June, 1985, pp. 181–5.

William Veeder, *Mary Shelley & Frankenstein: The Fate of Androgyny*, Unversity of Chicago Press, 1986.

Ellen Moers, 'Female Gothic', in Levine and Knoepflmacher, op. cit., pp. 77–87.

David E. Musselwhite, '*Frankenstein*: The making of a monster', in *Partings Welded Together: Politics and Desire in the Nineteenth-Century English Novel*, Methuen, London, 1987, pp. 43–74.

Chris Baldick, *In Frankenstein's Shadow: Myth, Monstrosity, and Nineteenth-century Writing*, Clarendon Press, Oxford, 1987.

Anne K. Mellor, *Mary Shelley: Her Life, Her Fiction, Her Monsters*, Routledge, New York and London, 1988.

Jean-Jacques Lecercle, *Frankenstein: mythe et philosophie*, Presses universitaires de France, 1988.

Audrey A. Fisch, Anne K. Mellor, Esther H. Schor (eds.), *The Other Mary Shelley: Beyond Frankenstein*, Oxford University Press, 1993.

Maurice Hindle, *Mary Shelley's Frankenstein, Penguin Critical Study*, 1994.

RELATED WORKS

Frank Darvall, *Popular Disturbances and Public Order in Regency England*, Oxford University Press, London, 1934.

E. P. Thompson, *The Making of the English Working Class*, Penguin, Harmondsworth, 1970.

Malcolm I. Thomis and Peter Holt, *Threats of Revolution in Britain, 1789–1848*, Macmillan, London, 1977.

Brian Easlea, *Fathering the Unthinkable: Masculinity, Scientists and the Nuclear Arms Race*, Pluto Press, 1983.

Marilyn Butler, *Romantics, Rebels and Reactionaries: English Literature and its Background, 1760–1830*, Oxford University Press, 1981.

H. T. Dickinson, *British Radicalism and the French Revolution, 1789–1815*, Blackwell, Oxford, 1985.

J. R. Dinwiddy, *From Luddism to the First Reform Bill: Reform in England, 1810–1832*, Blackwell, Oxford, 1986.

MARY WOLLSTONECRAFT SHELLEY:
A CHRONOLOGY

1797   William Godwin and Mary Wollstonecraft marry on 29
        March. Mary W. Godwin is born on 30 August; her
        mother dies ten days later.

1801   [Age 4] William Godwin and Mrs Mary Jane Clairmont
        marry on 21 December. Mrs Clairmont brings with her
        a son Charles (aged 7) and daughter Jane (4), later
        called Claire, to join young Mary and Fanny Imlay
        (daughter of Mary Wollstonecraft by Gilbert Imlay).

1807   [Age 10] Godwin family move to Skinner Street, Hol-
        born.

1812   [Age 14–15] On 3 January, Percy Bysshe Shelley,
        recently married to Harriet Westbrook, starts a cor-
        respondence with Godwin, whose ideas he reveres. He
        becomes a regular visitor to his house in the autumn,
        during Mary's absence. She has gone for a long stay with
        the Baxter family in Dundee, but meets Percy and Har-
        riet on a brief visit home on 11 November.

1814   [Age 16–17] Mary returns home in May and begins a
        relationship with Percy Shelley. On 28 July they elope to
        the Continent, taking with them Claire Clairmont. On
        30 November Harriet Shelley gives birth to Charles, her
        second child. Mary, Percy and Claire return to England
        in September.

1815   [Age 17] In February, Mary gives premature birth to a
        daughter who dies, unnamed, a few days later. By August
        Mary and Percy have settled at Bishops Gate, Windsor.

1816   [Age 18–19] In January, Mary gives birth to a son,
        William. The family, along with Claire, leave England

for Geneva in early May. They meet Byron (with whom Claire has already formed a liaison) and take up residence next to him at Montalègre, near Cologny. Mary begins to write *Frankenstein* in June. In July, Mary and Percy visit and explore the Mer de Glace at Chamonix, a major inspiration for Mary's novel. In September they return to England. On 9 October, Fanny Imlay, Mary's half-sister, commits suicide. Two months later Harriet Shelley is found drowned. Mary and Percy marry in London on 30 December.

1817   [Age 19–20] In March the Shelleys, with Claire and her daughter Allegra (by Byron), move to Marlow. On 14 May *Frankenstein* is completed. Mary gives birth to a daughter, Clara, in September. *History of a Six Weeks' Tour* is published in November.

1818   [Age 20–21] *Frankenstein* is published at the beginning of January. Mary, Percy, Claire and the children all leave for Italy on the 11 March. In June they settle for two months at Bagni di Lucca, moving to Este in September. Baby Clara dies in Venice. Whilst there they visit Byron. In December they travel south to Rome and settle in Naples for the winter. Mary and Percy go sightseeing together.

1819   [Age 21–2] In March they return to Rome. More tragedy as their son William dies in June: so far all Mary's children have perished. At this time Mary writes the semi-autobiographical *Mathilda*, a novella on the theme of father–daughter incestuous love which is not, however, destined to be published in her own lifetime. They depart for Leghorn. Having moved to Florence for her approaching confinement, Mary gives birth to a son, Percy Florence, in November. He will be the only Shelley child to survive.

1821   [Age 23–4] In April they return to Bagni di San Giuliano for the summer. In October they move to Pisa, with Edward and Jane Williams and Lord Byron as near neighbours. Mary sends her novel *Castruccio* (later entitled *Valperga*) to London for publication.

1822   [Age 24–5] In May, the Shelleys settle with the Williamses at Casa Magni, near Lerici. One month later, Mary almost dies from a miscarriage, but is saved by the quick-thinking efforts of her husband. In early July Percy and Edward sail to Leghorn to meet Leigh Hunt, but are lost at sea in a storm on the return journey. In September Mary joins the Hunts and Byron at Geneva.

1823   [Age 25] *Valperga* is published in February. The second edition of *Frankenstein* is published. In August Mary returns to London.

1824   [Age 26] In the spring Mary begins work on *The Last Man*, a novel set in the twenty-first century and purporting to be the narrative of the lone survivor in a world decimated by plague. Byron dies in Greece. Mary's edition of Percy Shelley's *Posthumous Poems* is published but suppressed at the insistence of Sir Timothy Shelley, his father.

1824–39 [Age 26–41] During these years, Mary Shelley writes numerous articles and stories for various magazines and journals, including the *London Magazine*, the *Westminster Review* and the *Keepsake*.

1826   [Age 28–9] *The Last Man* is published in February. Percy Florence becomes heir to the Shelley title and estate in September when Charles Bysshe, Shelley's son by Harriet, dies.

1830   [Age 32] *Perkin Warbeck*, Mary's fourth novel, is published.

1832   [Age 35] Percy Florence is entered at Harrow.

1835   [Age 37] Volume I of the *Lives of the Most Eminent Literary and Scientific Men of Italy, Spain and Portugal* for Lardner's *Cabinet Cyclopaedia* is published. Mary contributes the lives of Petrarch, Boccaccio and Machiavelli. In March *Lodore* is published. In October Volume II of the *Lives* is published, Mary writing essays on Alfieri, Foscolo, Goldoni, Monti and Metastasio.

1836   [Age 38] William Godwin dies on 7 April.

1837   [Age 39] *Falkner*, Mary's last novel, is published. In July, Percy Florence is entered at Trinity College, Cambridge. Volume III of the *Lives*, including essays by Mary on Calderon, Cervantes, and Lope de Vega.

1838–9   [Age 40–41] Mary continues to exercise her exceptional biographical talents by writing and publishing numerous essays for the *Lives of the Most Eminent Literary and Scientific Men of France* (2 vols.) for Lardner's *Cabinet Cyclopaedia*. They include essays on Montaigne, Rabelais, Corneille, Molière, Pascal, Racine, Voltaire, Rousseau, Condorcet, as well as Eminent Literary and Scientific Women, Mme Roland and Mme de Stael.

1839   [Age 41] Mary prepares and publishes an edition of Percy Shelley's *Poetical Works*. Although Sir Timothy still forbids her to write a biography of the poet, she is able to include biographical material in her notes to the poems. Percy Shelley's *Essays, Letters and Translations* are also published.

1844   [Age 46] *Rambles in Germany and Italy*, a book based on Mary's Continental tours with Percy Florence and his friends between 1840 and 1843, is published.

1851   [Age 53] Mary Wollstonecraft Shelley dies on 1 February at Chester Square, London. She is buried between the remains of her mother and father in St Peter's Churchyard, Bournemouth.

FRANKENSTEIN;

OR,

THE MODERN PROMETHEUS.

—◆—

IN THREE VOLUMES.

—◆—

Did I request thee, Maker, from my clay
To mould me man ? Did I solicit thee
From darkness to promote me ?——
                            PARADISE LOST.

—

VOL. I.

————————

London:
PRINTED FOR
LACKINGTON, HUGHES, HARDING, MAVOR, & JONES,
FINSBURY SQUARE.

—

1818.

TO

WILLIAM GODWIN

Author of *Political Justice, Caleb Williams*, &c.

THESE VOLUMES

Are respectfully inscribed

BY

THE AUTHOR

AUTHOR'S INTRODUCTION
TO THE STANDARD NOVELS EDITION
(1831)

The publishers of the Standard Novels, in selecting *Frankenstein* for one of their series, expressed a wish that I should furnish them with some account of the origin of the story. I am the more willing to comply, because I shall thus give a general answer to the question, so very frequently asked me. 'How I, then a young girl, came to think of and to dilate upon so very hideous an idea?' It is true that I am very averse to bringing myself forward in print; but as my account will only appear as an appendage to a former production, and as it will be confined to such topics as have connexion with my authorship alone, I can scarcely accuse myself of a personal intrusion.

It is not singular that, as the daughter of two persons of distinguished literary celebrity,[1] I should very early in life have thought of writing. As a child I scribbled; and my favourite pastime during the hours given me for recreation was to 'write stories'. Still, I had a dearer pleasure than this, which was the formation of castles in the air – the indulging in waking dreams – the following up trains of thought, which had for their subject the formation of a succession of imaginary incidents. My dreams were at once more fantastic and agreeable than my writings. In the latter I was a close imitator – rather doing as others had done than putting down the suggestions of my own mind. What I wrote was intended at least for one other eye – my childhood's companion and friend; but my dreams were all my own; I accounted for them to nobody; they were my refuge when annoyed – my dearest pleasure when free.

I lived principally in the country as a girl, and passed a considerable time in Scotland. I made occasional visits to the more picturesque parts; but my habitual residence was on the blank and dreary northern shores of the Tay, near Dundee. Blank and dreary on retrospection I call them; they were not so to me then. They were the eyry[2] of freedom, and the pleasant region where unheeded I could commune with the creatures of my fancy. I wrote then – but in a most common-place style. It was beneath the trees of the grounds belonging to our house, or on the bleak sides of the woodless mountains near, that my true compositions, the airy flights of my imagination, were born and fostered. I did not make myself the heroine of my tales. Life appeared to me too common-place an affair as regarded myself. I could not figure to myself that romantic woes or wonderful events would ever be my lot; but I was not confined to my own identity, and I could people the hours with creations far more interesting to me at that age than my own sensations.

After this my life became busier, and reality stood in place of fiction. My husband, however, was from the first, very anxious that I should prove myself worthy of my parentage, and enrol myself on the page of fame. He was for ever inciting me to obtain literary reputation, which even on my own part I cared for then, though since I have become infinitely indifferent to it. At this time he desired that I should write, not so much with the idea that I could produce any thing worthy of notice, but that he might himself judge how far I possessed the promise of better things hereafter. Still I did nothing. Travelling, and the cares of a family, occupied my time; and study, in the way of reading or improving my ideas in communication with his far more cultivated mind, was all of literary employment that engaged my attention.

In the summer of 1816, we visited Switzerland and became the neighbours of Lord Byron. At first we spent our pleasant hours on the lake, or wandering on its shores; and Lord Byron, who was writing the third canto of *Childe Harold*, was the only one among us who put his thoughts upon paper. These, as he brought them successively to us, clothed in all the light and harmony of poetry, seemed to stamp as divine the glories of heaven and earth, whose influences we partook with him.

But it proved a wet, ungenial summer, and incessant rain often confined us for days to the house. Some volumes of ghost stories, translated from the German into French, fell into our hands. There was the *History of the Inconstant Lover*, who, when he thought to clasp the bride to whom he had pledged his vows, found himself in the arms of the pale ghost of her whom he had deserted. There was the tale of the sinful founder of his race whose miserable doom it was to bestow the kiss of death on all the younger sons of his fated house, just when they reached the age of promise. His gigantic, shadowy form, clothed like the ghost in *Hamlet*, in complete armour, but with the beaver up, was seen at midnight, by the moon's fitful beams, to advance slowly along the gloomy avenue. The shape was lost beneath the shadow of the castle walls; but soon a gate swung back, a step was heard, the door of the chamber opened, and he advanced to the couch of the blooming youths, cradled in healthy sleep. Eternal sorrow sat upon his face as he bent down and kissed the forehead of the boys, who from that hour withered like flowers snapt upon the stalk. I have not seen these stories since then; but their incidents are as fresh in my mind as if I had read them yesterday.

'We will each write a ghost story', said Lord Byron; and his proposition was acceded to. There were four of us. The noble author began a tale, a fragment of which he printed at the end of his poem of *Mazeppa*. Shelley, more apt to embody ideas and sentiments in the radiance of brilliant imagery, and in the music of the most melodious verse that adorns our language, than to invent the machinery of a story, commenced one founded on the experiences of his early life. Poor Polidori had some terrible idea about a skull-headed lady who was so punished for peeping through a keyhole – what to see I forget – something very shocking and wrong of course; but when she was reduced to a worse condition than the renowned Tom of Coventry, he did not know what to do with her and was obliged to dispatch her to the tomb of the Capulets,³ the only place for which she was fitted. The illustrious poets also, annoyed by the platitude of prose, speedily relinquished their uncongenial task.

I busied myself *to think of a story*, – a story to rival those which had excited us to this task. One which would speak to the mysterious fears of our nature and awaken thrilling horror – one to make

7

the reader dread to look round, to curdle the blood, and quicken the beatings of the heart. If I did not accomplish these things, my ghost story would be unworthy of its name. I thought and pondered – vainly. I felt that blank incapability of invention which is the greatest misery of authorship, when dull Nothing replies to our anxious invocations. 'Have you thought of a story?' I was asked each morning, and each morning I was forced to reply with a mortifying negative.

Every thing must have a beginning, to speak in Sanchean phrase;[4] and that beginning must be linked to something that went before. The Hindoos give the world an elephant to support it, but they make the elephant stand upon a tortoise. Invention, it must be humbly admitted, does not consist in creating out of void, but out of chaos; the materials must, in the first place, be afforded: it can give form to dark, shapeless substances, but cannot bring into being the substance itself. In all matters of discovery and invention, even of those that appertain to the imagination, we are continually reminded of the story of Columbus and his egg.[5] Invention consists in the capacity of seizing on the capabilities of a subject: and in the power of moulding and fashioning ideas suggested to it.

Many and long were the conversations between Lord Byron and Shelley, to which I was a devout but nearly silent listener. During one of these, various philosophical doctrines were discussed, and among others the nature of the principle of life, and whether there was any probability of its ever being discovered and communicated. They talked of the experiments of Dr Darwin[6] (I speak not of what the Doctor really did, or said that he did, but, as more to my purpose, of what was then spoken of as having been done by him), who preserved a piece of vermicelli in a glass case, till by some extraordinary means it began to move with voluntary motion. Not thus, after all, would life be given. Perhaps a corpse would be re-animated; galvanism[7] had given token of such things: perhaps the component parts of a creature might be manufactured, brought together, and endued with vital warmth.

Night waned upon this talk, and even the witching hour had gone by, before we retired to rest. When I placed my head on my pillow, I did not sleep, nor could I be said to think. My imagination, unbidden, possessed and guided me, gifting the successive images that arose in my mind with a vividness far beyond the usual bounds of reverie. I saw – with shut eyes, but acute mental vision – I saw the pale student of unhallowed arts kneeling beside the thing he had put together. I saw the hideous phantasm of a man stretched out, and then, on the working of some powerful engine, show signs of life, and stir with an uneasy, half-vital motion. Frightful must it be; for supremely frightful would be the effect of any human endeavour to mock the stupendous mechanism of the Creator of the world. His success would terrify the artist; he would rush away from his odious handywork, horror-stricken. He would hope that, left to itself, the slight spark of life which he had communicated would fade; that this thing, which had received such imperfect animation would subside into dead matter; and he might sleep in the belief that the silence of the grave would quench forever the transient existence of the hideous corpse which he had looked upon as the cradle of life. He sleeps; but he is awakened; he opens his eyes; behold, the horrid thing stands at his bedside, opening his curtains and looking on him with yellow, watery, but speculative eyes.

I opened mine in terror. The idea so possessed my mind, that a thrill of fear ran through me, and I wished to exchange the ghastly image of my fancy for the realities around. I see them still; the very room, the dark *parquet*, the closed shutters, with the moonlight struggling through, and the sense I had that the glassy lake and white high Alps were beyond. I could not so easily get rid of my hideous phantom; still it haunted me. I must try to think of something else. I recurred to my ghost story – my tiresome, unlucky ghost story! O! if I could only contrive one which would frighten my reader as I myself had been frightened that night!

Swift as light and as cheering was the idea that broke in upon me. 'I have found it! What terrified me will terrify others; and I need only describe the spectre which had haunted my midnight pillow.' On the morrow I announced that I had *thought of a story*. I began that day with the words. 'It was on a dreary night of November,' making only a transcript of the grim terrors of my waking dream.

At first I thought but a few pages – of a short tale; but Shelley urged me to develope the idea at greater length. I certainly did not owe the suggestion of one incident, nor scarcely of one train of feeling, to my husband, and yet but for his incitement it would never have taken the form in which it was presented to the world. From this declaration I must except the preface. As far as I can recollect, it was entirely written by him.

And now, once again, I bid my hideous progeny go forth and prosper. I have an affection for it, for it was the offspring of happy days, when death and grief were but words, which found no true echo in my heart. Its several pages speak of many a walk, many a drive, and many a conversation, when I was not alone; and my companion was one who, in this world, I shall never see more. But this is for myself; my readers have nothing to do with these associations.

I will add but one word as to the alterations I have made. They are principally those of style. I have changed no portion of the story nor introduced any new ideas or circumstances. I have mended the language where it was so bald as to interfere with the interest of the narrative; and these changes occur almost exclusively in the beginning of the first volume. Throughout they are entirely confined to such parts as are mere adjuncts to the story, leaving the core and substance of it untouched.

M.W.S.

London, October 15th, 1831.

PREFACE

(by P. B. Shelley, 1818)

The event on which this fiction is founded, has been supposed, by Dr Darwin, and some of the physiological writers of Germany, as not of impossible occurrence. I shall not be supposed as according the remotest degree of serious faith to such an imagination; yet, in assuming it has the basis of a work of fancy, I have not considered myself as merely weaving a series of supernatural terrors. The event on which the interest of the story depends is exempt from the disadvantages of a mere tale of spectres or enchantment. It was recommended by the novelty of the situations which it develops, and, however impossible as a physical fact, affords a point of view to the imagination for the delineating of human passions more comprehensive and commanding than any which the ordinary relations of existing events can yield.

I have thus endeavoured to preserve the truth of the elementary principles of human nature, while I have not scrupled to innovate upon their combinations. The *Iliad*, the tragic poetry of Greece, – Shakespeare in *The Tempest* and *Midsummer Night's Dream*, – and most especially Milton, in *Paradise Lost*, conform to this rule; and the most humble novelist, who seeks to confer or receive amusement from his labours, may, without presumption, apply to prose fictions a licence, or rather a rule, from the adoption of which so many exquisite combinations of human feeling have resulted in the highest specimens of poetry.

The circumstance on which my story rests was suggested in casual conversation. It was commenced partly as a source of amusement, and partly as an expedient for exercising any untried resources of mind. Other motives were mingled with these as the work proceeded. I am by no means indifferent to the manner in which whatever moral tendencies exist in the sentiments or characters it contains shall affect the reader; yet my chief concern in this respect has been limited to the avoiding the enervating effects of the novels of the present day, and to the exhibition of the amiableness of domestic affection, and the excellence of universal virtue. The opinions which naturally spring from the character and situation of the hero are by no means to be conceived as existing always in my own conviction; nor is any inference justly to be drawn from the following pages as prejudicing any philosophical doctrine of whatever kind.

It is a subject also of additional interest to the author, that this story was begun in the majestic region where the scene is principally laid, and in society which cannot cease to be regretted. I passed the summer of 1816 in the environs of Geneva. The season was cold and rainy, and in the evenings we crowded around a blazing wood fire, and occasionally amused ourselves with some German stories of ghosts which happened to fall into our hands. These tales excited in us a playful desire of imitation. Two other friends (a tale from the pen of one of whom would be far more acceptable to the public than any thing I can ever hope to produce) and myself agreed to write each a story, founded on some super-natural occurrence.

The weather, however, suddenly became serene; and my two friends left me on a journey among the Alps and lost, in the magnificent scenes which they present, all memory of their ghostly visions. The following tale is the only one which has been completed.

MARLOW
September 1817

VOLUME ONE

LETTER I

═══════

To Mrs Saville, England.

St Petersburgh, Dec. 11th, 17–.

You will rejoice to hear that no disaster has accompanied the commencement of an enterprise which you have regarded with such evil forebodings. I arrived here yesterday; and my first task is to assure my dear sister of my welfare, and increasing confidence in the success of my undertaking.

I am already far north of London; and as I walk in the streets of Petersburgh, I feel a cold northern breeze play upon my cheeks, which braces my nerves, and fills me with delight. Do you understand this feeling? This breeze, which has travelled from the regions towards which I am advancing, gives me a foretaste of those icy climes. Inspirited by this wind of promise, my day dreams become more fervent and vivid. I try in vain to be persuaded that the pole is the seat of frost and desolation; it ever presents itself to my imagination as the region of beauty and delight. There, Margaret, the sun is for ever visible, its broad disk just skirting the horizon, and diffusing a perpetual splendour. There – for with your leave, my sister, I will put some trust in preceding navigators – there snow and frost are banished; and, sailing over a calm sea, we may be wafted to a land surpassing in wonders and in beauty every region hitherto discovered on the habitable globe. Its productions and features may be without example, as the phenomena of the heavenly bodies undoubtedly are in those undiscovered solitudes. What may not be expected in a country of eternal light? I may there discover the wondrous power which attracts the needle; and may regulate a thousand celestial observations, that require only this voyage to render their seeming eccentricities consistent for ever. I shall satiate my ardent curiosity with the sight of a part of the world never before visited, and may tread a land never before imprinted by the foot of man. These are my enticements, and they are sufficient to conquer all fear of danger or death, and to induce me to commence this laborious voyage with the joy a child feels when he embarks in a little boat, with his holiday mates, on an expedition of discovery up his native river. But, supposing all these conjectures to be false, you cannot contest the inestimable benefit which I shall confer on all mankind to the last generation, by discovering a passage near the pole to those countries, to reach which at present so many months are requisite; or by ascertaining the secret of the magnet, which, if at all possible, can only be effected by an undertaking such as mine.

These reflections have dispelled the agitation with which I began my letter, and I feel my heart glow with an enthusiasm which elevates me to heaven; for nothing contributes so much to tranquillize the mind as a steady purpose – a point on which the soul may fix its intellectual eye. This expedition has been the favourite dream of my early years. I have read with ardour the accounts of the various voyages which have been made in the prospect of arriving at the North Pacific Ocean through the seas which surround the pole. You may remember that a history of all the voyages made for purposes of discovery composed the whole of our good uncle Thomas's library. My education was neglected, yet I was passionately fond of reading. These volumes were my study day and night, and my familiarity with them increased that regret which I had felt, as a child, on learning that my father's dying injunction had forbidden my uncle to allow me to embark in a seafaring life.

These visions faded when I perused, for the first time, those poets whose effusions, entranced my soul, and lifted it to heaven. I also became a poet, and for one year lived in a Paradise of my own creation; I imagined that I also might obtain a niche in the temple where the names of Homer and Shakespeare are consecrated. You are well acquainted with my failure, and how heavily I bore the disappointment. But just at that time I inherited the fortune of my cousin, and my thoughts were turned into the channel of their earlier bent.

Six years have passed since I resolved on my present undertaking. I can, even now, remember the hour from which I dedicated myself to this great enterprise. I commenced by inuring my body to hardship. I accompanied the whale-fishers on several expeditions to the North Sea; I voluntarily endured cold, famine, thirst, and want of sleep; I often worked harder than the common sailors during the day, and devoted my nights to the study of mathematics, the theory of medicine, and those branches of physical science from which a naval adventure might derive the greatest practical advantage. Twice I actually hired myself as an under-mate in a Greenland whaler, and acquitted myself to admiration. I must own I felt a little proud, when my captain offered me the second dignity in the vessel and intreated me to remain with the greatest earnestness so valuable did he consider my services.

And now, dear Margaret, do I not deserve to accomplish some great purpose? My life might have been passed in ease and luxury; but I preferred glory to every enticement that wealth placed in my path. Oh, that some encouraging voice would answer in the affirmative! My courage and my resolution is firm; but my hopes fluctuate, and my spirits are often depressed. I am about to proceed on a long and difficult voyage, the emergencies of which will demand all my fortitude: I am required not only to raise the spirits of others, but sometimes to sustain my own, when theirs are failing.

This is the most favourable period for travelling in Russia. They fly quickly over the snow in their sledges; the motion is pleasant, and, in my opinion, far more agreeable than that of an English stage-coach. The cold is not excessive, if you are wrapped in furs – a dress which I have already adopted; for there is a great difference between walking the deck and remaining seated motionless for hours, when no exercise prevents the blood from actually freezing in your veins. I have no ambition to lose my life on the post-road between St Petersburgh and Archangel.

I shall depart for the latter town in a fortnight or three weeks; and my intention is to hire a ship there, which can easily be done by paying the insurance for the owner, and to engage as many sailors as I think necessary among those who are accustomed to the whale-fishing. I do not intend to sail until the month of June; and when shall I return? Ah, dear sister, how can I answer this question? If I succeed, many, many months, perhaps years, will pass before you and I may meet. If I fail, you will see me again soon, or never.

Farewell, my dear, excellent Margaret. Heaven shower down blessings on you, and save me, that I may again and again testify my gratitude for all your love and kindness.

Your affectionate brother,

R. WALTON

LETTER II

To Mrs Saville, England.

Archangel, March 28th, 17–.

How slowly the time passes here, encompassed as I am by frost
and snow! yet a second step is taken towards my enterprise. I
have hired a vessel, and am occupied in collecting my sailors;
those whom I have already engaged, appear to be men on whom
I can depend and are certainly possessed of dauntless courage.

But I have one want which I have never yet been able to
satisfy; and the absence of the object of which I now feel as a
most severe evil. I have no friend, Margaret: when I am glowing
with the enthusiasm of success, there will be none to participate
my joy; if I am assailed by disappointment, no one will endeavour
to sustain me in dejection. I shall commit my thoughts to paper,
it is true; but that is a poor medium for the communication of
feeling. I desire the company of a man who could sympathise
with me; whose eyes would reply to mine. You may deem me
romantic, my dear sister, but I bitterly feel the want of a friend. I
have no one near me, gentle yet courageous, possessed of a cultivated as well as of a capacious mind, whose tastes are like my own,
to approve or amend my plans. How would such a friend repair
the faults of your poor brother! I am too ardent in execution, and
too impatient of difficulties. But it is a still greater evil to me that
I am self-educated: for the first fourteen years of my life I ran
wild on a common, and read nothing but our uncle Thomas's
books of voyages. At that age I became acquainted with the
celebrated poets of our own country; but it was only when it had
ceased to be in my power to derive its most important benefits
from such a conviction, that I perceived the necessity of becoming
acquainted with more languages than that of my native country.
Now I am twenty-eight and am in reality more illiterate than

many schoolboys of fifteen. It is true that I have thought more, and that my day dreams are more extended and magnificent, but they want (as the painters call it) *keeping*;[8] and I greatly need a friend who would have sense enough not to despise me as romantic, and affection enough for me to endeavour to regulate my mind.

Well, these are useless complaints; I shall certainly find no friend on the wide ocean, nor even here in Archangel, among merchants and seamen. Yet some feelings, unallied to the dross of human nature, beat even in these rugged bosoms. My lieutenant, for instance, is a man of wonderful courage and enterprise; he is madly desirous of glory: or rather, to word my phrase more characteristically, of advancement in his profession. He is an Englishman, and in the midst of national and professional prejudices, unsoftened by cultivation, retains some of the noblest endowments of humanity. I first became acquainted with him on board a whale vessel: finding that he was unemployed in this city, I easily engaged him to assist in my enterprise.

The master is a person of an excellent disposition, and is remarkable in the ship for his gentleness and the mildness of his discipline. This circumstance, added to his well-known integrity and dauntless courage, made me very desirous to engage him. A youth passed in solitude, my best years spent under your gentle and feminine fosterage, has so refined the groundwork of my character that I cannot overcome an intense distaste to the usual brutality exercised on board ship: I have never believed it to be necessary, and when I heard of a mariner equally noted for his kindliness of heart and the respect and obedience paid to him by his crew, I felt myself peculiarly fortunate in being able to secure his services. I heard of him first in rather a romantic manner, from a lady who owes to him the happiness of her life. This, briefly, is his story. Some years ago he loved a young Russian lady of moderate fortune; and having amassed a considerable sum in prize-money, the father of the girl consented to the match. He saw his mistress once before the destined ceremony; but she was bathed in tears, and, throwing herself at his feet, intreated him to spare her, confessing at the time that she loved another, but that he was poor, and that her father would never consent to the union. My generous friend reassured the suppliant, and on being informed of the name of her lover, instantly abandoned his pursuit. He had already bought a farm with his money, on which he had designed to pass the remainder of his life; but he bestowed the whole on his rival, together with the remains of his prize-money to purchase stock, and then himself solicited the young woman's father to consent to her marriage with her lover. But the old man decidedly refused, thinking himself bound in honour to my friend; who, when he found the father inexorable, quitted his country, nor returned until he heard that his former mistress was married according to her inclinations. 'What a noble fellow!' you will exclaim. He is so; but then he is wholly uneducated: he is as silent as a Turk, and a kind of ignorant carelessness attends him, which, while it renders his conduct the more astonishing, detracts from the interest and sympathy which otherwise he would command.

Yet do not suppose, because I complain a little, or because I can conceive a consolation for my toils which I may never know, that I am wavering in my resolutions. Those are as fixed as fate, and my voyage is only now delayed until the weather shall permit my embarkation. The winter has been dreadfully severe, but the spring promises well, and it is considered as a remarkably early season; so that perhaps I may sail sooner than I expected. I shall do nothing rashly: you know me sufficiently to confide in my prudence and considerateness whenever the safety of others is committed to my care.

I cannot describe to you my sensations on the near prospect of my undertaking. It is impossible to communicate to you a conception of the trembling sensation, half pleasurable and half fearful, with which I am preparing to depart. I am going to unexplored regions to 'the land of mist and snow'; but I shall kill no albatross, therefore do not be alarmed for my safety, or if I should come back to you as worn and woeful as the 'Ancient Mariner'. You will smile at my allusion; but I will disclose a secret. I have often attributed my attachment to, my passionate enthusiasm for, the dangerous mysteries of ocean, to that production of the most imaginative of modern poets. There is something at work in my soul, which I do not understand. I am practically industrious – painstaking; a workman to execute with perseverance and labour:

– but besides this, there is a love for the marvellous, a belief in the marvellous, intertwined in all my projects, which hurries me out of the common pathways of men, even to the wild sea and un-visited regions I am about to explore.

But to return to dearer considerations. Shall I meet you again, after having traversed immense seas, and returned by the most southern cape of Africa or America? I dare not expect such success, yet I cannot bear to look on the reverse of the picture. Continue for the present to write to me by every opportunity: I may receive your letters on some occasions when I need them most to support my spirits. I love you very tenderly. Remember me with affection, should you never hear from me again.

Your affectionate brother,
ROBERT WALTON.

LETTER III

═══

To Mrs Saville, England.

July 7th, 17–.

MY DEAR SISTER,

I write a few lines in haste to say that I am safe – and well advanced on my voyage. This letter will reach England by a merchantman now on its homeward voyage from Archangel; more fortunate than I, who may not see my native land, perhaps, for many years. I am, however, in good spirits: my men are bold, and apparently firm of purpose, nor do the floating sheets of ice that continually pass us, indicating the dangers of the region towards which we are advancing, appear to dismay them. We have already reached a very high latitude; but it is the height of summer, and although not so warm as in England, the southern gales, which blow us speedily towards those shores which I so ardently desire to attain, breathe a degree of renovating warmth which I had not expected.

No incidents have hitherto befallen us that would make a figure in a letter. One or two stiff gales, and the springing of a leak, are accidents which experienced navigators scarcely remember to record; and I shall be well content if nothing worse happen to us during our voyage.

Adieu, my dear Margaret. Be assured, that for my own sake, as well as yours, I will not rashly encounter danger. I will be cool, persevering and prudent.

But success *shall* crown my endeavours. Wherefore not? Thus far I have gone, tracing a secure way over the pathless seas: the very stars themselves being witnesses and testimonies of my triumph. Why not still proceed over the untamed yet obedient element? What can stop the determined heart and resolved will of man?

My swelling heart involuntarily pours itself out thus. But I must finish. Heaven bless my beloved sister!

R.W.

LETTER IV

To Mrs Saville, England.

August 5th, 17–.

So strange an accident has happened to us that I cannot forbear recording it, although it is very probable that you will see me before these papers can come into your possession.

Last Monday (July 31st) we were nearly surrounded by ice, which closed in the ship on all sides, scarcely leaving her the sea-room in which she floated. Our situation was somewhat danger-ous, especially as we were compassed round by a very thick fog. We accordingly lay to, hoping that some change would take place in the atmosphere and weather.

About two o'clock the mist cleared away, and we beheld, stretched out in every direction, vast and irregular plains of ice, which seemed to have no end. Some of my comrades groaned, and my own mind began to grow watchful with anxious thoughts, when a strange sight suddenly attracted our attention, and diverted our solicitude from our own situations. We perceived a low carriage, fixed on a sledge and drawn by dogs, pass on towards the north, at the distance of half a mile; a being which had the shape of a man, but apparently of gigantic stature, sat in the sledge, and guided the dogs. We watched the rapid progress of the traveller with our telescopes until he was lost among the distant inequalities of the ice.

This appearance excited our unqualified wonder. We were, as we believed, many hundred miles from any land; but this appari-tion seemed to denote that it was not, in reality, so distant as we had supposed. Shut in, however, by ice, it was impossible to follow his track, which we had observed with the greatest atten-tion.

About two hours after this occurrence we heard the ground

sea;[9] and before night the ice broke, and freed our ship. We, however, lay to until the morning, fearing to encounter in the dark those large loose masses which float about after the breaking up of the ice. I profited of this time to rest for a few hours.

In the morning, however, as soon as it was light, I went upon deck and found all the sailors busy on one side of the vessel, apparently talking to some one in the sea. It was, in fact, a sledge, like that we had seen before, which had drifted towards us in the night on a large fragment of ice. Only one dog remained alive; but there was a human being within it, whom the sailors were persuading to enter the vessel. He was not as the other traveller seemed to be, a savage inhabitant of some undiscovered island, but an European. When I appeared on deck, the master said, 'Here is our captain, and he will not allow you to perish on the open sea.'

On perceiving me, the stranger addressed me in English, although with a foreign accent. 'Before I come on board your vessel,' said he, 'will you have the kindness to inform me whither you are bound?'

You may conceive my astonishment on hearing such a question addressed to me from a man on the brink of destruction and to whom I should have supposed that my vessel would have been a resource which he would not have exchanged for the most precious wealth the earth can afford. I replied, however, that we were on a voyage of discovery towards the northern pole.

Upon hearing this he appeared satisfied, and consented to come on board. Good God! Margaret, if you had seen the man who thus capitulated for his safety, your surprise would have been boundless. His limbs were nearly frozen, and his body dreadfully emaciated by fatigue and suffering. I never saw a man in so wretched a condition. We attempted to carry him into the cabin; but as soon as he had quitted the fresh air, he fainted. We accordingly brought him back to the deck, and restored him to animation by rubbing him with brandy and forcing him to swallow a small quantity. As soon as he showed signs of life, we wrapped him up in blankets and placed him near the chimney of the kitchen stove. By slow degrees he recovered, and ate a little soup which restored him wonderfully.

Two days passed in this manner before he was able to speak; and I often feared that his sufferings had deprived him of understanding. When he had in some measure recovered, I removed him to my own cabin, and attended on him as much as my duty would permit. I never saw a more interesting creature; his eyes have generally an expression of wildness, and even madness, but there are moments when, if any one performs an act of kindness towards him or does him any the most trifling service, his whole countenance is lighted up, as it were, with a beam of benevolence and sweetness that I never saw equalled. But he is generally melancholy and despairing; and sometimes he gnashes his teeth; as if impatient of the weight of woes that oppresses him.

When my guest was a little recovered, I had great trouble to keep off the men, who wished to ask him a thousand questions; but I would not allow him to be tormented by their idle curiosity, in a state of body and mind whose restoration evidently depended upon entire repose. Once, however, the lieutenant asked why he had come so far upon the ice in so strange a vehicle?

His countenance instantly assumed an aspect of the deepest gloom; and he replied, 'To seek one who fled from me.'

'And did the man whom you pursued travel in the same fashion?'

'Yes.'

'Then I fancy we have seen him, for the day before we picked you up, we saw some dogs drawing a sledge, with a man in it, across the ice.'

This aroused the stranger's attention, and he asked a multitude of questions concerning the route which the daemon, as he called him, had pursued. Soon after, when he was alone with me, he said, 'I have, doubtless, excited your curiosity, as well as that of these good people; but you are too considerate to make enquiries.'

'Certainly; it would indeed be very impertinent and inhuman in me to trouble you with any inquisitiveness of mine.'

'And yet you rescued me from a strange and perilous situation: you have benevolently restored me to life.'

Soon after this he enquired if I thought that the breaking up of the ice had destroyed the other sledge? I replied, that I could not answer with any degree of certainty, for the ice had not broken until near midnight, and the traveller might have arrived at a place of safety before that time; but of this I could not judge.

From this time a new spirit of life animated the decaying frame of the stranger. He manifested the greatest eagerness to be upon deck, to watch for the sledge which had before appeared; but I have persuaded him to remain in the cabin, for he is far too weak to sustain the rawness of the atmosphere. I have promised that some one should watch for him and give him instant notice if any new object should appear in sight.

Such is my journal of what relates to this strange occurrence up to the present day. The stranger has gradually improved in health, but is very silent, and appears uneasy when anyone except myself enters the cabin. Yet his manners are so conciliating and gentle, that the sailors are all interested in him, although they have had very little communication with him. For my own part, I begin to love him as a brother; and his constant and deep grief fills me with sympathy and compassion. He must have been a noble creature in his better days, being even now in wreck so attractive and amiable.

I said in one of my letters, my dear Margaret, that I should find no friend on the wide ocean; yet I have found a man who, before his spirit had been broken by misery, I should have been happy to have possessed as the brother of my heart.

I shall continue my journal concerning the stranger at intervals, should I have any fresh incidents to record.

August 13th, 17–.

My affection for my guest increases every day. He excites at once my admiration and my pity to an astonishing degree. How can I see so noble a creature destroyed by misery, without feeling the most poignant grief? He is so gentle, yet so wise; his mind is so cultivated, and when he speaks, although his words are culled with the choicest art, yet they flow with rapidity and unparalleled eloquence.

He is now much recovered from his illness, and is continually on the deck, apparently watching for the sledge that preceded his own. Yet, although unhappy, he is not so utterly occupied by his own misery but that he interests himself deeply in the projects of others. He has frequently conversed with me on mine, which I have communicated to him without disguise. He entered attentively into all my arguments in favour of my eventual success, and into every minute detail of the measures I had taken to secure it. I was easily led by the sympathy which he evinced, to use the language of my heart, to give utterance to the burning ardour of my soul; and to say, with all the fervour that warmed me, how gladly I would sacrifice my fortune, my existence, my every hope, to the furtherance of my enterprise. One man's life or death were but a small price to pay for the acquirement of the knowledge which I sought for the dominion I should acquire and transmit over the elemental foes of our race. As I spoke, a dark gloom spread over my listener's countenance. At first I perceived that he tried to suppress his emotion; he placed his hands before his eyes, and my voice quivered and failed me as I beheld tears trickle fast from between his fingers – a groan burst from his heaving breast. I paused; at length he spoke, in broken accents – 'Unhappy man! Do you share my madness? Have you drunk also of the intoxicating draught? Hear me – let me reveal my tale, and you will dash the cup from your lips!'

Such words, you may imagine, strongly excited my curiosity; but the paroxysm of grief that had seized the stranger overcame his weakened powers, and many hours of repose and tranquil conversation were necessary to restore his composure.

Having conquered the violence of his feelings, he appeared to despise himself for being the slave of passion; and quelling the dark tyranny of despair, he led me again to converse concerning myself personally. He asked me the history of my earlier years. The tale was quickly told: but it awakened various trains of reflection. I spoke of my desire of finding a friend – of my thirst for a more intimate sympathy with a fellow mind than had ever fallen to my lot; and expressed my conviction that a man could boast of little happiness, who did not enjoy this blessing.

'I agree with you,' replied the stranger; 'we are unfashioned creatures, but half made up, if one wiser, better, dearer than ourselves – such a friend ought to be – do not lend his aid to

27

perfectionate our weak and faulty natures. I once had a friend, the most noble of human creatures, and am entitled, therefore, to judge respecting friendship. You have hope, and the world before you, and have no cause for despair. But I – I have lost every thing and cannot begin life anew.'

As he said this his countenance became expressive of a calm, settled grief, that touched me to the heart. But he was silent, and presently retired to his cabin.

Even broken in spirit as he is, no one can feel more deeply than he does the beauties of nature. The starry sky, the sea, and every sight afforded by these wonderful regions, seems still to have the power of elevating his soul from earth. Such a man has a double existence: he may suffer misery and be overwhelmed by disappointments, yet, when he has retired into himself, he will be like a celestial spirit, that has a halo around him, within whose circle no grief or folly ventures.

Will you smile at the enthusiasm I express concerning this divine wanderer? You would not, if you saw him. You have been tutored and refined by books and retirement from the world, and you are therefore somewhat fastidious; but this only renders you the more fit to appreciate the extraordinary merits of this wonderful man. Sometimes I have endeavoured to discover what quality it is which he possesses, that elevates him so immeasurably above any other person I ever knew. I believe it to be an intuitive discernment; a quick but never-failing power of judgment; a penetration into the causes of things, unequalled for clearness and precision; add to this a facility of expression, and a voice whose varied intonations are soul-subduing music.

August 19th, 17–.

Yesterday the stranger said to me, 'You may easily perceive, Captain Walton, that I have suffered great and unparalled misfortunes. I had determined, at one time, that the memory of these evils should die with me, but you have won me to alter my determination. You seek for knowledge and wisdom, as I once did; and I ardently hope that the gratification of your wishes may not be a serpent to sting you, as mine has been. I do not know that the relation of my disasters will be useful to you; yet, when I reflect that you are pursuing the same course, exposing yourself to the same dangers which have rendered me what I am, I imagine that you may deduce an apt moral from my tale; one that may direct you if you succeed in your undertaking, and console you in case of failure. Prepare to hear of occurrences which are usually deemed marvellous. Were we among the tamer scenes of nature, I might fear to encounter your unbelief, perhaps your ridicule; but many things will appear possible in these wild and mysterious regions, which would provoke the laughter of those unacquainted with the ever-varied powers of nature; – nor can I doubt but that my tale conveys in its series internal evidence of the truth of the events of which it is composed.'

You may easily imagine that I was much gratified by the offered communication, yet I could not endure that he should renew his grief by a recital of his misfortunes. I felt the greatest eagerness to hear the promised narrative, partly from curiosity, and partly from a strong desire to ameliorate his fate, if it were in my power. I expressed these feelings in my answer.

'I thank you,' he replied, 'for your sympathy, but it is useless; my fate is nearly fulfilled. I wait but for one event, and then I shall repose in peace. I understand your feeling,' continued he, perceiving that I wished to interrupt him: 'but you are mistaken, my friend, if thus you will allow me to name you; nothing can alter my destiny; listen to my history, and you will perceive how irrevocably it is determined.'

He then told me, that he would commence his narrative the next day, when I should be at leisure. This promise drew from me the warmest thanks. I have resolved every night, when I am not imperatively occupied by my duties, to record, as nearly as possible in his own words, what he has related during the day. If I should be engaged, I will at least make notes. This manuscript will doubtless afford you the greatest pleasure: but to me, who know him and who hear it from his own lips – with what interest and sympathy shall I read it in some future day! Even now, as I commence my task, his full-toned voice swells in my ears; his lustrous eyes dwell on me with all their melancholy sweetness; I see his thin hand raised in animation, while the lineaments of his face are irradiated by the soul within. Strange and harrowing must be his story, frightful the storm which embraced the gallant vessel on its course and wrecked it – thus!

CHAPTER I

I am by birth a Genevese, and my family is one of the most distinguished of that republic. My ancestors had been for many years counsellors and syndics;[10] and my father had filled several public situations with honour and reputation. He was respected by all who knew him, for his integrity and indefatigable attention to public business. He passed his younger days perpetually occupied by the affairs of his country; a variety of circumstances had prevented his marrying early, nor was it until the decline of life that he became a husband and the father of a family.

As the circumstances of his marriage illustrate his character, I cannot refrain from relating them. One of his most intimate friends was a merchant who, from a flourishing state, fell, through numerous mischances, into poverty. This man, whose name was Beaufort, was of a proud and unbending disposition and could not bear to live in poverty and oblivion in the same country where he had formerly been distinguished for his rank and magnificence. Having paid his debts, therefore, in the most honourable manner, he retreated with his daughter to the town of Lucerne, where he lived unknown and in wretchedness. My father loved Beaufort with the truest friendship, and was deeply grieved by his retreat in these unfortunate circumstances. He bitterly deplored the false pride which led his friend to a conduct so little worthy of the affection that united them. He lost no time in endeavouring to seek him out, with the hope of persuading him to begin the world again through his credit and assistance.

Beaufort had taken effectual measures to conceal himself; and it was ten months before my father discovered his abode. Overjoyed at this discovery, he hastened to the house, which was situated in a mean street near the Reuss. But when he entered, misery and despair alone welcomed him. Beaufort had saved but a very small sum of money from the wreck of his fortunes, but it was sufficient to provide him with sustenance for some months, and in the mean time he hoped to procure some respectable employment in a merchant's house. The interval was, consequently, spent in inaction; his grief only became more deep and rankling, when he had leisure for reflection; and at length it took so fast hold of his mind, that at the end of three months he lay on a bed of sickness, incapable of any exertion.

His daughter attended him with the greatest tenderness; but she saw with despair that their little fund was rapidly decreasing, and that there was no other prospect of support. But Caroline Beaufort possessed a mind of an uncommon mould, and her courage rose to support her in her adversity. She procured plain work; she plaited straw; and by various means contrived to earn a pittance scarcely sufficient to support life.

Several months passed in this manner. Her father grew worse; her time was more entirely occupied in attending him; her means of subsistence decreased; and in the tenth month her father died in her arms, leaving her an orphan and a beggar. This last blow overcame her, and she knelt by Beaufort's coffin, weeping bitterly, when my father entered the chamber. He came like a protecting spirit to the poor girl, who committed herself to his care; and after the interment of his friend he conducted her to Geneva, and placed her under the protection of a relation. Two years after this event Caroline became his wife.

There was a considerable difference between the ages of my parents, but this circumstance seemed to unite them only closer in bonds of devoted affection. There was a sense of justice in my father's upright mind, which rendered it necessary that he should approve highly to love strongly. Perhaps during former years he had suffered from the late-discovered unworthiness of one beloved, and so was disposed to set a greater value on tried worth. There was a show of gratitude and worship in his attachment to my mother, differing wholly from the doating fondness of age, for it was inspired by reverence for her virtues and a desire to be the means of, in some degree, recompensing her for the sorrows she had endured, but which gave inexpressible grace to his behaviour to her. Every thing was made to yield to her wishes and her convenience. He strove to shelter her, as a fair exotic is sheltered by the gardener, from every rougher wind, and to surround her with all that could tend to excite pleasurable emotion in her soft and benevolent mind. Her health, and even the tranquillity of her hitherto constant spirit, had been shaken by what she had gone through. During the two years that had elapsed previous to their marriage my father had gradually relinquished all his public functions; and immediately after their union they sought the pleasant climate of Italy, and the change of scene and interest attendant on a tour through that land of wonders, as a restorative for her weakened frame.

From Italy they visited Germany and France. I, their eldest child, was born at Naples, and as an infant accompanied them in their rambles. I remained for several years their only child. Much as they were attached to each other, they seemed to draw inexhaustible stores of affection from a very mine of love to bestow them upon me. My mother's tender caresses and my father's smile of benevolent pleasure while regarding me, are my first recollections. I was their plaything and their idol, and something better – their child, the innocent and helpless creature bestowed on them by Heaven, whom to bring up to good, and whose future lot it was in their hands to direct to happiness or misery, according as they fulfilled their duties towards me. With this deep consciousness of what they owed towards the being to which they had given life, added to the active spirit of tenderness that animated both, it may be imagined that while during every hour of my infant life I received a lesson of patience, of charity, and of self-control, I was so guided by a silken cord that all seemed but one train of enjoyment to me.

For a long time I was their only care. My mother had much desire to have a daughter, but I continued their single offspring. When I was about five years old, while making an excursion beyond the frontiers of Italy, they passed a week on the shores of the Lake of Como. Their benevolent disposition often made them enter the cottages of the poor. This, to my mother, was more than a duty; it was a necessity, a passion – remembering what she had suffered, and how she had been relieved, – for her to act in her turn the guardian angel to the afflicted. During one of their walks a poor cot in the foldings of a vale attracted their notice as being singularly disconsolate, while the number of half-clothed children gathered about it spoke of penury in its worst shape. One day, when my father had gone by himself to Milan, my mother, accompanied by me, visited this abode. She found a peasant and his wife, hard working, bent down by care and labour, distributing a scanty meal to five hungry babes. Among these there was one which attracted my mother far above all the rest. She appeared of a different stock. The four others were dark-eyed, hardy little vagrants; this child was thin, and very fair. Her hair was the brightest living gold, and despite the poverty of her clothing, seemed to set a crown of distinction on her head. Her brow was clear and ample, her blue eyes cloudless, and her lips and the moulding of her face so expressive of sensibility and sweetness that none could behold her without looking on her as of a distinct species, a being heaven-sent, and bearing a celestial stamp in all her features.

The peasant woman, perceiving that my mother fixed eyes of wonder and admiration on this lovely girl, eagerly communicated her history. She was not her child, but the daughter of a Milanese nobleman. Her mother was a German, and had died on giving her birth. The infant had been placed with these good people to nurse: they were better off then. They had not been long married, and their eldest child was but just born. The father of their charge was one of those Italians nursed in the memory of the antique glory of Italy – one among the *schiavi ognor frementi*,[11] who exerted himself to obtain the liberty of his country. He became the victim of its weakness. Whether he had died, or still lingered in the dungeons of Austria, was not known. His property was confiscated; his child became an orphan and a beggar. She continued with her foster parents, and bloomed in their rude abode, fairer than a garden rose among dark-leaved brambles.

When my father returned from Milan, he found playing with me in the hall of our villa a child fairer than a pictured cherub – a creature who seemed to shed radiance from her looks and whose form and motions were lighter than the chamois of the hills. The apparition was soon explained. With his permission my mother prevailed on her rustic guardians to yield their charge to her. They were fond of the sweet orphan. Her presence had seemed a blessing to them, but it would be unfair to her to keep her in poverty and want, when Providence afforded her such powerful protection. They consulted their village priest, and the result was that Elizabeth Lavenza became the inmate of my parents' house – my more than sister – the beautiful and adored companion of all my occupations and my pleasures.

Everyone loved Elizabeth. The passionate and most reverential attachment with which all regarded her became, while I shared it, my pride and my delight. On the evening previous to her being brought to my home, my mother had said playfully, 'I have a pretty present for my Victor – tomorrow he shall have it.' And when, on the morrow, she presented Elizabeth to me as her promised gift, I, with childish seriousness, interpreted her words literally and looked upon Elizabeth as mine – mine to protect, love, and cherish. All praises bestowed on her I received as made to a possession of my own. We called each other familiarly by the name of cousin. No word, no expression could body forth the kind of relation in which she stood to me – my more than sister, since till death she was to be mine only.

CHAPTER II

We were brought up together; there was not quite a year difference in our ages. I need not say that we were strangers to any species of disunion or dispute. Harmony was the soul of our companionship, and the diversity and contrast that subsisted in our characters drew us nearer together. Elizabeth was of a calmer and more concentrated disposition; but, with all my ardour, I was capable of a more intense application, and was more deeply smitten with the thirst for knowledge. She busied herself with following the aerial creations of the poets; and in the majestic and wondrous scenes which surrounded our Swiss home – the sublime shapes of the mountains; the changes of the seasons; tempest and calm; the silence of winter, and the life and turbulence of our Alpine summers – she found ample scope for admiration and delight. While my companion contemplated with a serious and satisfied spirit the magnificent appearances of things, I delighted in investigating their causes. The world was to me a secret which I desired to divine. Curiosity, earnest research to learn the hidden laws of nature, gladness akin to rapture, as they were unfolded to me, are among the earliest sensations I can remember.

On the birth of a second son, my junior by seven years, my parents gave up entirely their wandering life, and fixed themselves in their native country. We possessed a house in Geneva, and a *campagne*[12] on Belrive, the eastern shore of the lake, at the distance of rather more than a league[13] from the city. We resided principally in the latter, and the lives of my parents were passed in considerable seclusion. It was my temper to avoid a crowd, and to attach myself fervently to a few. I was indifferent, therefore, to my schoolfellows in general; but I united myself in the bonds of the closest friendship to one among them. Henry Clerval was the son of a merchant of Geneva. He was a boy of singular talent and fancy. He loved enterprise, hardship, and even danger for its own sake. He was deeply read in books of chivalry and romance. He

36

composed heroic songs, and began to write many a tale of enchantment and knightly adventure. He tried to make us act plays and to enter into masquerades, in which the characters were drawn from the heroes of Roncesvalles, of the Round Table of King Arthur, and the chivalrous train who shed their blood to redeem the holy sepulchre from the hands of the infidels.

No human being could have passed a happier childhood than myself. My parents were possessed by the very spirit of kindness and indulgence. We felt that they were not the tyrants to rule our lot according to their caprice, but the agents and creators of all the many delights which we enjoyed. When I mingled with other families, I distinctly discerned how peculiarly fortunate my lot was, and gratitude assisted the development of filial love.

My temper was sometimes violent, and my passions vehement; but by some law in my temperature[14] they were turned not towards childish pursuits but to an eager desire to learn, and not to learn all things indiscriminately. I confess that neither the structure of languages, nor the code of governments, nor the politics of various states possessed attractions for me. It was the secrets of heaven and earth that I desired to learn; and whether it was the outward substance of things, or the inner spirit of nature and the mysterious soul of man that occupied me, still my enquiries were directed to the metaphysical, or in its highest sense, the physical secrets of the world.

Meanwhile Clerval occupied himself, so to speak, with the moral relations of things. The busy stage of life, the virtues of heroes, and the actions of men were his theme; and his hope and his dream was to become one among those whose names are recorded in story, as the gallant and adventurous benefactors of our species. The saintly soul of Elizabeth shone like a shrine-dedicated lamp in our peaceful home. Her sympathy was ours; her smile, her soft voice, the sweet glance of her celestial eyes, were ever there to bless and animate us. She was the living spirit of love to soften and attract: I might have become sullen in my study, rough through the ardour of my nature, but that she was there to subdue me to a semblance of her own gentleness. And Clerval – could aught ill entrench on the noble spirit of Clerval – yet he might not have been so perfectly humane, so thoughtful in his generosity – so full of kindness and tenderness amidst his passion for adventurous exploit, had she not unfolded to him the real loveliness of beneficence, and made the doing good the end and aim of his soaring ambition.

I feel exquisite pleasure in dwelling on the recollections of childhood, before misfortune had tainted my mind, and changed its bright visions of extensive usefulness into gloomy and narrow reflections upon self. Besides, in drawing the picture of my early days, I also record those events which led, by insensible steps, to my after tale of misery: for when I would account to myself for the birth of that passion, which afterwards ruled my destiny, I find it arise, like a mountain river, from ignoble and almost forgotten sources; but, swelling as it proceeded, it became the torrent which, in its course, has swept away all my hopes and joys.

Natural philosophy[15] is the genius that has regulated my fate; I desire, therefore, in this narration, to state those facts which led to my predilection for that science. When I was thirteen years of age we all went on a party of pleasure to the baths near Thonon: the inclemency of the weather obliged us to remain a day confined to the inn. In this house I chanced to find a volume of the works of Cornelius Agrippa.[16] I opened it with apathy; the theory which he attempts to demonstrate, and the wonderful facts which he relates soon changed this feeling into enthusiasm. A new light seemed to dawn upon my mind, and, bounding with joy, I communicated my discovery to my father. My father looked carelessly at the titlepage of my book and said, 'Ah! Cornelius Agrippa! My dear Victor, do not waste your time upon this; it is sad trash.'

If, instead of this remark, my father had taken the pains to explain to me that the principles of Agrippa had been entirely exploded, and that a modern system of science had been introduced, which possessed much greater powers than the ancient, because the powers of the latter were chimerical, while those of the former were real and practical; under such circumstances I should certainly have thrown Agrippa aside and have contented my imagination, warmed as it was, by returning with greater ardour to my former studies. It is even possible that the train of my ideas would never have received the fatal impulse that led to my ruin. But the cursory glance my father had taken of my volume by no means assured me that he was acquainted with its contents; and I continued to read with the greatest avidity.

When I returned home my first care was to procure the whole works of this author, and afterwards of Paracelsus and Albertus Magnus.[17] I read and studied the wild fancies of these writers with delight; they appeared to me treasures known to few besides myself. I have described myself as always having been imbued with a fervent longing to penetrate the secrets of nature. In spite of the intense labour and wonderful discoveries of modern philosophers, I always came from my studies discontented and unsatisfied. Sir Isaac Newton is said to have avowed that he felt like a child picking up shells beside the great and unexplored ocean of truth. Those of his successors in each branch of natural philosophy with whom I was acquainted, appeared even to my boy's apprehensions, as tyros engaged in the same pursuit.

The untaught peasant beheld the elements around him, and was acquainted with their practical uses. The most learned philosopher knew little more. He had partially unveiled the face of Nature, but her immortal lineaments were still a wonder and a mystery. He might dissect, anatomise, and give names; but, not to speak of a final cause, causes in their secondary and tertiary grades were utterly unknown to him. I had gazed upon the fortifications and impediments that seemed to keep human beings from entering the citadel of nature, and rashly and ignorantly I had repined.

But here were books, and here were men who had penetrated deeper and knew more. I took their word for all that they averred, and I became their disciple. It may appear strange that such should arise in the eighteenth century; but while I followed the routine of education in the schools of Geneva, I was, to a great degree, self-taught with regard to my favourite studies. My father was not scientific, and I was left to struggle with a child's blindness, added to a student's thirst for knowledge. Under the guidance of my new preceptors, I entered with the greatest diligence into the search of the philosopher's stone and the elixir of life; but the latter soon obtained my undivided attention. Wealth was an inferior object; but what glory would attend the discovery, if I could banish disease from the human frame and render man invulnerable to any but a violent death!

Nor were these my only visions. The raising of ghosts or devils, was a promise liberally accorded by my favourite authors, the fulfilment of which I most eagerly sought; and if my incantations were always unsuccessful, I attributed the failure rather to my own inexperience and mistake, than to a want of skill or fidelity in my instructors. And thus for a time I was occupied by exploded systems, mingling, like an unadept, a thousand contradictory theories, and floundering desperately in a very slough of multifarious knowledge, guided by an ardent imagination and childish reasoning, till an accident again changed the current of my ideas.

When I was about fifteen years old we had retired to our house near Belrive, when we witnessed a most violent and terrible thunder-storm. It advanced from behind the mountains of Jura; and the thunder burst at once with frightful loudness from various quarters of the heavens. I remained, while the storm lasted, watching its progress with curiosity and delight. As I stood at the door, on a sudden I beheld a stream of fire issue from an old and beautiful oak, which stood about twenty yards from our house; and so soon as the dazzling light vanished, the oak had disappeared, and nothing remained but a blasted stump. When we visited it the next morning, we found the tree shattered in a singular manner. It was not splintered by the shock, but entirely reduced to thin ribbons of wood. I never beheld anything so utterly destroyed.

Before this I was not unacquainted with the more obvious laws of electricity. On this occasion a man of great research in natural philosophy was with us, and, excited by this catastrophe, he entered on the explanation of a theory which he had formed on the subject of electricity and galvanism, which was at once new and astonishing to me. All that he said threw greatly into the shade Cornelius Agrippa, Albertus Magnus, and Paracelsus, the lords of my imagination; but by some fatality the overthrow of these men disinclined me to pursue my accustomed studies. It seemed to me as if nothing would or could ever be known. All that had so long engaged my attention suddenly grew despicable. By one of those caprices of the mind, which we are perhaps most subject to in early youth, I at once gave up my former occupations, set down natural history and all its progeny as a deformed and abortive creation, and entertained the greatest disdain for a would-be science which could never even step within the threshold of real knowledge. In this mood of mind I betook myself to the mathematics, and the branches of study appertaining to that science, as being built upon secure foundations, and so worthy of my consideration.

Thus strangely are our souls constructed, and by such slight ligaments are we bound to prosperity or ruin. When I look back, it seems to me as if this almost miraculous change of inclination and will was the immediate suggestion of the guardian angel of my life – the last effort made by the spirit of preservation to avert the storm that was even then hanging in the stars, and ready to envelope me. Her victory was announced by an unusual tranquillity and gladness of soul, which followed the relinquishing of my ancient and latterly tormenting studies. It was thus that I was to be taught to associate evil with their prosecution, happiness with their disregard.

It was a strong effort of the spirit of good; but it was ineffectual. Destiny was too potent, and her immutable laws had decreed my utter and terrible destruction.

CHAPTER III

When I had attained the age of seventeen, my parents resolved, that I should become a student at the university of Ingolstadt. I had hitherto attended the schools of Geneva; but my father thought it necessary, for the completion of my education, that I should be made acquainted with other customs than those of my native country. My departure was therefore fixed at an early date; but, before the day resolved upon could arrive, the first misfortune of my life occurred – an omen, as it were, of my future misery.

Elizabeth had caught the scarlet fever; her illness was severe, and she was in the greatest danger. During her illness, many arguments had been urged to persuade my mother to refrain from attending upon her. She had, at first, yielded to our in-treaties, but when she heard that the life of her favourite was menaced, she could no longer control her anxiety. She attended her sickbed; – her watchful attentions triumphed over the malignity of the distemper, – Elizabeth was saved, but the consequences of this imprudence were fatal to her preserver. On the third day my mother sickened; her fever was accompanied by the most alarming symptoms, and the looks of her medical attendants prognosticated the worst event. On her death-bed the fortitude and benignity of this best of women did not desert her. She joined the hands of Elizabeth and myself: – 'My children,' she said, 'my firmest hopes of future happiness were placed on the prospect of your union. This expectation will now be the consolation of your father. Elizabeth, my love, you must supply my place to my younger children. Alas! I regret that I am taken from you; and, happy and beloved as I have been, is it not hard to quit you all? But these are not thoughts befitting me; I will endeavour to resign myself cheerfully to death, and will indulge a hope of meeting you in another world.'

She died calmly; and her countenance expressed affection even in death. I need not describe the feelings of those whose dearest ties are rent by that most irreparable evil; the void that presents itself to the soul; and the despair that is exhibited on the countenance. It is so long before the mind can persuade itself that she, whom we saw every day, and whose very existence appeared a part of our own, can have departed forever – that the brightness of a beloved eye can have been extinguished, and the sound of a voice so familiar and dear to the ear can be hushed, never more to be heard. These are the reflections of the first days; but when the lapse of time proves the reality of the evil, then the actual bitterness of grief commences. Yet from whom has not that rude hand rent away some dear connexion? and why should I describe a sorrow which all have felt, and must feel? The time at length arrives when grief is rather an indulgence than a necessity; and the smile that plays upon the lips, although it may be deemed a sacrilege, is not banished. My mother was dead, but we had still duties which we ought to perform; we must continue our course with the rest, and learn to think ourselves fortunate, whilst one remains whom the spoiler had not seized.

My departure for Ingolstadt, which had been deferred by these events, was now again determined upon. I obtained from my father a respite of some weeks. It appeared to me sacrilege so soon to leave the repose, akin to death, of the house of mourning and to rush into the thick of life. I was new to sorrow, but it did not the less alarm me. I was unwilling to quit the sight of those that remained to me; and above all, I desired to see my sweet Elizabeth in some degree consoled.

She indeed veiled her grief, and strove to act the comforter to us all. She looked steadily on life, and assumed its duties with courage and zeal. She devoted herself to those whom she had been taught to call her uncle and cousins. Never was she so enchanting as at this time, when she recalled the sunshine of her smiles and spent them upon us. She forgot even her own regret in her endeavours to make us forget.

The day of my departure at length arrived. Clerval spent the last evening with us. He had endeavoured to persuade his father to permit him to accompany me and to become my fellow student; but in vain. His father was a narrow-minded trader, and saw idleness and ruin in the aspirations and ambition of his son. Henry deeply felt the misfortune of being debarred from a liberal education. He said little; but when he spoke, I read in his kindling eye and in his animated glance a restrained but firm resolve, not to be chained to the miserable details of commerce.

We sat late. We could not tear ourselves away from each other, nor persuade ourselves to say the word 'Farewell!' It was said; and we retired under the pretence of seeking repose, each fancying that the other was deceived: but when at morning's dawn I descended to the carriage which was to convey me away, they were all there – my father again to bless me, Clerval to press my hand once more, my Elizabeth to renew her intreaties that I would write often, and to bestow the last feminine attentions on her playmate and friend.

I threw myself into the chaise that was to convey me away and indulged in the most melancholy reflections. I, who had ever been surrounded by amiable companions, continually engaged in endeavouring to bestow mutual pleasure, I was now alone. In the university, whither I was going, I must form my own friends and be my own protector. My life had hitherto been remarkably secluded and domestic; and this had given me invincible repugnance to new countenances. I loved my brothers, Elizabeth, and Clerval; these were 'old familiar faces,'[18] but I believed myself totally unfitted for the company of strangers. Such were my reflections as I commenced my journey; but as I proceeded, my spirits and hopes rose. I ardently desired the acquisition of knowledge. I had often, when at home, thought it hard to remain during my youth cooped up in one place, and had longed to enter the world, and take my station among other human beings. Now my desires were complied with, and it would, indeed, have been folly to repent.

I had sufficient leisure for these and many other reflections during my journey to Ingolstadt, which was long and fatiguing. At length the high white steeple of the town met my eyes. I alighted, and was conducted to my solitary apartment, to spend the evening as I pleased.

The next morning I delivered my letters of introduction, and paid a visit to some of the principal professors. Chance – or rather the evil influence, the Angel of Destruction, which asserted omnipotent sway over me from the moment I turned my reluctant steps from my father's door – led me first to M. Krempe, professor of natural philosophy. He was an uncouth man, but deeply imbued in the secrets of his science. He asked me several questions concerning my progress in the different branches of science appertaining to natural philosophy. I replied carelessly; and, partly in contempt, mentioned the names of my alchymists as the principal authors I had studied. The professor stared. 'Have you,' he said, 'really spent your time in studying such nonsense?'

I replied in the affirmative. 'Every minute,' continued M. Krempe with warmth, 'every instant that you have wasted on those books is utterly and entirely lost. You have burdened your memory with exploded systems and useless names. Good God! In what desert land have you lived, where no one was kind enough to inform you that these fancies which you have so greedily imbibed are a thousand years old and as musty as they are ancient? I little expected, in this enlightened and scientific age, to find a disciple of Albertus Magnus and Paracelsus. My dear sir, you must begin your studies entirely anew.'

So saying, he stept aside, and wrote down a list of several books treating of natural philosophy, which he desired me to procure; and dismissed me after mentioning that in the beginning of the following week he intended to commence a course of lectures upon natural philosophy in its general relations, and that M. Waldman, a fellow-professor, would lecture upon chemistry the alternate days that he omitted.

I returned home, not disappointed, for I have said that I had long considered those authors useless whom the professor reprobated; but I returned, not at all the more inclined to recur to these studies in any shape. M. Krempe was a little squat man, with a gruff voice and a repulsive countenance; the teacher, therefore, did not prepossess me in favour of his pursuits. In rather a too philosophical and connected a strain, perhaps, I have given an account of the conclusions I had come to concerning them in my early years. As a child, I had not been content with the results promised by the modern professors of natural science. With a confusion of ideas only to be accounted for by my extreme youth, and my want of a guide on such matters, I had retrod the steps of knowledge along the paths of time, and exchanged the discoveries of recent enquirers for the dreams of forgotten alchymists. Besides, I had a contempt for the uses of modern natural philosophy. It was very different, when the masters of the science sought immortality and power; such views, although futile, were grand; but now the scene was changed. The ambition of the enquirer seemed to limit itself to the annihilation of those visions on which my interest in science was chiefly founded. I was required to exchange chimeras of boundless grandeur for realities of little worth.

Such were my reflections during the first two or three days of my residence at Ingolstadt, which were chiefly spent in becoming acquainted with the localities, and the principal residents in my new abode. But as the ensuing week commenced, I thought of the information which M. Krempe had given me concerning the lectures. And although I could not consent to go and hear that little conceited fellow deliver sentences out of a pulpit, I recollected what he had said of M. Waldman, whom I had never seen, as he had hitherto been out of town.

Partly from curiosity, and partly from idleness, I went into the lecturing room, which M. Waldman entered shortly after. This professor was very unlike his colleague. He appeared about fifty years of age, but with an aspect expressive of the greatest benevolence; a few grey hairs covered his temples, but those at the back of his head were nearly black. His person was short, but remarkably erect; and his voice the sweetest I had ever heard. He began his lecture by a recapitulation of the history of chemistry and the various improvements made by different men of learning, pronouncing with fervour the names of the most distinguished discoverers. He then took a cursory view of the present state of the science, and explained many of its elementary terms. After having made a few preparatory experiments, he concluded with a panegyric upon modern chemistry, the terms of which I shall never forget: –

'The ancient teachers of this science,' said he, 'promised impossibilities, and performed nothing. The modern masters promise very little; they know that metals cannot be transmuted, and that the elixir of life is a chimera. But these philosophers, whose hands seem only made to dabble in dirt, and their eyes to pore over the microscope or crucible, have indeed performed miracles. They penetrate into the recesses of nature, and show how she works in her hiding-places. They ascend into the heavens: they have discovered how the blood circulates, and the nature of the air we breathe. They have acquired new and almost unlimited powers; they can command the thunders of heaven, mimic the earthquake, and even mock the invisible world with its own shadows.'

Such were the professor's words – rather let me say such the words of the fate – enounced to destroy me. As he went on I felt as if my soul were grappling with a palpable enemy; one by one the various keys were touched which formed the mechanism of my being: chord after chord was sounded, and soon my mind was filled with one thought, one conception, one purpose. So much has been done, exclaimed the soul of Frankenstein, – more, far more, will I achieve: treading in the steps already marked, I will pioneer a new way, explore unknown powers, and unfold to the world the deepest mysteries of creation.

I closed not my eyes that night. My internal being was in a state of insurrection and turmoil; I felt that order would thence arise, but I had no power to produce it. By degrees, after the morning's dawn, sleep came. I awoke, and my yesternight's thoughts were as a dream. There only remained a resolution to return to my ancient studies and to devote myself to a science for which I believed myself to possess a natural talent. On the same day, I paid M. Waldman a visit. His manners in private were even more mild and attractive than in public; for there was a certain dignity in his mien during his lecture, which in his own house was replaced by the greatest affability and kindness. I gave him pretty nearly the same account of my former pursuits as I had given to his fellow-professor. He heard with attention the little narration concerning my studies, and smiled at the names of Cornelius Agrippa and Paracelsus, but without the contempt that M. Krempe had exhibited. He said that 'these were men to whose indefatigable zeal modern philosophers were indebted for most of the foundations of their knowledge. They had left to us, as an easier task to give new names, and arrange in connected classifications the facts which they in a great degree had been the instruments of bringing to light. The labours of men of genius, however erroneously directed, scarcely ever fail in ultimately turning to the solid advantage of mankind.' I listened to his statement, which was delivered without any presumption or affectation; and then added that his lecture had removed any prejudices against modern chemists; I expressed myself in measured terms, with the modesty and deference due from a youth to his instructor, without letting escape (inexperience in life would have made me ashamed) any of the enthusiasm which stimulated my intended labours. I requested his advice concerning the books I ought to procure.

'I am happy,' said M. Waldman, 'to have gained a disciple; and if your application equals your ability, I have no doubt of your success. Chemistry is that branch of natural philosophy in which the greatest improvements have been and may be made: it is on that account that I have made it my peculiar study; but at the same time, I have not neglected the other branches of science. A man would make but a very sorry chemist if he attended to that department of human knowledge alone. If your wish is to become really a man of science, and not merely a petty experimentalist, I should advise you to apply to every branch of natural philosophy, including mathematics.'

He then took me into his laboratory and explained to me the uses of his various machines; instructing me as to what I ought to procure, and promising me the use of his own when I should have advanced far enough in the science not to derange their mechanism. He also gave me the list of books which I had requested; and I took my leave.

Thus ended a day memorable to me: it decided my future destiny.

CHAPTER IV

From this day natural philosophy, and particularly chemistry, in the most comprehensive sense of the term, became nearly my sole occupation. I read with ardour those works, so full of genius and discrimination, which modern enquirers have written on these subjects. I attended the lectures, and cultivated the acquaintance, of the men of science of the university; and I found even in M. Krempe a great deal of sound sense and real information, combined, it is true, with a repulsive physiognomy and manners, but not on that account the less valuable. In M. Waldman I found a true friend. His gentleness was never tinged by dogmatism, and his instructions were given with an air of frankness and good nature, that banished every idea of pedantry. In a thousand ways he smoothed for me the path of knowledge, and made the most abstruse enquiries clear and facile to my apprehension. My application was at first fluctuating and uncertain; it gained strength as I proceeded, and soon became so ardent and eager, that the stars often disappeared in the light of morning whilst I was yet engaged in my laboratory.

As I applied so closely, it may be easily conceived that my progress was rapid. My ardour was indeed the astonishment of the students, and my proficiency that of the masters. Professor Krempe often asked me, with a sly smile, how Cornelius Agrippa went on? whilst M. Waldman expressed the most heartfelt exultation in my progress. Two years passed in this manner, during which I paid no visit to Geneva, but was engaged, heart and soul, in the pursuit of some discoveries which I hoped to make. None but those who have experienced them can conceive of the enticements of science. In other studies you go as far as others have gone before you, and there is nothing more to know; but in a scientific pursuit there is continual food for discovery and wonder. A mind of moderate capacity, which closely pursued one study must infallibly arrive at great proficiency in that study; and

I, who continually sought the attainment of one object of pursuit and was solely wrapt up in this, improved so rapidly, that, at the end of two years, I made some discoveries in the improvement of some chemical instruments, which procured me great esteem and admiration at the university. When I had arrived at this point and had become as well acquainted with the theory and practice of natural philosophy as depended on the lessons of any of the professors at Ingolstadt, my residence there being no longer conducive to my improvements, I thought of returning to my friends and my native town, when an incident happened that protracted my stay.

One of the phenomena which had peculiarly attracted my attention was the structure of the human frame, and, indeed, any animal endued with life. Whence, I often asked myself, did the principle of life proceed? It was a bold question, and one which has ever been considered as a mystery; yet with how many things are we upon the brink of becoming acquainted, if cowardice or carelessness did not restrain our enquiries. I revolved these circumstances in my mind, and determined thenceforth to apply myself more particularly to those branches of natural philosophy which relate to physiology. Unless I had been animated by an almost supernatural enthusiasm, my application to this study would have been irksome, and almost intolerable. To examine the causes of life, we must first have recourse to death. I became acquainted with the science of anatomy: but this was not sufficient; I must also observe the natural decay and corruption of the human body. In my education my father had taken the greatest precautions that my mind should be impressed with no supernatural horrors. I do not ever remember to have trembled at a tale of superstition, or to have feared the apparition of a spirit. Darkness had no effect upon my fancy; and a churchyard was to me merely the receptacle of bodies deprived of life, which, from being the seat of beauty and strength, had become food for the worm. Now I was led to examine the cause and progress of this decay, and forced to spend days and nights in vaults and charnel-houses. My attention was fixed upon every object the most insupportable to the delicacy of the human feelings. I saw how the fine form of man was degraded and wasted; I beheld the corruption of death succeed to the blooming cheek of life; I saw how the worm inherited the wonders of the eye and brain. I paused, examining and analysing all the minutiae of causation, as exemplified in the change from life to death, and death to life, until from the midst of this darkness a sudden light broke in upon me – a light so brilliant and wondrous, yet so simple, that while I became dizzy with the immensity of the prospect which it illustrated, I was surprised, that among so many men of genius who had directed their enquiries towards the same science, that I alone should be reserved to discover so astonishing a secret.

Remember, I am not recording the vision of a madman. The sun does not more certainly shine in the heavens, than that which I now affirm is true. Some miracle might have produced it, yet the stages of the discovery were distinct and probable. After days and nights of incredible labour and fatigue, I succeeded in discovering the cause of generation and life; nay, more, I became myself capable of bestowing animation upon lifeless matter.

The astonishment which I had at first experienced on this discovery soon gave place to delight and rapture. After so much time spent in painful labour, to arrive at once at the summit of my desires, was the most gratifying consummation of my toils. But this discovery was so great and overwhelming, that all the steps by which I had been progressively led to it were obliterated, and I beheld only the result. What had been the study and desire of the wisest men since the creation of the world was now within my grasp. Not that, like a magic scene, it all opened upon me at once: the information I had obtained was of a nature rather to direct my endeavours so soon as I should point them towards the object of my search, than to exhibit that object already accomplished. I was like the Arabian who had been buried with the dead[19] and found a passage to life, aided only by one glimmering and seemingly ineffectual light.

I see by your eagerness and the wonder and hope which your eyes express, my friend, that you expect to be informed of the secret with which I am acquainted; that cannot be: listen patiently until the end of my story, and you will easily perceive why I am reserved upon that subject. I will not lead you on, unguarded and ardent as I then was, to your destruction and infallible misery. Learn from me, if not by my precepts, at least by my example, how dangerous is the acquirement of knowledge and how much happier that man is who believes his native town to be the world, than he who aspires to become greater than his nature will allow.

When I found so astonishing a power placed within my hands, I hesitated a long time concerning the manner in which I should employ it. Although I possessed the capacity of bestowing animation, yet to prepare a frame for the reception of it, with all its intricacies of fibres, muscles, and veins, still remained a work of inconceivable difficulty and labour. I doubted at first whether I should attempt the creation of a being like myself, or one of simpler organisation; but my imagination was too much exalted by my first success to permit me to doubt of my ability to give life to an animal as complex and wonderful as man. The materials at present within my command hardly appeared adequate to so arduous an undertaking; but I doubted not that I should ultimately succeed. I prepared myself for a multitude of reverses; my operations might be incessantly baffled, and at last my work be imperfect: yet, when I considered the improvement which every day takes place in science and mechanics, I was encouraged to hope my present attempts would at least lay the foundations of future success. Nor could I consider the magnitude and complexity of my plan as any argument of its impracticability. It was with these feelings that I began the creation of a human being. As the minuteness of the parts formed a great hindrance to my speed, I resolved, contrary to my first intention, to make the being of a gigantic stature; that is to say, about eight feet in height, and proportionably large. After having formed this determination and having spent some months in successfully collecting and arranging my materials, I began.

No one can conceive the variety of feelings which bore me onwards, like a hurricane, in the first enthusiasm of success. Life and death appeared to me ideal bounds, which I should first break through, and pour a torrent of light into our dark world. A new species would bless me as its creator and source; many happy and excellent natures would owe their being to me. No father could claim the gratitude of his child so completely as I should deserve theirs. Pursuing these reflections, I thought, that if I could bestow animation upon lifeless matter, I might in process of time (although I now found it impossible) renew life where death had apparently devoted the body to corruption.

These thoughts supported my spirits, while I pursued my undertaking with unremitting ardour. My cheek had grown pale with study, and my person had become emaciated with confinement. Sometimes, on the very brink of certainty, I failed; yet still I clung to the hope which the next day or the next hour might realise. One secret which I alone possessed was the hope to which I had dedicated myself; and the moon gazed on my midnight labours, while, with unrelaxed and breathless eagerness, I pursued nature to her hiding-places. Who shall conceive the horrors of my secret toil as I dabbled among the unhallowed damps of the grave or tortured the living animal to animate the lifeless clay? My limbs now tremble, and my eyes swim with the remembrance; but then a resistless, and almost frantic impulse, urged me forward; I seemed to have lost all soul or sensation but for this one pursuit. It was indeed but a passing trance, that only made me feel with renewed acuteness so soon as, the unnatural stimulus ceasing to operate, I had returned to my old habits. I collected bones from charnel-houses and disturbed, with profane fingers, the tremendous secrets of the human frame. In a solitary chamber, or rather cell, at the top of the house, and separated from all the other apartments by a gallery and staircase, I kept my workshop of filthy creation: my eyeballs were starting from their sockets in attending to the details of my employment. The dissecting room and the slaughter-house furnished many of my materials; and often did my human nature turn with loathing from my occupation, whilst, still urged on by an eagerness which perpetually increased, I brought my work near to a conclusion.

The summer months passed while I was thus engaged, heart and soul, in one pursuit. It was a most beautiful season; never did the fields bestow a more plentiful harvest, or the vines yield a more luxuriant vintage: but my eyes were insensible to the charms of nature. And the same feelings which made me neglect the scenes around me caused me also to forget those friends who were so many miles absent, and whom I had not seen for so long a time. I knew my silence disquieted them; and I well remembered the words of my father: 'I know that while you are pleased with yourself, you will think of us with affection, and we shall hear regularly from you. You must pardon me if I regard any interruption in your correspondence as a proof that your other duties are equally neglected.'

I knew well therefore what would be my father's feelings; but I could not tear my thoughts from my employment, loathsome in itself, but which had taken an irresistible hold of my imagination. I wished, as it were, to procrastinate all that related to my feelings of affection until the great object, which swallowed up every habit of my nature, should be completed.

I then thought that my father would be unjust if he ascribed my neglect to vice, or faultiness on my part, but I am now convinced that he was justified in conceiving that I should not be altogether free from blame. A human being in perfection ought always to preserve a calm and peaceful mind, and never to allow passion or a transitory desire to disturb his tranquillity. I do not think that the pursuit of knowledge is an exception to this rule. If the study to which you apply yourself has a tendency to weaken your affections, and to destroy your taste for those simple pleasures in which no alloy can possibly mix, then that study is certainly unlawful, that is to say, not befitting the human mind. If this rule were always observed; if no man allowed any pursuit whatsoever to interfere with the tranquillity of his domestic affections, Greece had not been enslaved; Caesar would have spared his country; America would have been discovered more gradually; and the empires of Mexico and Peru had not been destroyed.

But I forget that I am moralising in the most interesting part of my tale, and your looks remind me to proceed.

My father made no reproach in his letters, and only took notice of my silence by enquiring into my occupations more particularly than before. Winter, spring, and summer passed away during my labours; but I did not watch the blossom or the expanding leaves – sights which before always yielded me supreme delight – so deeply was I engrossed in my occupation. The leaves of that year had withered before my work drew to a close; and now every day showed me more plainly how well I had succeeded.

But my enthusiasm was checked by my anxiety, and I appeared rather like one doomed by slavery to toil in the mines, or any other unwholesome trade than an artist occupied by his favourite employment. Every night I was oppressed by a slow fever, and I became nervous to a most painful degree; the fall of a leaf startled me, and I shunned my fellow-creatures as if I had been guilty of a crime. Sometimes I grew alarmed at the wreck I perceived that I had become; the energy of my purpose alone sustained me: my labours would soon end, and I believed that exercise and amusement would then drive away incipient disease; and I promised myself both of these when my creation should be complete.

CHAPTER V

It was on a dreary night of November, that I beheld the accomplishment of my toils. With an anxiety that almost amounted to agony, I collected the instruments of life around me, that I might infuse a spark of being into the lifeless thing that lay at my feet. It was already one in the morning; the rain pattered dismally against the panes, and my candle was nearly burnt out, when, by the glimmer of the half-extinguished light, I saw the dull yellow eye of the creature open; it breathed hard, and a convulsive motion agitated its limbs.

How can I describe my emotions at this catastrophe, or how delineate the wretch whom with such infinite pains and care I had endeavoured to form? His limbs were in proportion, and I had selected his features as beautiful. Beautiful! – Great God! His yellow skin scarcely covered the work of muscles and arteries beneath; his hair was of a lustrous black, and flowing; his teeth of pearly whiteness; but these luxuriances only formed a more horrid contrast with his watery eyes, that seemed almost of the same colour as the dun-white sockets in which they were set, his shrivelled complexion and straight black lips.

The different accidents of life are not so changeable as the feelings of human nature. I had worked hard for nearly two years, for the sole purpose of infusing life into an inanimate body. For this I had deprived myself of rest and health. I had desired it with an ardour that far exceeded moderation; but now that I had finished, the beauty of the dream vanished, and breathless horror and disgust filled my heart. Unable to endure the aspect of the being I had created, I rushed out of the room, and continued a long time traversing my bedchamber, unable to compose my mind to sleep. At length lassitude succeeded to the tumult I had before endured; and I threw myself on the bed in my clothes, endeavouring to seek a few moments of forgetfulness. But it was in vain: I slept, indeed, but I was disturbed by the wildest dreams.

I thought I saw Elizabeth, in the bloom of health, walking in the streets of Ingolstadt. Delighted and surprised, I embraced her, but as I imprinted the first kiss on her lips, they became livid with the hue of death; her features appeared to change, and I thought that I held the corpse of my dead mother in my arms; a shroud enveloped her form, and I saw the grave-worms crawling in the folds of flannel. I started from my sleep with horror; a cold dew covered my forehead, my teeth chattered, and every limb became convulsed: when, by the dim and yellow light of the moon, as it forced its way through the window shutters, I beheld the wretch – the miserable monster whom I had created. He held up the curtain of the bed; and his eyes, if eyes they may be called, were fixed on me. His jaws opened, and he muttered some inarticulate sounds, while a grin wrinkled his cheeks. He might have spoken, but I did not hear; one hand was stretched out, seemingly to detain me, but I escaped, and rushed downstairs. I took refuge in the courtyard belonging to the house which I inhabited; where I remained during the rest of the night, walking up and down in the greatest agitation, listening attentively, catching and fearing each sound as if it were to announce the approach of the demoniacal corpse to which I had so miserably given life.

Oh! no mortal could support the horror of that countenance. A mummy again endued with animation could not be so hideous as that wretch. I had gazed on him while unfinished; he was ugly then; but when those muscles and joints were rendered capable of motion, it became a thing such as even Dante could not have conceived.

I passed the night wretchedly. Sometimes my pulse beat so quickly and hardly that I felt the palpitation of every artery; at others, I nearly sank to the ground through languor and extreme weakness. Mingled with this horror, I felt the bitterness of disappointment; dreams that had been my food and pleasant rest for so long a space were now become a hell to me; and the change was so rapid, the overthrow so complete!

Morning, dismal and wet, at length dawned, and discovered to my sleepless and aching eyes the church of Ingolstadt, its white steeple and clock, which indicated the sixth hour. The porter opened the gates of the court, which had that night been my asylum, and I issued into the streets, pacing them with quick steps, as if I sought to avoid the wretch whom I feared every turning of the street would present to my view. I did not dare return to the apartment which I inhabited, but felt impelled to hurry on, although drenched by the rain which poured from a black and comfortless sky.

I continued walking in this manner for some time, endeavouring by bodily exercise to ease the load that weighed upon my mind. I traversed the streets without any clear conception of where I was or what I was doing. My heart palpitated in the sickness of fear, and I hurried on with irregular steps, not daring to look about me:

> Like one, on a lonesome road who,
>   Doth walk in fear and dread,
> And, having once turned round, walks on,
>   And turns no more his head;
> Because he knows a frightful fiend
>   Doth close behind him tread.*

Continuing thus, I came at length opposite to the inn at which the various diligences and carriages usually stopped. Here I paused, I knew not why; but I remained some minutes with my eyes fixed on a coach that was coming towards me from the other end of the street. As it drew nearer I observed that it was the Swiss diligence: it stopped just where I was standing; and, on the door being opened, I perceived Henry Clerval, who, on seeing me, instantly sprung out. 'My dear Frankenstein,' exclaimed he, 'how glad I am to see you! how fortunate that you should be here at the very moment of my alighting!'

Nothing could equal my delight on seeing Clerval; his presence brought back to my thoughts my father, Elizabeth, and all those scenes of home so dear to my recollection. I grasped his hand, and in a moment forgot my horror and misfortune; I felt suddenly, and for the first time during many months, calm and serene joy. I welcomed my friend, therefore, in the most cordial manner, and

* Coleridge's *Ancient Mariner* [author's footnote].

58

we walked towards my college. Clerval continued talking for some time about our mutual friends and his own good fortune in being permitted to come to Ingolstadt. 'You may easily believe,' said he, 'how great was the difficulty to persuade my father that all necessary knowledge was not comprised in the noble art of book-keeping; and, indeed, I believe I left him incredulous to the last, for his constant answer to my unwearied intreaties was the same as that to the Dutch schoolmaster in *The Vicar of Wakefield*: "I have ten thousand florins a year without Greek, I eat heartily without Greek."[20] But his affection for me at length overcame his dislike of learning, and he has permitted me to undertake a voyage of discovery to the land of knowledge.'

'It gives me the greatest delight to see you; but tell me how you left my father, brothers, and Elizabeth.'

'Very well, and very happy, only a little uneasy that they hear from you so seldom. By the by, I mean to lecture you a little upon their account myself – But, my dear Frankenstein,' continued he, stopping short and gazing full in my face, 'I did not before remark how very ill you appear; so thin and pale; and look as if you had been watching for several nights.'

'You have guessed right; I have lately been so deeply engaged in one occupation, that I have not allowed myself sufficient rest, as you see; but I hope, I sincerely hope, that all these employments are now at an end, and that I am at length free.'

I trembled excessively; I could not endure to think of, and far less to allude to, the occurrences of the preceding night. I walked with a quick pace, and we soon arrived at my college. I then reflected, and the thought made me shiver, that the creature whom I had left in my apartment might still be there, alive and walking about. I dreaded to behold this monster; but I feared still more that Henry should see him. Intreating him, therefore, to remain a few minutes at the bottom of the stairs, I darted up towards my own room. My hand was already on the lock of the door before I recollected myself. I then paused; and a cold shivering came over me. I threw the door forcibly open, as children are accustomed to do when they expect a spectre to stand in waiting for them on the other side; but nothing appeared. I stepped fearfully in: the apartment was empty; and my bedroom was also freed from its hideous guest. I could hardly believe that so great a good fortune could have befallen me; but when I became assured that my enemy had indeed fled, I clapped my hands for joy and ran down to Clerval.

We ascended into my room, and the servant presently brought breakfast; but I was unable to contain myself. It was not joy only that possessed me; I felt my flesh tingle with excess of sensitiveness, and my pulse beat rapidly. I was unable to remain for a single instant in the same place; I jumped over the chairs, clapped my hands, and laughed aloud. Clerval at first attributed my unusual spirits to joy on his arrival, but when he observed me more attentively, he saw a wildness in my eyes for which he could not account; and my loud, unrestrained, heartless laughter frightened and astonished him.

'My dear Victor,' cried he, 'what, for God's sake, is the matter? do not laugh in that manner. How ill you are! What is the cause of all this?'

'Do not ask me,' cried I, putting my hands before my eyes, for I thought I saw the dreaded spectre glide into the room; '*he* can tell. – Oh, save me! save me!' I imagined that the monster seized me; I struggled furiously and fell down in a fit.

Poor Clerval! what must have been his feelings? A meeting, which he anticipated with such joy, so strangely turned to bitterness. But I was not the witness of his grief; for I was lifeless, and did not recover my senses for a long, long time.

This was the commencement of a nervous fever, which confined me for several months. During all that time Henry was my only nurse. I afterwards learned that, knowing my father's advanced age, and unfitness for so long a journey, and how wretched my sickness would make Elizabeth, he spared them this grief by concealing the extent of my disorder. He knew that I could not have a more kind and attentive nurse than himself; and, firm in the hope he felt of my recovery, he did not doubt that, instead of doing harm, he performed the kindest action that he could towards them.

But I was in reality very ill; and surely nothing but the unbounded and unremitting attentions of my friend could have restored me to life. The form of the monster on whom I had

bestowed existence was forever before my eyes, and I raved incessantly concerning him. Doubtless my words surprised Henry; he
at first believed them to be the wanderings of my disturbed
imagination; but the pertinacity with which I continually
recurred to the same subject, persuaded him that my disorder
indeed owed its origin to some uncommon and terrible event.

By very slow degrees, and with frequent relapses that alarmed
and grieved my friend, I recovered. I remember the first time I
became capable of observing outward objects with any kind of
pleasure, I perceived that the fallen leaves had disappeared and
that the young buds were shooting forth from the trees that
shaded my window. It was a divine spring; and the season contributed greatly to my convalescence. I felt also sentiments of joy
and affection revive in my bosom; my gloom disappeared, and in
a short time I became as cheerful as before I was attacked by the
fatal passion.

'Dearest Clerval,' exclaimed I, 'how kind, how very good you
are to me. This whole winter, instead of being spent in study, as
you promised yourself, has been consumed in my sick room. How
shall I ever repay you? I feel the greatest remorse for the disappointment of which I have been the occasion; but you will forgive me.'

'You will repay me entirely, if you do not discompose yourself,
but get well as fast as you can; and since you appear in such good
spirits, I may speak to you on one subject, may I not?'

I trembled. One subject! What could it be? Could he allude to
an object on whom I dared not even think?

'Compose yourself,' said Clerval, who observed my change of
colour, 'I will not mention it if it agitates you; but your father
and cousin would be very happy if they received a letter from
you in your own handwriting. They hardly know how ill you
have been, and are uneasy at your long silence.'

'Is that all, my dear Henry? How could you suppose that my
first thought would not fly towards those dear, dear friends whom
I love, and who are so deserving of my love?'

'If this is your present temper, my friend, you will perhaps be
glad to see a letter that has been lying here some days for you: it
is from your cousin, I believe.'

CHAPTER VI

Clerval then put the following letter into my hands. It was from my own Elizabeth: –

MY DEAREST COUSIN,

You have been ill, very ill, and even the constant letters of dear kind Henry are not sufficient to reassure me on your account. You are forbidden to write – to hold a pen; yet one word from you, dear Victor, is necessary to calm our apprehensions. For a long time I have thought that each post would bring this line, and my persuasions have restrained my uncle from undertaking a journey to Ingolstadt. I have prevented his encountering the inconveniences and perhaps dangers of so long a journey, yet how often have I regretted not being able to perform it myself! I figure to myself that the task of attending on your sickbed has devolved on some mercenary old nurse, who could never guess your wishes, nor minister to them with the care and affection of your poor cousin. Yet that is over now: Clerval writes that indeed you are getting better. I eagerly hope that you will confirm this intelligence soon in your own handwriting.

Get well – and return to us. You will find a happy, cheerful home, and friends who love you dearly. Your father's health is vigorous, and he asks but to see you, but to be assured that you are well; and not a care will ever cloud his benevolent countenance. How pleased you would be to remark the improvement of our Ernest! He is now sixteen, and full of activity and spirit. He is desirous to be a true Swiss, and to enter into foreign service, but we cannot part with him, at least until his elder brother return to us. My uncle is not pleased with the idea of a military career in a distant country, but Ernest never had your powers of application. He looks upon study as an odious fetter; his time is spent in the open air, climbing the hills or rowing on the lake. I fear that he will become an idler, unless we yield the point, and permit him to enter on the profession which he has selected.

Little alteration, except the growth of our dear children, has taken place since you left us. The blue lake, and snow-clad mountains – they never change; and I think our placid home and our contented hearts are regulated by the same immutable laws. My trifling occupations take up my time and amuse me, and I am rewarded for any exertions by seeing none but happy, kind faces around me. Since you left us, but one change has taken place in our little household. Do you remember on what occasions Justine Moritz entered our family? Probably you do not; I will relate her history, therefore, in a few words. Madame Moritz, her mother, was a widow with four children, of whom Justine was the third. This girl had always been the favourite of her father; but, through a strange perversity, her mother could not endure her, and after the death of M. Moritz, treated her very ill. My aunt observed this, and when Justine was twelve years of age, prevailed on her mother to allow her to live at our house. The republican institutions of our country have produced simpler and happier manners than those which prevail in the great monarchies that surround it. Hence there is less distinction between the several classes of its inhabitants; and the lower orders, being neither so poor nor so despised, their manners are more refined and moral. A servant in Geneva does not mean the same thing as a servant in France and England. Justine, thus received in our family, learned the duties of a servant; a condition which, in our fortunate country, does not include the idea of ignorance, and a sacrifice of the dignity of a human being.

Justine, you may remember, was a great favourite of yours; and I recollect you once remarked that if you were in an ill humour, one glance from Justine could dissipate it, for the same reason that Ariosto gives concerning the beauty of Angelica[21] – she looked so frank-hearted and happy. My aunt conceived a great attachment for her, by which she was induced to give her an education superior to that which she had at first intended. This benefit was fully repaid; Justine was the most grateful little creature in the world: I do not mean that she made any professions; I never heard one pass her lips, but you could see by her eyes that she almost adored her protectress. Although her disposition was gay, and in many respects inconsiderate, yet she paid the greatest attention to every gesture of my aunt. She thought her the model of all excellence and endeavoured to imitate her phraseology and manners, so that even now she often reminds me of her.

When my dearest aunt died, every one was too much occupied in their own grief to notice poor Justine, who had attended her illness with the most anxious affection. Poor Justine was very ill, but other trials were reserved for her.

One by one, her brothers and sister died; and her mother, with the exception of her neglected daughter, was left childless. The conscience of the woman was troubled; she began to think that the deaths of her favourites were a judgment from heaven to chastise her partiality. She was a Roman catholic; and I believe her confessor confirmed the idea which she had conceived. Accordingly, a few months after your departure for Ingolstadt, Justine was called home by her repentant mother. Poor girl! she wept when she quitted our house; she was much altered since the death of my aunt; grief had given softness and a winning mildness to her manners which had before been remarkable for vivacity. Nor was her residence at her mother's house of a nature to restore her gaiety. The poor woman was very vacillating in her repentance. She sometimes begged Justine to forgive her unkindness but much oftener accused her of having caused the deaths of her brothers and sister. Perpetual fretting at length threw Madame Moritz into a decline, which at first increased her irritability, but she is now at peace forever. She died on the first approach of cold weather, at the beginning of this last winter. Justine has returned to us, and I assure you I love her tenderly. She is very clever and gentle, and extremely pretty; as I mentioned before, her mien and her expressions continually remind me of my dear aunt.

I must say also a few words to you, my dear cousin, of little darling William. I wish you could see him; he is very tall of his age, with sweet laughing blue eyes, dark eyelashes, and curling hair. When he smiles, two little dimples appear on each cheek, which are rosy with health. He has already had one or two little *wives*, but Louisa Biron is his favourite, a pretty little girl of five years of age.

Now, dear Victor, I dare say you wish to be indulged in a little gossip concerning the good people of Geneva. The pretty Miss Mansfield has already received the congratulatory visits on her approaching marriage with a young Englishman, John Melbourne, Esq. Her ugly sister, Manon, married M. Duvillard, the rich banker, last autumn. Your favourite school-fellow, Louis Manoir, has suffered misfortunes since the departure of Clerval from Geneva. But he has already recovered his spirits and is reported to be on the point of marrying a very lively, pretty Frenchwoman, Madame Tavernier. She is a widow, and much older than Manoir; but she is very much admired and a favourite with every body.

I have written myself into better spirits, dear cousin; but my anxiety returns upon me as I conclude. Write, dearest Victor – one line – one word will be a blessing to us. Ten thousand thanks to Henry for his kindness, his affection, and his many letters: we are sincerely grateful. Adieu! my cousin, take care of yourself; and, I intreat you, write!

ELIZABETH LAVENZA
Geneva, March 18th, 17–.

'Dear, dear Elizabeth!' I exclaimed, when I had read her letter, 'I will write instantly, and relieve them from the anxiety they must feel.' I wrote, and this exertion greatly fatigued me; but my convalescence had commenced, and proceeded regularly. In another fortnight I was able to leave my chamber.

One of my first duties on my recovery was to introduce Clerval to the several professors of the university. In doing this, I underwent a kind of rough usage, ill befitting the wounds that my mind had sustained. Ever since the fatal night, the end of my labours, and the beginning of my misfortunes, I had conceived a violent antipathy even to the name of natural philosophy. When I was otherwise quite restored to health, the sight of a chemical instrument would renew all the agony of my nervous symptoms. Henry saw this and had removed all my apparatus from my view. He had also changed my apartment, for he perceived that I had acquired a dislike for the room which had previously been my laboratory. But these cares of Clerval were made of no avail when I visited the professors. M. Waldman inflicted torture when he praised, with kindness and warmth, the astonishing progress I had made in the sciences. He soon perceived that I disliked the subject; but not guessing the real cause, he attributed my feelings to modesty and changed the subject from my improvement to the science itself, with a desire, as I evidently saw, of drawing me out. What could I do? He meant to please, and he tormented me. I felt as if he had placed carefully, one by one, in my view those instruments which were to be afterwards used in putting me to a slow and cruel death. I writhed under his words, yet dared not exhibit the pain I felt. Clerval, whose eyes and feelings were always quick in discerning the sensations of others, declined the subject, alleging, in excuse, his total ignorance; and the conversation took a more general turn. I thanked my friend from my heart, but I did not speak. I saw plainly that he was surprised, but he never attempted to draw my secret from me; and although I loved him with a mixture of affection and reverence that knew no bounds, yet I could never persuade myself to confide to him that event which was so often present to my recollection, but which I feared the detail to another would only impress more deeply.

M. Krempe was not equally docile; and in my condition at that time, of almost insupportable sensitiveness, his harsh, blunt encomiums gave me even more pain than the benevolent approbation of M. Waldman. 'D—n the fellow!' cried he; 'why, M. Clerval, I assure you he has outstript us all. Ay, stare if you please; but it is nevertheless true. A youngster who, but a few years ago, believed in Cornelius Agrippa as firmly as in the Gospel, has now set himself at the head of the university; and if he is not soon pulled down, we shall all be out of countenance. — Ay, ay,' continued he, observing my face expressive of suffering, 'M. Frankenstein is modest, an excellent quality in a young man. Young men should be diffident of themselves, you know, M. Clerval: I was myself when young, but that wears out in a very short time.'

M. Krempe had now commenced a eulogy on himself, which

happily turned the conversation from a subject that was so annoying to me.

Clerval had never sympathised in my tastes for natural science; and his literary pursuits differed wholly from whose which had occupied me. He came to the university with the design of making himself complete master of the Oriental languages, as thus he should open a field for the plan of life he had marked out for himself. Resolved to pursue no inglorious career, he turned his eyes towards the East as affording scope for his spirit of enterprise. The Persian, Arabic, and Sanscrit languages engaged his attention, and I was easily induced to enter on the same studies. Idleness had ever been irksome to me, and now that I wished to fly from reflection and hated my former studies, I felt great relief in being the fellow pupil with my friend, and found not only instruction but consolation in the works of the Orientalists. I did not, like him, attempt a critical knowledge of their dialects, for I did not contemplate making any other use of them than temporary amusement. I read merely to understand their meaning, and they well repaid my labours. Their melancholy is soothing, and their joy elevating, to a degree I never experienced in studying the authors of any other country. When you read their writings, life appears to consist in a warm sun and a garden of roses, in the smiles and frowns of a fair enemy, and the fire that consumes your own heart. How different from the manly and heroical poetry of Greece and Rome!

Summer passed away in these occupations, and my return to Geneva was fixed for the latter end of autumn; but being delayed by several accidents, winter and snow arrived, the roads were deemed impassable, and my journey was retarded until the ensuing spring. I felt this delay very bitterly; for I longed to see my native town and my beloved friends. My return had only been delayed so long from an unwillingness to leave Clerval in a strange place before he had become acquainted with any of its inhabitants. The winter, however, was spent cheerfully, and although the spring was uncommonly late, when it came its beauty compensated for its dilatoriness.

The month of May had already commenced, and I expected the letter daily which was to fix the date of my departure, when

Henry proposed a pedestrian tour in the environs of Ingolstadt, that I might bid a personal farewell to the country I had so long inhabited. I acceded with pleasure to this proposition: I was fond of exercise, and Clerval had always been my favourite companion in the rambles of this nature that I had taken among the scenes of my native country.

We passed a fortnight in these perambulations: my health and spirits had long been restored, and they gained additional strength from the salubrious air I breathed, the natural incidents of our progress, and the conversation of my friend. Study had before secluded me from the intercourse of my fellow-creatures, and rendered me unsocial, but Clerval called forth the better feelings of my heart; he again taught me to love the aspect of nature, and the cheerful faces of children. Excellent friend! how sincerely did you love me and endeavour to elevate my mind until it was on a level with your own! A selfish pursuit had cramped and narrowed me, until your gentleness and affection warmed and opened my senses; I became the same happy creature who, a few years ago, loved and beloved by all, had no sorrow or care. When happy, inanimate nature had the power of bestowing on me the most delightful sensations. A serene sky and verdant fields filled me with ecstasy. The present season was indeed divine; the flowers of spring bloomed in the hedges, while those of summer were already in bud. I was undisturbed by thoughts which during the preceding year had pressed upon me, notwithstanding my endeavours to throw them off, with an invincible burden.

Henry rejoiced in my gaiety, and sincerely sympathised in my feelings: he exerted himself to amuse me, while he expressed the sensations that filled his soul. The resources of his mind on this occasion were truly astonishing: his conversation was full of imagination; and very often, in imitation of the Persian and Arabic writers, he invented tales of wonderful fancy and passion. At other times, he repeated my favourite poems, or drew me out into arguments, which he supported with great ingenuity.

We returned to our college on a Sunday afternoon: the peasants were dancing, and everyone we met appeared gay and happy. My own spirits were high, and I bounded along with feelings of unbridled joy and hilarity.

CHAPTER VII

On my return, I found the following letter from my father: –

MY DEAR VICTOR,

You have probably waited impatiently for a letter to fix the date of your return to us; and I was at first tempted to write only a few lines, merely mentioning the day on which I should expect you. But that would be a cruel kindness, and I dare not do it. What would be your surprise, my son, when you expect a happy and glad welcome, to behold, on the contrary, tears and wretchedness? And how, Victor, can I relate our misfortune? Absence cannot have rendered you callous to our joys and griefs; and how shall I inflict pain on my long-absent son? I wish to prepare you for the woeful news, but I know it is impossible; even now your eye skims over the page, to seek the words which are to convey to you the horrible tidings.

William is dead! – that sweet child, whose smiles delighted and warmed my heart, who was so gentle, yet so gay! Victor, he is murdered!

I will not attempt to console you; but will simply relate the circumstances of the transaction.

Last Thursday (May 7th) I, my niece, and your two brothers went to walk in Plainpalais. The evening was warm and serene, and we prolonged our walk farther than usual. It was already dusk before we thought of returning; and then we discovered that William and Ernest, who had gone on before, were not to be found. We accordingly rested on a seat until they should return. Presently Ernest came, and enquired if we had seen his brother: he said that he had been playing with him, that William had run away to hide himself, and that he vainly sought for him, and afterwards waited for him a long time, but he did not return.

This account rather alarmed us, and we continued to search for him until night fell, when Elizabeth conjectured that he might have returned to the house. He was not there. We returned again, with torches, for I could not rest when I thought that my sweet boy had lost himself and was exposed to all the damps and dews of night; Elizabeth also suffered extreme anguish. About five in the morning I discovered my lovely boy, whom the night before I had seen blooming and active in health, stretched on the grass livid and motionless: the print of the murderer's finger was on his neck.

He was conveyed home, and the anguish that was visible in my countenance betrayed the secret to Elizabeth. She was very earnest to see the corpse. At first I attempted to prevent her, but she persisted, and entering the room where it lay, hastily examined the neck of the victim, and clasping her hands, exclaimed, 'Oh, God! I have murdered my darling child!'

She fainted, and was restored with extreme difficulty. When she again lived, it was only to weep and sigh. She told me that that same evening William had teased her to let him wear a very valuable miniature that she possessed of your mother. This picture is gone, and was doubtless the temptation which urged the murderer to the deed. We have no trace of him at present, although our exertions to discover him are unremitted; but they will not restore my beloved William!

Come, dearest Victor; you alone can console Elizabeth. She weeps continually and accuses herself unjustly as the cause of his death; her words pierce my heart. We are all unhappy, but will not that be an additional motive for you, my son, to return and be our comforter? Your dear mother! Alas, Victor! I now say, Thank God she did not live to witness the cruel, miserable death of her youngest darling!

Come, Victor; not brooding thoughts of vengeance against the assassin, but with feelings of peace and gentleness, that will heal, instead of festering, the wounds of our minds. Enter the house of mourning, my friend, but with kindness and affection for those who love you, and not with hatred for your enemies.

Your affectionate and afflicted father,
ALPHONSE FRANKENSTEIN
Geneva, May 12th, 17–.

Clerval, who had watched my countenance as I read this letter, was surprised to observe the despair that succeeded to the joy I at first expressed on receiving news from my friends. I threw the letter on the table, and covered my face with my hands.

'My dear Frankenstein,' exclaimed Henry, when he perceived me weep with bitterness, 'are we always to be unhappy? My dear friend, what has happened?'

I motioned to him to take up the letter, while I walked up and down the room in the extremest agitation. Tears also gushed from the eyes of Clerval, as he read the account of my misfortune.

'I can offer you no consolation, my friend,' said he; 'your disaster is irreparable. What do you intend to do?'

'To go instantly to Geneva: come with me, Henry, to order the horses.'

During our walk Clerval endeavoured to say a few words of consolation; he could only express his heartfelt sympathy. 'Poor William!' said he. 'Dear lovely child, he now sleeps with his angel mother! Who that had seen him bright and joyous in his young beauty, but must weep over his untimely loss! To die so miserably; to feel the murderer's grasp! How much more a murderer, that could destroy such radiant innocence! Poor little fellow! one only consolation have we; his friends mourn and weep, but he is at rest. The pang is over, his sufferings are at an end forever. A sod covers his gentle form, and he knows no pain. He can no longer be a subject for pity; we must reserve that for his miserable survivors.'

Clerval spoke thus as we hurried through the streets; the words impressed themselves on my mind, and I remembered them afterwards in solitude. But now, as soon as the horses arrived, I hurried into a cabriolet and bade farewell to my friend.

My journey was very melancholy. At first I wished to hurry on, for I longed to console and sympathise with my loved and sorrowing friends; but when I drew near my native town, I slackened my progress. I could hardly sustain the multitude of feelings that crowded into my mind. I passed through scenes familiar to my youth, but which I had not seen for nearly six years. How altered every thing might be during that time! One sudden and desolating change had taken place; but a thousand

little circumstances might have by degrees worked other alterations, which, although they were done more tranquilly, might not
be the less decisive. Fear overcame me; I dared not advance,
dreading a thousand nameless evils that made me tremble, although I was unable to define them.

I remained two days at Lausanne, in this painful state of mind.
I contemplated the lake: the waters were placid: all around was
calm; and the snowy mountains, 'the palaces of nature',[22] were
not changed. By degrees the calm and heavenly scene restored
me, and I continued my journey towards Geneva.

The road ran by the side of the lake, which became narrower
as I approached my native town. I discovered more distinctly the
black sides of Jura, and the bright summit of Mont Blanc. I wept
like a child. 'Dear mountains! My own beautiful lake! How do
you welcome your wanderer? Your summits are clear; the sky
and lake are blue and placid. Is this to prognosticate peace, or to
mock at my unhappiness?'

I fear, my friend, that I shall render myself tedious by dwelling
on these preliminary circumstances; but they were days of comparative happiness, and I think of them with pleasure. My country, my beloved country! who but a native can tell the delight
I took in again beholding thy streams, thy mountains, and, more
than all, thy lovely lake!

Yet, as I drew nearer home, grief and fear again overcame me.
Night also closed around; and when I could hardly see the dark
mountains, I felt still more gloomily. The picture appeared a vast
and dim scene of evil, and I foresaw obscurely that I was destined
to become the most wretched of human beings. Alas! I prophesied
truly, and failed only in one single circumstance, that in all the
misery I imagined and dreaded, I did not conceive the hundredth
part of the anguish I was destined to endure.

It was completely dark when I arrived in the environs of
Geneva; the gates of the town were already shut; and I was
obliged to pass the night at Secheron, a village at the distance of
half a league from the city. The sky was serene; and as I was
unable to rest, I resolved to visit the spot where my poor William
had been murdered. As I could not pass through the town, I was
obliged to cross the lake in a boat to arrive at Plainpalais. During

this short voyage I saw the lightnings playing on the summit of Mont Blanc in the most beautiful figures. The storm appeared to approach rapidly; and, on landing, I ascended a low hill, that I might observe its progress. It advanced; the heavens were clouded, and I soon felt the rain coming slowly in large drops, but its violence quickly increased.

I quitted my seat and walked on, although the darkness and storm increased every minute and the thunder burst with a terrific crash over my head. It was echoed from Salêve, the Juras, and the Alps of Savoy; vivid flashes of lightning dazzled my eyes, illuminating the lake, making it appear like a vast sheet of fire; then for an instant every thing seemed of a pitchy darkness, until the eye recovered itself from the preceding flash. The storm, as is often the case in Switzerland, appeared at once in various parts of the heavens. The most violent storm hung exactly north of the town, over that part of the lake which lies between the promontory of Belrive and the village of Copêt. Another storm enlightened Jura with faint flashes; and another darkened and sometimes disclosed the Môle, a peaked mountain to the east of the lake.

While I watched the tempest, so beautiful yet terrific, I wandered on with a hasty step. This noble war in the sky elevated my spirits; I clasped my hands and exclaimed aloud, 'William, dear angel! this is thy funeral, this thy dirge!' As I said these words, I perceived in the gloom a figure which stole from behind a clump of trees near me; I stood fixed, gazing intently: I could not be mistaken. A flash of lightning illuminated the object, and discovered its shape plainly to me; its gigantic stature, and the deformity of its aspect, more hideous than belongs to humanity, instantly informed me that it was the wretch, the filthy daemon to whom I had given life. What did he there? Could he be (I shuddered at the conception) the murderer of my brother? No sooner did that idea cross my imagination, than I became convinced of its truth; my teeth chattered, and I was forced to lean against a tree for support. The figure passed me quickly, and I lost it in the gloom. Nothing in human shape could have destroyed that fair child. *He* was the murderer! I could not doubt it. The mere presence of the idea was an irresistible proof of the fact. I

73

thought of pursuing the devil; but it would have been in vain, for another flash discovered him to me hanging among the rocks of the nearly perpendicular ascent of Mount Salêve, a hill that bound Plainpalais on the south. He soon reached the summit, and disappeared.

I remained motionless. The thunder ceased, but the rain still continued, and the scene was enveloped in an impenetrable darkness. I revolved in my mind the events which I had until now sought to forget: the whole train of my progress towards the creation; the appearance of the work of my own hands alive at my bedside; its departure. Two years had now nearly elapsed since the night on which he first received life; and was this his first crime? Alas! I had turned loose into the world a depraved wretch, whose delight was in carnage and misery; had he not murdered my brother?

No one can conceive the anguish I suffered during the remainder of the night, which I spent, cold and wet, in the open air. But I did not feel the inconvenience of the weather; my imagination was busy in scenes of evil and despair. I considered the being whom I had cast among mankind, and endowed with the will and power to effect purposes of horror, such as the deed which he had now done, nearly in the light of my own vampire, my own spirit let loose from the grave, and forced to destroy all that was dear to me.

Day dawned; and I directed my steps towards the town. The gates were open, and I hastened to my father's house. My first thought was to discover what I knew of the murderer, and cause instant pursuit to be made. But I paused when I reflected on the story that I had to tell. A being whom I myself had formed, and endued with life, had met me at midnight among the precipices of an inaccessible mountain. I remembered also the nervous fever with which I had been seized just at the time that I dated my creation, and which would give an air of delirium to a tale otherwise so utterly improbable. I well knew that if any other had communicated such a relation to me, I should have looked upon it as the ravings of insanity. Besides, the strange nature of the animal would elude all pursuit, even if I were so far credited as to persuade my relatives to commence it. And then of what use would be pursuit? Who could arrest a creature capable of scaling the overhanging sides of Mont Salêve? These reflections determined me, and I resolved to remain silent.

It was about five in the morning when I entered my father's house. I told the servants not to disturb the family, and went into the library to attend their usual hour of rising.

Six years had elapsed, passed as a dream but for one indelible trace, and I stood in the same place where I had last embraced my father before my departure for Ingolstadt. Beloved and venerable parent! He still remained to me. I gazed on the picture of my mother which stood over the mantel-piece. It was an historical subject, painted at my father's desire, and represented Caroline Beaufort in an agony of despair, kneeling by the coffin of her dead father. Her garb was rustic, and her cheek pale; but there was an air of dignity and beauty, that hardly permitted the sentiment of pity. Below this picture was a miniature of William; and my tears flowed when I looked upon it. While I was thus engaged, Ernest entered: he had heard me arrive, and hastened to welcome me. He expressed a sorrowful delight to see me. 'Welcome, my dearest Victor,' said he. 'Ah! I wish you had come three months ago, and then you would have found us all joyous and delighted. You come to us now to share a misery which nothing can alleviate; yet your presence will, I hope, revive our father, who seems sinking under his misfortune; and your persuasions will induce poor Elizabeth to cease her vain and tormenting self-accusations. – Poor William! he was our darling and our pride!'

Tears, unrestrained, fell from my brother's eyes; a sense of mortal agony crept over my frame. Before, I had only imagined the wretchedness of my desolated home; the reality came on me as a new and a not less terrible disaster. I tried to calm Ernest; I enquired more minutely concerning my father, and her I named my cousin.

'She most of all,' said Ernest, 'requires consolation; she accused herself of having caused the death of my brother, and that made her very wretched. But since the murderer has been discovered –'

'The murderer discovered! Good God! how can that be? who could attempt to pursue him? It is impossible; one might as well try to overtake the winds or confine a mountain-stream with a straw. I saw him too; he was free last night!'

'I do not know what you mean,' replied my brother, in accents of wonder, 'but to us the discovery we have made completes our misery. No one would believe it at first; and even now Elizabeth will not be convinced, notwithstanding all the evidence. Indeed, who would credit that Justine Moritz, who was so amiable and fond of all the family, could suddenly become capable of so frightful, so appalling a crime?'

'Justine Moritz! Poor, poor girl, is she the accused? But it is wrongfully; every one knows that; no one believes it, surely, Ernest?'

'No one did at first; but several circumstances came out that have almost forced conviction upon us; and her own behaviour has been so confused as to add to the evidence of facts a weight that, I fear, leaves no hope for doubt. But she will be tried today, and you will then hear all.'

He related that, the morning on which the murder of poor William had been discovered, Justine had been taken ill, and confined to her bed for several days. During this interval one of the servants, happening to examine the apparel she had worn on the night of the murder, had discovered in her pocket the picture of my mother, which had been judged to be the temptation of the murderer. The servant instantly showed it to one of the others, who, without saying a word to any of the family, went to a magistrate; and, upon their deposition, Justine was apprehended. On being charged with the fact, the poor girl confirmed the suspicion in a great measure by her extreme confusion of manner.

This was a strange tale, but it did not shake my faith, and I replied earnestly, 'You are all mistaken; I know the murderer. Justine, poor, good Justine, is innocent.'

At that instant my father entered. I saw unhappiness deeply impressed on his countenance, but he endeavoured to welcome me cheerfully; and after we had exchanged our mournful greeting, would have introduced some other topic than that of our disaster, had not Ernest exclaimed, 'Good God, Papa! Victor says that he knows who was the murderer of poor William.'

'We do also, unfortunately,' replied my father; 'for indeed I had rather have been forever ignorant than have discovered so much depravity and ingratitude in one I valued so highly.'

'My dear father, you are mistaken; Justine is innocent.'

'If she is, God forbid that she should suffer as guilty. She is to be tried today, and I hope, I sincerely hope, that she will be acquitted.'

This speech calmed me. I was firmly convinced in my own mind that Justine, and indeed every human being, was guiltless of this murder. I had no fear, therefore, that any circumstantial evidence could be brought forward strong enough to convict her. My tale was not one to announce publicly; its astounding horror would be looked upon as madness by the vulgar. Did any one indeed exist, except I, the creator, who would believe, unless his senses convinced him, in the existence of the living monument of presumption[23] and rash ignorance which I had let loose upon the world?

We were soon joined by Elizabeth. Time had altered her since I last beheld her; it had endowed her with loveliness surpassing the beauty of her childish years. There was the same candour, the same vivacity, but it was allied to an expression more full of sensibility and intellect. She welcomed me with the greatest affection. 'Your arrival, my dear cousin,' said she, 'fills me with hope. You perhaps will find some means to justify my poor guiltless Justine. Alas! who is safe, if she be convicted of crime? I rely on her innocence as certainly as I do upon my own. Our misfortune is doubly hard to us; we have not only lost that lovely darling boy, but this poor girl, whom I sincerely love, is to be torn away by even a worse fate. If she is condemned, I never shall know joy more. But she will not, I am sure she will not; and then I shall be happy again, even after the sad death of my little William.'

'She is innocent, my Elizabeth,' said I, 'and that shall be proved; fear nothing, but let your spirits be cheered by the assurance of her acquittal.'

'How kind and generous you are! every one else believes in her guilt, and that made me wretched, for I knew that it was impossible: and to see every one else prejudiced in so deadly a manner rendered me hopeless and despairing.' She wept.

'Dearest niece,' said my father, 'dry your tears. If she is, as you believe, innocent, rely on the justice of our laws, and the activity with which I shall prevent the slightest shadow of partiality.'

CHAPTER VIII

We passed a few sad hours, until eleven o'clock, when the trial was to commence. My father and the rest of the family being obliged to attend as witnesses, I accompanied them to the court. During the whole of this wretched mockery of justice I suffered living torture. It was to be decided, whether the result of my curiosity and lawless devices would cause the death of my fellow-beings: one a smiling babe full of innocence and joy; the other far more dreadfully murdered, with every aggravation of infamy that could make the murder memorable in horror. Justine also was a girl of merit, and possessed qualities which promised to render her life happy; now all was to be obliterated in an ignominious grave, and I the cause! A thousand times rather would I have confessed myself guilty of the crime ascribed to Justine; but I was absent when it was committed, and such a declaration would have been considered as the ravings of a madman, and would not have exculpated her who suffered through me.

The appearance of Justine was calm. She was dressed in mourning; and her countenance, always engaging, was rendered, by the solemnity of her feelings, exquisitely beautiful. Yet she appeared confident in innocence and did not tremble, although gazed on and execrated by thousands; for all the kindness which her beauty might otherwise have excited was obliterated in the minds of the spectators by the imagination of the enormity she was supposed to have committed. She was tranquil, yet her tranquillity was evidently constrained; and as her confusion had before been adduced as a proof of her guilt, she worked up her mind to an appearance of courage. When she entered the court she threw her eyes round it, and quickly discovered where we were seated. A tear seemed to dim her eye when she saw us; but she quickly recovered herself, and a look of sorrowful affection seemed to attest her utter guiltlessness.

The trial began; and after the advocate against her had stated the charge, several witnesses were called. Several strange facts combined against her, which might have staggered any one who had not such proof of her innocence as I had. She had been out the whole of the night on which the murder had been committed, and towards morning had been perceived by a market-woman not far from the spot where the body of the murdered child had been afterwards found. The woman asked her what she did there; but she looked very strangely, and only returned a confused and unintelligible answer. She returned to the house about eight o'clock; and when one enquired where she had passed the night, she replied that she had been looking for the child and demanded earnestly if any thing had been heard concerning him. When shown the body, she fell into violent hysterics, and kept her bed for several days. The picture was then produced, which the servant had found in her pocket; and when Elizabeth, in a faltering voice, proved that it was the same which, an hour before the child had been missed, she had placed round his neck, a murmur of horror and indignation filled the court.

Justine was called on for her defence. As the trial proceeded, her countenance had altered. Surprise, horror, and misery were strongly expressed. Sometimes she struggled with her tears; but when she was desired to plead, she collected her powers, and spoke in an audible although variable voice.

'God knows,' she said, 'how entirely I am innocent. But I do not pretend that my protestations should acquit me: I rest my innocence on a plain and simple explanation of the facts which have been adduced against me; and I hope the character I have always borne will incline my judges to a favourable interpretation, where any circumstance appears doubtful or suspicious.'

She then related that, by the permission of Elizabeth, she had passed the evening of the night on which the murder had been committed at the house of an aunt at Chêne, a village situated at about a league from Geneva. On her return, at about nine o'clock, she met a man who asked her if she had seen any thing of the child who was lost. She was alarmed by this account, and passed several hours in looking for him, when the gates of Geneva were shut, and she was forced to remain several hours of the night in a barn belonging to a cottage, being unwilling to call up the inhabitants, to whom she was well known. Most of the night she spent here watching; towards morning she believed that she slept for a few minutes; some steps disturbed her, and she awoke. It was dawn, and she quitted her asylum, that she might again endeavour to find my brother. If she had gone near the spot where his body lay, it was without her knowledge. That she had been bewildered when questioned by the market-woman was not surprising, since she had passed a sleepless night and the fate of poor William was yet uncertain. Concerning the picture she could give no account.

'I know,' continued the unhappy victim, 'how heavily and fatally this one circumstance weighs against me, but I have no power of explaining it; and when I have expressed my utter ignorance, I am only left to conjecture concerning the probabilities by which it might have been placed in my pocket. But here also I am checked. I believe that I have no enemy on earth, and none surely would have been so wicked as to destroy me wantonly. Did the murderer place it there? I know of no opportunity afforded him for so doing; or, if I had, why should he have stolen the jewel, to part with it again so soon?

'I commit my cause to the justice of my judges, yet I see no room for hope. I beg permission to have a few witnesses examined concerning my character; and if their testimony shall not overweigh my supposed guilt, I must be condemned, although I would pledge my salvation on my innocence.'

Several witnesses were called who had known her for many years, and they spoke well of her; but fear and hatred of the crime of which they supposed her guilty rendered them timorous, and unwilling to come forward. Elizabeth saw even this last resource, her excellent dispositions and irreproachable conduct, about to fail the accused, when, although violently agitated, she desired permission to address the court.

'I am,' said she, 'the cousin of the unhappy child who was murdered, or rather his sister, for I was educated by and have lived with his parents ever since and even long before, his birth. It may therefore be judged indecent in me to come forward on this occasion; but when I see a fellow creature about to perish through the cowardice of her pretended friends, I wish to be allowed to speak, that I may say what I know of her character. I am well acquainted with the accused. I have lived in the same house with her, at one time for five, and at another for nearly two years. During all that period she appeared to me the most amiable and benevolent of human creatures. She nursed Madame Frankenstein, my aunt, in her last illness, with the greatest affection and care, and afterwards attended her own mother during a tedious illness, in a manner that excited the admiration of all who knew her; after which she again lived in my uncle's house, where she was beloved by all the family. She was warmly attached to the child who is now dead, and acted towards him like a most affectionate mother. For my own part, I do not hesitate to say that, notwithstanding all the evidence produced against her, I believe and rely on her perfect innocence. She had no temptation for such an action: as to the bauble on which the chief proof rests, if she had earnestly desired it, I should have willingly given it to her; so much do I esteem and value her.'

A murmur of approbation followed Elizabeth's simple and powerful appeal; but it was excited by her generous interference, and not in favour of poor Justine, on whom the public indignation was turned with renewed violence, charging her with the blackest ingratitude. She herself wept as Elizabeth spoke, but she did not answer. My own agitation and anguish was extreme during the whole trial. I believed in her innocence; I knew it. Could the daemon who had (I did not for a minute doubt) murdered my brother also in his hellish sport have betrayed the innocent to death and ignominy? I could not sustain the horror of my situation, and when I perceived that the popular voice and the countenances of the judges had already condemned my unhappy victim, I rushed out of the court in agony. The tortures of the accused did not equal mine; she was sustained by innocence, but the fangs of remorse tore my bosom and would not forego their hold.

I passed a night of unmingled wretchedness. In the morning I went to the court; my lips and throat were parched. I dared not ask the fatal question; but I was known, and the officer guessed the cause of my visit. The ballots had been thrown; they were all black, and Justine was condemned.

I cannot pretend to describe what I then felt. I had before experienced sensations of horror; and I have endeavoured to bestow upon them adequate expressions, but words cannot convey an idea of the heart-sickening despair that I then endured. The person to whom I addressed myself added, that Justine had already confessed her guilt. 'That evidence,' he observed, 'was hardly required in so glaring a case, but I am glad of it; and, indeed, none of our judges like to condemn a criminal upon circumstantial evidence, be it ever so decisive.'

This was strange and unexpected intelligence; what could it mean? Had my eyes deceived me? And was I really as mad as the whole world would believe me to be, if I disclosed the object of my suspicions? I hastened to return home, and Elizabeth eagerly demanded the result.

'My cousin,' replied I, 'it is decided as you may have expected; all judges had rather that ten innocent should suffer than that one guilty should escape. But she has confessed.'

This was a dire blow to poor Elizabeth, who had relied with firmness upon Justine's innocence. 'Alas!' said she. 'How shall I ever again believe in human goodness? Justine, whom I loved and esteemed as my sister, how could she put on those smiles of innocence only to betray? her mild eyes seemed incapable of any severity or guile, and yet she has committed a murder.'

Soon after we heard that the poor victim had expressed a desire to see my cousin. My father wished her not to go, but said that he left it to her own judgment and feelings to decide. 'Yes,' said Elizabeth, 'I will go, although she is guilty; and you, Victor, shall accompany me: I cannot go alone.' The idea of this visit was torture to me, yet I could not refuse.

We entered the gloomy prison chamber and beheld Justine sitting on some straw at the farther end; her hands were manacled, and her head rested on her knees. She rose on seeing us enter; and when we were left alone with her, she threw herself at the feet of Elizabeth, weeping bitterly. My cousin wept also.

'Oh, Justine!' said she. 'Why did you rob me of my last consolation? I relied on your innocence, and although I was then very wretched, I was not so miserable as I am now.'

'And do you also believe that I am so very, very wicked? Do you also join with my enemies to crush me, to condemn me as a murderer?' Her voice was suffocated with sobs.

'Rise, my poor girl,' said Elizabeth; 'why do you kneel, if you are innocent? I am not one of your enemies; I believed you guiltless, notwithstanding every evidence, until I heard that you had yourself declared your guilt. That report, you say, is false; and be assured, dear Justine, that nothing can shake my confidence in you for a moment, but your own confession.'

'I did confess; but I confessed a lie. I confessed, that I might obtain absolution; but now that falsehood lies heavier at my heart than all my other sins. The God of heaven forgive me! Ever since I was condemned, my confessor has besieged me; he threatened and menaced, until I almost began to think that I was the monster that he said I was. He threatened excommunication and hell fire in my last moments if I continued obdurate. Dear lady, I had none to support me; all looked on me as a wretch doomed to ignominy and perdition. What could I do? In an evil hour I subscribed to a lie; and now only am I truly miserable.'

She paused, weeping, and then continued – 'I thought with horror, my sweet lady, that you should believe your Justine, whom your blessed aunt had so highly honoured and whom you loved, was a creature capable of a crime which none but the devil himself could have perpetrated. Dear William! Dearest blessed child! I soon shall see you again in heaven, where we shall all be happy; and that consoles me, going as I am to suffer ignominy and death.'

'Oh, Justine! Forgive me for having for one moment distrusted you. Why did you confess? But do not mourn, dear girl. Do not fear. I will proclaim, I will prove your innocence. I will melt the stony hearts of your enemies by my tears and prayers. You shall not die! You, my playfellow, my companion, my sister, perish on the scaffold! No! No! I never could survive so horrible a misfortune.'

Justine shook her head mournfully. 'I do not fear to die,' she said; 'that pang is past. God raises my weakness and gives me courage to endure the worst. I leave a sad and bitter world; and if you remember me and think of me as of one unjustly condemned, I am resigned to the fate awaiting me. Learn from me, dear lady, to submit in patience to the will of heaven!'

During this conversation I had retired to the corner of the

prison room, where I could conceal the horrid anguish that posses-sed me. Despair! Who dared talk of that? The poor victim, who on the morrow was to pass the awful boundary between life and death, felt not, as I did, such deep and bitter agony. I gnashed my teeth and ground them together, uttering a groan that came from my inmost soul. Justine started. When she saw who it was, she approached me and said, 'Dear sir, you are very kind to visit me; you, I hope, do not believe that I am guilty?'

I could not answer. 'No, Justine,' said Elizabeth; 'he is more convinced of your innocence than I was; for even when he heard that you had confessed, he did not credit it.'

'I truly thank him. In these last moments I feel the sincerest gratitude towards those who think of me with kindness. How sweet is the affection of others to such a wretch as I am! It removes more than half my misfortune; and I feel as if I could die in peace, now that my innocence is acknowledged by you, dear lady, and your cousin.'

Thus the poor sufferer tried to comfort others and herself. She indeed gained the resignation she desired. But I, the true mur-derer, felt the never-dying worm alive in my bosom, which allowed of no hope or consolation. Elizabeth also wept and was unhappy; but hers also was the misery of innocence, which, like a cloud that passes over the fair moon, for a while hides but cannot tarnish its brightness. Anguish and despair had penetrated into the core of my heart; I bore a hell within me which nothing could extinguish. We stayed several hours with Justine; and it was with great difficulty that Elizabeth could tear herself away. 'I wish,' cried she, 'that I were to die with you; I cannot live in this world of misery.'

Justine assumed an air of cheerfulness, while she with difficulty repressed her bitter tears. She embraced Elizabeth and said, in a voice of half-suppressed emotion, 'Farewell, sweet lady, dearest Elizabeth, my beloved and only friend; may Heaven, in its bounty, bless and preserve you; may this be the last misfortune that you will ever suffer! Live, and be happy, and make others so.'

And on the morrow Justine died. Elizabeth's heart-rending eloquence failed to move the judges from their settled conviction in the criminality of the saintly sufferer. My passionate and indignant appeals were lost upon them. And when I received their cold answers and heard the harsh, unfeeling reasoning of these men, my purposed avowal died away on my lips. Thus I might proclaim myself a madman, but not revoke the sentence passed upon my wretched victim. She perished on the scaffold as a murderess!

From the tortures of my own heart, I turned to contemplate the deep and voiceless grief of my Elizabeth. This also was my doing! And my father's woe, and the desolation of that late so smiling home – all was the work of my thrice-accursed hands! Ye weep, unhappy ones; but these are not your last tears! Again shall you raise the funeral wail, and the sound of your lamentations shall again and again be heard! Frankenstein, your son, your kinsman, your early, much-loved friend; he who would spend each vital drop of blood for your sakes – who has no thought nor sense of joy, except as it is mirrored also in your dear countenances – who would fill the air with blessings and spend his life in serving you – he bids you weep – to shed countless tears; happy beyond his hopes, if thus inexorable fate be satisfied, and if the destruction pause before the peace of the grave have succeeded to your sad torments!

Thus spoke my prophetic soul, as, torn by remorse, horror, and despair, I beheld those I loved spend vain sorrow upon the graves of William and Justine, the first hapless victims to my unhallowed arts.

END OF VOLUME ONE

VOLUME TWO

CHAPTER I

Nothing is more painful to the human mind than, after the feelings have been worked up by a quick succession of events, the dead calmness of inaction and certainty which follows and deprives the soul both of hope and fear. Justine died; she rested; and I was alive. The blood flowed freely in my veins, but a weight of despair and remorse pressed on my heart, which nothing could remove. Sleep fled from my eyes; I wandered like an evil spirit, for I had committed deeds of mischief beyond description horrible, and more, much more (I persuaded myself) was yet behind. Yet my heart overflowed with kindness, and the love of virtue. I had begun life with benevolent intentions, and thirsted for the moment when I should put them in practice and make myself useful to my fellow beings. Now all was blasted: instead of that serenity of conscience which allowed me to look back upon the past with self-satisfaction, and from thence to gather promise of new hopes, I was seized by remorse and the sense of guilt, which hurried me away to a hell of intense tortures, such as no language can describe.

This state of mind preyed upon my health, which had perhaps never entirely recovered from the first shock it had sustained. I shunned the face of man; all sound of joy or complacency was torture to me; solitude was my only consolation – deep, dark, deathlike solitude.

My father observed with pain the alteration perceptible in my disposition and habits, and endeavoured by arguments, deduced from the feelings of his serene conscience and guiltless life, to inspire me with fortitude, and awaken in me the courage to dispel the dark cloud which brooded over me. 'Do you think,

Victor,' said he, 'that I do not suffer also? No one could love a child more than I loved your brother' – tears came into his eyes as he spoke – 'but is it not a duty to the survivors that we should refrain from augmenting their unhappiness by an appearance of immoderate grief? It is also a duty owed to yourself; for excessive sorrow prevents improvement or enjoyment, or even the discharge of daily usefulness, without which no man is fit for society.'

This advice, although good, was totally inapplicable to my case; I should have been the first to hide my grief and console my friends, if remorse had not mingled its bitterness, and terror its alarm, with my other sensations. Now I could only answer my father with a look of despair, and endeavour to hide myself from his view.

About this time we retired to our house at Belrive. This change was particularly agreeable to me. The shutting of the gates regularly at ten o'clock and the impossibility of remaining on the lake after that hour, had rendered our residence within the walls of Geneva very irksome to me. I was now free. Often, after the rest of the family had retired for the night, I took the boat and passed many hours upon the water. Sometimes, with my sails set, I was carried by the wind; and sometimes, after rowing into the middle of the lake, I left the boat to pursue its own course, and gave way to my own miserable reflections. I was often tempted, when all was at peace around me, and I the only unquiet thing that wandered restless in a scene so beautiful and heavenly – if I except some bat, or the frogs, whose harsh and interrupted croaking was heard only when I approached the shore – often, I say, I was tempted to plunge into the silent lake, that the waters might close over me and my calamities forever. But I was restrained, when I thought of the heroic and suffering Elizabeth, whom I tenderly loved, and whose existence was bound up in mine. I thought also of my father and surviving brother: should I by my base desertion leave them exposed and unprotected to the malice of the fiend whom I had let loose among them?

At these moments I wept bitterly, and wished that peace would revisit my mind only that I might afford them consolation and happiness. But that could not be. Remorse extinguished every hope. I had been the author of unalterable evils, and I lived in daily fear lest the monster whom I had created should perpetrate some new wickedness. I had an obscure feeling that all was not over, and that he would still commit some signal crime, which by its enormity should almost efface the recollection of the past. There was always scope for fear, so long as anything I loved remained behind. My abhorrence of this fiend cannot be conceived. When I thought of him I gnashed my teeth, my eyes became inflamed, and I ardently wished to extinguish that life which I had so thoughtlessly bestowed. When I reflected on his crimes and malice, my hatred and revenge burst all bounds of moderation. I would have made a pilgrimage to the highest peak of the Andes, could I, when there, have precipitated him to their base. I wished to see him again, that I might wreak the utmost extent of abhorrence on his head, and avenge the deaths of William and Justine.

Our house was the house of mourning. My father's health was deeply shaken by the horror of the recent events. Elizabeth was sad and desponding; she no longer took delight in her ordinary occupations; all pleasure seemed to her sacrilege toward the dead; eternal woe and tears she then thought was the just tribute she should pay to innocence so blasted and destroyed. She was no longer that happy creature who in earlier youth wandered with me on the banks of the lake, and talked with ecstasy of our future prospects. The first of these sorrows which are sent to wean us from the earth, had visited her, and its dimming influence quenched her dearest smiles.

'When I reflect, my dear cousin,' said she, 'on the miserable death of Justine Moritz, I no longer see the world and its works as they before appeared to me. Before, I looked upon the accounts of vice and injustice, that I read in books or heard from others as tales of ancient days or imaginary evils; at least they were remote and more familiar to reason than to the imagination; but now misery has come home, and men appear to me as monsters thirsting for each other's blood. Yet I am certainly unjust. Every body believed that poor girl to be guilty; and if she could have committed the crime for which she suffered, assuredly she would have been the most depraved of human creatures. For the sake of a few jewels, to have murdered the son of her benefactor and friend, a child whom she had nursed from its birth, and appeared to love as if it had been her own! I could not consent to the death of any human being; but certainly I should have thought such a creature unfit to remain in the society of men. But she was innocent. I know, I feel, she was innocent; you are of the same opinion, and that confirms me. Alas! Victor, when falsehood can look so like the truth, who can assure themselves of certain happiness? I feel as if I were walking on the edge of a precipice, towards which thousands are crowding, and endeavouring to plunge me into the abyss. William and Justine were assassinated, and the murderer escapes: he walks about the world free, and perhaps respected. But even if I were condemned to suffer on the scaffold for the same crimes, I would not change places with such a wretch.'

I listened to this discourse with the extremest agony. I, not in deed, but in effect, was the true murderer. Elizabeth read my anguish in my countenance, and kindly taking my hand, said, 'My dearest friend, you must calm yourself. These events have affected me, God knows how deeply; but I am not so wretched as you are. There is an expression of despair, and sometimes of revenge, in your countenance that makes me tremble. Dear Victor, banish these dark passions. Remember the friends around you, who centre all their hopes in you. Have we lost the power of rendering you happy? Ah! while we love – while we are true to each other, here in this land of peace and beauty, your native country, we may reap every tranquil blessing – what can disturb our peace?'

And could not such words from her whom I fondly prized before every other gift of fortune, suffice to chase away the fiend that lurked in my heart? Even as she spoke I drew near to her, as if in terror; lest at that very moment the destroyer had been near to rob me of her.

Thus not the tenderness of friendship, nor the beauty of earth, nor of heaven, could redeem my soul from woe: the very accents of love were ineffectual. I was encompassed by a cloud which no beneficial influence could penetrate. The wounded deer dragging its fainting limbs to some untrodden brake,[24] there to gaze upon the arrow which had pierced it, and to die – was but a type of me.

Sometimes I could cope with the sullen despair that overwhelmed me: but sometimes the whirlwind passions of my soul drove me to seek, by bodily exercise and by change of place, some relief from my intolerable sensations. It was during an access[25] of this kind that I suddenly left my home, and bending my steps towards the near Alpine valleys, sought in the magnificence, the eternity of such scenes, to forget myself and my ephemeral, because human, sorrows. My wanderings were directed towards the valley of Chamounix. I had visited it frequently during my boyhood. Six years had passed since then: *I* was a wreck – but nought had changed in those savage and enduring scenes.

I performed the first part of my journey on horseback. I afterwards hired a mule, as the more sure-footed and least liable to receive injury on these rugged roads. The weather was fine: it was about the middle of the month of August, nearly two months after the death of Justine; that miserable epoch from which I dated all my woe. The weight upon my spirit was sensibly lightened as I plunged yet deeper in the ravine of Arve. The immense mountains and precipices that overhung me on every side – the sound of the river raging among the rocks, and the dashing of the waterfalls around, spoke of a power mighty as Omnipotence – and I ceased to fear, or to bend before any being less almighty than that which had created and ruled the elements, here displayed in their most terrific guise. Still, as I ascended higher, the valley assumed a more magnificent and astonishing character. Ruined castles hanging on the precipices of piny mountains; the impetuous Arve, and cottages every here and there peeping forth from among the trees, formed a scene of singular beauty. But it was augmented and rendered sublime by the mighty Alps, whose white and shining pyramids and domes towered above all, as belonging to another earth, the habitations of another race of beings.

I passed the bridge of Pélissier, where the ravine, which the river forms, opened before me, and I began to ascend the mountain that overhangs it. Soon after I entered the valley of Chamounix. This valley is more wonderful and sublime, but not so beautiful and picturesque, as that of Servox, through which I had just passed. The high and snowy mountains were its immediate boundaries; but I saw no more ruined castles and fertile fields. Immense glaciers approached the road; I heard the rumbling thunder of the falling avalanche and marked the smoke of its passage. Mont Blanc, the supreme and magnificent Mont Blanc, raised itself from the surrounding *aiguilles*,[26] and its tremendous *dôme* overlooked the valley.

A tingling long-lost sense of pleasure often came across me during this journey. Some turn in the road, some new object suddenly perceived and recognised, reminded me of days gone by, and were associated with the light-hearted gaiety of boyhood. The very winds whispered in soothing accents, and maternal nature bade me weep no more. Then again the kindly influence ceased to act – I found myself fettered again to grief and indulging in all the misery of reflection. Then I spurred on my animal, striving so to forget the world, my fears, and more than all, myself – or, in a more desperate fashion, I alighted and threw myself on the grass, weighed down by horror and despair.

At length I arrived at the village of Chamounix. Exhaustion succeeded to the extreme fatigue both of body and of mind which I had endured. For a short space of time I remained at the window, watching the pallid lightnings that played above Mont Blanc, and listening to the rushing of the Arve, which pursued its noisy way beneath. The same lulling sounds acted as a lullaby to my too keen sensations: when I placed my head upon my pillow, sleep crept over me; I felt it as it came and blest the giver of oblivion.

CHAPTER II

I spent the following day roaming through the valley. I stood beside the sources of the Arveiron, which take their rise in a glacier, that with slow pace is advancing down from the summit of the hills, to barricade the valley. The abrupt sides of vast mountains were before me; the icy wall of the glacier overhung me; a few shattered pines were scattered around; and the solemn silence of this glorious presence-chamber of imperial Nature was broken only by the brawling waves or the fall of some vast fragment, the thunder sound of the avalanche or the cracking, reverberated along the mountains, of the accumulated ice, which, through the silent working of immutable laws, was ever and anon rent and torn, as if it had been but a plaything in their hands. These sublime and magnificent scenes afforded me the greatest consolation that I was capable of receiving. They elevated me from all littleness of feeling; and although they did not remove my grief, they subdued and tranquillised it. In some degree, also, they diverted my mind from the thoughts over which it had brooded for the last month. I retired to rest at night; my slumbers, as it were, waited on and ministered to by the assemblance of grand shapes which I had contemplated during the day. They congregated round me; the unstained snowy mountain-top, the glittering pinnacle, the pine woods, and ragged bare ravine, the eagle, soaring amidst the clouds – they all gathered round me and bade me be at peace.

Where had they fled when the next morning I awoke? All of soul-inspiring fled with sleep, and dark melancholy clouded every thought. The rain was pouring in torrents, and thick mists hid the summits of the mountains, so that I even saw not the faces of those mighty friends. Still I would penetrate their misty veil and seek them in their cloudy retreats. What were rain and storm to me? My mule was brought to the door, and I resolved to ascend to the summit of Montanvert. I remembered the effect that the

93

view of the tremendous and ever-moving glacier had produced upon my mind when I first saw it. It had then filled me with a sublime ecstasy, that gave wings to the soul, and allowed it to soar from the obscure world to light and joy. The sight of the awful and majestic in nature had indeed always the effect of solemnising my mind and causing me to forget the passing cares of life. I determined to go without a guide, for I was well acquainted with the path, and the presence of another would destroy the solitary grandeur of the scene.

The ascent is precipitous, but the path is cut into continual and short windings, which enable you to surmount the perpendicularity of the mountain. It is a scene terrifically desolate. In a thousand spots the traces of the winter avalanche may be perceived, where trees lie broken and strewed on the ground; some entirely destroyed, others bent, leaning upon the jutting rocks of the mountain or transversely upon other trees. The path, as you ascend higher, is intersected by ravines of snow, down which stones continually roll from above; one of them is particularly dangerous, as the slightest sound, such as even speaking in a loud voice, produces a concussion of air sufficient to draw destruction upon the head of the speaker. The pines are not tall or luxuriant, but they are sombre and add an air of severity to the scene. I looked on the valley beneath; vast mists were rising from the rivers which ran through it and curling in thick wreaths around the opposite mountains, whose summits were hid in the uniform clouds, while rain poured from the dark sky, and added to the melancholy impression I received from the objects around me. Alas! why does man boast of sensibilities superior to those apparent in the brute; it only renders them more necessary beings.[27] If our impulses were confined to hunger, thirst, and desire, we might be nearly free; but now we are moved by every wind that blows and a chance word or scene that that word may convey to us.

> We rest; a dream has power to poison sleep.
> We rise; one wand'ring thought pollutes the day.
> We feel, conceive, or reason; laugh or weep,
> Embrace fond woe, or cast our cares away;

It is the same: for, be it joy or sorrow,
  The path of its departure still is free.
Man's yesterday may ne'er be like his morrow;
  Nought may endure but mutability![28]

It was nearly noon when I arrived at the top of the ascent. For some time I sat upon the rock that overlooks the sea of ice. A mist covered both that and the surrounding mountains. Presently a breeze dissipated the cloud, and I descended upon the glacier. The surface is very uneven, rising like the waves of a troubled sea, descending low, and interspersed by rifts that sink deep. The field of ice is almost a league in width, but I spent nearly two hours in crossing it. The opposite mountain is a bare perpendicular rock. From the side where I now stood Montanvert was exactly opposite, at the distance of a league; and above it rose Mont Blanc, in awful majesty. I remained in a recess of the rock, gazing on this wonderful and stupendous scene. The sea, or rather the vast river of ice, wound among its dependent mountains, whose aerial summits hung over its recesses. Their icy and glittering peaks shone in the sunlight over the clouds. My heart, which was before sorrowful, now swelled with something like joy; I exclaimed – 'Wandering spirits, if indeed ye wander, and do not rest in your narrow beds, allow me this faint happiness, or take me, as your companion, away from the joys of life.'

As I said this, I suddenly beheld the figure of a man, at some distance, advancing towards me with superhuman speed. He bounded over the crevices in the ice, among which I had walked with caution; his stature, also, as he approached, seemed to exceed that of man. I was troubled: a mist came over my eyes, and I felt a faintness seize me; but I was quickly restored by the cold gale of the mountains. I perceived, as the shape came nearer (sight tremendous and abhorred!) that it was the wretch whom I had created. I trembled with rage and horror, resolving to wait his approach, and then close with him in mortal combat. He approached; his countenance bespoke bitter anguish, combined with disdain and malignity, while its unearthly ugliness rendered it almost too horrible for human eyes. But I scarcely observed this; rage and hatred had at first deprived me of utterance, and I recovered only to overwhelm him with words expressive of furious detestation and contempt.

'Devil,' I exclaimed, 'do you dare approach me? and do not you fear the fierce vengeance of my arm wreaked on your miserable head? Begone, vile insect! or rather, stay, that I may trample you to dust! and, oh! that I could, with the extinction of your miserable existence, restore those victims whom you have so diabolically murdered!'

'I expected this reception,' said the daemon. 'All men hate the wretched; how, then, must I be hated, who am miserable beyond all living things! Yet you, my creator, detest and spurn me, thy creature, to whom thou art bound by ties only dissoluble by the annihilation of one of us. You purpose to kill me. How dare you sport thus with life? Do your duty towards me, and I will do mine towards you and the rest of mankind. If you will comply with my conditions, I will leave them and you at peace; but if you refuse, I will glut the maw of death, until it be satiated with the blood of your remaining friends.'

'Abhorred monster! fiend that thou art! the tortures of hell are too mild a vengeance for thy crimes. Wretched devil! you reproach me with your creation; come on, then, that I may extinguish the spark which I so negligently bestowed.'

My rage was without bounds; I sprang on him, impelled by all the feelings which can arm one being against the existence of another.

He easily eluded me, and said –

'Be calm! I intreat you to hear me, before you give vent to your hatred on my devoted head. Have I not suffered enough, that you seek to increase my misery? Life, although it may only be an accumulation of anguish, is dear to me, and I will defend it. Remember, thou hast made me more powerful than thyself; my height is superior to thine, my joints more supple. But I will not be tempted to set myself in opposition to thee. I am thy creature, and I will be even mild and docile to my natural lord and king, if thou wilt also perform thy part, the which thou owest me. Oh, Frankenstein, be not equitable to every other and trample upon me alone, to whom thy justice, and even thy clemency and affection, is most due. Remember, that I am thy creature; I ought to be thy Adam, but I am rather the fallen angel, whom thou drivest from joy for no misdeed. Everywhere I see bliss, from which I alone am irrevocably excluded. I was benevolent and good; misery made me a fiend. Make me happy, and I shall again be virtuous.'

'Begone! I will not hear you. There can be no community between you and me; we are enemies. Begone, or let us try our strength in a fight in which one must fall.'

'How can I move thee? Will no intreaties cause thee to turn a favourable eye upon thy creature, who implores thy goodness and compassion? Believe me, Frankenstein: I was benevolent; my soul glowed with love and humanity; but am I not alone, miserably alone? You, my creator, abhor me; what hope can I gather from your fellow-creatures, who owe me nothing? they spurn and hate me. The desert mountains and dreary glaciers are my refuge. I have wandered here many days; the caves of ice, which I only do not fear, are a dwelling to me, and the only one which man does not grudge. These bleak skies I hail, for they are kinder to me than your fellow beings. If the multitude of mankind knew of my existence, they would do as you do, and arm themselves for my destruction. Shall I not then hate them who abhor me? I will keep no terms with my enemies. I am miserable, and they shall share my wretchedness. Yet it is in your power to recompense me, and deliver them from an evil which it only remains for you to make so great, that not only you and your family, but thousands of others, shall be swallowed up in the whirlwinds of its rage. Let your compassion be moved, and do not disdain me. Listen to my tale: when you have heard that, abandon or commiserate me, as you shall judge that I deserve. But hear me. The guilty are allowed, by human laws, bloody as they are, to speak in their own defence before they are condemned. Listen to me, Frankenstein. You accuse me of murder, and yet you would, with a satisfied conscience, destroy your own creature. Oh, praise the eternal justice of man! Yet I ask you not to spare me: listen to me; and then, if you can, and if you will, destroy the work of your hands.'

'Why do you call to my remembrance,' I rejoined, 'circumstances, of which I shudder to reflect, that I have been the miserable origin and author? Cursed be the day, abhorred devil, in which you first saw light! Cursed (although I curse myself) be the hands that formed you! You have made me wretched beyond expression. You have left me no power to consider whether I am just to you, or not. Begone! relieve me from the sight of your detested form.'

'Thus I relieve thee, my creator,' he said, and placed his hated hands before my eyes, which I flung from me with violence; 'thus I take from thee a sight which you abhor. Still thou canst listen to me and grant me thy compassion. By the virtues that I once possessed, I demand this from you. Hear my tale; it is long and strange, and the temperature of this place is not fitting to your fine sensations; come to the hut upon the mountain. The sun is yet high in the heavens; before it descends to hide itself beyond yon snowy precipices, and illuminate another world, you will have heard my story and can decide. On you it rests, whether I quit forever the neighbourhood of man and lead a harmless life, or become the scourge of your fellow creatures, and the author of your own speedy ruin.'

As he said this, he led the way across the ice: I followed. My heart was full, and I did not answer him; but as I proceeded, I weighed the various arguments that he had used, and determined at least to listen to his tale. I was partly urged by curiosity, and compassion confirmed my resolution. I had hitherto supposed him to be the murderer of my brother, and I eagerly sought a confirmation or denial of this opinion. For the first time, also, I felt what the duties of a creator towards his creature were, and that I ought to render him happy before I complained of his wickedness. These motives urged me to comply with his demand. We crossed the ice, therefore, and ascended the opposite rock. The air was cold, and the rain again began to descend: we entered the hut, the fiend with an air of exultation, I with a heavy heart and depressed spirits. But I consented to listen, and seating myself by the fire which my odious companion had lighted, he thus began his tale.

CHAPTER III

'It is with considerable difficulty that I remember the original era of my being: all the events of that period appear confused and indistinct. A strange multiplicity of sensations seized me, and I saw, felt, heard, and smelt at the same time; and it was, indeed, a long time before I learned to distinguish between the operations of my various senses. By degrees, I remember, a stronger light pressed upon my nerves, so that I was obliged to shut my eyes. Darkness then came over me, and troubled me; but hardly had I felt this when, by opening my eyes, as I now suppose, the light poured in upon me again. I walked and, I believe, descended; but I presently found a great alteration in my sensations. Before, dark and opaque bodies had surrounded me, impervious to my touch or sight; but I now found that I could wander on at liberty, with no obstacles which I could not either surmount or avoid. The light became more and more oppressive to me; and the heat wearying me as I walked, I sought a place where I could receive shade. This was the forest near Ingolstadt; and here I lay by the side of a brook resting from my fatigue, until I felt tormented by hunger and thirst. This roused me from my nearly dormant state, and I ate some berries which I found hanging on the trees or lying on the ground. I slaked my thirst at the brook; and then lying down, was overcome by sleep.

'It was dark when I awoke; I felt cold also, and half frightened, as it were, instinctively, finding myself so desolate. Before I had quitted your apartment, on a sensation of cold, I had covered myself with some clothes; but these were insufficient to secure me from the dews of night. I was a poor, helpless, miserable wretch; I knew, and could distinguish, nothing; but feeling pain invade me on all sides, I sat down and wept.

'Soon a gentle light stole over the heavens, and gave me a sensation of pleasure. I started up and beheld a radiant form rise from among the trees.* I gazed with a kind of wonder. It moved slowly, but it enlightened my path, and I again went out in search of berries. I was still cold when under one of the trees I found a huge cloak, with which I covered myself, and sat down upon the ground. No distinct ideas occupied my mind; all was confused. I felt light, and hunger, and thirst, and darkness; innumerable sounds rang in my ears, and on all sides various scents saluted me: the only object that I could distinguish was the bright moon, and I fixed my eyes on that with pleasure.

'Several changes of day and night passed, and the orb of night had greatly lessened, when I began to distinguish my sensations from each other. I gradually saw plainly the clear stream that supplied me with drink, and the trees that shaded me with their foliage. I was delighted when I first discovered that a pleasant sound, which often saluted my ears, proceeded from the throats of the little winged animals who had often intercepted the light from my eyes. I began also to observe, with greater accuracy, the forms that surrounded me, and to perceive the boundaries of the radiant roof of light which canopied me. Sometimes I tried to imitate the pleasant songs of the birds, but was unable. Sometimes I wished to express my sensations in my own mode, but the uncouth and inarticulate sounds which broke from me frightened me into silence again.

'The moon had disappeared from the night, and again, with a lessened form, showed itself, while I still remained in the forest. My sensations had by this time become distinct, and my mind received every day additional ideas. My eyes became accustomed to the light and to perceive objects in their right forms; I distinguished the insect from the herb, and by degrees, one herb from another. I found that the sparrow uttered none but harsh notes, whilst those of the blackbird and thrush were sweet and enticing.

'One day, when I was oppressed by cold, I found a fire which had been left by some wandering beggars, and was overcome with delight at the warmth I experienced from it. In my joy I thrust my hand into the live embers, but quickly drew it out

---

* The moon [author's footnote].

again with a cry of pain. How strange, I thought, that the same cause should produce such opposite effects! I examined the materials of the fire, and to my joy found it to be composed of wood. I quickly collected some branches; but they were wet and would not burn. I was pained at this; and sat still watching the operation of the fire. The wet wood which I had placed near the heat dried, and itself became inflamed. I reflected on this; and by touching the various branches, I discovered the cause, and busied myself in collecting a great quantity of wood, that I might dry it and have a plentiful supply of fire. When night came on and brought sleep with it, I was in the greatest fear lest my fire should be extinguished. I covered it carefully with dry wood and leaves, and placed wet branches upon it; and then, spreading my cloak, I lay on the ground, and sunk into sleep.

'It was morning when I awoke, and my first care was to visit the fire. I uncovered it, and a gentle breeze quickly fanned it into a flame. I observed this also and contrived a fan of branches, which roused the embers when they were nearly extinguished. When night came again I found, with pleasure, that the fire gave light as well as heat; and that the discovery of this element was useful to me in my food, for I found some of the offals that the travellers had left had been roasted, and tasted much more savoury than the berries I gathered from the trees. I tried, therefore, to dress my food in the same manner, placing it on the live embers. I found that the berries were spoiled by this operation, and the nuts and roots much improved.

'Food, however, became scarce; and I often spent the whole day searching in vain for a few acorns to assuage the pangs of hunger. When I found this, I resolved to quit the place that I had hitherto inhabited, to seek for one where the few wants I experienced would be more easily satisfied. In this emigration, I exceedingly lamented the loss of the fire which I had obtained through accident, and knew not how to reproduce it. I gave several hours to the serious consideration of this difficulty; but I was obliged to relinquish all attempts to supply it; and, wrapping myself up in my cloak, I struck across the wood towards the setting sun. I passed three days in these rambles, and at length discovered the open country. A great fall of snow had taken place the night before, and the fields were of one uniform white; the appearance was disconsolate, and I found my feet chilled by the cold damp outside that covered the ground.

'It was about seven in the morning, and I longed to obtain food and shelter; at length I perceived a small hut, on a rising ground, which had doubtless been built for the convenience of some shepherd. This was a new sight to me; and I examined the structure; with great curiosity. Finding the door open, I entered. An old man sat in it, near a fire, over which he was preparing his breakfast. He turned on hearing a noise; and perceiving me, shrieked loudly, and quitting the hut, ran across the fields with a speed of which his debilitated form hardly appeared capable. His appearance, different from any I had ever before seen, and his flight, somewhat surprised me. But I was enchanted by the appearance of the hut: here the snow and rain could not penetrate; the ground was dry; and it presented to me then as exquisite and divine a retreat as Pandaemonium appeared to the daemons of hell[29] after their sufferings in the lake of fire. I greedily devoured the remnants of the shepherd's breakfast, which consisted of bread, cheese, milk, and wine; the latter, however, I did not like. Then, overcome by fatigue, I lay down among some straw, and fell asleep.

'It was noon when I awoke; and, allured by the warmth of the sun, which shone brightly on the white ground, I determined to recommence my travels; and, depositing the remains of the peasant's breakfast in a wallet I found, I proceeded across the fields for several hours, until at sunset I arrived at a village. How miraculous did this appear! the huts, the neater cottages, and stately houses engaged my admiration by turns. The vegetables in the gardens, the milk and cheese that I saw placed at the windows of some of the cottages, allured my appetite. One of the best of these I entered; but I had hardly placed my foot within the door before the children shrieked, and one of the women fainted. The whole village was roused; some fled, some attacked me, until, grievously bruised by stones and many other kinds of missile weapons, I escaped to the open country and fearfully took refuge in a low hovel, quite bare, and making a wretched appearance after the palaces I had beheld in the village. This hovel, however, joined a cottage of a neat and pleasant appearance;

but, after my late dearly bought experience, I dared not enter it. My place of refuge was constructed of wood, but so low that I could with difficulty sit upright in it. No wood, however, was placed on the earth which formed the floor, but it was dry; and although the wind entered it by innumerable chinks, I found it an agreeable asylum from the snow and rain.

'Here then I retreated, and lay down happy to have found a shelter, however miserable, from the inclemency of the season, and still more from the barbarity of man.

'As soon as morning dawned, I crept from my kennel, that I might view the adjacent cottage and discover if I could remain in the habitation I had found. It was situated against the back of the cottage and surrounded on the sides which were exposed by a pig-sty and a clear pool of water. One part was open, and by that I had crept in; but now I covered every crevice by which I might be perceived with stones and wood, yet in such a manner that I might move them on occasion to pass out: all the light I enjoyed came through the sty, and that was sufficient for me.

'Having thus arranged my dwelling and carpeted it with clean straw, I retired; for I saw the figure of a man at a distance, and I remembered too well my treatment the night before, to trust myself in his power. I had first, however, provided for my sustenance for that day by a loaf of coarse bread, which I purloined, and a cup with which I could drink, more conveniently than from my hand, of the pure water which flowed by my retreat. The floor was a little raised, so that it was kept perfectly dry, and by its vicinity to the chimney of the cottage it was tolerably warm.

'Being thus provided, I resolved to reside in this hovel until something should occur which might alter my determination. It was indeed a paradise compared to the bleak forest, my former residence, the rain-dropping branches, and dank earth. I ate my breakfast with pleasure and was about to remove a plank to procure myself a little water when I heard a step, and looking through a small chink, I beheld a young creature, with a pail on her head, passing before my hovel. The girl was young and of gentle demeanour, unlike, what I have since found cottagers and farm-house servants to be. Yet she was meanly dressed, a coarse blue petticoat and a linen jacket being her only grab; her fair hair was plaited, but not adorned: she looked patient, yet sad. I lost sight of her; and in about a quarter of an hour she returned bearing the pail, which was now partly filled with milk. As she walked along, seemingly incommoded by the burden, a young man met her, whose countenance expressed a deeper despondence. Uttering a few sounds with an air of melancholy, he took the pail from her head and bore it to the cottage himself. She followed, and they disappeared. Presently I saw the young man again, with some tools in his hand, cross the field behind the cottage; and the girl was also busied, sometimes in the house and sometimes in the yard.

'On examining my dwelling, I found that one of the windows of the cottage had formerly occupied a part of it, but the panes had been filled up with wood. In one of these was a small and almost imperceptible chink, through which the eye could just penetrate. Through this crevice a small room was visible, white-washed and clean, but very bare of furniture. In one corner, near a small fire, sat an old man, leaning his head on his hands in a disconsolate attitude. The young girl was occupied in arranging the cottage; but presently she took something out of a drawer, which employed her hands, and she sat down beside the old man, who, taking up an instrument, began to play, and to produce sounds sweeter than the voice of the thrush or the nightingale. It was a lovely sight, even to me, poor wretch! who had never beheld aught beautiful before. The silver hair and benevolent countenance of the aged cottager won my reverence, while the gentle manners of the girl enticed my love. He played a sweet mournful air, which I perceived drew tears from the eyes of his amiable companion, of which the old man took no notice, until she sobbed audibly; he then pronounced a few sounds, and the fair creature, leaving her work, knelt at his feet. He raised her, and smiled with such kindness and affection that I felt sensations of a peculiar and overpowering nature: they were a mixture of pain and pleasure, such as I had never before experienced, either from hunger or cold, warmth or food; and I withdrew from the window, unable to bear these emotions.

'Soon after this the young man returned, bearing on his shoulders a load of wood. The girl met him at the door, helped to relieve him of his burden, and taking some of the fuel into the cottage, placed it on the fire; then she and the youth went apart into a nook of the cottage, and he showed her a large loaf and a piece of cheese. She seemed pleased, and went into the garden for some roots and plants, which she placed in water, and then upon the fire. She afterwards continued her work, whilst the young man went into the garden, and appeared busily employed in digging and pulling up roots. After he had been employed thus about an hour, the young woman joined him, and they entered the cottage together.

'The old man had, in the mean time, been pensive; but on the appearance of his companions he assumed a more cheerful air, and they sat down to eat. The meal was quickly despatched. The young woman was again occupied in arranging the cottage; the old man walked before the cottage in the sun for a few minutes, leaning on the arm of the youth. Nothing could exceed in beauty the contrast between these two excellent creatures. One was old, with silver hairs and a countenance beaming with benevolence and love: the younger was slight and graceful in his figure, and his features were moulded with the finest symmetry; yet his eyes and attitude expressed the utmost sadness and despondency. The old man returned to the cottage; and the youth, with tools different from those he had used in the morning, directed his steps across the fields.

'Night quickly shut in; but to my extreme wonder, I found that the cottagers had a means of prolonging light by the use of tapers, and was delighted to find that the setting of the sun did not put an end to the pleasure I experienced in watching my human neighbours. In the evening, the young girl and her companion were employed in various occupations which I did not understand; and the old man again took up the instrument which produced the divine sounds that had enchanted me in the morning. So soon as he had finished the youth began, not to play, but to utter sounds that were monotonous, and neither resembling the harmony of the old man's instrument nor the songs of the birds: I since found that he read aloud, but at that time I knew nothing of the science of words or letters.

'The family, after having been thus occupied for a short time, extinguished their lights and retired, as I conjectured, to rest.'

CHAPTER IV

'I lay on my straw, but I could not sleep. I thought of the occurrences of the day. What chiefly struck me was the gentle manners of these people; and I longed to join them, but dared not. I remembered too well the treatment I had suffered the night before from the barbarous villagers, and resolved, whatever course of conduct I might hereafter think it right to pursue, that for the present I would remain quietly in my hovel, watching, and endeavouring to discover the motives which influenced their actions.

'The cottagers arose the next morning before the sun. The young woman arranged the cottage and prepared the food; and the youth departed after the first meal.

'This day was passed in the same routine as that which preceded it. The young man was constantly employed out of doors, and the girl in various laborious occupations within. The old man, whom I soon perceived to be blind, employed his leisure hours on his instrument or in contemplation. Nothing could exceed the love and respect which the younger cottagers exhibited towards their venerable companion. They performed towards him every little office of affection and duty with gentleness; and he rewarded them by his benevolent smiles.

'They were not entirely happy. The young man and his companion often went apart, and appeared to weep. I saw no cause for their unhappiness; but I was deeply affected by it. If such lovely creatures were miserable, it was less strange that I, an imperfect and solitary being, should be wretched. Yet why were these gentle beings unhappy? They possessed a delightful house (for such it was in my eyes) and every luxury; they had a fire to warm them when chill, and delicious viands when hungry; they were dressed in excellent clothes; and, still more, they enjoyed one another's company and speech, interchanging each day looks of affection and kindness. What did their tears imply? Did they really express pain? I was at first unable to solve these questions; but perpetual attention and time explained to me many appearances which were at first enigmatic.

'A considerable period elapsed before I discovered one of the causes of the uneasiness of this amiable family: it was poverty, and they suffered that evil in a very distressing degree. Their nourishment consisted entirely of the vegetables of their garden and the milk of one cow, which gave very little during the winter, when its masters could scarcely procure food to support it. They often, I believe, suffered the pangs of hunger very poignantly, especially the two younger cottagers; for several times they placed food before the old man when they reserved none for themselves.

'This trait of kindness moved me sensibly. I had been accustomed, during the night, to steal a part of their store for my own consumption; but when I found that in doing this I inflicted pain on the cottagers, I abstained, and satisfied myself with berries, nuts, and roots, which I gathered from a neighbouring wood.

'I discovered also another means through which I was enabled to assist their labours. I found that the youth spent a great part of each day in collecting wood for the family fire; and, during the night I often took his tools, the use of which I quickly discovered, and brought home firing sufficient for the consumption of several days.

'I remember, the first time that I did this, the young woman, when she opened the door in the morning, appeared greatly astonished on seeing a great pile of wood on the outside. She uttered some words in a loud voice, and the youth joined her, who also expressed surprise. I observed, with pleasure, that he did not go to the forest that day, but spent it in repairing the cottage and cultivating the garden.

'By degrees I made a discovery of still greater moment. I found that these people possessed a method of communicating their experience and feelings to one another by articulate sounds. I perceived that the words they spoke sometimes produced pleasure or pain, smiles or sadness, in the minds and countenances of the hearers. This was indeed a godlike science, and I ardently desired to become acquainted with it. But I was baffled in every attempt

I made for this purpose. Their pronunciation was quick; and the words they uttered, not having any apparent connection with visible objects, I was unable to discover any clue by which I could unravel the mystery of their reference. By great application, however, and after having remained during the space of several revolutions of the moon in my hovel, I discovered the names that were given to some of the most familiar objects of discourse; I learned and applied the words, "fire", "milk", "bread", and "wood". I learned also the names of the cottagers themselves. The youth and his companion had each of them several names, but the old man had only one, which was "father". The girl was called "sister", or "Agatha", and the youth "Felix", "brother", or "son". I cannot describe the delight I felt when I learned the ideas appropriated to each of these sounds, and was able to pronounce them. I distinguished several other words without being able as yet to understand or apply them; such as "good", "dearest", "unhappy".

'I spent the winter in this manner. The gentle manners and beauty of the cottagers greatly endeared them to me: when they were unhappy, I felt depressed; when they rejoiced, I sympathised in their joys. I saw few human beings besides them; and if any other happened to enter the cottage, their harsh manners and rude gait only enhanced to me the superior accomplishments of my friends. The old man, I could perceive, often endeavoured to encourage his children, as sometimes I found that he called them, to cast off their melancholy. He would talk in a cheerful accent, with an expression of goodness that bestowed pleasure even upon me. Agatha listened with respect, her eyes sometimes filled with tears, which she endeavoured to wipe away unperceived; but I generally found that her countenance and tone were more cheerful after having listened to the exhortations of her father. It was not thus with Felix. He was always the saddest of the group, and, even to my unpractised senses, he appeared to have suffered more deeply than his friends. But if his countenance was more sorrowful, his voice was more cheerful than that of his sister, especially when he addressed the old man.

'I could mention innumerable instances which, although slight, marked the dispositions of these amiable cottagers. In the midst of poverty and want, Felix carried with pleasure to his sister the first little white flower that peeped out from beneath the snowy ground. Early in the morning, before she had risen, he cleared away the snow that obstructed her path to the milk-house, drew water from the well, and brought the wood from the out-house, where, to his perpetual astonishment, he found his store always replenished by an invisible hand. In the day, I believe, he worked sometimes for a neighbouring farmer, because he often went forth and did not return until dinner, yet brought no wood with him. At other times he worked in the garden; but as there was little to do in the frosty season, he read to the old man and Agatha.

'This reading had puzzled me extremely at first; but, by degrees, I discovered that he uttered many of the same sounds when he read, as when he talked. I conjectured, therefore, that he found on the paper signs for speech which he understood, and I ardently longed to comprehend these also; but how was that possible when I did not even understand the sounds for which they stood as signs? I improved, however, sensibly in this science, but not sufficiently to follow up any kind of conversation, although I applied my whole mind to the endeavour: for I easily perceived that, although I eagerly longed to discover myself[30] to the cottagers, I ought not to make the attempt until I had first become master of their language; which knowledge might enable me to make them overlook the deformity of my figure; for with this also the contrast perpetually presented to my eyes had made me acquainted.

'I had admired the perfect forms of my cottagers – their grace, beauty, and delicate complexions: but how was I terrified, when I viewed myself in a transparent pool! At first I started back, unable to believe that it was indeed I who was reflected in the mirror; and when I became fully convinced that I was in reality the monster that I am, I was filled with the bitterest sensations of despondence and mortification. Alas! I did not yet entirely know the fatal effects of this miserable deformity.

'As the sun became warmer, and the light of day longer, the snow vanished, and I beheld the bare trees and the black earth. From this time Felix was more employed; and the heart-moving indications of impending famine disappeared. Their food, as I afterwards found, was coarse, but it was wholesome; and they procured a sufficiency of it. Several new kinds of plants sprang up in the garden, which they dressed; and these signs of comfort increased daily as the season advanced.

'The old man, leaning on his son, walked each day at noon, when it did not rain, as I found it was called when the heavens poured forth its water. This frequently took place; but a high wind quickly dried the earth, and the season became far more pleasant than it had been.

'My mode of life in my hovel was uniform. During the morning I attended the motions of the cottagers; and when they were dispersed in various occupations, I slept: the remainder of the day was spent in observing my friends. When they had retired to rest, if there was any moon or the night was star-light, I went into the woods and collected my own food and fuel for the cottage. When I returned, as often as it was necessary, I cleared their path from the snow and performed those offices that I had seen done by Felix. I afterwards found that these labours, performed by an invisible hand, greatly astonished them; and once or twice I heard them, on these occasions, utter the words "good spirit", "wonderful"; but I did not then understand the signification of these terms.

'My thoughts now became more active, and I longed to discover the motives and feelings of these lovely creatures; I was inquisitive to know why Felix appeared so miserable and Agatha so sad. I thought (foolish wretch!) that it might be in my power to restore happiness to these deserving people. When I slept or was absent, the forms of the venerable blind father, the gentle Agatha, and the excellent Felix, flitted before me. I looked upon them as superior beings, who would be the arbiters of my future destiny. I formed in my imagination a thousand pictures of presenting myself to them, and their reception of me. I imagined that they would be disgusted, until, by my gentle demeanour and conciliating words, I should first win their favour, and afterwards their love.

'These thoughts exhilarated me and led me to apply with fresh ardour to the acquiring the art of language. My organs were indeed harsh, but supple; and although my voice was very unlike the soft music of their tones, yet I pronounced such words as I understood with tolerable ease. It was as the ass and the lap-dog;[31] yet surely the gentle ass whose intentions were affectionate, although his manners were rude, deserved better treatment than blows and execration.

'The pleasant showers and genial warmth of spring greatly altered the aspect of the earth. Men, who before this change seemed to have been hid in caves, dispersed themselves, and were employed in various arts of cultivation. The birds sang in more cheerful notes, and the leaves began to bud forth on the trees. Happy, happy earth! fit habitation for gods, which, so short a time before, was bleak, damp, and unwholesome. My spirits were elevated by the enchanting appearance of nature; the past was blotted from my memory, the present was tranquil, and the future gilded by bright rays of hope, and anticipations of joy.'

CHAPTER V

'I now hasten to the more moving part of my story. I shall relate events, that impressed me with feelings which, from what I had been, have made me what I am.

'Spring advanced rapidly; the weather became fine and the skies cloudless. It surprised me, that what before was desert and gloomy should now bloom with the most beautiful flowers and verdure. My senses were gratified and refreshed by a thousand scents of delight, and a thousand sights of beauty.

'It was on one of these days, when my cottagers periodically rested from labour – the old man played on his guitar, and the children listened to him – that I observed the countenance of Felix was melancholy beyond expression; he sighed frequently; and once his father paused in his music, and I conjectured by his manner that he enquired the cause of his son's sorrow. Felix replied in a cheerful accent, and the old man was recommencing his music when some-one tapped at the door.

'It was a lady on horseback, accompanied by a countryman as a guide. The lady was dressed in a dark suit, and covered with a thick black veil. Agatha asked a question, to which the stranger only replied by pronouncing, in a sweet accent, the name of Felix. Her voice was musical but unlike that of either of my friends. On hearing this word, Felix came up hastily to the lady, who, when she saw him, threw up her veil, and I beheld a countenance of angelic beauty and expression. Her hair of a shining raven black, and curiously braided; her eyes were dark, but gentle, although animated; her features of a regular proportion, and her complexion wondrously fair, each cheek tinged with a lovely pink.

'Felix seemed ravished with delight when he saw her, every trait of sorrow vanished from his face, and it instantly expressed a degree of ecstatic joy, of which I could hardly have believed it capable; his eyes sparkled, as his cheek flushed with pleasure; and at that moment I thought him as beautiful as the stranger. She appeared affected by different feelings; wiping a few tears from her lovely eyes, she held out her hand to Felix, who kissed it rapturously and called her, as well as I could distinguish, his sweet Arabian. She did not appear to understand him, but smiled. He assisted her to dismount, and dismissing her guide, conducted her into the cottage. Some conversation took place between him and his father; and the young stranger knelt at the old man's feet and would have kissed his hand, but he raised her, and embraced her affectionately.

'I soon perceived, that although the stranger uttered articulate sounds, and appeared to have a language of her own, she was neither understood by, nor herself understood, the cottagers. They made many signs which I did not comprehend; but I saw that her presence diffused gladness through the cottage, dispelling their sorrow as the sun dissipates the morning mists. Felix seemed peculiarly happy, and with smiles of delight welcomed his Arabian. Agatha, the ever-gentle Agatha, kissed the hands of the lovely stranger; and pointing to her brother, made signs which appeared to me to mean that he had been sorrowful until she came. Some hours passed thus, while they, by their countenances, expressed joy, the cause of which I did not comprehend. Presently I found, by the frequent recurrence of some sound which the stranger repeated after them, that she was endeavouring to learn their language; and the idea instantly occurred to me that I should make use of the same instructions to the same end. The stranger learned about twenty words at the first lesson, most of them, indeed, were those which I had before understood, but I profited by the others.

'As night came on, Agatha and the Arabian retired early. When they separated, Felix kissed the hand of the stranger and said, "Good night, sweet Safie." He sat up much longer, conversing with his father; and by the frequent repetition of her name, I conjectured that their lovely guest was the subject of their conversation. I ardently desired to understand them, and bent every faculty towards that purpose, but found it utterly impossible.

'The next morning Felix went out to his work; and, after the usual occupations of Agatha were finished, the Arabian sat at the feet of the old man, and taking his guitar, played some airs so entrancingly beautiful that they at once drew tears of sorrow and delight from my eyes. She sang, and her voice flowed in a rich cadence, swelling or dying away, like a nightingale of the woods.

'When she had finished, she gave the guitar to Agatha, who at first declined it. She played a simple air, and her voice accompanied it in sweet accents, but unlike the wondrous strain of the stranger. The old man appeared enraptured and said some words, which Agatha endeavoured to explain to Safie, and by which he appeared to wish to express that she bestowed on him the greatest delight by her music.

'The days now passed as peaceably as before, with the sole alteration that joy had taken place of sadness in the countenances of my friends. Safie was always gay and happy; she and I improved rapidly in the knowledge of language, so that in two months I began to comprehend most of the words uttered by my protectors.

'In the meanwhile also the black ground was covered with herbage, and the green banks interspersed with innumerable flowers, sweet to the scent and the eyes, stars of pale radiance among the moonlight woods; the sun became warmer, the nights clear and balmy; and my nocturnal rambles were an extreme pleasure to me, although they were considerably shortened by the late setting and early rising of the sun, for I never ventured abroad during daylight, fearful of meeting with the same treatment I had formerly endured in the first village which I entered.

'My days were spent in close attention, that I might more speedily master the language; and I may boast that I improved more rapidly than the Arabian, who understood very little and conversed in broken accents, whilst I comprehended and could imitate almost every word that was spoken.

'While I improved in speech, I also learned the science of letters as it was taught to the stranger; and this opened before me a wide field for wonder and delight.

'The book from which Felix instructed Safie was Volney's *Ruins of Empires*.[32] I should not have understood the purport of this book had not Felix, in reading it, given very minute explanations. He had chosen this work, he said, because the declamatory style was framed in imitation of the eastern authors. Through this work I obtained a cursory knowledge of history and a view of the several empires at present existing in the world; it gave me an insight into the manners, governments, and religions of the different nations of the earth. I heard of the slothful Asiatics; of the stupend-ous genius and mental activity of the Grecians; of the wars and wonderful virtue of the early Romans – of their subsequent de-generating – of the decline of that mighty empire, of chivalry, Christianity, and kings. I heard of the discovery of the American hemisphere and wept with Safie over the hapless fate of its original inhabitants.

'These wonderful narrations inspired me with strange feelings. Was man, indeed, at once so powerful, so virtuous, and magnifi-cent, yet so vicious and base? He appeared at one time a mere scion of the evil principle, and at another as all that can be conceived as noble and godlike. To be a great and virtuous man appeared the highest honour that can befall a sensitive being; to be base and vicious, as many on record have been, appeared the lowest degradation, a condition more abject than that of the blind mole or harmless worm. For a long time I could not conceive how one man could go forth to murder his fellow, or even why there were laws and governments; but when I heard details of vice and bloodshed, my wonder ceased, and I turned away with disgust and loathing.

'Every conversation of the cottagers now opened new wonders to me. While I listened to the instructions which Felix bestowed upon the Arabian, the strange system of human society was ex-plained to me. I heard of the division of property, of immense wealth and squalid poverty; of rank, descent, and noble blood.

'The words induced me to turn towards myself. I learned that the possessions most esteemed by your fellow creatures were, high and unsullied descent united with riches. A man might be re-spected with only one of these advantages; but without either he was considered, except in very rare instances, as a vagabond and a slave, doomed to waste his powers for the profits of the chosen few! And what was I? Of my creation and creator I was absolutely ignorant, but I knew that I possessed no money, no friends, no kind of property. I was, besides, endued with a figure hideously deformed and loathsome; I was not even of the same nature as man. I was more agile than they and could subsist upon coarser diet; I bore the extremes of heat and cold with less injury to my frame; my stature far exceeded theirs. When I looked around I saw and heard of none like me. Was I, then, a monster, a blot upon the earth, from which all men fled and whom all men disowned?

'I cannot describe to you the agony that these reflections inflicted upon me: I tried to dispel them, but sorrow only increased with knowledge. Oh, that I had forever remained in my native wood, nor known nor felt beyond the sensations of hunger, thirst and heat!

'Of what a strange nature is knowledge! It clings to the mind, when it has once seized on it, like a lichen on the rock. I wished sometimes to shake off all thought and feeling; but I learned that there was but one means to overcome the sensation of pain, and that was death – a state which I feared yet did not understand. I admired virtue and good feelings and loved the gentle manners and amiable qualities of my cottagers, but I was shut out from intercourse with them, except through means which I obtained by stealth, when I was unseen and unknown, and which rather increased than satisfied the desire I had of becoming one among my fellows. The gentle words of Agatha and the animated smiles of the charming Arabian, were not for me. The mild exhortations of the old man, and the lively conversation of the loved Felix were not for me. Miserable, unhappy wretch!

'Other lessons were impressed upon me even more deeply. I heard of the difference of sexes; and the birth and growth of children; how the father doated on the smiles of the infant, and the lively sallies of the older child; how all the life and cares of the mother were wrapped up in the precious charge; how the mind of youth expanded and gained knowledge; of brother, sister, and all the various relationships which bind one human being to another in mutual bonds.

'But where were my friends and relations? No father had watched my infant days, no mother had blessed me with smiles and caresses; or if they had, all my past life was now a blot, a blind vacancy in which I distinguished nothing. From my earliest remembrance I had been as I then was in height and proportion. I had never yet seen a being resembling me, or who claimed any intercourse with me. What was I? The question again recurred, to be answered only with groans.

'I will soon explain to what these feeling tended; but allow me now to return to the cottagers, whose story excited in me such various feelings of indignation, delight, and wonder, but which all terminated in additional love and reverence for my protectors (for so I loved, in an innocent, half-painful self-deceit, to call them).'

CHAPTER VI

'Some time elapsed before I learned the history of my friends. It was one which could not fail to impress itself deeply on my mind, unfolding as it did a number of circumstances, each interesting and wonderful to one so utterly inexperienced as I was.

'The name of the old man was De Lacey. He was descended from a good family in France, where he had lived for many years in affluence, respected by his superiors and beloved by his equals. His son was bred in the service of his country; and Agatha had ranked with ladies of the highest distinction. A few months before my arrival they had lived in a large and luxurious city called Paris, surrounded by friends and possessed of every enjoyment which virtue, refinement of intellect, or taste, accompanied by a moderate fortune, could afford.

'The father of Safie had been the cause of their ruin. He was a Turkish merchant, and had inhabited Paris for many years, when, for some reason which I could not learn, he became obnoxious to the government. He was seized and cast into prison the very day that Safie arrived from Constantinople to join him. He was tried and condemned to death. The injustice of his sentence was very flagrant; all Paris was indignant; and it was judged that his religion and wealth rather than the crime alleged against him had been the cause of his condemnation.

'Felix had accidentally been present at the trial; his horror and indignation were uncontrollable when he heard the decision of the court. He made, at that moment, a solemn vow to deliver him and then looked around for the means. After many fruitless attempts to gain admittance to the prison, he found a strongly grated window in an unguarded part of the building, which lighted the dungeon of the unfortunate Mahometan; who, loaded with chains, waited in despair the execution of the barbarous sentence. Felix visited the grate at night and made known to the prisoner his intentions in his favour. The Turk, amazed and delighted, endeavoured to kindle the zeal of his deliverer by promises of reward and wealth. Felix rejected his offers with contempt; yet when he saw the lovely Safie, who was allowed to visit her father and who, by her gestures, expressed her lively gratitude, the youth could not help owning to his own mind that the captive possessed a treasure which would fully reward his toil and hazard.

'The Turk quickly perceived the impression that his daughter had made on the heart of Felix and endeavoured to secure him more entirely in his interests by the promise of her hand in marriage, so soon as he should be conveyed to a place of safety. Felix was too delicate to accept his offer; yet he looked forward to the probability of the event as to the consummation of his happiness.

'During the ensuing days, while the preparations were going forward for the escape of the merchant, the zeal of Felix was warmed by several letters that he received from this lovely girl, who found means to express her thoughts in the language of her lover by the aid of an old man, a servant of her father who understood French. She thanked him in the most ardent terms for his intended services towards her parent; and at the same time she gently deplored her own fate.

'I have copies of these letters; for I found means, during my residence in the hovel, to procure the implements of writing; and the letters were often in the hands of Felix or Agatha. Before I depart, I will give them to you, they will prove the truth of my tale; but at present, as the sun is already far declined, I shall only have time to repeat the substance of them to you.

'Safie related that her mother was a Christian Arab, seized and made a slave by the Turks; recommended by her beauty, she had won the heart of the father of Safie, who married her. The young girl spoke in high and enthusiastic terms of her mother, who, born in freedom, spurned the bondage to which she was now reduced. She instructed her daughter in the tenets of her religion and taught her to aspire to higher powers of intellect and an independence of spirit forbidden to the female followers of Mahomet. This lady died; but her lessons were indelibly impressed on the mind of Safie, who sickened at the prospect of again returning to Asia and being immured within the walls of a harem, allowed only to occupy herself with infantile amusements, ill-suited to the temper of her soul, now accustomed to grand ideas and a noble emulation of virtue. The prospect of marrying a Christian and remaining in a country where women were allowed to take a rank in society was enchanting to her.

'The day for the execution of the Turk was fixed; but on the night previous to it he quitted his prison, and before morning was distant many leagues from Paris. Felix had procured passports in the name of his father, sister, and himself. He had previously communicated his plan to the former, who aided the deceit by quitting his house, under the pretence of a journey and concealing himself, with his daughter, in an obscure part of Paris.

'Felix conducted the fugitives through France to Lyons and across Mont Cenis to Leghorn, where the merchant had decided to wait a favourable opportunity of passing into some part of the Turkish dominions.

'Safie resolved to remain with her father until the moment of his departure, before which time the Turk renewed his promise that she should be united to his deliverer; and Felix remained with them in expectation of that event; and in the mean time he enjoyed the society of the Arabian, who exhibited towards him the simplest and tenderest affection. They conversed with one another through the means of an interpreter, and sometimes with the interpretation of looks; and Safie sang to him the divine airs of her native country.

'The Turk allowed this intimacy to take place, and encouraged the hopes of the youthful lovers, while in his heart he had formed far other plans. He loathed the idea that his daughter should be united to a Christian; but he feared the resentment of Felix if he should appear lukewarm; for he knew that he was still in the power of his deliverer if he should choose to betray him to the Italian state which they inhabited. He revolved a thousand plans by which he should be enabled to prolong the deceit until it might be no longer necessary, and secretly to take his daughter with him when he departed. His plans were facilitated by the news which arrived from Paris.

'The government of France were greatly enraged at the escape of their victim and spared no pains to detect and punish his deliverer. The plot of Felix was quickly discovered, and De Lacey and Agatha were thrown into prison. The news reached Felix and roused him from his dream of pleasure. His blind and aged father and his gentle sister lay in a noisome dungeon while he enjoyed the free air and the society of her whom he loved. This idea was torture to him. He quickly arranged with the Turk that if the latter should find a favourable opportunity for escape before Felix could return to Italy, Safie should remain as a boarder at a convent at Leghorn; and then, quitting the lovely Arabian, he hastened to Paris, and delivered himself up to the vengeance of the law, hoping to free De Lacey and Agatha by this proceeding.

'He did not succeed. They remained confined for five months before the trial took place; the result of which deprived them of their fortune and condemned them to a perpetual exile from their native country.

'They found a miserable asylum in the cottage in Germany, where I discovered them. Felix soon learned that the treacherous Turk, for whom he and his family endured such unheard-of oppression, on discovering that his deliverer was thus reduced to poverty and ruin, became a traitor to good feeling and honour and had quitted Italy with his daughter, insultingly sending Felix a pittance of money to aid him, as he said, in some plan of future maintenance.

'Such were the events that preyed on the heart of Felix and rendered him, when I first saw him, the most miserable of his family. He could have endured poverty; and while this distress had been the meed of his virtue, he gloried in it; but the ingratitude of the Turk and the loss of his beloved Safie, were misfortunes more bitter and irreparable. The arrival of the Arabian now infused new life into his soul.

'When the news reached Leghorn that Felix was deprived of his wealth and rank, the merchant commanded his daughter to think no more of her lover, but to prepare to return to her native country. The generous nature of Safie was outraged by this command; she attempted to expostulate with her father, but he left her angrily, reiterating his tyrannical mandate.

'A few days after, the Turk entered his daughter's apartment and told her hastily that he had reason to believe that his residence at Leghorn had been divulged and that he should speedily be delivered up to the French government; he had, consequently, hired a vessel to convey him to Constantinople, for which city he should sail in a few hours. He intended to leave his daughter under the care of a confidential servant, to follow at her leisure with the greater part of his property, which had not yet arrived at Leghorn.

'When alone, Safie resolved in her own mind the plan of conduct that it would become her to pursue in this emergency. A residence in Turkey was abhorrent to her; her religion and her feelings were alike averse to it. By some papers of her father which fell into her hands she heard of the exile of her lover and learnt the name of the spot where he then resided. She hesitated some time, but at length she formed her determination. Taking with her some jewels that belonged to her and a sum of money, she quitted Italy with an attendant, a native of Leghorn, but who understood the common language of Turkey, and departed for Germany.

'She arrived in safety at a town about twenty leagues from the cottage of De Lacey, when her attendant fell dangerously ill. Safie nursed her with the most devoted affection; but the poor girl died, and the Arabian was left alone, unacquainted with the language of the country and utterly ignorant of the customs of the world. She fell, however, into good hands. The Italian had mentioned the name of the spot for which they were bound; and after her death, the woman of the house in which they had lived took care that Safie should arrive in safety at the cottage of her lover.'

CHAPTER VII

'Such was the history of my beloved cottagers. It impressed me deeply. I learned, from the views of social life which it developed, to admire their virtues and to deprecate the vices of mankind.

'As yet I looked upon crime as a distant evil; benevolence and generosity were ever present before me, inciting within me a desire to become an actor in the busy scene where so many admirable qualities were called forth and displayed. But in giving an account of the progress of my intellect, I must not omit a circumstance which occurred in the beginning of the month of August of the same year.

'One night, during my accustomed visit to the neighbouring wood, where I collected my own food and brought home firing for my protectors, I found on the ground a leathern portmanteau, containing several articles of dress and some books. I eagerly seized the prize, and returned with it to my hovel. Fortunately the books were written in the language, the elements of which I had acquired at the cottage; they consisted of *Paradise Lost*, a volume of Plutarch's *Lives*, and the *Sorrows of Werter*.³³ The possession of these treasures gave me extreme delight; I now continually studied and exercised my mind upon these histories, whilst my friends were employed in their ordinary occupations.

'I can hardly describe to you the effect of these books. They produced in me an infinity of new images and feelings, that sometimes raised me to ecstasy, but more frequently sunk me into the lowest dejection. In the *Sorrows of Werter*, besides the interest of its simple and affecting story, so many opinions are canvassed, and so many lights thrown upon what had hitherto been to me obscure subjects, that I found in it a never-ending source of speculation and astonishment. The gentle and domestic manners it described, combined with lofty sentiments and feelings, which had for their object something out of self, accorded well with my experience among my protectors, and with the wants which were forever alive in my own bosom. But I thought Werter himself a more divine being than I had ever beheld or imagined; his character contained no pretension, but it sunk deep. The disquisitions upon death and suicide were calculated to fill me with wonder. I did not pretend to enter into the merits of the case, yet I inclined towards the opinions of the hero, whose extinction I wept, without precisely understanding it.

'As I read, however, I applied much personally to my own feelings and condition. I found myself similar, yet at the same time strangely unlike to the beings concerning whom I read, and to whose conversation I was a listener. I sympathised with and partly understood them, but I was unformed in mind; I was dependent on none, and related to none. "The path of my departure was free,"[34] and there was none to lament my annihilation. My person was hideous and my stature gigantic. What did this mean? Who was I? What was I? Whence did I come? What was my destination? These questions continually recurred, but I was unable to solve them.

'The volume of Plutarch's *Lives* which I possessed, contained the histories of the first founders of the ancient republics. This book had a far different effect upon me from the *Sorrows of Werter*. I learned from Werter's imaginations despondency and gloom: but Plutarch taught me high thoughts; he elevated me above the wretched sphere of my own reflections, to admire and love the heroes of past ages. Many things I read surpassed my understanding and experience. I had a very confused knowledge of kingdoms, wide extents of country, mighty rivers, and boundless seas. But I was perfectly unacquainted with towns, and large assemblages of men. The cottage of my protectors had been the only school in which I had studied human nature; but this book developed new and mightier scenes of action. I read of men concerned in public affairs, governing or massacring their species. I felt the greatest ardour for virtue rise within me, and abhorrence for vice, as far as I understood the signification of those terms, relative as they were, as I applied them, to pleasure and pain alone. Induced by these feelings, I was of course led to admire peaceable lawgivers, Numa, Solon, and Lycurgus, in preference to Romulus and Theseus. The patriarchal lives of my protectors caused these impressions to take a firm hold on my mind; perhaps, if my first introduction to humanity had been made by a young soldier, burning for glory and slaughter, I should have been imbued with different sensations.

'But *Paradise Lost* excited different and far deeper emotions. I read it, as I had read the other volumes which had fallen into my hands, as a true history. It moved every feeling of wonder and awe, that the picture of an omnipotent God warring with his creatures was capable of exciting. I often referred the several situations, as their similarity struck me, to my own. Like Adam, I was apparently united by no link to any other being in existence; but his state was far different from mine in every other respect. He had come forth from the hands of God a perfect creature, happy and prosperous, guarded by the especial care of his Creator; he was allowed to converse with and acquire knowledge from beings of a superior nature: but I was wretched, helpless, and alone. Many times I considered Satan as the fitter emblem of my condition; for often, like him, when I viewed the bliss of my protectors, the bitter gall of envy rose within me.

'Another circumstance strengthened and confirmed these feelings. Soon after my arrival in the hovel, I discovered some papers in the pocket of the dress which I had taken from your laboratory. At first I had neglected them; but now that I was able to decipher the characters in which they were written, I began to study them with diligence. It was your journal of the four months that preceded my creation. You minutely described in these papers every step you took in the progress of your work; this history was mingled with accounts of domestic occurrences. You doubtless recollect these papers. Here they are. Every thing is related in them which bears reference to my accursed origin; the whole detail of that series of disgusting circumstances which produced it is set in view; the minutest description of my odious and loathsome person is given, in language which painted your own horrors and rendered mine indelible. I sickened as I read. "Hateful day when I received life!" I exclaimed in agony. "Accursed creator! Why did you form a monster so hideous that even *you* turned from me in disgust? God, in pity, made man beautiful and alluring, after his own image; but my form is a filthy type of yours, more horrid even from the very resemblance. Satan had his companions, fellow-devils, to admire and encourage him; but I am solitary and abhorred."

'These were the reflections of my hours of despondency and solitude; but when I contemplated the virtues of the cottagers, their amiable and benevolent dispositions, I persuaded myself that when they should become acquainted with my admiration of their virtues, they would compassionate me and overlook my personal deformity. Could they turn from their door one, however monstrous, who solicited their compassion and friendship? I resolved, at least, not to despair, but in every way to fit myself for an interview with them, which would decide my fate. I postponed this attempt for some months longer; for the importance attached to its success inspired me with a dread lest I should fail. Besides, I found that my understanding improved so much with every day's experience that I was unwilling to commence this undertaking until a few more months should have added to my sagacity.

'Several changes, in the mean time, took place in the cottage. The presence of Safie diffused happiness among its inhabitants; and I also found that a greater degree of plenty reigned there. Felix and Agatha spent more time in amusement and conversation, and were assisted in their labours by servants. They did not appear rich, but they were contented and happy; their feelings were serene and peaceful, while mine became every day more tumultuous. Increase of knowledge only discovered to me more clearly what a wretched outcast I was. I cherished hope, it is true; but it vanished when I beheld my person reflected in water, or my shadow in the moonshine, even as that frail image and that inconstant shade.

'I endeavoured to crush these fears, and to fortify myself for the trial which in a few months I resolved to undergo; and sometimes I allowed my thoughts, unchecked by reason, to ramble in the fields of Paradise, and dared to fancy amiable and lovely creatures sympathising with my feelings and cheering my gloom; their angelic countenances breathed smiles of consolation. But it was all a dream; no Eve soothed my sorrows nor shared my thoughts; I was alone. I remembered Adam's supplication to his Creator. But where was mine? He had abandoned me, and in the bitterness of my heart I cursed him.

'Autumn passed thus. I saw, with surprise and grief, the leaves decay and fall, and nature again assume the barren and bleak appearance it had worn when I first beheld the woods and the lovely moon. Yet I did not heed the bleakness of the weather; I was better fitted by my conformation for the endurance of cold than heat. But my chief delights were the sight of the flowers, the birds, and all the gay apparel of summer; when those deserted me, I turned with more attention towards the cottagers. Their happiness was not decreased by the absence of summer. They loved and sympathised with one another; and their joys, depending on each other, were not interrupted by the casualties that took place around them. The more I saw of them, the greater became my desire to claim their protection and kindness; my heart yearned to be known and loved by these amiable creatures; to see their sweet looks directed towards me with affection was the utmost limit of my ambition. I dared not think that they would turn them from me with disdain and horror. The poor that stopped at their door were never driven away. I asked, it is true, for greater treasures than a little food or rest: I required kindness and sympathy; but I did not believe myself unworthy of it.

'The winter advanced, and an entire revolution of the seasons had taken place since I awoke into life. My attention, at this time, was solely directed towards my plan of introducing myself into the cottage of my protectors. I revolved many projects; but that on which I finally fixed was, to enter the dwelling when the blind old man should be alone. I had sagacity enough to discover, that the unnatural hideousness of my person was the chief object of horror with those who had formerly beheld me. My voice, although harsh, had nothing terrible in it; I thought, therefore, that if in the absence of his children, I could gain the good-will and mediation of the old De Lacey, I might by his means be tolerated by my younger protectors.

'One day, when the sun shone on the red leaves that strewed the ground, and diffused cheerfulness, although it denied warmth, Safie, Agatha, and Felix departed on a long country walk, and the old man, at his own desire, was left alone in the cottage. When his children had departed, he took up his guitar, and played several mournful but sweet airs, more sweet and mournful than I had ever heard him play before. At first his countenance was illuminated with pleasure, but, as he continued, thoughtfulness and sadness succeeded; at length, laying aside the instrument, he sat absorbed in reflection.

'My heart beat quick; this was the hour and moment of trial, which would decide my hopes, or realise my fears. The servants were gone to a neighbouring fair. All was silent in and around the cottage: it was an excellent opportunity; yet, when I proceeded to execute my plan, my limbs failed me, and I sank to the ground. Again I rose; and, exerting all the firmness of which I was master, removed the planks which I had placed before my hovel to conceal my retreat. The fresh air revived me, and, with renewed determination, I approached the door of their cottage.

'I knocked. "Who is there?" said the old man – "Come in."

'I entered; "Pardon this intrusion", said I; "I am a traveller in want of a little rest; you would greatly oblige me if you would allow me to remain a few minutes before the fire."

'"Enter," said De Lacey, "and I will try in what manner I can to relieve your wants; but, unfortunately, my children are from home, and as I am blind, I am afraid I shall find it difficult to procure food for you."

'"Do not trouble yourself, my kind host; I have food; it is warmth and rest only that I need."

'I sat down, and a silence ensued. I knew that every minute was precious to me, yet I remained irresolute in what manner to commence the interview; when the old man addressed me. "By your language, stranger, I suppose you are my countryman; – are you French?"

'"No; but I was educated by a French family, and understand that language only. I am now going to claim the protection of some friends, whom I sincerely love, and of whose favour I have some hopes."

'"Are they Germans?"

'"No, they are French. But let us change the subject. I am an unfortunate and deserted creature; I look around, and I have no relation or friend upon earth. These amiable people to whom I go have never seen me, and know little of me. I am full of fears, for if I fail there, I am an outcast in the world forever."

' "Do not despair. To be friendless is indeed to be unfortunate; but the hearts of men, when unprejudiced by any obvious self-interest, are full of brotherly love and charity. Rely, therefore, on your hopes; and if these friends are good and amiable, do not despair."

' "They are kind – they are the most excellent creatures in the world; but unfortunately, they are prejudiced against me. I have good dispositions; my life has been hitherto harmless and in some degree beneficial; but a fatal prejudice clouds their eyes, and where they ought to see a feeling and kind friend, they behold only a detestable monster."

' "That is indeed unfortunate; but if you are really blameless, cannot you undeceive them?"

' "I am about to undertake that task; and it is on that account that I feel so many overwhelming terrors. I tenderly love these friends; I have, unknown to them, been for many months in the habits of daily kindness towards them; but they believe that I wish to injure them, and it is that prejudice which I wish to overcome."

' "Where do these friends reside?"

' "Near this spot."

'The old man paused and then continued, "If you will unreservedly confide to me the particulars of your tale, I perhaps may be of use in undeceiving them. I am blind and cannot judge of your countenance, but there is something in your words which persuades me that you are sincere. I am poor and an exile, but it will afford me true pleasure to be in any way serviceable to a human creature."

' "Excellent man! I thank you and accept your generous offer. You raise me from the dust by this kindness; and I trust that, by your aid, I shall not be driven from the society and sympathy of your fellow-creatures."

' "Heaven forbid! Even if you were really criminal, for that can only drive you to desperation, and not instigate you to virtue. I also am unfortunate; I and my family have been condemned, although innocent; judge, therefore, if I do not feel for your misfortunes."

' "How can I thank you, my best and only benefactor? From

your lips first have I heard the voice of kindness directed towards me; I shall be forever grateful; and your present humanity assures me of success with those friends whom I am on the point of meeting."

'"May I know the names and residence of those friends?"

'I paused. This, I thought, was the moment of decision, which was to rob me of, or bestow happiness on me forever. I struggled vainly for firmness sufficient to answer him, but the effort destroyed all my remaining strength; I sank on the chair and sobbed aloud. At that moment I heard the steps of my younger protectors. I had not a moment to lose, but, seizing the hand of the old man, I cried, "Now is the time! Save and protect me! You and your family are the friends whom I seek. Do not you desert me in the hour of trial!"

'"Great God!" exclaimed the old man, "who are you?"

'At that instant the cottage door was opened, and Felix, Safie, and Agatha entered. Who can describe their horror and consternation on beholding me? Agatha fainted, and Safie, unable to attend to her friend, rushed out of the cottage. Felix darted forward, and with supernatural force tore me from his father, to whose knees I clung: in a transport of fury, he dashed me to the ground and struck me violently with a stick. I could have torn him limb from limb, as the lion rends the antelope. But my heart sunk within me as with bitter sickness, and I refrained. I saw him on the point of repeating his blow, when, overcome by pain and anguish, I quitted the cottage, and in the general tumult escaped unperceived to my hovel.'

CHAPTER VIII

'Cursed, cursed creator! Why did I live? Why, in that instant, did I not extinguish the spark of existence which you had so wantonly bestowed? I know not; despair had not yet taken possession of me; my feelings were those of rage and revenge. I could with pleasure have destroyed the cottage and its inhabitants, and have glutted myself with their shrieks and misery.

'When night came I quitted my retreat and wandered in the wood; and now, no longer restrained by the fear of discovery, I gave vent to my anguish in fearful howlings. I was like a wild beast that had broken the toils, destroying the objects that obstructed me and ranging through the wood with a staglike swiftness. O! what a miserable night I passed! the cold stars shone in mockery, and the bare trees waved their branches above me: now and then the sweet voice of a bird burst forth amidst the universal stillness. All, save I, were at rest or in enjoyment: I, like the archfiend, bore a hell within me, and finding myself unsympathised with, wished to tear up the trees, spread havoc and destruction around me, and then to have sat down and enjoyed the ruin.

'But this was a luxury of sensation that could not endure; I became fatigued with excess of bodily exertion, and sank on the damp grass in the sick impotence of despair. There was none among the myriads of men that existed who would pity or assist me; and should I feel kindness towards my enemies? No: from that moment I declared ever-lasting war against the species, and, more than all, against him who had formed me, and sent me forth to this insupportable misery.

'The sun rose; I heard the voices of men and knew that it was impossible to return to my retreat during that day. Accordingly I hid myself in some thick underwood, determining to devote the ensuing hours to reflection on my situation.

'The pleasant sunshine, and the pure air of day, restored me to some degree of tranquillity; and when I considered what had passed at the cottage, I could not help believing that I had been too hasty in my conclusions. I had certainly acted imprudently. It was apparent that my conversation had interested the father in my behalf, and I was a fool in having exposed my person to the horror of his children. I ought to have familiarised the old De Lacey to me, and by degrees to have discovered myself to the rest of his family, when they should have been prepared for my approach. But I did not believe my errors to be irretrievable, and after much consideration I resolved to return to the cottage, seek the old man, and by my representations win him to my party.

'These thoughts calmed me, and in the afternoon I sank into a profound sleep; but the fever of my blood did not allow me to be visited by peaceful dreams. The horrible scene of the preceding day was forever acting before my eyes; the females were flying, and the enraged Felix tearing me from his father's feet. I awoke exhausted; and finding that it was already night, I crept forth from my hiding-place, and went in search of food.

'When my hunger was appeased, I directed my steps towards the well-known path that conducted to the cottage. All there was at peace. I crept into my hovel, and remained in silent expectation of the accustomed hour when the family arose. That hour passed, the sun mounted high in the heavens, but the cottagers did not appear. I trembled violently, apprehending some dreadful misfortune. The inside of the cottage was dark, and I heard no motion; I cannot describe the agony of this suspense.

'Presently two countrymen passed by; but pausing near the cottage, they entered into conversation, using violent gesticulations; but I did not understand what they said, as they spoke the language of the country, which differed from that of my protectors. Soon after, however, Felix approached with another man; I was surprised, as I knew that he had not quitted the cottage that morning, and waited anxiously to discover, from his discourse, the meaning of these unusual appearances.

'"Do you consider," said his companion to him, "that you will be obliged to pay three months' rent and to lose the produce of your garden? I do not wish to take any unfair advantage, and I beg therefore that you will take some days to consider of your determination."

'"It is utterly useless," replied Felix; "we can never again inhabit your cottage. The life of my father is in the greatest danger, owing to the dreadful circumstance that I have related. My wife and my sister will never recover from their horror. I intreat you not to reason with me any more. Take possession of your tenement, and let me fly from this place."

'Felix trembled violently as he said this. He and his companion entered the cottage, in which they remained for a few minutes, and then departed. I never saw any of the family of De Lacey more.

'I continued for the remainder of the day in my hovel in a state of utter and stupid despair. My protectors had departed, and had broken the only link that held me to the world. For the first time the feelings of revenge and hatred filled my bosom, and I did not strive to control them; but allowing myself to be borne away by the stream, I bent my mind towards injury and death. When I thought of my friends, of the mild voice of De Lacey, the gentle eyes of Agatha, and the exquisite beauty of the Arabian, these thoughts vanished and a gush of tears somewhat soothed me. But again when I reflected that they had spurned and deserted me, anger returned, a rage of anger, and unable to injure anything human, I turned my fury towards inanimate objects. As night advanced I placed a variety of combustibles around the cottage; and, after having destroyed every vestige of cultivation in the garden, I waited with forced impatience until the moon had sunk to commence my operations.

'As the night advanced, a fierce wind arose from the woods, and quickly dispersed the clouds that had loitered in the heavens; the blast tore along like a mighty avalanche and produced a kind of insanity in my spirits, that burst all bounds of reason and reflection. I lighted the dry branch of a tree and danced with fury around the devoted cottage, my eyes still fixed on the western horizon, the edge of which the moon nearly touched. A part of its orb was at length hid, and I waved my brand; it sank, and with a loud scream I fired the straw, and heath, and bushes, which I had collected. The wind fanned the fire, and the cottage was quickly enveloped by the flames, which clung to it and licked it with their forked and destroying tongues.

'As soon as I was convinced that no assistance could save any part of the habitation, I quitted the scene, and sought for refuge in the woods.

'And now, with the world before me, whither should I bend my steps? I resolved to fly far from the scene of my misfortunes; but to me, hated and despised, every country must be equally horrible. At length the thought of you crossed my mind. I learned from your papers that you were my father, my creator; and to whom could I apply with more fitness than to him who had given me life? Among the lessons that Felix had bestowed upon Safie, geography had not been omitted: I had learned from these the relative situations of the different countries of the earth. You had mentioned Geneva as the name of your native town; and towards this place I resolved to proceed.

'But how was I to direct myself? I knew that I must travel in a south-westerly direction to reach my destination; but the sun was my only guide. I did not know the names of the towns that I was to pass through, nor could I ask information from a single human being; but I did not despair. From you only could I hope for succour, although towards you I felt no sentiment but that of hatred. Unfeeling, heartless creator! You had endowed me with perceptions and passions and then cast me abroad an object for the scorn and horror of mankind. But on you only had I any claim for pity and redress, and from you I determined to seek that justice which I vainly attempted to gain from any other being that wore the human form.

'My travels were long, and the sufferings I endured intense. It was late in autumn when I quitted the district where I had so long resided. I travelled only at night, fearful of encountering the visage of a human being. Nature decayed around me, and the sun became heatless; rain and snow poured around me; mighty rivers were frozen; the surface of the earth was hard and chill, and bare, and I found no shelter. Oh, earth! how often did I imprecate curses on the cause of my being! The mildness of my nature had fled, and all within me was turned to gall and bitterness. The nearer I approached to your habitation, the more deeply did I feel the spirit of revenge enkindled in my heart. Snow fell, and the waters were hardened, but I rested not. A few incidents now and then directed me, and I possessed a map of the country; but I often wandered wide from my path. The agony of my feelings allowed me no respite: no incident occurred from which my rage and misery could not extract its food; but a circumstance that happened when I arrived on the confines of Switzerland, when the sun had recovered its warmth and the earth again began to look green, confirmed in an especial manner the bitterness and horror of my feelings.

'I generally rested during the day, and travelled only when I was secured by night from the view of man. One morning, however, finding that my path lay through a deep wood, I ventured to continue my journey after the sun had risen; the day, which was one of the first of spring, cheered even me by the loveliness of its sunshine and the balminess of the air. I felt emotions of gentleness and pleasure, that had long appeared dead, revive within me. Half surprised by the novelty of these sensations, I allowed myself to be borne away by them, and, forgetting my solitude and deformity, dared to be happy. Soft tears again bedewed my cheeks, and I even raised my humid eyes with thankfulness towards the blessed sun, which bestowed such joy upon me.

'I continued to wind among the paths of the wood, until I came to its boundary, which was skirted by a deep and rapid river, into which many of the trees bent their branches, now budding with the fresh spring. Here I paused, not exactly knowing what path to pursue, when I heard the sound of voices, that induced me to conceal myself under the shade of a cypress. I was scarcely hid, when a young girl came running towards the spot where I was concealed, laughing, as if she ran from some one in sport. She continued her course along the precipitous sides of the river, when suddenly her foot slipt, and she fell into the rapid stream. I rushed from my hiding-place, and, with extreme labour from the force of the current, saved her, and dragged her to shore. She was senseless; and I endeavoured, by every means in my power, to restore animation, when I was suddenly interrupted by the approach of a rustic, who was probably the person from whom she had playfully fled. On seeing me, he darted towards me, and tearing the girl from my arms, hastened towards the deeper parts of the wood. I followed speedily, I hardly knew why;

but when the man saw me draw near, he aimed a gun, which he carried, at my body, and fired. I sank to the ground, and my injurer, with increased swiftness, escaped into the wood.

'This was then the reward of my benevolence! I had saved a human being from destruction, and as a recompense I now writhed under the miserable pain of a wound which shattered the flesh and bone. The feelings of kindness and gentleness, which I had entertained but a few moments before, gave place to hellish rage and gnashing of teeth. Inflamed by pain, I vowed eternal hatred and vengeance to all mankind. But the agony of my wound overcame me; my pulses paused, and I fainted.

'For some weeks I led a miserable life in the woods, endeavouring to cure the wound which I had received. The ball had entered my shoulder, and I knew not whether it had remained there or passed through; at any rate I had no means of extracting it. My sufferings were augmented also by the oppressive sense of the injustice and ingratitude of their infliction. My daily vows rose for revenge – a deep and deadly revenge, such as would alone compensate for the outrages and anguish I had endured.

'After some weeks my wound healed, and I continued my journey. The labours I endured were no longer to be alleviated by the bright sun or gentle breezes of spring; all joy was but a mockery which insulted my desolate state, and made me feel more painfully that I was not made for the enjoyment of pleasure.

'But my toils now drew near a close, and in two months from this time, I reached the environs of Geneva.

'It was evening when I arrived, and I retired to a hiding-place among the fields that surround it, to meditate in what manner I should apply to you. I was oppressed by fatigue and hunger, and far too unhappy to enjoy the gentle breezes of evening, or the prospect of the sun setting behind the stupendous mountains of Jura.

'At this time a slight sleep relieved me from the pain of reflection, which was disturbed by the approach of a beautiful child, who came running into the recess I had chosen, with all the sportiveness of infancy. Suddenly, as I gazed on him, an idea seized me that this little creature was unprejudiced, and had lived too short a time to have imbibed a horror of deformity. If, therefore, I could seize him and educate him as my companion and friend, I should not be so desolate in this peopled earth.

'Urged by this impulse, I seized on the boy as he passed and drew him towards me. As soon as he beheld my form, he placed his hands before his eyes, and uttered a shrill scream; I drew his hand forcibly from his face and said, "Child, what is the meaning of this? I do not intend to hurt you; listen to me."

'He struggled violently. "Let me go," he cried; "monster! ugly wretch! you wish to eat me and tear me to pieces – You are an ogre – Let me go, or I will tell my papa."

'"Boy, you will never see your father again; you must come with me."

'"Hideous monster! let me go. My papa is a syndic – he is M. Frankenstein – he will punish you. You dare not keep me."

'"Frankenstein! you belong then to my enemy – to him towards whom I have sworn eternal revenge; you shall be my first victim."

'The child still struggled, and loaded me with epithets which carried despair to my heart; I grasped his throat to silence him, and in a moment he lay dead at my feet.

'I gazed on my victim, and my heart swelled with exultation and hellish triumph; clapping my hands, I exclaimed, "I too can create desolation; my enemy is not invulnerable; this death will carry despair to him, and a thousand other miseries shall torment and destroy him."

'As I fixed my eyes on the child, I saw something glittering on his breast. I took it; it was a portrait of a most lovely woman. In spite of my malignity, it softened and attracted me. For a few moments I gazed with delight on her dark eyes, fringed by deep lashes, and her lovely lips; but presently my rage returned: I remembered that I was forever deprived of the delights that such beautiful creatures could bestow; and that she whose resemblance I contemplated would, in regarding me, have changed that air of divine benignity to one expressive of disgust and affright.

'Can you wonder that such thoughts transported me with rage? I only wonder that at that moment, instead of venting my sensations in exclamations and agony, I did not rush among mankind, and perish in the attempt to destroy them.

'While I was overcome by these feelings, I left the spot where I had committed the murder, and seeking a more secluded hiding-place, I entered a barn which had appeared to me to be empty. A woman was sleeping on some straw; she was young: not indeed so beautiful as her whose portrait I held; but of an agreeable aspect and blooming in the loveliness of youth and health. Here, I thought, is one of those whose joy-imparting smiles are bestowed on all but me. And then I bent over her, and whispered, "Awake, fairest, thy lover is near – he who would give his life but to obtain one look of affection from thine eyes: my beloved, awake!"

'The sleeper stirred; a thrill of terror ran through me. Should she indeed awake, and see me, and curse me, and denounce the murderer? Thus would she assuredly act, if her darkened eyes opened, and she beheld me. The thought was madness; it stirred the fiend within me – not I, but she, shall suffer; the murder I have committed because I am forever robbed of all that she could give me, she shall atone. The crime had its source in her: be hers the punishment! Thanks to the lessons of Felix and the sanguinary laws of man, I had learned how to work mischief. I bent over her and placed the portrait securely in one of the folds of her dress. She moved again, and I fled.

'For some days I haunted the spot where these scenes had taken place; sometimes wishing to see you, sometimes resolved to quit the world and its miseries forever. At length I wandered towards these mountains, and have ranged through their immense recesses, consumed by a burning passion which you alone can gratify. We may not part until you have promised to comply with my requisition. I am alone, and miserable; man will not associate with me; but one as deformed and horrible as myself would not deny herself to me. My companion must be of the same species, and have the same defects. This being you must create.'

CHAPTER IX

The being finished speaking, and fixed his looks upon me in the expectation of a reply. But I was bewildered, perplexed, and unable to arrange my ideas sufficiently to understand the full extent of his proposition. He continued.

'You must create a female for me, with whom I can live in the interchange of those sympathies necessary for my being. This you alone can do; and I demand it of you as a right which you must not refuse to concede.'

The latter part of his tale had kindled anew in me the anger that had died away while he narrated his peaceful life among the cottagers, and, as he said this, I could no longer suppress the rage that burned within me.

'I do refuse it,' I replied; 'and no torture shall ever extort a consent from me. You may render me the most miserable of men, but you shall never make me base in my own eyes. Shall I create another like yourself, whose joint wickedness might desolate the world? Begone! I have answered you; you may torture me, but I will never consent.'

'You are in the wrong,' replied the fiend; 'and, instead of threatening, I am content to reason with you. I am malicious because I am miserable. Am I not shunned and hated by all mankind? You, my creator, would tear me to pieces, and triumph; remember that, and tell me why I should pity man more than he pities me? You would not call it murder, if you could precipitate me into one of those ice-rifts, and destroy my frame, the work of your own hands. Shall I respect man when he contemns me? Let him live with me in the interchange of kindness; and, instead of injury I would bestow every benefit upon him with tears of gratitude at his acceptance. But that cannot be; the human senses are insurmountable barriers to our union. Yet mine shall not be the submission of abject slavery. I will revenge my injuries: if I cannot inspire love, I will cause fear, and chiefly towards you my arch-enemy, because my creator, do I swear inextinguishable hatred. Have a care: I will work at your destruction, nor finish until I desolate your heart, so that you shall curse the hour of your birth.'

A fiendish rage animated him as he said this; his face was wrinkled into contortions too horrible for human eyes to behold; but presently he calmed himself and proceeded.

'I intended to reason. This passion is detrimental to me; for you do not reflect that *you* are the cause of its excess. If any being felt emotions of benevolence towards me, I should return them an hundred and an hundredfold; for that one creature's sake I would make peace with the whole kind! But I now indulge in dreams of bliss that cannot be realised. What I ask of you is reasonable and moderate; I demand a creature of another sex, but as hideous as myself; the gratification is small, but it is all that I can receive, and it shall content me. It is true, we shall be monsters, cut off from all the world; but on that account we shall be more attached to one another. Our lives will not be happy, but they will be harmless, and free from the misery I now feel. Oh! my creator, make me happy; let me feel gratitude towards you for one benefit! Let me see that I excite the sympathy of some existing thing; do not deny me my request!'

I was moved. I shuddered when I thought of the possible consequences of my consent, but I felt that there was some justice in his argument. His tale, and the feelings he now expressed, proved him to be a creature of fine sensations; and did I not as his maker, owe him all the portion of happiness that it was in my power to bestow? He saw my change of feeling and continued.

'If you consent, neither you nor any other human being shall ever see us again: I will go to the vast wilds of South America. My food is not that of man; I do not destroy the lamb and the kid to glut my appetite; acorns and berries afford me sufficient nourishment. My companion will be of the same nature as myself, and will be content with the same fare. We shall make our bed of dried leaves; the sun will shine on us as on man, and will ripen our food. The picture I present to you is peaceful and human, and you must feel that you could deny it only in the wantonness of power and cruelty. Pitiless as you have been towards me, I now see compassion in your eyes; let me seize the favourable moment and persuade you to promise what I so ardently desire.'

'You propose,' replied I, 'to fly from the habitations of man, to dwell in those wilds where the beasts of the field will be your only companions. How can you, who long for the love and sympathy of man, persevere in this exile? You will return, and again seek their kindness, and you will meet with their detestation; your evil passions will be renewed, and you will then have a companion to aid you in the task of destruction. This may not be: cease to argue the point, for I cannot consent.'

'How inconstant are your feelings! but a moment ago you were moved by my representations, and why do you again harden yourself to my complaints? I swear to you, by the earth which I inhabit, and by you that made me, that with the companion you bestow I will quit the neighbourhood of man, and dwell, as it may chance, in the most savage of places. My evil passions will have fled, for I shall meet with sympathy! my life will flow quietly away, and in my dying moments I shall not curse my maker.'

His words had a strange effect upon me. I compassionated him and sometimes felt a wish to console him; but when I looked upon him, when I saw the filthy mass that moved and talked, my heart sickened and my feelings were altered to those of horror and hatred. I tried to stifle these sensations; I thought, that as I could not sympathise with him, I had no right to withhold from him the small portion of happiness which was yet in my power to bestow.

'You swear,' I said, 'to be harmless; but have you not already shown a degree of malice that should reasonably make me distrust you? May not even this be a feint that will increase your triumph by affording a wider scope for your revenge?'

'How is this? I must not be trifled with: and I demand an answer. If I have no ties and no affections, hatred and vice must be my portion; the love of another will destroy the cause of my crimes, and I shall become a thing of whose existence every one will be ignorant. My vices are the children of a forced solitude that I abhor; and my virtues will necessarily arise when I live in communion with an equal. I shall feel the affections of a sensitive being, and become linked to the chain of existence and events, from which I am now excluded.'

I paused some time to reflect on all he had related, and the various arguments which he had employed. I thought of the promise of virtues which he had displayed on the opening of his existence, and the subsequent blight of all kindly feeling by the loathing and scorn which his protectors had manifested towards him. His power and threats were not omitted to my calculations: a creature who could exist in the ice-caves of the glaciers, and hide himself from pursuit among the ridges of inaccessible precipices, was a being possessing faculties it would be vain to cope with. After a long pause of reflection, I concluded that the justice due both to him and my fellow creatures demanded of me that I should comply with his request. Turning to him, therefore, I said –

'I consent to your demand, on your solemn oath to quit Europe forever, and every other place in the neighbourhood of man, as soon as I shall deliver into your hands a female who will accompany you in your exile.'

'I swear,' he cried, 'by the sun, and by the blue sky of Heaven, and by the fire of love that burns my heart, that if you grant my prayer, while they exist you shall never behold me again. Depart to your home, and commence your labours: I shall watch their progress with unutterable anxiety; and fear not but that when you are ready I shall appear.'

Saying this, he suddenly quitted me, fearful, perhaps, of any change in my sentiments. I saw him descend the mountain with greater speed than the flight of an eagle, and quickly lost among the undulations of the sea of ice.

His tale had occupied the whole day, and the sun was upon the verge of the horizon when he departed. I knew that I ought to hasten my descent towards the valley, as I should soon be encompassed in darkness; but my heart was heavy, and my steps slow. The labour of winding among the little paths of the mountain and fixing my feet firmly as I advanced, perplexed me, occupied as I was by the emotions which the occurrences of the day had produced. Night was far advanced when I came to the half way resting-place and seated myself beside the fountain. The stars shone at intervals, as the clouds passed from over them; the dark pines rose before me, and every here and there a broken tree lay on the ground: it was a scene of wonderful solemnity and stirred strange thoughts within me. I wept bitterly; and clasping my hands in agony, I exclaimed, 'Oh! stars and clouds and winds, ye are all about to mock me: if ye really pity me, crush sensation and memory; let me become as nought; but if not, depart, depart, and leave me in darkness.'

These were wild and miserable thoughts; but I cannot describe to you how the eternal twinkling of the stars weighed upon me, and how I listened to every blast of wind, as if it were a dull ugly siroc[35] on its way to consume me.

Morning dawned before I arrived at the village of Chamounix; I took no rest, but returned immediately to Geneva. Even in my own heart I could give no expression to my sensations – they weighed on me with a mountain's weight, and their excess destroyed my agony beneath them. Thus I returned home, and entering the house, presented myself to the family. My haggard and wild appearance awoke intense alarm; but I answered no questions, scarcely did I speak. I felt as if I were placed under a ban – as if I had no right to claim their sympathies – as if never more might I enjoy companionship with them. Yet even thus I loved them to adoration; and to save them, I resolved to dedicate myself to my most abhorred task. The prospect of such an occupation made every other circumstance of existence pass before me like a dream, and that thought only had to me the reality of life.

END OF VOLUME TWO

VOLUME THREE

CHAPTER I

Day after day, week after week, passed away on my return to Geneva; and I could not collect the courage to recommence my work. I feared the vengeance of the disappointed fiend, yet I was unable to overcome my repugnance to the task which was enjoined me. I found that I could not compose a female without again devoting several months to profound study and laborious disquisition. I had heard of some discoveries having been made by an English philosopher, the knowledge of which was material to my success, and I sometimes thought of obtaining my father's consent to visit England for this purpose; but I clung to every pretence of delay, and shrank from taking the first step in an undertaking whose immediate necessity began to appear less absolute to me. A change indeed had taken place in me: my health, which had hitherto declined, was now much restored; and my spirits, when unchecked by the memory of my unhappy promise, rose proportionably. My father saw this change with pleasure, and he turned his thoughts towards the best method of eradicating the remains of my melancholy, which every now and then would return by fits, and with a devouring blackness overcast the approaching sunshine. At these moments I took refuge in the most perfect solitude. I passed whole days on the lake alone in a little boat, watching the clouds, and listening to the rippling of the waves, silent and listless. But the fresh air and bright sun seldom failed to restore me to some degree of composure; and, on my return, I met the salutations of my friends with a readier smile and a more cheerful heart.

It was after my return from one of these rambles that my father, calling me aside, thus addressed me –

'I am happy to remark, my dear son, that you have resumed your former pleasures, and seem to be returning to yourself. And yet you are still unhappy, and still avoid our society. For some time I was lost in conjecture as to the cause of this; but yesterday an idea struck me, and if it is well founded, I conjure you to avow it. Reserve on such a point would be not only useless, but draw down treble misery on us all.'

I trembled violently at his exordium, and my father continued –

'I confess, my son, that I have always looked forward to your marriage with our dear Elizabeth as the tie of our domestic comfort, and the stay of my declining years. You were attached to each other from your earliest infancy; you studied together, and appeared, in dispositions and tastes, entirely suited to one another. But so blind is the experience of man, that what I conceived to be the best assistants to my plan may have entirely destroyed it. You, perhaps, regard her as your sister, without any wish that she might become you wife. Nay, you may have met with another whom you may love; and considering yourself as bound in honour to Elizabeth, this struggle may occasion the poignant misery which you appear to feel.'

'My dear father, re-assure yourself. I love my cousin tenderly and sincerely. I never saw any woman who excited, as Elizabeth does, my warmest admiration and affection. My future hopes and prospects are entirely bound up in the expectation of our union.'

'The expression of your sentiments of this subject, my dear Victor, gives me more pleasure than I have for some time experienced. If you feel thus, we shall assuredly be happy, however present events may cast a gloom over us. But it is this gloom which appears to have taken so strong a hold of your mind, that I wish to dissipate. Tell me, therefore, whether you object to an immediate solemnisation of the marriage. We have been unfortunate, and recent events have drawn us from that every-day tranquillity befitting my years and infirmities. You are younger; yet I do not suppose, possessed as you are of a competent fortune, that an early marriage would at all interfere with any future plans of honour and utility that you may have formed. Do not suppose, however, that I wish to dictate happiness to you, or that a delay on your part would cause me any serious uneasiness.

Interpret my words with candour and answer me, I conjure you, with confidence and sincerity.'

I listened to my father in silence, and remained for some time incapable of offering any reply. I revolved rapidly in my mind a multitude of thoughts, and endeavoured to arrive at some conclusion. Alas! to me the idea of an immediate union with my Elizabeth was one of horror and dismay. I was bound by a solemn promise, which I had not yet fulfilled, and dared not break; or if I did, what manifold miseries might not impend over me and my devoted family! Could I enter into a festival with this deadly weight yet hanging round my neck, and bowing me to the ground? I must perform my engagement, and let the monster depart with his mate, before I allowed myself to enjoy the delight of a union from which I expected peace.

I remembered also the necessity imposed upon me of either journeying to England, or entering into a long correspondence with those philosophers of that country, whose knowledge and discoveries were of indispensable use to me in my present undertaking. The latter method of obtaining the desired intelligence was dilatory and unsatisfactory: besides, I had an insurmountable aversion to the idea of engaging myself in my loathsome task in my father's house, while in habits of familiar intercourse with those I loved. I knew that a thousand fearful accidents might occur, the slightest of which would disclose a tale to thrill all connected with me with horror. I was aware also that I should often lose all self-command, all capacity of hiding the harrowing sensations that would possess me during the progress of my unearthly occupation. I must absent myself from all I loved while thus employed. Once commenced, it would quickly be achieved, and I might be restored to my family in peace and happiness. My promise fulfilled, the monster would depart forever. Or (so my fond fancy imaged) some accident might meanwhile occur to destroy him, and put an end to my slavery forever.

These feelings dictated my answer to my father. I expressed a wish to visit England; but concealing the true reasons of this request, I clothed my desires under a guise which excited no suspicion, while I urged my desire with an earnestness that easily induced my father to comply. After so long a period of an absorbing melancholy, that resembled madness in its intensity and effects, he was glad to find that I was capable of taking pleasure in the idea of such a journey, and he hoped that change of scene and varied amusement would, before my return, have restored me entirely to myself.

The duration of my absence was left to my own choice; a few months, or at most a year, was the period contemplated. One paternal kind precaution he had taken to ensure my having a companion. Without previously communicating with me, he had, in concert with Elizabeth, arranged that Clerval should join me in Strasburgh. This interfered with the solitude I coveted for the prosecution of my task; yet at the commencement of my journey the presence of my friend could in no way be an impediment, and truly I rejoiced that thus I should be saved many hours of lonely, maddening reflection. Nay, Henry might stand between me and the intrusion of my foe. If I were alone, would he not at times force his abhorred presence on me, to remind me of my task or to contemplate its progress?

To England, therefore, I was bound, and it was understood that my union with Elizabeth should take place immediately on my return. My father's age rendered him extremely averse to delay. For myself, there was one reward I promised myself from my detested toils – one consolation for my unparalleled sufferings; it was the prospect of that day when, enfranchised from my miserable slavery, I might claim Elizabeth, and forget the past in union with her.

I now made arrangements for my journey; but one feeling haunted me, which filled me with fear and agitation. During my absence I should leave my friends unconscious of the existence of their enemy, and unprotected from his attacks, exasperated as he might be by my departure. But he had promised to follow me wherever I might go; and would he not accompany me to England? This imagination was dreadful in itself, but soothing, inasmuch as it supposed the safety of my friends. I was agonised with the idea of the possibility that the reverse of this might happen. But through the whole period during which I was the slave of my creature I allowed myself to be governed by the impulses of the moment; and my present sensations strongly intimated that the fiend would follow me, and exempt my family from the danger of his machinations.

It was in the latter end of September that I again quitted my native country. My journey had been my own suggestion, and Elizabeth, therefore, acquiesced; but she was filled with disquiet at the idea of my suffering, away from her, the inroads of misery and grief. It had been her care which provided me a companion in Clerval – and yet a man is blind to a thousand minute circumstances, which call forth a woman's sedulous attention. She longed to bid me hasten my return – a thousand conflicting emotions rendered her mute, as she bade me a tearful, silent farewell.

I threw myself into the carriage that was to convey me away, hardly knowing whither I was going, and careless of what was passing around. I remembered only, and it was with a bitter anguish that I reflected on it, to order that my chemical instruments should be packed to go with me. Filled with dreary imaginations, I passed through many beautiful and majestic scenes, but me eyes were fixed and unobserving. I could only think of the bourne of my travels, and the work which was to occupy me whilst they endured.

After some days spent in listless indolence, during which I traversed many leagues, I arrived at Strasburgh where I waited two days for Clerval. He came. Alas, how great was the contrast between us! He was alive to every new scene; joyful when he saw the beauties of the setting sun, and more happy when he beheld it rise and recommence a new day. He pointed out to me the shifting colours of the landscape, and the appearances of the sky. 'This is what it is to live,' he cried; 'now I enjoy existence! But you, my dear Frankenstein, wherefore are you desponding and sorrowful?' In truth, I was occupied by gloomy thoughts, and neither saw the descent of the evening star, nor the golden sunrise reflected in the Rhine. – And you, my friend, would be far more amused with the journal of Clerval, who observed the scenery with an eye of feeling and delight, than in listening to my reflections. I, a miserable wretch, haunted by a curse that shut up every avenue to enjoyment.

We had agreed to descend the Rhine in a boat from Strasburgh to Rotterdam, whence we might take shipping for London.

During this voyage we passed many willowy islands, and saw several beautiful towns. We stayed a day at Mannheim, and, on the fifth from our departure from Strasburgh, arrived at Mayence. The course of the Rhine below Mayence becomes much more picturesque. The river descends rapidly, and winds between hills, not high, but steep, and of beautiful forms. We saw many ruined castles standing on the edges of precipices, surrounded by black woods, high and inaccessible. This part of the Rhine, indeed, presents a singularly variegated landscape. In one spot you view rugged hills, ruined castles overlooking tremendous precipices, with the dark Rhine rushing beneath; and, on the sudden turn of a promontory, flourishing vineyards with green sloping banks and a meandering river and populous towns occupy the scene.

We travelled at the time of the vintage, and heard the song of the labourers, as we glided down the stream. Even I, depressed in mind, and my spirits continually agitated by gloomy feelings, even I was pleased. I lay at the bottom of the boat, and, as I gazed on the cloudless blue sky, I seemed to drink in a tranquillity to which I had long been a stranger. And if these were my sensations, who can describe those of Henry? He felt as if he had been transported to Fairy-land and enjoyed a happiness seldom tasted by man. 'I have seen,' he said, 'the most beautiful scenes of my own country; I have visited the lakes of Lucerne and Uri, where the snowy mountains descend almost perpendicularly to the water, casting black and impenetrable shades, which would cause a gloomy and mournful appearance were it not for the most verdant islands that relieve the eye by their gay appearance; I have seen this lake agitated by a tempest, when the wind tore up whirlwinds of water and gave you an idea of what the water-spout must be on the great ocean; and the waves dash with fury the base of the mountain, where the priest and his mistress were overwhelmed by an avalanche and where their dying voices are still said to be heard amid the pauses of the nightly wind; I have seen the mountains of La Valais, and the Pays de Vaud: but this country, Victor, pleases me more than all those wonders. The mountains of Switzerland are more majestic and strange; but there is a charm in the banks of this divine river, that I never before saw equalled. Look at that castle which overhangs yon precipice; and that also on the island, almost concealed amongst the foliage of those lovely trees; and now that group of labourers coming from among their vines; and that village half hid in the recess of the mountain. Oh, surely the spirit that inhabits and guards this place has a soul more in harmony with man than those who pile the glacier, or retire to the inaccessible peaks of the mountains of our own country.'

Clerval! beloved friend! Even now it delights me to record your words, and to dwell on the praise of which you are so eminently deserving. He was a being formed in the 'very poetry of nature'.[36] His wild and enthusiastic imagination was chastened by the sensibility of his heart. His soul overflowed with ardent affections, and his friendship was of that devoted and wondrous nature that the worldly-minded teach us to look for only in the imagination. But even human sympathies were not sufficient to satisfy his eager mind. The scenery of external nature, which others regard only with admiration, he loved with ardour: –

> The sounding cataract
> Haunted him like a passion: the tall rock,
> The mountain, and the deep and gloomy wood,
> Their colours and their forms, were then to him
> An appetite; a feeling, and a love,
> That had no need of a remoter charm,
> By thought supplied, or any interest
> Unborrow'd from the eye.*

And where does he now exist? Is this gentle and lovely being lost forever? Has this mind, so replete with ideas, imaginations fanciful and magnificent, which formed a world, whose existence depended on the life of its creator – has this mind perished? Does it now only exist in my memory? No, it is not thus; your form so divinely wrought, and beaming with beauty, has decayed, but your spirit still visits and consoles your unhappy friend.

Pardon this gush of sorrow; these ineffectual words are but a slight tribute to the unexampled worth of Henry, but they soothe

---

* Wordsworth's Tintern Abbey [author's footnote].

my heart, overflowing with the anguish which his remembrance creates. I will proceed with my tale.

Beyond Cologne we descended to the plains of Holland; and we resolved to post the remainder of our way; for the wind was contrary, and the stream of the river was too gentle to aid us.

Our journey here lost the interest arising from beautiful scenery, but we arrived in a few days at Rotterdam; whence we proceeded by sea to England. It was on a clear morning, in the latter days of December, that I first saw the white cliffs of Britain. The banks of the Thames presented a new scene; they were flat, but fertile, and almost every town was marked by the remembrance of some story. We saw Tilbury Fort, and remembered the Spanish Armada; Gravesend, Woolwich, and Greenwich – places which I had heard of even in my country.

At length we saw the numerous steeples of London, St Paul's towering above all, and the Tower, famed in English history.

CHAPTER II

London was our present point of rest; we determined to remain several months in this wonderful and celebrated city. Clerval desired the intercourse of the men of genius and talent who flourished at this time; but this was with me a secondary object; I was principally occupied with the means of obtaining the information necessary for the completion of my promise, and quickly availed myself of the letters of introduction that I had brought with me, addressed to the most distinguished natural philosopher.

If this journey had taken place during my days of study and happiness, it would have afforded me inexpressible pleasure. But a blight had come over my existence, and I only visited these people for the sake of the information they might give me on the subject in which my interest was so terribly profound. Company was irksome to me; when alone, I could fill my mind with the sights of heaven and earth; the voice of Henry soothed me, and I could thus cheat myself into a transitory peace. But busy, uninteresting, joyous faces brought back despair to my heart. I saw an insurmountable barrier placed between me and my fellow-men; this barrier was sealed with the blood of William and Justine, and to reflect on the events connected with those names filled my soul with anguish.

But in Clerval I saw the image of my former self; he was inquisitive, and anxious to gain experience and instruction. The difference of manners which he observed was to him an inexhaustible source of instruction and amusement. He was also pursuing an object he had long had in view. His design was to visit India, in the belief that he had in his knowledge of its various languages, and in the views he had taken of its society, the means of materially assisting the progress of European colonisation and trade. In Britain only could he further the execution of his plan. He was forever busy; and the only check to his enjoyments was my sorrowful and dejected mind. I tried to conceal this as much as possible, that I might not debar him from the pleasures natural to one, who was entering on a new scene of life, undisturbed by any care or bitter recollection. I often refused to accompany him, alleging another engagement, that I might remain alone. I now also began to collect the materials necessary for my new creation, and this was to me like the torture of single drops of water continually falling on the head. Every thought that was devoted to it was an extreme anguish, and every word that I spoke in allusion to it caused my lips to quiver, and my heart to palpitate.

After passing some months in London, we received a letter from a person in Scotland, who had formerly been our visitor at Geneva. He mentioned the beauties of his native country, and asked us if those were not sufficient allurements to induce us to prolong our journey as far north as Perth, where he resided. Clerval eagerly desired to accept this invitation; and I, although I abhorred society, wished to view again mountains and streams, and all the wondrous works with which Nature adorns her chosen dwelling-places.

We had arrived in England at the beginning of October, and it was now February. We accordingly determined to commence our journey towards the north at the expiration of another month. In this expedition we did not intend to follow the great road to Edinburgh, but to visit Windsor, Oxford, Matlock, and the Cumberland lakes, resolving to arrive at the completion of this tour about the end of July. I packed up my chemical instruments and the materials I had collected, resolving to finish my labours in some obscure nook in the northern highlands of Scotland.

We quitted London on the 27th of March and remained a few days at Windsor, rambling in its beautiful forest. This was a new scene to us mountaineers; the majestic oaks, the quantity of game, and the herds of stately deer, were all novelties to us.

From thence we proceeded to Oxford. As we entered this city, our minds were filled with the remembrance of the events that had been transacted there more than a century and a half before. It was here that Charles I had collected his forces. This city had remained faithful to him, after the whole nation had forsaken his cause to join the standard of parliament and liberty. The memory of that unfortunate king, and his companions, the amiable Falkland, the insolent Goring,[37] his queen and son, gave a peculiar interest to every part of the city, which they might be supposed to have inhabited. The spirit of elder days found a dwelling here, and we delighted to trace its footsteps. If these feelings had not found an imaginary gratification, the appearance of the city had yet in itself sufficient beauty to obtain our admiration. The colleges are ancient and picturesque; the streets are almost magnificent; and the lovely Isis, which flows beside it through meadows of exquisite verdure, is spread forth into a placid expanse of waters, which reflects its majestic assemblage of towers, and spires, and domes, embosomed among aged trees.

I enjoyed this scene; and yet my enjoyment was embittered both by the memory of the past, and the anticipation of the future. I was formed for peaceful happiness. During my youthful days discontent never visited my mind; and if I was ever overcome by *ennui,* the sight of what is beautiful in nature, or the study of what is excellent and sublime in the productions of man, could always interest my heart, and communicate elasticity to my spirits. But I am a blasted tree; the bolt has entered my soul; and I felt then that I should survive to exhibit what I shall soon cease to be – a miserable spectacle of wrecked humanity, pitiable to others, and intolerable to myself.

We passed a considerable period at Oxford, rambling among its environs, and endeavouring to identify every spot which might relate to the most animating epoch of English history. Our little voyages of discovery were often prolonged by the successive objects that presented themselves. We visited the tomb of the illustrious Hampden,[38] and the field on which that patriot fell. For a moment my soul was elevated from its debasing and miserable fears, to contemplate the divine ideas of liberty and self-sacrifice, of which these sights were the monuments and the remembrancers. For an instant I dared to shake off my chains, and look around me with a free and lofty spirit; but the iron had eaten into my flesh, and I sank again, trembling and hopeless, into my miserable self.

We left Oxford with regret, and proceeded to Matlock, which was our next place of rest. The country in the neighbourhood of this village resembled, to a greater degree, the scenery of Switzerland; but every thing is on a lower scale, and the green hills want the crown of distant white Alps, which always attend on the piny mountains of my native country. We visited the wondrous cave, and the little cabinets of natural history, where the curiosities are disposed in the same manner as in the collections at Servox and Chamounix. The latter name made me tremble when pronounced by Henry; and I hastened to quit Matlock, with which that terrible scene was thus associated.

From Derby, still journeying northwards, we passed two months in Cumberland and Westmorland. I could now almost fancy myself among the Swiss mountains. The little patches of snow which yet lingered on the northern sides of the mountains, the lakes, and the dashing of the rocky streams, were all familiar and dear sights to me. Here also we made some acquaintances, who almost contrived to cheat me into happiness. The delight of Clerval was proportionably greater than mine; his mind expanded in the company of men of talent, and he found in his own nature greater capacities and resources than he could have imagined himself to have possessed while he associated with his inferiors. 'I could pass my life here,' said he to me; 'and among these mountains I should scarcely regret Switzerland and the Rhine.'

But he found that a traveller's life is one that includes much pain amidst its enjoyments. His feelings are forever on the stretch; and when he begins to sink into repose, he finds himself obliged to quit that on which he rests in pleasure for something new, which again engages his attention, and which also he forsakes for other novelties.

We had scarcely visited various lakes of Cumberland and Westmorland, and conceived an affection for some of the inhabitants, when the period of our appointment with our Scotch friend approached, and we left them to travel on. For my own part I was not sorry. I had now neglected my promise for some time, and I feared the effects of the daemon's disappointment. He might remain in Switzerland, and wreak his vengeance on my relatives. This idea pursued me, and tormented me at every moment from which I might otherwise have snatched repose and peace. I waited for my letters with feverish impatience: if they were delayed, I was miserable, and overcome by a thousand fears; and when they arrived and I saw the superscription of Elizabeth or my father, I hardly dared to read and ascertain my fate. Sometimes I thought that the fiend followed me, and might expedite my remissness by murdering my companion. When these thoughts possessed me, I would not quit Henry for a moment, but followed him as his shadow, to protect him from the fancied rage of his destroyer. I felt as if I had committed some great crime, the consciousness of which haunted me. I was guiltless, but I had indeed drawn down a horrible curse upon my head, as mortal as that of crime.

I visited Edinburgh with languid eyes and mind; and yet that city might have interested the most unfortunate being. Clerval did not like it so well as Oxford: for the antiquity of the latter city was more pleasing to him. But the beauty and regularity of the new town of Edinburgh, its romantic castle and its environs, the most delightful in the world, Arthur's Seat, St Bernard's Well, and the Pentland Hills, compensated him for the change, and filled him with cheerfulness and admiration. But I was impatient to arrive at the termination of my journey.

We left Edinburgh in a week, passing through Coupar, St Andrew's, and along the banks of the Tay, to Perth, where our friend expected us. But I was in no mood to laugh and talk with strangers, or enter into their feelings or plans with the good humour expected from a guest; and accordingly I told Clerval that I wished to make the tour of Scotland alone. 'Do you,' said I, 'enjoy yourself, and let this be our rendezvous. I may be absent a month or two; but do not interfere with my motions, I intreat you: leave me to peace and solitude for a short time; and when I return, I hope it will be with a lighter heart, more congenial to your own temper.'

Henry wished to dissuade me; but seeing me bent on this plan, ceased to remonstrate. He intreated me to write often. 'I had rather be with you,' he said, 'in your solitary rambles, than with these Scotch people, whom I do not know: hasten, then, my dear friend, to return, that I may again feel myself somewhat at home, which I cannot do in your absence.'

Having parted from my friend, I determined to visit some remote spot of Scotland, and finish my work in solitude. I did not doubt but that the monster followed me, and would discover himself to me when I should have finished, that he might receive his companion.

With this resolution I traversed the northern highlands, and fixed on one of the remotest of the Orkneys as the scene of my labours. It was a place fitted for such a work, being hardly more than a rock, whose high sides were continually beaten upon by the waves. The soil was barren, scarcely affording pasture for a few miserable cows, and oatmeal for its inhabitants, which consisted of five persons, whose gaunt and scraggy limbs gave tokens of their miserable fare. Vegetables and bread, when they indulged in such luxuries, and even fresh water, was to be procured from the mainland, which was about five miles distant.

On the whole island there were but three miserable huts, and one of these was vacant when I arrived. This I hired. It contained but two rooms, and these exhibited all the squalidness of the most miserable penury. The thatch had fallen in, the walls were unplastered, and the door was off its hinges. I ordered it to be repaired, bought some furniture, and took possession; an incident which would, doubtless, have occasioned some surprise had not all the senses of the cottagers been benumbed by want and squalid poverty. As it was, I lived ungazed at and unmolested, hardly thanked for the pittance of food and clothes which I gave; so much does suffering blunt even the coarsest sensations of men.

In this retreat I devoted the morning to labour; but in the evening, when the weather permitted, I walked on the stony beach of the sea to listen to the waves as they roared and dashed at my feet. It was a monotonous yet everchanging scene. I thought of Switzerland; it was far different from this desolate and appalling landscape. Its hills are covered with veins, and its cottages are scattered thickly in the plains. Its fair lakes reflect a blue and gentle sky; and, when troubled by the winds, their tumult is but as the play of a lively infant, when compared to the roarings of the giant ocean.

In this manner I distributed my occupations when I first arrived; but as I proceeded in my labour, it became every day more horrible and irksome to me. Sometimes I could not prevail on myself to enter my laboratory for several days; and at other times I toiled day and night in order to complete my work. It was, indeed, a filthy process in which I was engaged. During my first experiment, a kind of enthusiastic frenzy had blinded me to the horror of my employment; my mind was intently fixed on the consummation of my labour, and my eyes shut to the horror of my proceedings. But now I went to it in cold blood, and my heart often sickened at the work of my hands.

Thus situated, employed in the most detestable occupation, immersed in a solitude where nothing could for an instant call my attention from the actual scene in which I was engaged, my spirits became unequal; I grew restless and nervous. Every moment I feared to meet my persecutor. Sometimes I sat with my eyes fixed on the ground, fearing to raise them, lest they should encounter the object which I so much dreaded to behold. I feared to wander from the sight of my fellow-creatures, lest when alone he should come to claim his companion.

In the mean time I worked on, and my labour was already considerably advanced. I looked towards its completion with a tremulous and eager hope, which I dared not trust myself to question, but which was intermixed with obscure forebodings of evil, that made my heart sicken in my bosom.

CHAPTER III

I sat one evening in my laboratory; the sun had set, and the moon was just rising from the sea; I had not sufficient light for my employment, and I remained idle, in a pause of consideration of whether I should leave my labour for the night, or hasten its conclusion by an unremitting attention to it. As I sat, a train of reflection occurred to me, which led me to consider the effects of what I was now doing. Three years before I was engaged in the same manner, and had created a fiend whose unparalleled barbarity had desolated my heart, and filled it forever with the bitterest remorse. I was now about to form another being, of whose dispositions I was alike ignorant; she might become ten thousand times more malignant than her mate, and delight, for its own sake, in murder and wretchedness. He had sworn to quit the neighbourhood of man, and hide himself in deserts; but she had not; and she, who in all probability was to become a thinking and reasoning animal, might refuse to comply with a compact made before her creation. They might even hate each other; the creature who already lived loathed his own deformity, and might he not conceive a greater abhorrence for it when it came before his eyes in the female form? She also might turn with disgust from him to the superior beauty of man; she might quit him, and he be again alone, exasperated by the fresh provocation of being deserted by one of his own species.

Even if they were to leave Europe, and inhabit the deserts of the new world, yet one of the first results of those sympathies for which the daemon thirsted would be children, and a race of devils would be propagated upon the earth, who might make the very existence of the species of man a condition precarious and full of terror. Had I a right, for my own benefit, to inflict this curse upon everlasting generations? I had before been moved by the sophisms of the being I had created; I had been struck senseless by his fiendish threats: but now, for the first time, the wickedness of my promise burst upon me; I shuddered to think that future ages might curse me as their pest, whose selfishness had not hesitated to buy its own peace at the price, perhaps, of the existence of the whole human race.

I trembled, and my heart failed within me, when, on looking up, I saw, by the light of the moon, the daemon at the casement. A ghastly grin wrinkled his lips as he gazed on me, where I sat fulfilling the task which he had allotted to me. Yes, he had followed me in my travels; he had loitered in forests, hid himself in caves, or taken refuge in wide and desert heaths; and he now came to mark my progress, and claim the fulfilment of my promise.

As I looked on him, his countenance expressed the utmost extent of malice and treachery. I thought with a sensation of madness on my promise of creating another like to him, and trembling with passion, tore to pieces the thing on which I was engaged. The wretch saw me destroy the creature on whose future existence he depended for happiness, and, with a howl of devilish despair and revenge, withdrew.

I left the room, and, locking the door, made a solemn vow in my own heart never to resume my labours; and then, with trembling steps, I sought my own apartment. I was alone; none were near me to dissipate the gloom, and relieve me from the sickening oppression of the most terrible reveries.

Several hours passed, and I remained near my window gazing on the sea; it was almost motionless, for the winds were hushed, and all nature reposed under the eye of the quiet moon. A few fishing vessels alone specked the water, and now and then the gentle breeze wafted the sound of voices as the fishermen called to one another. I felt the silence, although I was hardly conscious of its extreme profundity, until my ear was suddenly arrested by the paddling of oars near the shore, and a person landed close to my house.

In a few minutes after, I heard the creaking of my door, as if some one endeavoured to open it softly. I trembled from head to foot; I felt a presentiment of who it was, and wished to rouse one of the peasants who dwelt in a cottage not far from mine; but I was overcome by the sensation of helplessness, so often felt in frightful dreams, when you in vain endeavour to fly from an impending danger, and was rooted to the spot.

Presently I heard the sound of footsteps along the passage; the door opened, and the wretch whom I dreaded appeared. Shutting the door, he approached me and said in a smothered voice –

'You have destroyed the work which you began; what is it that you intend? Do you dare to break your promise? I have endured toil and misery: I left Switzerland with you; I crept along the shores of the Rhine, among its willow islands, and over the summits of its hills. I have dwelt many months in the heaths of England, and among the deserts of Scotland. I have endured incalculable fatigue, and cold, and hunger, do you dare destroy my hopes?'

'Begone! I do break my promise; never will I create another like yourself, equal in deformity and wickedness.'

'Slave, I before reasoned with you, but you have proved yourself unworthy of my condescension. Remember that I have power; you believe yourself miserable, but I can make you so wretched that the light of day will be hateful to you. You are my creator, but I am your master – obey!'

'The hour of my irresolution is past, and the period of your power is arrived. Your threats cannot move me to do an act of wickedness; but they confirm me in a determination of not creating you a companion in vice. Shall I, in cool blood, set loose upon the earth a daemon, whose delight is in death and wretchedness? Begone! I am firm, and your words will only exasperate my rage.'

The monster saw my determination in my face, and gnashed his teeth in the impotence of anger. 'Shall each man,' cried he, 'find a wife for his bosom, and each beast have his mate, and I be alone? I had feelings of affection, and they were requited by detestation and scorn. Man! you may hate, but beware! your hours will pass in dread and misery, and soon the bolt will fall which must ravish from you your happiness forever. Are you to be happy, while I grovel in the intensity of my wretchedness? You can blast my other passions, but revenge remains – revenge, henceforth dearer than light or food! I may die, but first you, my tyrant and tormentor, shall curse the sun that gazes on your misery. Beware; for I am fearless, and therefore powerful. I will watch with the wiliness of a snake, that I may sting with its venom. Man, you shall repent of the injuries you inflict.'

'Devil, cease; and do not poison the air with these sounds of malice. I have declared my resolution to you, and I am no coward to bend beneath words. Leave me; I am inexorable.'

'It is well. I go; but remember, I shall be with you on your wedding-night.'

I started forward, and exclaimed, 'Villain! Before you sign my death-warrant, be sure that you are yourself safe.'

I would have seized him; but he eluded me, and quitted the house with precipitation. In a few moments I saw him in his boat, which shot across the waters with an arrowy swiftness, and was soon lost amidst the waves.

All was again silent; but his words rang in my ears. I burned with rage to pursue the murderer of my peace, and precipitate him into the ocean. I walked up and down my room hastily and perturbed, while my imagination conjured up a thousand images to torment and sting me. Why had I not followed him, and closed with him in mortal strife? But I had suffered him to depart, and he had directed his course towards the mainland. I shuddered to think who might be the next victim sacrificed to his insatiate revenge. And then I thought again of his words – '*I will be with you on your wedding-night*.' That then was the period fixed for the fulfilment of my destiny. In that hour I should die, and at once satisfy and extinguish his malice. The prospect did not move me to fear; yet when I thought of my beloved Elizabeth, – of her tears and endless sorrow, when she should find her lover so barbarously snatched from her, – tears, the first I had shed for many months, streamed from my eyes, and I resolved not to fall before my enemy without a bitter struggle.

The night passed away, and the sun rose from the ocean; my feelings became calmer, if it may be called calmness, when the violence of rage sinks into the depths of despair. I left the house, the horrid scene of the last night's contention, and walked on the beach of the sea, which I almost regarded as an insuperable barrier between me and my fellow-creatures; nay, a wish that such should prove the fact stole across me. I desired that I might

pass my life on that barren rock, wearily, it is true, but uninter-
rupted by any sudden shock of misery. If I returned, it was to be
sacrificed, or to see those whom I most loved die under the grasp
of a daemon whom I had myself created.

I walked about the isle like a restless spectre, separated from all
it loved, and miserable in the separation. When it became noon,
and the sun rose higher, I lay down on the grass, and was
overpowered by a deep sleep. I had been awake the whole of the
preceding night, my nerves were agitated, and my eyes inflamed
by watching and misery. The sleep into which I now sunk refreshed me; and when I awoke, I again felt as if I belonged to a
race of human beings like myself, and I began to reflect upon
what had passed with greater composure; yet still the words of
the fiend rung in my ears like a death-knell; they appeared like a
dream, yet distinct and oppressive as a reality.

The sun had far descended, and I still sat on the shore, satisfying my appetite, which had become ravenous, with an oaten
cake, when I saw a fishing-boat land close to me, and one of the
men brought me a packet; it contained letters from Geneva, and
one from Clerval entreating me to join him. He said that he was
wearing away his time fruitlessly where he was; that letters from
the friends he had formed in London desired his return to complete the negotiation they had entered into for his Indian enterprise. He could not any longer delay his departure; but as his
journey to London might be followed, even sooner than he now
conjectured, by his longer voyage, he entreated me to bestow as
much of my society on him as I could spare. He besought me,
therefore, to leave my solitary isle, and to meet him at Perth, that
we might proceed southwards together. This letter in a degree
recalled me to life, and I determined to quit my island at the
expiration of two days.

Yet, before I departed, there was a task to perform, on which I
shuddered to reflect: I must pack up my chemical instruments;
and for that purpose I must enter the room which had been the
scene of my odious work, and I must handle those utensils, the
sight of which was sickening to me. The next morning, at day-
break, I summoned sufficient courage, and unlocked the door of
my laboratory. The remains of the half-finished creature, whom I

had destroyed, lay scattered on the floor, and I almost felt as if I had mangled the living flesh of a human being. I paused to collect myself, and then entered the chamber. With trembling hand I conveyed the instruments out of the room; but I reflected that I ought not to leave the relics of my work to excite the horror and suspicion of the peasants; and I accordingly put them into a basket, with a great quantity of stones, and, laying them up, determined to throw them into the sea that very night; and in the mean time I sat upon the beach, employed in cleaning and arranging my chemical apparatus.

Nothing could be more complete than the alteration that had taken place in my feelings since the night of the appearance of the daemon. I had before regarded my promise with a gloomy despair, as a thing that, with whatever consequences, must be fulfilled; but I now felt as if a film had been taken from before my eyes, and that I, for the first time, saw clearly. The idea of renewing my labours did not for one instant occur to me; the threat I had heard weighed on my thoughts, but I did not reflect that a voluntary act of mine could avert it. I had resolved in my own mind, that to create another like the fiend I had first made would be an act of the basest and most atrocious selfishness; and I banished from my mind every thought that could lead to a different conclusion.

Between two and three in the morning the moon rose; and I then, putting my basket aboard a little skiff, sailed out about four miles from the shore. The scene was perfectly solitary: a few boats were returning towards land, but I sailed away from them. I felt as if I was about the commission of a dreadful crime, and avoided with shuddering anxiety any encounter with my fellow-creatures. At one time the moon, which had before been clear, was suddenly overspread by a thick cloud, and I took advantage of the moment of darkness and cast my basket into the sea: I listened to the gurgling sound as it sunk, and then sailed away from the spot. The sky became clouded; but the air was pure, although chilled by the north-east breeze that was then rising. But it refreshed me, and filled me with such agreeable sensations, that I resolved to prolong my stay on the water; and, fixing the rudder in a direct position, stretched myself at the bottom of the boat. Clouds hid the moon, every-thing was obscure, and I heard only the sound of the boat, as its keel cut through the waves; the murmur lulled me, and in a short time I slept soundly.

I do not know how long I remained in this situation, but when I awoke I found that the sun had already mounted considerably. The wind was high, and the waves continually threatened the safety of my little skiff. I found that the wind was north-east, and must have driven me far from the coast from which I had embarked. I endeavoured to change my course, but quickly found that if I again made the attempt, the boat would be instantly filled with water.

Thus situated, my only resource was to drive before the wind. I confess that I felt a few sensations of terror. I had no compass with me, and was so slenderly acquainted with the geography of this part of the world, that the sun was of little benefit to me. I might be driven into the wide Atlantic, and feel all the tortures of starvation, or be swallowed up in the immeasurable waters that roared and buffeted around me. I had already been out many hours, and felt the torment of a burning thirst, a prelude to my other sufferings. I looked on the heavens, which were covered by clouds that flew before the wind, only to be replaced by others: I looked upon the sea, it was to be my grave. 'Fiend,' I exclaimed, 'your task is already fulfilled!' I thought of Elizabeth, of my father, and of Clerval; all left behind, on whom the monster might satisfy his sanguinary and merciless passions. This idea plunged me into a reverie, so despairing and frightful, that even now, when the scene is on the point of closing before me forever, I shudder to reflect on it.

Some hours passed thus; but by degrees, as the sun declined towards the horizon, the wind died away into a gentle breeze, and the sea became free from breakers. But these gave place to a heavy swell; I felt sick, and hardly able to hold the rudder, when suddenly I saw a line of high land towards the south.

Almost spent, as I was, by fatigue, and the dreadful suspense I endured for several hours, this sudden certainty of life rushed like a flood of warm joy to my heart, and tears gushed from my eyes.

How mutable are our feelings, and how strange is that clinging love we have of life even in the excess of misery! I constructed another sail with a part of my dress, and eagerly steered my course towards the land. It had a wild and rocky appearance, but, as I approached nearer, I easily perceived the traces of cultivation. I saw vessels near the shore, and found myself suddenly transported back to the neighbourhood of civilised man. I carefully traced the windings of the land, and hailed a steeple which I at length saw issuing from behind a small promontory. As I was in a state of extreme debility, I resolved to sail directly towards the town, as a place where I could most easily procure nourishment. Fortunately I had money with me. As I turned the promontory, I perceived a small neat town and a good harbour, which I entered, my heart bounding with joy at my unexpected escape.

As I was occupied in fixing the boat and arranging the sails, several people crowded towards the spot. They seemed much surprised at my appearance, but instead of offering me any assistance, whispered together with gestures that at any other time might have produced in me a slight sensation of alarm. As it was, I merely remarked that they spoke English; and I therefore addressed them in that language. 'My good friends,' said I, 'will you be so kind as to tell me the name of this town, and inform me where I am?'

'You will know that soon enough,' replied a man with a hoarse voice. 'May be you are come to a place that will not prove much to your taste; but you will not be consulted as to your quarters, I promise you.'

I was exceedingly surprised on receiving so rude an answer from a stranger; and I was also disconcerted on perceiving the frowning and angry countenances of his companions. 'Why do you answer me so roughly?' I replied; 'surely it is not the custom of Englishmen to receive strangers so inhospitably.'

'I do not know,' said the man, 'what the custom of the English may be; but it is the custom of the Irish to hate villains.'

While this strange dialogue continued, I perceived the crowd rapidly increase. Their faces expressed a mixture of curiosity and anger, which annoyed, and in some degree alarmed me. I enquired the way to the inn; but no one replied. I then moved forward, and a murmuring sound arose from the crowd as they followed and surrounded me; when an ill-looking man approaching, tapped me on the shoulder, and said, 'Come, sir, you must follow me to Mr Kirwin's, to give an account of yourself.'

'Who is Mr Kirwin? Why am I to give an account of myself? Is not this a free country?'

'Ay, sir, free enough for honest folks. Mr Kirwin is a magistrate; and you are to give an account of the death of a gentleman who was found murdered here last night.'

This answer startled me; but I presently recovered myself. I was innocent; that could easily be proved: accordingly I followed my conductor in silence and was led to one of the best houses in the town. I was ready to sink from fatigue and hunger; but, being surrounded by a crowd, I thought it politic to rouse all my strength, that no physical debility might be construed into apprehension or conscious guilt. Little did I then expect the calamity that was in a few moments to overwhelm me, and extinguish in horror and despair all fear of ignominy or death.

I must pause here; for it requires all my fortitude to recall the memory of the frightful events which I am about to relate, in proper detail, to my recollection.

CHAPTER IV

I was soon introduced into the presence of the magistrate, an old benevolent man, with calm and mild manners. He looked upon me, however, with some degree of severity; and then, turning towards my conductors, he asked who appeared as witnesses on this occasion.

About half a dozen men came forward; and, one being selected by the magistrate, he deposed, that he had been out fishing the night before with his son and brother-in-law, Daniel Nugent, when, about ten o'clock, they observed a strong northerly blast rising, and they accordingly put in for port. It was a very dark night, as the moon had not yet risen; they did not land at the harbour, but, as they had been accustomed, at a creek about two miles below. He walked on first, carrying a part of the fishing tackle, and his companions followed him at some distance. As he was proceeding along the sands, he struck his foot against something, and fell at his length on the ground. His companions came up to assist him; and, by the light of their lantern, they found that he had fallen on the body of a man, who was to all appearance dead. Their first supposition was, that it was the corpse of some person who had been drowned, and was thrown on shore by the waves, but, on examination, they found that the clothes were not wet, and even that the body was not then cold. They instantly carried it to the cottage of an old woman near the spot, and endeavoured, but in vain, to restore it to life. It appeared to be a handsome young man, about five and twenty years of age. He had apparently been strangled; for there was no sign of any violence, except the black mark of fingers on his neck.

The first part of his deposition did not in the least interest me; but when the mark of the fingers was mentioned, I remembered the murder of my brother and felt myself extremely agitated; my limbs trembled, and a mist came over my eyes, which obliged me to lean on a chair for support. The magistrate observed me with a keen eye, and of course drew an unfavourable augury from my manner.

The son confirmed his father's account: but when Daniel Nugent was called, he swore positively that just before the fall of his companion, he saw a boat, with a single man in it, at a short distance from the shore; and, as far as he could judge by the light of a few stars, it was the same boat in which I had just landed.

A woman deposed, that she lived near the beach, and was standing at the door of her cottage, waiting for the return of the fishermen, about an hour before she heard of the discovery of the body, when she saw a boat with only one man, in it push off from that part of the shore where the corpse was afterwards found.

Another woman confirmed the account of the fishermen having brought the body into her house; it was not cold. They put it into a bed and rubbed it; and Daniel went to the town for an apothecary, but life was quite gone.

Several other men were examined concerning my landing; and they agreed that, with the strong north wind that had arisen during the night, it was very probable that I had beaten about for many hours, and had been obliged to return nearly to the same spot from which I had departed. Besides, they observed that it appeared that I had brought the body from another place, and it was likely, that as I did not appear to know the shore, I might have put into the harbour ignorant of the distance of the town of *** from the place where I had deposited the corpse.

Mr Kirwin, on hearing this evidence, desired that I should be taken into the room where the body lay for interment, that it might be observed what effect the sight of it would produce upon me. This idea was probably suggested by the extreme agitation I had exhibited when the mode of the murder had been described. I was accordingly conducted, by the magistrate and several other persons, to the inn. I could not help being struck by the strange coincidences that had taken place during this eventful night; but, knowing that I had been conversing with several persons in the island I had inhabited about the time that the body had been found, I was perfectly tranquil as to the consequences of the affair.

I entered the room where the corpse lay, and was led up to the coffin. How can I describe my sensations of beholding it? I feel yet parched with horror, nor can I reflect on that terrible moment without shuddering and agony. The examination, the presence of the magistrate and witnesses, passed like a dream from my memory, when I saw the lifeless form of Henry Clerval stretched before me. I gasped for breath; and throwing myself on the body, I exclaimed, 'Have my murderous machinations deprived you also, my dearest Henry, of life? Two I have already destroyed; other victims await their destiny: but you, Clerval, my friend, my benefactor –'

The human frame could no longer support the agonies that I endured, and I was carried out of the room in strong convulsions.

A fever succeeded to this. I lay for two months on the point of death: my ravings, as I afterwards heard, were frightful; I called myself the murderer of William, of Justine, and of Clerval. Sometimes I intreated my attendants to assist me in the destruction of the fiend by whom I was tormented; and at others, I felt the fingers of the monster already grasping my neck, and screamed aloud with agony and terror. Fortunately, as I spoke my native language, Mr Kirwin alone understood me; but my gestures and bitter cries were sufficient to affright the other witnesses.

Why did I not die? More miserable than man ever was before, why did I not sink into forgetfulness and rest? Death snatches away many blooming children, the only hopes of their doating parents: how many brides and youthful lovers have been one day in the bloom of health and hope, and the next a prey for worms and the decay of the tomb! Of what materials was I made, that I could thus resist so many shocks, which, like the turning of the wheel, continually renewed the torture?

But I was doomed to live; and in two months, found myself as awaking from a dream, in a prison, stretched on a wretched bed, surrounded by gaolers, turnkeys, bolts, and all the miserable apparatus of a dungeon. It was morning, I remember, when I thus awoke to understanding: I had forgotten the particulars of what had happened, and only felt as if some great misfortune had suddenly overwhelmed me; but when I looked around, and saw the barred windows, and the squalidness of the room in which I was, all flashed across my memory, and I groaned bitterly.

This sound disturbed an old woman who was sleeping in a chair beside me. She was a hired nurse, the wife of one of the turnkeys, and her countenance expressed all those bad qualities which often characterise that class. The lines of her face were hard and rude, like that of persons accustomed to see without sympathising in sights of misery. Her tone expressed her entire indifference; she addressed me in English, and the voice struck me as one that I had heard during my sufferings: –

'Are you better now, sir?' said she.

I replied in the same language, with a feeble voice, 'I believe I am; but if it all be true, if indeed I did not dream, I am sorry that I am still alive to feel this misery and horror.'

'For that matter,' replied the old woman, 'if you mean about the gentleman you murdered, I believe that it were better for you if you were dead, for I fancy it will go hard for you! However, that's none of my business; I am sent to nurse you and get you well; I do my duty with a safe conscience; it were well if everybody did the same.'

I turned with loathing from the woman who could utter so unfeeling a speech to a person just saved, on the very edge of death; but I felt languid, and unable to reflect on all that had passed. The whole series of my life appeared to me as a dream; I sometimes doubted if indeed it were all true, for it never presented itself to my mind with the force of reality.

As the images that floated before me became more distinct, I grew feverish; a darkness pressed around me: no one was near me who soothed me with the gentle voice of love; no dear hand supported me. The physician came and prescribed medicines, and the old woman prepared them for me; but utter carelessness was visible in the first, and the expression of brutality was strongly marked in the visage of the second. Who could be interested in the fate of a murderer, but the hangman who would gain his fee?

These were my first reflections; but I soon learned that Mr Kirwin had shown me extreme kindness. He had caused the best room in the prison to be prepared for me (wretched indeed was the best); and it was he who had provided a physician and a nurse. It is true, he seldom came to see me, for although he ardently desired to relieve the sufferings of every human creature, he did not wish to be present at the agonies and miserable ravings of a murderer. He came, therefore, sometimes to see that I was not neglected; but his visits were short, and with long intervals.

One day, while I was gradually recovering, I was seated in a chair, my eyes half open, and my cheeks livid like those in death. I was overcome by gloom and misery, and often reflected I had better seek death than desire to remain in a world which to me was replete with wretchedness. At one time I considered whether I should not declare myself guilty, and suffer the penalty of the law, less innocent than poor Justine had been. Such were my thoughts, when the door of my apartment was opened, and Mr Kirwin entered. His countenance expressed sympathy and compassion; he drew a chair close to mine and addressed me in French –

'I fear that this place is very shocking to you; can I do anything to make you more comfortable?'

'I thank you, but all that you mention is nothing to me: on the whole earth there is no comfort which I am capable of receiving.'

'I know that the sympathy of a stranger can be but of little relief to one borne down as you are by so strange a misfortune. But you will, I hope, soon quit this melancholy abode; for, doubtless, evidence can easily be brought to free you from the criminal charge.'

'That is my least concern: I am, by a course of strange events, become the most miserable of mortals. Persecuted and tortured as I am and have been, can death be any evil to me?'

'Nothing indeed could be more unfortunate and agonising than the strange chances that have lately occurred. You were thrown, by some surprising accident, on this shore, renowned for its hospitality; seized immediately, and charged with murder. The first sight that was presented to your eyes was the body of your friend, murdered in so unaccountable a manner, and placed, as it were, by some fiend across your path.'

As Mr Kirwin said this, notwithstanding the agitation I endured on this retrospect of my sufferings, I also felt considerable surprise at the knowledge he seemed to possess concerning me. I suppose some astonishment was exhibited in my countenance; for Mr Kirwin hastened to say –

'Immediately upon your being taken ill, all the papers that were on your person were brought me, and I examined them that I might discover some trace by which I could send to your relations an account of your misfortune and illness. I found several letters, and, among others, one which I discovered from its commencement to be from your father. I instantly wrote to Geneva: nearly two months have elapsed since the departure of my letter: – But you are ill, even now you tremble: you are unfit for agitation of any kind.'

'This suspense is a thousand times worse than the most horrible event: tell me what new scene of death has been acted, and whose I am now to lament?'

'Your family is perfectly well,' said Mr Kirwin, with gentleness: 'and some one, a friend, is come to visit you.'

I know not by what chain of thought, the idea presented itself, but it instantly darted into my mind that the murderer had come to mock at my misery, and taunt me with the death of Clerval, as a new incitement for me to comply with his hellish desires. I put my hand before my eyes, and cried out in agony –

'Oh! Take him away! I cannot see him; for God's sake, do not let him enter!'

Mr Kirwin regarded me with a troubled countenance. He could not help regarding my exclamation as a presumption of my guilt, and said, in rather a severe tone –

'I should have thought, young man, that the presence of your father would have been welcome instead of inspiring such violent repugnance.'

'My father!' cried I, while every feature and every muscle was relaxed from anguish to pleasure: 'is my father indeed come? How kind, how very kind! But where is he, why does he not hasten to me?'

My change of manner surprised and pleased the magistrate; perhaps he thought that my former exclamation was a momentary return of delirium, and now he instantly resumed his former benevolence. He rose, and quitted the room with my nurse, and in a moment my father entered it.

Nothing, at this moment, could have given me greater pleasure than the arrival of my father. I stretched out my hand to him and cried –

'Are you, then, safe – and Elizabeth – and Ernest?'

My father calmed me with assurances of their welfare, and endeavoured, by dwelling on these subjects so interesting to my heart, to raise my desponding spirits; but he soon felt that a prison cannot be the abode of cheerfulness. 'What a place is this that you inhabit, my son!' said he, looking mournfully at the barred windows, and wretched appearance of the room. 'You travelled to seek happiness, but a fatality seems to pursue you. And poor Clerval –'

The name of my unfortunate and murdered friend was an agitation too great to be endured in my weak state; I shed tears.

'Alas! yes, my father,' replied I; 'some destiny of the most horrible kind hangs over me, and I must live to fulfil it, or surely I should have died on the coffin of Henry.'

We were not allowed to converse for any length of time, for the precarious state of my health rendered every precaution necessary that could ensure tranquillity. Mr Kirwin came in, and insisted that my strength should not be exhausted by too much exertion. But the appearance of my father was to me like that of my good angel, and I gradually recovered my health.

As my sickness quitted me, I was absorbed by a gloomy and black melancholy, that nothing could dissipate. The image of Clerval was forever before me, ghastly and murdered. More than once the agitation into which these reflections threw me made my friends dread a dangerous relapse. Alas! why did they preserve so miserable and detested a life? It was surely that I might fill my destiny, which is now drawing to a close. Soon, oh! very soon, will death extinguish these throbbings, and relieve me from the mighty weight of anguish that bears me to the dust; and, in executing the award of justice, I shall also sink to rest. Then the appearance of death was distant, although the wish was ever present to my thoughts; and I often sat for hours motionless and speechless, wishing for some mighty revolution that might bury me and my destroyer in its ruins.

The season of the assizes approached. I had already been three months in prison; and although I was still weak and in continual danger of a relapse, I was obliged to travel nearly a hundred miles to the county-town, where the court was held. Mr Kirwin charged himself with every care of collecting witnesses, and arranging my defence. I was spared the disgrace of appearing publicly as a criminal, as the case was not brought before the court that decides on life and death. The grand jury rejected the bill, on its being proved that I was on the Orkney Islands at the hour the body of my friend was found; and a fortnight after my removal I was liberated from prison.

My father was enraptured on finding me freed from the vexations of a criminal charge, that I was again allowed to breathe the fresh atmosphere, and permitted to return to my native country. I did not participate in these feelings; for to me the walls of a dungeon or a palace were alike hateful. The cup of life was poisoned for ever; and although the sun shone upon me, as upon the happy and gay of heart, I saw around me nothing but a dense and frightful darkness, penetrated by no light but the glimmer of two eyes that glared upon me. Sometimes they were the expressive eyes of Henry, languishing in death, the dark orbs nearly covered by the lids, and the long black lashes that fringed them; sometimes it was the watery, clouded eyes of the monster, as I first saw them in my chamber at Ingolstadt.

My father tried to awaken in me the feelings of affection. He talked of Geneva, which I should soon visit – of Elizabeth and Ernest; but these words only drew deep groans from me. Sometimes, indeed, I felt a wish for happiness; and thought, with melancholy delight of my beloved cousin; or longed, with a devouring *maladie du pays,*[39] to see once more the blue lake and rapid Rhone, that had been so dear to me in early childhood: but my general state of feeling was a torpor, in which a prison was as welcome a residence as the divinest scene in nature; and these fits were seldom interrupted but by paroxysms of anguish and despair. At these moments I often endeavoured to put an end to the existence I loathed; and it required unceasing attendance and vigilance to restrain me from committing some dreadful act of violence.

Yet one duty remained to me, the recollection of which finally triumphed over my selfish despair. It was necessary that I should return without delay to Geneva, there to watch over the lives of those I so fondly loved; and to lie in wait for the murderer, that if any chance led me to the place of his concealment, or if he dared again to blast me by his presence, I might, with unfailing aim, put an end to the existence of the monstrous Image which I had endued with the mockery of a soul still more monstrous. My father still desired to delay our departure, fearful that I could not sustain the fatigues of a journey: for I was a shattered wreck – the shadow of a human being. My strength was gone. I was a mere skeleton; and fever night and day preyed upon my wasted frame.

Still, as I urged our leaving Ireland with such inquietude and impatience, my father thought it best to yield. We took our passage on board a vessel bound for Havre-de-Grâce, and sailed with a fair wind from the Irish shores. It was midnight. I lay on the deck, looking at the stars, and listening to the dashing of the waves. I hailed the darkness that shut Ireland from my sight; and my pulse beat with a feverish joy when I reflected that I should soon see Geneva. The past appeared to me in the light of a frightful dream; yet the vessel in which I was, the wind that blew me from the detested shore of Ireland, and the sea which surrounded me, told me too forcibly that I was deceived by no vision, and that Clerval, my friend and dearest companion, had fallen a victim to me and the monster of my creation. I repassed, in my memory, my whole life – my quiet happiness while residing with my family in Geneva, the death of my mother, and my departure for Ingolstadt. I remembered, shuddering, the mad enthusiasm that hurried me on to the creation of my hideous enemy, and I called to mind the night in which he first lived. I was unable to pursue the train of thought; a thousand feelings pressed upon me, and I wept bitterly.

Ever since my recovery from the fever, I had been in the custom of taking every night a small quantity of laudanum;[40] for it was by means of this drug only that I was enabled to gain the rest necessary for the preservation of life. Oppressed by the recollection of my various misfortunes, I now swallowed double my usual quantity, and soon slept profoundly. But sleep did not afford me respite from thought and misery; my dreams presented a thousand objects that scared me. Towards morning I was possessed by a kind of nightmare; I felt the fiend's grasp in my neck; and could not free myself from it; groans and cries rang in my ears. My father, who was watching over me, perceiving my rest-

lessness, awoke me; the dashing waves were around: the cloudy
sky above; the fiend was not here: a sense of security, a feeling
that a truce was established between the present hour and the
irresistible, disastrous future, imparted to me a kind of calm
forgetfulness, of which the human mind is by its structure peculiarly susceptible.

CHAPTER V

The voyage came to an end. We landed, and proceeded to Paris. I soon found that I had overtaxed my strength, and that I must repose before I could continue my journey. My father's care and attentions were indefatigable; but he did not know the origin of my sufferings, and sought erroneous methods to remedy the incurable ill. He wished me to seek amusement in society. I abhorred the face of man. Oh, not abhorred! they were my brethren, my fellow beings, and I felt attracted even to the most repulsive among them, as to creatures of an angelic nature and celestial mechanism. But I felt that I had no right to share their intercourse. I had unchained an enemy among them, whose joy it was to shed their blood, and to revel in their groans. How they would, each and all, abhor me, and hunt me from the world, did they know my unhallowed acts and the crimes which had their source in me!

My father yielded at length to my desire to avoid society, and strove by various arguments to banish my despair. Sometimes he thought that I felt deeply the degradation of being obliged to answer a charge of murder, and he endeavoured to prove to me the futility of pride.

'Alas! my father,' said I, 'how little do you know me. Human beings, their feelings and passions, would indeed be degraded if such a wretch as I felt pride. Justine, poor unhappy Justine, was as innocent as I, and she suffered the same charge; she died for it; and I am the cause of this – I murdered her. William, Justine, and Henry – they all died by my hands.'

My father had often, during my imprisonment, heard me make the same assertion; when I thus accused myself, he sometimes seemed to desire an explanation, and at others he appeared to consider it as the offspring of delirium, and that, during my illness, some idea of this kind had presented itself to my imagination, the remembrance of which I preserved in my convalescence.

I avoided explanation, and maintained a continual silence concerning the wretch I had created. I had a persuasion that I should be supposed mad; and this in itself would forever have chained my tongue. But, besides, I could not bring myself to disclose a secret which would fill my hearer with consternation, and make fear and unnatural horror the inmates of his breast. I checked, therefore, my impatient thirst for sympathy, and was silent when I would have given the world to have confided that fatal secret. Yet still words like those I have recorded would burst uncontrollably from me. I could offer no explanation of them; but their truth in part relieved the burden of my mysterious woe.

Upon this occasion my father said, with an expression of unbounded wonder, 'My dearest Victor, what infatuation is this? My dear son, I entreat you never to make such an assertion again.'

'I am not mad,' I cried energetically; 'the sun and the heavens, who have viewed my operations, can bear witness of my truth. I am the assassin of those most innocent victims; they died by my machinations. A thousand times would I have shed my own blood, drop by drop, to have saved their lives; but I could not, my father, indeed I could not sacrifice the whole human race.'

The conclusion of this speech convinced my father that my ideas were deranged, and he instantly changed the subject of our conversation, and endeavoured to alter the course of my thoughts. He wished as much as possible to obliterate the memory of the scenes that had taken place in Ireland, and never alluded to them, or suffered me to speak of my misfortunes.

As time passed away I became more calm; misery had her dwelling in my heart, but I no longer talked in the same incoherent manner of my own crimes; sufficient for me was the consciousness of them. By the utmost self-violence I curbed the imperious voice of wretchedness, which sometimes desired to declare itself to the whole world; and my manners were calmer and more composed than they had ever been since my journey to the sea of ice.

A few days before we left Paris on our way to Switzerland, I received the following letter from Elizabeth: –

MY DEAR FRIEND,

It gave me the greatest pleasure to receive a letter from my uncle dated at Paris; you are no longer at a formidable distance, and I may hope to see you in less than a fortnight. My poor cousin, how much you must have suffered! I expect to see you looking even more ill than when you quitted Geneva. This winter has been passed more miserably, tortured as I have been by anxious suspense; yet I hope to see peace in your countenance, and to find that your heart is not totally void of comfort and tranquillity.

Yet I fear that the same feelings now exist that made you so miserable a year ago, even perhaps augmented by time. I would not disturb you at this period, when so many misfortunes weigh upon you; but a conversation that I had with my uncle previous to his departure renders some explanation necessary before we meet.

Explanation! You may possibly say; what can Elizabeth have to explain? If you really say this, my questions are answered, and all my doubts satisfied. But you are distant from me, and it is possible that you may dread, and yet be pleased with this explanation; and, in a probability of this being the case, I dare not any longer postpone writing what, during your absence, I have often wished to express to you, but have never had the courage to begin.

You well know, Victor, that our union had been the favourite plan of your parents ever since our infancy. We were told this when young, and taught to look forward to it as an event that would certainly take place. We were affectionate playfellows during childhood, and, I believe, dear and valued friends to one another as we grew older. But as brother and sister often entertain a lively affection towards each other, without desiring a more intimate union, may not such also be our case? Tell me, dearest Victor, Answer me, I conjure you, by our mutual happiness, with simple truth – Do you not love another?

You have travelled: you have spent several years of your life at Ingolstadt; and I confess to you, my friend, that when I saw you last autumn so unhappy, flying to solitude, from the society of every creature, I could not help supposing that you might regret our connection, and believe yourself bound in honour to fulfil the wishes of your parents, although they opposed themselves to your inclinations. But this is false reasoning. I confess to you, my friend, that I love you, and that in my airy dreams of futurity you have been my constant friend and companion. But it is your happiness I desire as well as my own, when I declare to you that our marriage would render me eternally miserable, unless it were the dictate of your own free choice. Even now I weep to think that, borne down as you are by the cruellest misfortunes, you may stifle, by the word 'honour', all hope of that love and happiness which would alone restore you to yourself. I, who have so disinterested an affection for you, may increase your miseries tenfold by being an obstacle to your wishes. Ah! Victor, be assured that your cousin and playmate has too sincere a love for you not to be made miserable by this supposition. Be happy, my friend; and if you obey me in this one request, remain satisfied that nothing on earth will have the power to interrupt my tranquillity.

Do not let this letter disturb you; do not answer tomorrow, or the next day, or even until you come, if it will give you pain. My uncle will send me news of your health; and if I see but one smile on your lips when we meet, occasioned by this or any other exertion of mine, I shall need no other happiness.

ELIZABETH LAVENZA
Geneva, May 18th, 17–.

This letter revived in my memory what I had before forgotten, the threat of the fiend – '*I will be with you on your wedding-night!*' Such was my sentence, and on that night would the daemon employ every art to destroy me, and tear me from the glimpse of happiness which promised partly to console my sufferings. On that night he had determined to consummate his crimes by my death. Well, be it so; a deadly struggle would then assuredly take place, in which if he were victorious I should be at peace, and his power over me be at an end. If he were vanquished, I should be a free man. Alas! what freedom? Such as the peasant enjoys when his family have been massacred before his eyes, his cottage burnt, his lands laid waste, and he is turned adrift, homeless, penniless, and alone, but free. Such would be my liberty, except that in my Elizabeth I possessed a treasure; alas! balanced by those horrors of remorse and guilt, which would pursue me until death.

Sweet and beloved Elizabeth! I read and re-read her letter, and some softened feelings stole into my heart, and dared to whisper paradisiacal dreams of love and joy; but the apple was already eaten, and the angel's arm bared to drive me from all hope. Yet I would die to make her happy. If the monster executed his threat, death was inevitable; yet, again, I considered whether my marriage would hasten my fate. My destruction might indeed arrive a few months sooner; but if my torturer should suspect that I postponed it, influenced by his menaces, he would surely find other and perhaps more dreadful means of revenge. He had vowed *to be with me on my wedding-night*, yet he did not consider that threat as binding him to peace in the mean time, for as if to show me that he was not yet satiated with blood, he had murdered Clerval immediately after the enunciation of his threats. I resolved, therefore, that if my immediate union with my cousin would conduce either to hers or my father's happiness, my adversary's designs against my life should not retard it a single hour.

In this state of mind I wrote to Elizabeth. My letter was calm and affectionate. 'I fear, my beloved girl,' I said, 'little happiness remains for us on earth; yet all that I may one day enjoy is centred in you. Chase away your idle fears; to you alone do I consecrate my life, and my endeavours for contentment. I have one secret, Elizabeth, a dreadful one; when revealed to you, it will chill your frame with horror, and then, far from being surprised at my misery, you will only wonder that I survive what I have endured. I will confide this tale of misery and terror to you the day after our marriage shall take place, for, my sweet cousin, there must be perfect confidence between us. But until then, I conjure you, do not mention or allude to it. This I most earnestly intreat, and I know you will comply.'

In about a week after the arrival of Elizabeth's letter, we returned to Geneva. The sweet girl welcomed me with warm affection; yet tears were in her eyes; as she beheld my emaciated frame and feverish cheeks. I saw a change in her also. She was thinner, and had lost much of that heavenly vivacity that had before charmed me; but her gentleness, and soft looks of compassion, made her a more fit companion for one blasted and miserable as I was.

The tranquillity which I now enjoyed did not endure. Memory brought madness with it; and when I thought of what had passed, a real insanity possessed me; sometimes I was furious and burnt with rage; sometimes low and despondent. I neither spoke, nor looked at any one, but sat motionless, bewildered by the multitude of miseries that overcame me.

Elizabeth alone had the power to draw me from these fits; her gentle voice would soothe me when transported by passion, and inspire me with human feelings when sunk in torpor. She wept with me, and for me. When reason returned, she would remonstrate, and endeavour to inspire me with resignation. Ah! it is well for the unfortunate to be resigned, but for the guilty there is no peace. The agonies of remorse poison the luxury there is otherwise sometimes found in indulging the excess of grief.

Soon after my arrival, my father spoke of my immediate marriage with Elizabeth. I remained silent.

'Have you, then, some other attachment?'

'None on earth. I love Elizabeth and look forward to our union with delight. Let the day therefore be fixed; and on it I will consecrate myself, in life or death, to the happiness of my cousin.'

'My dear Victor, do not speak thus. Heavy misfortunes have befallen us, but let us only cling closer to what remains, and transfer our love for those whom we have lost to those who yet live. Our circle will be small, but bound close by the ties of affection and mutual misfortune. And when time shall have softened your despair, new and dear objects of care will be born to replace those of whom we have been so cruelly deprived.'

Such were the lessons of my father. But to me the remembrance of the threat returned: nor can you wonder that, omnipotent as the fiend had yet been in his deeds of blood, I should almost regard him as invincible; and that when he had pronounced the words '*I shall be with you on your wedding-night*', I should regard the threatened fate as unavoidable. But death was no evil to me, if the loss of Elizabeth were balanced with it; and I therefore, with a contented and even cheerful countenance, agreed with my father, that if my cousin would consent, the ceremony should take place in ten days, and thus put, as I imagined, the seal to my fate.

Great God! if for one instant I had thought what might be the hellish intention of my fiendish adversary, I would rather have banished myself for ever from my native country, and wandered a friendless outcast over the earth, than have consented to this miserable marriage. But, as if possessed of magic powers, the monster had blinded me to his real intentions; and when I thought that I had prepared only my own death, I hastened that of a far dearer victim.

As the period fixed for our marriage drew nearer, whether from cowardice or a prophetic feeling, I felt my heart sink within me. But I concealed my feelings by an appearance of hilarity, that brought smiles and joy to the countenance of my father, but hardly deceived the ever-watchful and nicer eye of Elizabeth. She looked forward to our union with placid contentment, not unmingled with a little fear, which past misfortunes had impressed, that what now appeared certain and tangible happiness, might soon dissipate into an airy dream, and leave no trace but deep and everlasting regret.

Preparations were made for the event, congratulatory visits were received, and all wore a smiling appearance. I shut up, as well as I could, in my own heart the anxiety that preyed there, and entered with seeming earnestness into the plans of my father, although they might only serve as the decorations of my tragedy. Through my father's exertions, a part of the inheritance of Elizabeth had been restored to her by the Austrian government. A small possession on the shores of Como belonged to her. It was agreed that, immediately after our union, we should proceed to Villa Lavenza, and spend our first days of happiness beside the beautiful lake near which it stood.

In the mean time I took every precaution to defend my person, in case the fiend should openly attack me. I carried pistols and a dagger constantly about me, and was ever on the watch to prevent artifice; and by these means gained a greater degree of tranquillity. Indeed, as the period approached, the threat appeared more as a delusion, not to be regarded as worthy to disturb my peace, while the happiness I hoped for in my marriage wore a greater appearance of certainty, as the day fixed for its solemnisation drew nearer, and I heard it continually spoken of as an occurrence which no accident could possibly prevent.

Elizabeth seemed happy; my tranquil demeanour contributed greatly to calm her mind. But on the day that was to fulfil my wishes and my destiny, she was melancholy, and a presentiment of evil pervaded her; and perhaps also she thought of the dreadful secret which I had promised to reveal to her on the following day. My father was in the mean time overjoyed, and in the bustle of preparation only recognised in the melancholy of his niece the diffidence of a bride.

After the ceremony was performed, a large party assembled at my father's; but it was agreed that Elizabeth and I should commence our journey by water, sleeping that night at Evian, and continuing our voyage on the following day. The day was fair, the wind favourable, all smiled on our nuptial embarkation.

Those were the last moments of my life during which I enjoyed the feeling of happiness. We passed rapidly along: the sun was hot, but we were sheltered from its rays by a kind of canopy, while we enjoyed the beauty of the scene, sometimes on one side of the lake, where we saw Mont Salêve, the pleasant banks of Montalègre, and at a distance, surmounting all, the beautiful Mont Blanc, and the assemblage of snowy mountains that in vain endeavour to emulate her; sometimes coasting the opposite banks, we saw the mighty Jura opposing its dark side to the ambition that would quit its native country, and an almost insurmountable barrier to the invader who should wish to enslave it.

I took the hand of Elizabeth. 'You are sorrowful, my love. Ah! if you knew what I have suffered, and what I may yet endure, you would endeavour to let me taste the quiet and freedom from despair that this one day at least permits me to enjoy.'

'Be happy, my dear Victor,' replied Elizabeth; 'there is, I hope, nothing to distress you; and be assured that if a lively joy is not painted in my face, my heart is contented. Something whispers to me not to depend too much on the prospect that is opened before us, but I will not listen to such a sinister voice. Observe how fast we move along, and how the clouds, which sometimes obscure and sometimes rise above the dome of Mont Blanc, render this scene of beauty still more interesting. Look also at the innumerable fish that are swimming in the clear waters, where we can distinguish every pebble that lies at the bottom. What a divine day! how happy and serene all nature appears!'

Thus Elizabeth endeavoured to divert her thoughts and mine from all reflection upon melancholy subjects. But her temper was fluctuating; joy for a few instants shone in her eyes, but it continually gave place to distraction and reverie.

The sun sank lower in the heavens; we passed the river Drance, and observed its path through the chasms of the higher, and the glens of the lower hills. The Alps here come closer to the lake, and we approached the amphitheatre of mountains which forms its eastern boundary. The spire of Evian shone under the woods that surrounded it, and the range of mountain above mountain by which it was overhung.

The wind, which had hitherto carried us along with amazing rapidity, sunk at sunset to a light breeze; the soft air just ruffled the water, and caused a pleasant motion among the trees as we approached the shore, from which it wafted the most delightful scent of flowers and hay. The sun sunk beneath the horizon as we landed; and as I touched the shore, I felt those cares and fears revive, which soon were to clasp me, and cling to me forever.

CHAPTER VI

It was eight o'clock when we landed; we walked for a short time on the shore, enjoying the transitory light, and then retired to the inn, and contemplated the lovely scene of waters, woods, and mountains, obscured in darkness, yet still displaying their black outlines.

The wind, which had fallen in the south, now rose with great violence in the west. The moon had reached her summit in the heavens and was beginning to descend; the clouds swept across it swifter than the flight of the vulture and dimmed her rays, while the lake reflected the scene of the busy heavens, rendered still busier by the restless waves that were beginning to rise. Suddenly a heavy storm of rain descended.

I had been calm during the day; but so soon as night obscured the shapes of objects, a thousand fears arose in my mind. I was anxious and watchful, while my right hand grasped a pistol which was hidden in my bosom; every sound terrified me; but I resolved that I would sell my life dearly, and not shrink from the conflict until my own life, or that of my adversary, was extinguished.

Elizabeth observed my agitation for some time in timid and fearful silence, but there was something in my glance which communicated terror to her, and trembling, she asked, 'What is it that agitates you, my dear Victor? What is it you fear?'

'Oh! peace, peace, my love,' replied I; 'this night, and all will be safe: but this night is dreadful, very dreadful.'

I passed an hour in this state of mind, when suddenly, I reflected how fearful the combat which I momentarily expected would be to my wife, and I earnestly intreated her to retire, resolving not to join her until I had obtained some knowledge as to the situation of my enemy.

She left me, and I continued some time walking up and down the passages of the house, and inspecting every corner that might afford a retreat to my adversary. But I discovered no trace of him, and was beginning to conjecture that some fortunate chance had intervened to prevent the execution of his menaces; when suddenly I heard a shrill and dreadful scream. It came from the room into which Elizabeth had retired. As I heard it, the whole truth rushed into my mind, my arms dropped, the motion of every muscle and fibre was suspended; I could feel the blood trickling in my veins, and tingling in the extremities of my limbs. This state lasted but for an instant; the scream was repeated, and I rushed into the room.

Great God! why did I not then expire! Why am I here to relate the destruction of the best hope, and the purest creature of earth? She was there, lifeless and inanimate, thrown across the bed, her head hanging down, and her pale and distorted features half covered by her hair. Every where I turn I see the same figure – her bloodless arms and relaxed form flung by the murderer on its bridal bier. Could I behold this, and live? Alas! life is obstinate, and clings closest where it is most hated. For a moment only did I lose recollection: I fell senseless on the ground.

When I recovered, I found myself surrounded by the people of the inn; their countenances expressed a breathless terror: but the horror of others appeared only as a mockery, a shadow of the feelings that oppressed me. I escaped from them to the room where lay the body of Elizabeth, my love, my wife, so lately living, so dear, so worthy. She had been moved from the posture in which I had first beheld her; and now, as she lay, her head upon her arm, and a handkerchief thrown across her face and neck, I might have supposed her asleep. I rushed towards her, and embraced her with ardour; but the deadly langour and coldness of the limbs told me, that what I now held in my arms had ceased to be the Elizabeth whom I had loved and cherished. The murderous mark of the fiends' grasp was on her neck, and the breath had ceased to issue from her lips.

While I still hung over her in the agony of despair. I happened to look up. The windows of the room had before been darkened, and I felt a kind of panic on seeing the pale yellow light of the moon illuminate the chamber. The shutters had been thrown back; and, with a sensation of horror not to be described. I saw at the open window a figure the most hideous and abhorred. A grin was on the face of the monster; he seemed to jeer, as with his fiendish finger he pointed towards the corpse of my wife. I rushed towards the window, and drawing a pistol from my bosom, fired: but he eluded me, leaped from his station, and, running with the swiftness of lightning, plunged into the lake.

The report of the pistol brought a crowd into the room. I pointed to the spot where he had disappeared, and we followed the track with boats; nets were cast, but in vain. After passing several hours, we returned hopeless, most of my companions believing it to have been a form conjured up by my fancy. After having landed, they proceeded to search the country, parties going in different directions among the woods and vines.

I attempted to accompany them, and proceeded a short distance from the house; but my head whirled round, my steps were like those of a drunken man, I fell at last in a state of utter exhaustion; a film covered my eyes, and my skin was parched with the heat of fever. In this state I was carried back, and placed on a bed, hardly conscious of what had happened; my eyes wandered round the room, as if to seek something that I had lost.

After an interval I arose, and, as if by instinct, crawled into the room where the corpse of my beloved lay. There were women weeping around; – I hung over it, and joined my sad tears to theirs – all this time no distinct idea presented itself to my mind; but my thoughts rambled to various subjects, reflecting confusedly on my misfortunes and their cause. I was bewildered, in a cloud of wonder and horror. The death of William, the execution of Justine, the murder of Clerval, and lastly of my wife; even at that moment I knew not that my only remaining friends were safe from the malignity of the fiend; my father even now might be writhing under his grasp, and Ernest might be dead at his feet. This idea made me shudder, and recalled me to action. I started up, and resolved to return to Geneva with all possible speed.

There were no horses to be procured, and I must return by the lake; but the wind was unfavourable and the rain fell in torrents. However, it was hardly morning, and I might reasonably hope to arrive by night. I hired men to row and took an oar myself; for I had always experienced relief from mental torment in bodily exercise. But the overflowing misery I now felt, and the excess of agitation that I endured, rendered me incapable of any exertion. I threw down the oar; and leaning my head upon my hands, gave way to every gloomy idea that arose. If I looked up, I saw scenes which were familiar to me in my happier time, and which I had contemplated but the day before in the company of her who was now but a shadow and a recollection. Tears streamed from my eyes. The rain had ceased for a moment, and I saw the fish play in the waters as they had done a few hours before; they had then been observed by Elizabeth. Nothing is so painful to the human mind as a great and sudden change. The sun might shine, or the clouds might lower: but nothing could appear to me as it had done the day before. A fiend had snatched from me every hope of future happiness: no creature had ever been so miserable as I was; so frightful an event is single in the history of man.

But why should I dwell upon the incidents that followed this last overwhelming event? Mine has been a tale of horrors; I have reached their *acme*, and what I must now relate can but be tedious to you. Know that, one by one, my friends were snatched away; I was left desolate. My own strength is exhausted; and I must tell, in a few words, what remains of my hideous narration.

I arrived at Geneva. My father and Ernest yet lived; but the former sunk under the tidings that I bore. I see him now, excellent and venerable old man! his eyes wandered in vacancy, for they had lost their charm and their delight – his Elizabeth, his more than daughter, whom he doated on with all that affection which a man feels, who in the decline of life, having few affections, clings more earnestly to those that remain. Cursed, cursed be the fiend that brought misery on his grey hairs, and doomed him to waste in wretchedness! He could not live under the horrors that were accumulated around him; the springs of existence suddenly gave way: he was unable to rise from his bed, and in a few days he died in my arms.

What then became of me? I know not; I lost sensation and chains and darkness were the only objects that pressed upon me. Sometimes, indeed, I dreamt that I wandered in flowery meadows and pleasant vales with the friends of my youth, but I awoke, and found myself in a dungeon. Melancholy followed, but by degrees

I gained a clear conception of my miseries and situation, and was then released from my prison. For they had called me mad; and during many months, as I understood, a solitary cell had been my habitation.

Liberty, however, had been an useless gift to me, had I not, as I awakened to reason, at the same time awakened to revenge. As the memory of past misfortunes pressed upon me, I began to reflect on their cause – the monster whom I had created, the miserable daemon whom I had sent abroad into the world for my destruction. I was possessed by a maddening rage when I thought of him, and desired and ardently prayed that I might have him within my grasp to wreak a great and signal revenge on his cursed head.

Nor did my hate long confine itself to useless wishes; I began to reflect on the best means of securing him; and for this purpose, about a month after my release, I repaired to a criminal judge in the town, and told him that I had an accusation to make; that I knew the destroyer of my family; and that I required him to exert his whole authority for the apprehension of the murderer.

The magistrate listened to me with attention and kindness: – 'Be assured sir,' said he, 'no pains or exertions on my part shall be spared to discover the villain.'

'I thank you,' replied I; 'listen, therefore, to the deposition that I have to make. It is indeed a tale so strange, that I should fear you would not credit it were there not something in truth which, however wonderful, forces conviction. The story is too connected to be mistaken for a dream, and I have no motive for falsehood.' My manner, as I thus addressed him, was impressive, but calm; I had formed in my own heart a resolution to pursue my destroyer to death; and this purpose quieted my agony, and for an interval reconciled me to life. I now related my history, briefly, but with firmness and precision, marking the dates with accuracy, and never deviating into invective or exclamation.

The magistrate appeared at first perfectly incredulous, but as I continued he became more attentive and interested; I saw him sometimes shudder with horror; at others a lively surprise, un-mingled with disbelief, was painted on his countenance.

When I had concluded my narration I said, 'This is the being whom I accuse, and for whose seizure and punishment I call upon you to exert your whole power. It is your duty as a magistrate, and I believe and hope that your feelings as a man will not revolt from the execution of those functions on this occasion.'

This address caused a considerable change in the physiognomy of my own auditor. He had heard my story with that half kind of belief that is given to a tale of spirits and supernatural events; but when he was called upon to act officially in consequence, the whole tide of his incredulity returned. He, however, answered mildly, 'I would willingly afford you every aid in your pursuit; but the creature of whom you speak appears to have powers which would put all my exertions to defiance. Who can follow an animal which can traverse the sea of ice, and inhabit caves and dens where no man would venture to intrude? Besides, some months have elapsed since the commission of his crimes, and no one can conjecture to what place he has wandered, or what region he may now inhabit.

'I do not doubt that he hovers near the spot which I inhabit; and if he has indeed taken refuge in the Alps, he may be hunted like the chamois, and destroyed as a beast of prey. But I perceive your thoughts: you do not credit my narrative, and do not intend to pursue my enemy with the punishment which is his desert.'

As I spoke, rage sparkled in my eyes; the magistrate was intimidated: – 'You are mistaken,' said he. 'I will exert myself; and if it is in my power to seize the monster, be assured that he shall suffer punishment proportionate to his crimes. But I fear, from what you have yourself described to be his properties, that this will prove impracticable; and thus, while every proper measure is pursued, you should make up your mind to disappointment.'

'That cannot be; but all that I can say will be of little avail. My revenge is of no moment to you; yet, while I allow it to be a vice, I confess that it is the devouring and only passion of my soul. My rage is unspeakable, when I reflect that the murderer, whom I have turned loose upon society, still exists. You refuse my just demand: I have but one resource; and I devote myself, either in my life or death, to his destruction.'

I trembled with excess of agitation as I said this; there was a frenzy in my manner, and something, I doubt not, of that haughty fierceness which the martyrs of old are said to have possessed. But to a Genevan magistrate, whose mind was occupied by far other ideas than those of devotion and heroism, this elevation of mind had much the appearance of madness. He endeavoured to soothe me as a nurse does a child, and reverted to my tale as the effects of delirium.

'Man,' I cried, 'how ignorant art thou in thy pride of wisdom! Cease; you know not what it is you say.'

I broke from the house angry and disturbed, and retired to meditate on some other mode of action.

CHAPTER VII

My present situation was one in which all voluntary thought was swallowed up and lost. I was hurried away by fury; revenge alone endowed me with strength and composure; it moulded my feelings, and allowed me to be calculating and calm, at periods when otherwise delirium or death would have been my portion.

My first resolution was to quit Geneva forever; my country, which, when I was happy and beloved, was dear to me, now, in my adversity, became hateful. I provided myself with a sum of money, together with a few jewels which had belonged to my mother, and departed.

And now my wanderings began, which are to cease but with life. I have traversed a vast portion of the earth, and have endured all the hardships which travellers, in deserts and barbarous countries, are wont to meet. How I have lived I hardly know; many times have I stretched my failing limbs upon the sandy plain, and prayed for death. But revenge kept me alive; I dared not die, and leave my adversary in being.

When I quitted Geneva, my first labour was to gain some clue by which I might trace the steps of my fiendish enemy. But my plan was unsettled; and I wandered many hours round the confines of the town, uncertain what path I should pursue. As night approached, I found myself at the entrance of the cemetery where William, Elizabeth, and my father reposed. I entered it, and approached the tomb which marked their graves. Every thing was silent, except the leaves of the trees, which were gently agitated by the wind; the night was nearly dark; and the scene would have been solemn and affecting even to an uninterested observer. The spirits of the departed seemed to flit around, and to cast a shadow, which was felt but not seen, around the head of the mourner.

The deep grief which this scene had at first excited quickly gave way to rage and despair. They were dead, and I lived; their murderer also lived, and to destroy him I must drag out my weary existence. I knelt on the grass, and kissed the earth, and with quivering lips exclaimed, 'By the sacred earth on which I kneel, by the shades that wander near me, by the deep and eternal grief that I feel, I swear; and by thee, O Night, and the spirits that preside over thee, to pursue the daemon, who caused this misery, until he or I shall perish in mortal conflict. For this purpose I will preserve my life: to execute this dear revenge will I again behold the sun, and tread the green herbage of earth, which otherwise should vanish from my eyes forever. And I call on you, spirits of the dead; and on you, wandering ministers of vengeance, to aid and conduct me in my work. Let the cursed and hellish monster drink deep of agony; let him feel the despair that now torments me.'

I had begun my adjuration with solemnity, and an awe which almost assured me that the shades of my murdered friends heard and approved my devotion; but the furies possessed me as I concluded, and rage choked my utterance.

I was answered through the stillness of night by a loud and fiendish laugh. It rang on my ears long and heavily; the mountains re-echoed it, and I felt as if all hell surrounded me with mockery and laughter. Surely in that moment I should have been possessed by frenzy, and have destroyed my miserable existence, but that my vow was heard, and that I was reserved for vengeance. The laughter died away; when a well-known and abhorred voice, apparently close to my ear, addressed me in an audible whisper, 'I am satisfied: miserable wretch! you have determined to live, and I am satisfied.'

I darted towards the spot from which the sound proceeded; but the devil eluded my grasp. Suddenly the broad disk of the moon arose, and shone full upon his ghastly and distorted shape, as he fled with more than mortal speed.

I pursued him; and for many months this has been my task. Guided by a slight clue, I followed the windings of the Rhône, but vainly. The blue Mediterranean appeared; and, by a strange chance, I saw the fiend enter by night, and hide himself in a vessel bound for the Black Sea. I took my passage in the same ship; but he escaped, I know not how.

Amidst the wilds of Tartary and Russia, although he still evaded me, I have ever followed in his track. Sometimes the peasants, scared by this horrid apparition, informed me of his path; sometimes he himself, who feared that if I lost all trace of him, I should despair and die, left some mark to guide me. The snows descended on my head, and I saw the print of his huge step on the white plain. To you first entering on life, to whom care is new, and agony unknown, how can you understand what I have felt and still feel? Cold, want, and fatigue, were the least pains which I was destined to endure; I was cursed by some devil, and carried about with me my eternal hell; yet still a spirit of good followed and directed my steps and, when I most murmured, would suddenly extricate me from seemingly insurmountable difficulties. Sometimes, when nature, overcome by hunger, sunk under the exhaustion, a repast was prepared for me in the desert, that restored and inspirited me. The fare was, indeed, coarse, such as the peasants of the country ate; but I will not doubt that it was set there by the spirits that I had invoked to aid me. Often, when all was dry, the heavens cloudless, and I was parched by thirst, a slight cloud would bedim the sky, shed the few drops that revived me, and vanish.

I followed, when I could, the courses of the rivers; but the daemon generally avoided these, as it was here that the population of the country chiefly collected. In other places human beings were seldom seen; and I generally subsisted on the wild animals that crossed my path. I had money with me, and gained the friendship of the villagers by distributing it; or I brought with me some food that I had killed, which, after taking a small part, I always presented to those who had provided me with fire and utensils for cooking.

My life, as it passed thus, was indeed hateful to me, and it was during sleep alone that I could taste joy. O blessed sleep! often, when most miserable, I sank to repose, and my dreams lulled me even to rapture. The spirits that guarded me had provided these moments, or rather hours, of happiness that I might retain strength to fulfil my pilgrimage. Deprived of this respite, I should have sunk under my hardships. During the day I was sustained and inspirited by the hope of night: for in sleep I saw my friends, my wife, and my beloved country; again I saw the benevolent countenance of my father, heard the silver tones of my Elizabeth's voice, and beheld Clerval enjoying health and youth. Often, when wearied by a toilsome march, I persuaded myself that I was dreaming until night should come, and that I should then enjoy reality in the arms of my dearest friends. What agonising fondness did I feel for them! how did I cling to their dear forms, as sometimes they haunted even my waking hours, and persuade myself that they still lived! At such moments vengeance, that burned within me, died in my heart, and I pursued my path towards the destruction of the daemon, more as a task enjoined by heaven, as the mechanical impulse of some power of which I was unconscious, than as the ardent desire of my soul.

What his feelings were whom I pursued I cannot know. Sometimes, indeed, he left marks in writing on the barks of the trees, or cut in stone, that guided me, and instigated my fury. 'My reign is not yet over' – these words were legible in one of these inscriptions – 'you live, and my power is complete. Follow me; I seek the everlasting ices of the north, where you will feel the misery of cold and frost, to which I am impassive. You will find near this place, if you follow not too tardily, a dead hare; eat and be refreshed. Come on, my enemy; we have yet to wrestle for our lives, but many hard and miserable hours must you endure until that period shall arrive.'

Scoffing devil! Again do I vow vengeance; again do I devote thee, miserable fiend, to torture and death. Never will I give up my search, until he or I perish; and then with what ecstasy shall I join my Elizabeth and my departed friends, who even now prepare for me the reward of my tedious toil and horrible pilgrimage!

As I still pursued my journey to the northward, the snows thickened, and the cold increased in a degree almost too severe to support. The peasants were shut up in their hovels, and only a few of the most hardy ventured forth to seize the animals whom starvation had forced from their hiding-places to seek for prey. The rivers were covered with ice, and no fish could be procured; and thus I was cut off from my chief article of maintenance.

The triumph of my enemy increased with the difficulty of my

labours. One inscription that he left was in these words: – 'Prepare! your toils only begin; wrap yourself in furs, and provide food, for we shall soon enter upon a journey where your sufferings will satisfy my everlasting hatred.'

My courage and perseverance were invigorated by these scoffing words; I resolved not to fail in my purpose; and, calling on Heaven to support me, I continued with unabated fervour to traverse immense deserts, until the ocean appeared at a distance, and formed the utmost boundary of the horizon. Oh! how unlike it was to the blue seasons of the south! Covered with ice, it was only to be distinguished from land by its superior wildness and ruggedness. The Greeks wept for joy when they beheld the Mediterranean from the hills of Asia, and hailed with rapture the boundary of their toils. I did not weep, but I knelt down, and, with a full heart, thanked my guiding spirit for conducting me in safety to the place where I hoped, notwithstanding my adversary's gibe, to meet and grapple with him.

Some weeks before this period I had procured a sledge and dogs, and thus traversed the snows with inconceivable speed. I know not whether the fiend possessed the same advantages; but I found that, as before I had daily lost ground in the pursuit, I now gained on him, so much so that when I first saw the ocean he was but one day's journey in advance, and I hoped to intercept him before he should reach the beach. With new courage, therefore, I pressed on, and in two days arrived at a wretched hamlet on the sea-shore. I enquired of the inhabitants concerning the fiend, and gained accurate information. A gigantic monster, they said, had arrived the night before, armed with a gun and many pistols; putting to flight the inhabitants of a solitary cottage, through fear of his terrific appearance. He had carried off their store of winter food, and, placing it in a sledge, to draw which he had seized on a numerous drove of trained dogs, he had harnessed them, and the same night, to the joy of the horror-struck villagers, had pursued his journey across the sea in a direction that led to no land; and they conjectured that he must speedily be destroyed by the breaking of the ice, or frozen by the eternal frosts.

On hearing this information, I suffered a temporary access of despair. He had escaped me; and I must commence a destructive and almost endless journey across the mountainous ices of the ocean, – amidst cold that few of the inhabitants could long endure and which I, the native of a genial and sunny climate, could not hope to survive. Yet at the idea that the fiend should live and be triumphant, my rage and vengeance returned, and, like a mighty tide, overwhelmed every other feeling. After a slight repose, during which the spirits of the dead hovered round, and instigated me to toil and revenge, I prepared for my journey.

I exchanged my land-sledge for one fashioned for the inequalities of the Frozen Ocean; and purchasing a plentiful stock of provisions, I departed from land.

I cannot guess how many days have passed since then; but I have endured misery, which nothing but the eternal sentiment of a just retribution burning within my heart could have enabled me to support. Immense and rugged mountains of ice often barred up my passage, and I often heard the thunder of the ground sea, which threatened my destruction. But again the frost came, and made the paths of the sea secure.

By the quantity of provision which I had consumed, I should guess that I had passed three weeks in this journey; and the continual protraction of hope, returning back upon the heart, often wrung bitter drops of despondency and grief from my eyes. Despair had indeed almost secured her prey, and I should soon have sunk beneath this misery. Once, after the poor animals that conveyed me had with incredible toil gained the summit of a sloping ice-mountain, and one, sinking under his fatigue, died, I viewed the expanse before me with anguish, when suddenly my eye caught a dark speck upon the dusky plain. I strained my sight to discover what it could be, and uttered a wild cry of ecstasy when I distinguished a sledge, and the distorted proportions of a well-known form within. Oh! with what a burning gush did hope revisit my heart! warm tears filled my eyes, which I hastily wiped away, that they might not intercept the view I had of the daemon; but still my sight was dimmed by the burning drops, until, giving way to the emotions that oppressed me, I wept aloud.

But this was not the time for delay: I disencumbered the dogs of their dead companion, gave them a plentiful portion of food;

and, after an hour's rest, which was absolutely necessary, and yet which was bitterly irksome to me, I continued my route. The sledge was still visible; nor did I again lose sight of it, except at the moments when for a short time some ice-rock concealed it with its intervening crags. I indeed perceptibly gained on it; and when, after nearly two days' journey, I beheld my enemy at no more than a mile distant, my heart bounded within me.

But now, when I appeared almost within grasp of my foe, my hopes were suddenly extinguished, and I lost all trace of him more utterly than I had ever done before. A ground sea was heard; the thunder of its progress, as the waters rolled and swelled beneath me, became every moment more ominous and terrific. I pressed on, but in vain. The wind arose; the sea roared; and, as with the mighty shock of an earthquake, it split, and cracked with a tremendous and overwhelming sound. The work was soon finished: in a few minutes a tumultuous sea rolled between me and my enemy, and I was left drifting on a scattered piece of ice, that was continually lessening, and thus preparing for me a hideous death.

In this manner many appalling hours passed; several of my dogs died; and I myself was about to sink under the accumulation of distress when I saw your vessel riding at anchor, and holding forth to me hopes of succour and life. I had no conception that vessels ever came so far north, and was astounded at the sight. I quickly destroyed part of my sledge to construct oars; and by these means was enabled, with infinite fatigue, to move my ice-raft in the direction of your ship. I had determined, if you were going southwards, still to trust myself to the mercy of the seas rather than abandon my purpose. I hoped to induce you to grant me a boat with which I could pursue my enemy. But your direction was northward. You took me on board when my vigour was exhausted, and I should soon have sunk under my multiplied hardships into a death which I still dread – for my task is unfulfilled.

Oh! when will my guiding spirit, in conducting me to the daemon, allow me the rest I so much desire; or must I die, and he yet live? If I do, swear to me, Walton, that he shall not escape; that you will seek him, and satisfy my vengeance in his death.

And do I dare to ask of you to undertake my pilgrimage, to endure the hardships that I have undergone? No; I am not so selfish. Yet, when I am dead, if he should appear; if the ministers of vengeance should conduct him to you, swear that he shall not live – swear that he shall not triumph over my accumulated woes and survive to add to the list of his dark crimes. He is eloquent and persuasive; and once his words had even power over my heart: but trust him not. His soul is as hellish as his form, full of treachery and fiendlike malice. Hear him not; call on the manes[41] of William, Justine, Clerval, Elizabeth, my father, and of the wretched Victor, and thrust your sword into his heart. I will hover near, and direct the steel aright.

WALTON, *in continuation*.

August 26th, 17–.

You have read this strange and terrific story, Margaret; and do you not feel your blood congeal with horror, like that which even now curdles mine? Sometimes, seized with sudden agony, he could not continue his tale; at others, his voice broken, yet piercing, uttered with difficulty the words so replete with anguish. His fine and lovely eyes were now lighted up with indignation, now subdued to downcast sorrow, and quenched in infinite wretchedness. Sometimes he commanded his countenance and tones, and related the most horrible incidents with a tranquil voice, suppressing every mark of agitation; then, like a volcano bursting forth, his face would suddenly change to an expression of the wildest rage, as he shrieked out imprecations on his persecutor.

His tale is connected, and told with an appearance of the simplest truth; yet I own to you that the letters of Felix and Safie, which he showed me, and the apparition of the monster seen from our ship, brought to me a greater conviction of the truth of his narrative than his asseverations, however earnest and connected. Such a monster has, then, real existence! I cannot doubt it; yet I am lost in surprise and admiration. Sometimes I endeavoured to gain from Frankenstein the particulars of his creature's formation: but on this point he was impenetrable.

'Are you mad, my friend?' said he; 'or whither does your senseless curiosity lead you? Would you also create for yourself and the world a demoniacal enemy? Peace, peace! learn my miseries, and do not seek to increase your own.'

Frankenstein discovered that I made notes concerning his history: he asked to see them, and then himself corrected and augmented them in many places; but principally in giving the life and spirit to the conversations he held with his enemy. 'Since you have preserved my narration,' said he, 'I would not that a mutilated one should go down to posterity.'

Thus has a week passed away, while I have listened to the strangest tale that ever imagination formed. My thoughts, and every feeling of my soul, have been drunk up by the interest for my guest, which this tale, and his own elevated and gentle manners, have created. I wish to soothe him; yet can I counsel one so infinitely miserable, so destitute of every hope of consolation, to live? Oh, no! the only joy that he can now know will be when he composes his shattered spirit to peace and death. Yet he enjoys one comfort, the offspring of solitude and delirium: he believes, that when in dreams he holds converse with his friends, and derives from that communion consolation for his miseries, or excitements to his vengeance, that they are not the creations of his fancy, but the beings themselves who visit him from the regions of a remote world. This faith gives a solemnity to his reveries that render them to me almost as imposing and interesting as truth.

Our conversations are not always confined to his own history and misfortunes. On every point of general literature he displays unbounded knowledge, and a quick and piercing apprehension. His eloquence is forcible and touching; nor can I hear him, when he relates a pathetic incident, or endeavours to move the passions of pity or love, without tears. What a glorious creature must he have been in the days of his prosperity, when he is thus noble and godlike in ruin! He seems to feel his own worth, and the greatness of his fall.

'When younger,' said he, 'I believed myself destined for some great enterprise. My feelings are profound; but I possessed a coolness of judgment that fitted me for illustrious achievements.

This sentiment of the worth of my nature supported me, when others would have been oppressed; for I deemed it criminal to throw away in useless grief those talents that might be useful to my fellow-creatures. When I reflected on the work I had completed, no less a one than the creation of a sensitive and rational animal, I could not rank myself with the herd of common projectors. But this thought, which supported me in the commencement of my career, now serves only to plunge me lower in the dust. All my speculations and hopes are as nothing; and, like the archangel who aspired to omnipotence, I am chained in an eternal hell. My imagination was vivid, yet my powers of analysis and application were intense; by the union of these qualities I conceived the idea, and executed the creation of a man. Even now I cannot recollect, without passion, my reveries while the work was incomplete. I trod heaven in my thoughts, now exulting in my powers, now burning with the idea of their effects. From my infancy I was imbued with high hopes and a lofty ambition; but how am I sunk! Oh! my friend, if you had known me as I once was, you would not recognise me in this state of degradation. Despondency rarely visited my heart; a high destiny seemed to bear me on, until I fell, never, never again to rise.'

Must I then lose this admirable being! I have longed for a friend; I have sought one who would sympathise with and love me. Behold, on these desert seas I have found such a one; but, I fear, I have gained him only to know his value, and lose him. I would reconcile him to life, but he repulses the idea.

'I thank you, Walton,' he said, 'for your kind intentions towards so miserable a wretch; but when you speak of new ties, and fresh affections, think you that any can replace those who are gone? Can any man be to me as Clerval was; or any woman another Elizabeth? Even where the affections are not strongly moved by any superior excellence, the companions of our childhood always possess a certain power over our minds, which hardly any later friend can obtain. They know our infantine dispositions, which, however they may be afterwards modified, are never eradicated; and they can judge of our actions with more certain conclusions as to the integrity of our motives. A sister or a brother can never, unless indeed such symptoms have been shown early, suspect the other of fraud or false dealing, when another friend, however strongly he may be attached, may, in spite of himself, be contemplated with suspicion. But I enjoyed friends, dear not only through habit and association, but from their own merits; and wherever I am, the soothing voice of my Elizabeth, and the conversation of Clerval, will be ever whispered in my ear. They are dead; and but one feeling in such a solitude can persuade me to preserve my life. If I were engaged in any high undertaking or design, fraught with extensive utility to my fellow-creatures, then could I live to fulfil it. But such is not my destiny; I must pursue and destroy the being to whom I gave existence; then my lot on earth will be fulfilled, and I may die.'

September 2nd.

MY BELOVED SISTER,

I write to you, encompassed by peril, and ignorant whether I am ever doomed to see again dear England, and the dearer friends that inhabit it. I am surrounded by mountains of ice, which admit of no escape, and threaten every moment to crush my vessel. The brave fellows, whom I have persuaded to be my companions, look towards me for aid; but I have none to bestow. There is something terribly appalling in our situation, yet my courage and hopes do not desert me. Yet it is terrible to reflect that the lives of all these men are endangered through me. If we are lost, my mad schemes are the cause.

And what, Margaret, will be the state of your mind? You will not hear of my destruction, and you will anxiously await my return. Years will pass, and you will have visitings of despair, and yet be tortured by hope. Oh! my beloved sister, the sickening failing of your heart-felt expectations is, in prospect, more terrible to me than my own death. But you have a husband, and lovely children; you may be happy: Heaven bless you, and make you so!

My unfortunate guest regards me with the tenderest compassion. He endeavours to fill me with hope; and talks as if life were a possession which he valued. He reminds me how often the same accidents have happened to other navigators, who have attempted this sea, and in spite of myself, he fills me with cheerful auguries. Even the sailors feel the power of his eloquence; when he speaks, they no longer despair; he rouses their energies, and, while they hear his voice, they believe these vast mountains of ice are molehills, which will vanish before the resolutions of man. These feelings are transitory; each day of expectation delayed fills them with fear, and I almost dread a mutiny caused by this despair.

September 5th.

A scene has just passed of such uncommon interest, that although it is highly probable that these papers may never reach you, yet I cannot forbear recording it.

We are still surrounded by mountains of ice, still in imminent danger of being crushed in their conflict. The cold is excessive, and many of my unfortunate comrades have already found a grave amidst this scene of desolation. Frankenstein has daily declined in health: a feverish fire still glimmers in his eyes; but he is exhausted, and when suddenly roused to any exertion, he speedily sinks again into apparent lifelessness.

I mentioned in my last letter the fears I entertained of a mutiny. This morning, as I sat watching the wan countenance of my friend – his eyes half closed, and his limbs hanging listlessly – I was roused by half a dozen of the sailors, who demanded admission into the cabin. They entered, and their leader addressed me. He told me that he and his companions had been chosen by the other sailors to come in deputation to me, to make me a requisition, which, in justice, I could not refuse. We were immured in ice, and should probably never escape; but they feared that if, as was possible, the ice should dissipate and a free passage be opened, I should be rash enough to continue my voyage, and lead them into fresh dangers, after they might happily have surmounted this. They insisted, therefore, that I should engage with a solemn promise, that if the vessel should be freed I would instantly direct my course southwards.

This speech troubled me. I had not despaired; nor had I yet conceived the idea of returning, if set free. Yet could I, in justice, or even in possibility, refuse this demand? I hesitated before I answered; when Frankenstein, who had at first been silent, and, indeed, appeared hardly to have force enough to attend, now roused himself; his eyes sparkled, and his cheeks flushed with momentary vigour. Turning towards the men, he said –

'What do you mean? What do you demand of your captain? Are you then so easily turned from your design? Did you not call this a glorious expedition? And wherefore was it glorious? Not because the way was smooth and placid as a southern sea, but because it was full of dangers and terror; because, at every new incident, your fortitude was to be called forth, and your courage exhibited; because danger and death surrounded it, and these you were to brave and overcome. For this was it a glorious, for this was it an honourable undertaking. You were hereafter to be hailed as the benefactors of your species; your names adored, as belonging to brave men who encountered death for honour, and the benefit of mankind. And now, behold, with the first imagination of danger, or, if you will, the first mighty and terrific trial of your courage, you shrink away, and are content to be handed down as men who had not strength enough to endure cold and peril; and so, poor souls, they were chilly and returned to their warm firesides. Why, that requires not this preparation; ye need not have come thus far, and dragged your captain to the shame of a defeat, merely to prove yourselves cowards. Oh! be men, or be more than men. Be steady to your purposes, and firm as a rock. This ice is not made of such stuff as your hearts may be; it is mutable, and cannot withstand you, if you say that it shall not. Do not return to your families with the stigma of disgrace marked on your brows. Return as heroes who have fought and conquered, and who know not what it is to turn their backs on the foe.'

He spoke this with a voice so modulated to the different feelings expressed in his speech, with an eye so full of lofty design and heroism, that can you wonder that these men were moved? They looked at one another, and were unable to reply. I spoke; I told them to retire, and consider of what had been said: that I would not lead them farther north if they strenuously desired the contrary; but that I hoped that, with reflection, their courage would return.

They retired, and I turned towards my friend, but he was sunk in languor, and almost deprived of life.

How all this will terminate, I know not; but I had rather die than return shamefully – my purpose unfulfilled. Yet I fear such will be my fate; the men, unsupported by ideas of glory and honour, can never willingly continue to endure their present hardships.

September 7th.

The die is cast; I have consented to return, if we are not destroyed. Thus are my hopes blasted by cowardice and indecision: I come back ignorant and disappointed. It requires more philosophy than I possess, to bear this injustice with patience.

September 12th.

It is past; I am returning to England. I have lost my hopes of utility and glory; – I have lost my friend. But I will endeavour to detail these bitter circumstances to you, my dear sister; and, while I am wafted towards England, and towards you, I will not despond.

September 9th, the ice began to move, and roarings like thunder were heard at a distance, as the islands split and cracked in every direction. We were in the most imminent peril; but, as we could only remain passive, my chief attention was occupied by my unfortunate guest, whose illness increased in such a degree that he was entirely confined to his bed. The ice cracked behind us, and was driven with force towards the north; a breeze sprung from the west, and on the 11th the passage towards the south became perfectly free. When the sailors saw this, and that their return to their native country was apparently assured, a shout of tumultuous joy broke from them, loud and long-continued. Frankenstein, who was dozing, awoke and asked the cause of the tumult. 'They shout,' I said, 'because they will soon return to England.'

'Do you then really return?'

'Alas! yes; I cannot withstand their demands. I cannot lead them unwillingly to danger, and I must return.'

'Do so, if you will; but I will not. You may give up your purpose, but mine is assigned to me by Heaven, and I dare not. I

208

am weak; but surely the spirits who assist my vengeance will endow me with sufficient strength.' Saying this, he endeavoured to spring from the bed, but the exertion was too great for him; he fell back and fainted.

It was long before he was restored; and I often thought that life was entirely extinct. At length he opened his eyes; he breathed with difficulty, and was unable to speak. The surgeon gave him a composing draught, and ordered us to leave him undisturbed. In the mean time he told me, that my friend had certainly not many hours to live.

His sentence was pronounced; and I could only grieve, and be patient. I sat by his bed, watching him; his eyes were closed, and I thought he slept; but presently he called to me in a feeble voice, and bidding me come near, said –

'Alas! the strength I relied on is gone; I feel that I shall soon die, and he, my enemy and persecutor, may still be in being. Think not, Walton, that in the last moments of my existence I feel that burning hatred, and ardent desire of revenge, I once expressed; but I feel myself justified in desiring the death of my adversary. During these last days I have been occupied in examining my past conduct; nor do I find it blameable. In a fit of enthusiastic madness I created a rational creature, and was bound towards him, to assure, as far as was in my power, his happiness and well-being. This was my duty; but there was another still paramount to that. My duties towards the beings of my own species had greater claims to my attention, because they included a greater proportion of happiness or misery. Urged by this view, I refused, and I did right in refusing, to create a companion for the first creature. He showed unparalleled malignity and selfishness, in evil; he destroyed my friends; he devoted to destruction beings who possessed exquisite sensations, happiness, and wisdom; nor do I know where this thirst for vengeance may end. Miserable himself, that he may render no other wretched, he ought to die. The task of his destruction was mine, but I have failed. When actuated by selfish and vicious motives, I asked you to undertake my unfinished work; and I renew this request now, when I am only induced by reason and virtue.

'Yet I cannot ask you to renounce your country and friends, to fulfil this task; and now that you are returning to England, you will have little chance of meeting with him. But the consideration of these points, and the well balancing of what you may esteem your duties, I leave to you; my judgment and ideas are already disturbed by the near approach of death. I dare not ask you to do what I think right, for I may still be misled by passion.

'That he should live to be an instrument of mischief disturbs me; in other respects, this hour, when I momentarily expect my release, is the only happy one which I have enjoyed for several years. The forms of the beloved dead flit before me, and I hasten to their arms. Farewell, Walton! Seek happiness in tranquillity, and avoid ambition, even if it be only the apparently innocent one of distinguishing yourself in science and discoveries. Yet why do I say this? I have myself been blasted in these hopes, yet another may succeed.'

His voice became faint as he spoke; and at length, exhausted by his effort, he sunk into silence. About half an hour afterwards he attempted again to speak, but was unable; he pressed my hand feebly, and his eyes closed forever, while the irradiation of a gentle smile passed away from his lips.

Margaret, what comment can I make on the untimely extinction of this glorious spirit? What can I say, that will enable you to understand the depth of my sorrow? All that I should express would be inadequate and feeble. My tears flow; my mind is overshadowed by a cloud of disappointment. But I journey towards England, and I may there find consolation.

I am interrupted. What do these sounds portend? It is midnight; the breeze blows fairly, and the watch on deck scarcely stir. Again there is a sound as of a human voice; but hoarser; it comes from the cabin where the remains of Frankenstein still lie. I must arise, and examine. Good night, my sister.

Great God! what a scene has just taken place! I am yet dizzy with the remembrance of it. I hardly know whether I shall have the power to detail it; yet the tale which I have recorded would be incomplete without this final and wonderful catastrophe.

I entered the cabin where lay the remains of my ill-fated and admirable friend. Over him hung a form which I cannot find words to describe: – gigantic in stature, yet uncouth and distorted in its proportions. As he hung over the coffin, his face was concealed by long locks of ragged hair; but one vast hand was extended, in colour and apparent texture like that of a mummy. When he heard the sound of my approach, he ceased to utter exclamations of grief and horror, and sprung towards the window. Never did I behold a vision so horrible as his face, of such loathsome, yet appalling hideousness. I shut my eyes, involuntarily, and endeavoured to recollect what were my duties with regard to this destroyer. I called on him to stay.

He paused, looking on me with wonder; and, again turning towards the lifeless form of his creator, he seemed to forget my presence, and every feature and gesture seemed instigated by the wildest rage of some uncontrollable passion.

'That is also my victim!' he exclaimed: 'in his murder my crimes are consummated; the miserable series of my being is wound to its close! Oh, Frankenstein! generous and self-devoted being! what does it avail that I now ask thee to pardon me? I, who irretrievably destroyed thee by destroying all thou lovedst. Alas! he is cold, he cannot answer me.'

His voice seemed suffocated; and my first impulses, which had suggested to me the duty of obeying the dying request of my friend, in destroying his enemy, were now suspended by a mixture of curiosity and compassion. I approached this tremendous being; I dared not again raise my eyes to his face, there was something so scaring and unearthly in his ugliness. I attempted to speak, but the words died away on my lips. The monster continued to utter wild and incoherent self-reproaches. At length I gathered resolution to address him in a pause of the tempest of his passion: 'Your repentance,' I said, 'is now superfluous. If you had listened to the voice of conscience, and heeded the stings of remorse, before you had urged your diabolical vengeance to this extremity, Frankenstein would yet have lived.'

'And do you dream?' said the daemon; 'do you think that I was then dead to agony and remorse? – He,' he continued, pointing to the corpse, 'he suffered not in the consummation of the deed – oh! not the ten-thousandth portion of the anguish that was mine during the lingering detail of its execution. A frightful selfishness hurried me on, while my heart was poisoned with remorse. Think you that the groans of Clerval were music to my ears? My heart was fashioned to be susceptible of love and sympathy; and when wrenched by misery to vice and hatred, it did not endure the violence of the change, without torture such as you cannot even imagine.

'After the murder of Clerval, I returned to Switzerland, heartbroken and overcome. I pitied Frankenstein; my pity amounted to horror: I abhorred myself. But when I discovered that he, the author at once of my existence and of its unspeakable torments, dared to hope for happiness; that while he accumulated wretchedness and despair upon me, he sought his own enjoyment in feelings and passions from the indulgence of which I was forever barred, then impotent envy and bitter indignation filled me with an insatiable thirst for vengeance. I recollected my threat, and resolved that it should be accomplished. I knew that I was preparing for myself a deadly torture; but I was the slave, not the master, of an impulse, which I detested, yet could not disobey. Yet when she died! – nay, then I was not miserable. I had cast off all feeling, subdued all anguish, to riot in the excess of my despair. Evil thenceforth became my good.[42] Urged thus far, I had no choice but to adapt my nature to an element which I had willingly chosen. The completion of my demoniacal design became an insatiable passion. And now it is ended; there is my last victim!'

I was at first touched by the expressions of his misery; yet, when I called to mind what Frankenstein had said of his powers of eloquence and persuasion, and when I again cast my eyes on the lifeless form of my friend, indignation was rekindled within me. 'Wretch!' I said, 'it is well that you come here to whine over the desolation that you have made. You throw a torch into a pile of buildings; and when they are consumed, you sit among the ruins, and lament the fall. Hypocritical fiend! if he whom you mourn still lived, still would he be the object, again would he become the prey, of your accursed vengeance. It is not pity that you feel; you lament only because the victim of your malignity is withdrawn from your power.'

'Oh, it is not thus – not thus,' interrupted the being; 'yet such must be the impression conveyed to you by what appears to be the purport of my actions. Yet I seek not a fellow-feeling in my misery. No sympathy may I ever find. When I first sought it, it was the love of virtue, the feelings of happiness and affection with which my whole being overflowed, that I wished to be participated. But now, that virtue has become to me a shadow, and that happiness and affection are turned into bitter and loathing despair, in what should I seek for sympathy? I am content to suffer alone, while my sufferings shall endure; when I die, I am well satisfied that abhorrence and opprobrium should load my memory. Once my fancy was soothed with dreams of virtue, of fame, and of enjoyment. Once I falsely hoped to meet with beings who, pardoning my outward form, would love me for the excellent qualities which I was capable of unfolding. I was nourished with high thoughts of honour and devotion. But now crime has degraded me beneath the meanest animal. No guilt, no mischief, no malignity, no misery, can be found comparable to mine. When I run over the frightful catalogue of my sins, I cannot believe that I am the same creature whose thoughts were once filled with sublime and transcendent visions of the beauty and the majesty of goodness. But it is even so; the fallen angel becomes a malignant devil. Yet even that enemy of God and man had friends and associates in his desolation; I am alone.

'You, who call Frankenstein your friend, seem to have a knowledge of my crimes and his misfortunes. But, in the detail which he gave you of them, he could not sum up the hours and months of misery which I endured, wasting in impotent passions. For while I destroyed his hopes, I did not satisfy my own desires. They were forever ardent and craving; still I desired love and fellowship, and I was still spurned. Was there no injustice in this? Am I to be thought the only criminal, when all human kind sinned against me? Why do you not hate Felix, who drove his friend from the door with contumely? Why do you not execrate the rustic who sought to destroy the saviour of his child? Nay, these are virtuous and immaculate beings! I, the miserable and the abandoned, am an abortion, to be spurned at, and kicked, and trampled on. Even now my blood boils at the recollection of this injustice.

'But it is true that I am a wretch. I have murdered the lovely and the helpless; I have strangled the innocent as they slept, and grasped to death his throat who never injured me or any other living thing. I have devoted my creator, the select specimen of all that is worthy of love and admiration among men, to misery; I have pursued him even to that irremediable ruin. There he lies, white and cold in death. You hate me; but your abhorrence cannot equal that with which I regard myself. I look on the hands which executed the deed; I think on the heart in which the imagination of it was conceived, and long for the moment when these hands will meet my eyes, when that imagination will haunt my thoughts no more.

'Fear not that I shall be the instrument of future mischief. My work is nearly complete. Neither yours nor any man's death is needed to consummate the series of my being, and accomplish that which must be done; but it requires my own. Do not think that I shall be slow to perform this sacrifice. I shall quit your vessel on the ice-raft which brought me thither, and shall seek the most northern extremity of the globe; I shall collect my funeral pile, and consume to ashes this miserable frame, that its remains may afford no light to any curious and unhallowed wretch, who would create such another as I have been. I shall die. I shall no longer feel the agonies which now consume me, or be the prey of feelings unsatisfied, yet unquenched. He is dead who called me into being; and when I shall be no more, the very remembrance of us both will speedily vanish. I shall no longer see the sun or stars, or feel the winds play on my cheeks. Light, feeling, and sense will pass away; and in this condition must I find my happiness. Some years ago, when the images which this world affords first opened upon me, when I felt the cheering warmth of summer and heard the rustling of the leaves and the warbling of the birds, and these were all to me, I should have wept to die; now it is my only consolation. Polluted by crimes, and torn by the bitterest remorse, where can I find rest but in death?

'Farewell! I leave you, and in you the last of human-kind whom these eyes will ever behold. Farewell, Frankenstein! If thou wert yet alive and yet cherished a desire of revenge against me, it would be better satiated in my life than in my destruction. But it was not so; thou didst seek my extinction, that I might not cause greater wretchedness; and if yet, in some mode unknown to me, thou hadst not ceased to think and feel, thou wouldst not desire against me a vengeance greater than that which I feel. Blasted as thou wert, my agony was still superior to thine; for the bitter sting of remorse will not cease to rankle in my wounds until death shall close them for ever.

'But soon,' he cried, with sad and solemn enthusiasm, 'I shall die, and what I now feel be no longer felt. Soon these burning miseries will be extinct. I shall ascend my funeral pile triumphantly, and exult in the agony of the torturing flames. The light of that conflagration will fade away; my ashes will be swept into the sea by the winds. My spirit will sleep in peace; or if it thinks, it will not surely think thus. Farewell.'

He sprung from the cabin window, as he said this, upon the ice-raft which lay close to the vessel. He was soon borne away by the waves, and lost in darkness and distance.

THE END

APPENDIX A:

SELECT COLLATION OF THE TEXTS OF 1831 AND 1818

━━━━━

Substantial variants between the texts of 1831 and 1818 are provided, together with a selection of significant revisions made by Percy Shelley at MS stage, which Mary Shelley adopted. Page and line numbers refer to passages cited from the present edition, and the relevant extracts, shown in italics, are abbreviated by ellipsis where longer than six words. The 1831 reading is followed by that of 1818, printed in roman type. Material that was new in 1831 is followed by the comment *Not in 1818*.

VOLUME ONE

18.21–32 *This circumstance, added . . . is his story.* He is, indeed, of so amiable a nature, that he will not hunt (a favourite, and almost the only amusement here), because he cannot endure to spill blood. He is, moreover, heroically generous.

19.31–20.5 *or if I . . . to dearer considerations. Not in 1818.*

21.25–22 *But success* shall *. . . my beloved sister! Not in 1818.*

26.4–5 *a new spirit . . . the greatest eagerness* the stranger seemed very eager

27.3–28.1 *frequently conversed with . . . and faulty natures.* asked me many questions concerning my design; and I have related my little history frankly to him. He appeared pleased with the confidence, and suggested several alterations in my plan, which I shall find exceedingly useful. There is no pedantry in his manner; but all he does appears to spring wholly from the interest he instinctively takes in the welfare of those who surround him. He is often overcome by gloom, and then he sits by himself, and tries to overcome all that is sullen or unsocial in his humour. These paroxysms pass from him like a cloud from before the sun, though his dejection never leaves him. I have endeavoured to win his confidence; and I trust that I have succeeded. One day I mentioned to him the desire I had always felt of finding a friend who might sympathise with me, and direct me by his counsel. I said, I did not belong to that class of men who are offended by advice. 'I am self-educated, and perhaps I hardly rely sufficiently upon my own powers. I wish therefore that my companion would be wiser and more experienced than myself, to confirm and support me; nor have I believed it impossible to find a true friend.'

'I agree with you,' replied the stranger, 'in believing that friendship is not only a desirable, but a possible acquisition.

28.18–28 *You would not . . . soul-subduing music.* If you do, you must have certainly lost that simplicity which was once your characteristic charm. Yet, if you will, smile at the warmth of my expressions, while I find every day new causes for repeating them.

29.1–12 *; yet, when I . . . I doubt but*, yet, if you are inclined, listen to my tale. I believe that the strange incidents connected with it will afford a view of nature, which may enlarge your faculties and understanding. You will hear of powers and occurrences, such as you have been accustomed to believe impossible; but I do not doubt

29.35–30.3 *Even now, as . . . wrecked it – thus!* Added 1831.

32.24–38.4 *There was a . . . his soaring ambition.* When my father became a husband and a parent, he found his time so occupied by the duties of his new situation, that he relinquished many of his public employments, and devoted himself to the education of his children. Of these I was the eldest, and the destined successor to all his labours and utility. No creature could have more tender parents than mine. My improvement and health were their constant care, especially as I remained for several years their only child. But before I continue my narrative, I must record an incident which took place when I was four years of age.

My father had a sister, whom he tenderly loved, and who had married early in life an Italian gentleman. Soon after her marriage, she had accompanied her husband into her [*sic*] native country, and for some years my father had very little communication with her. About the time I mentioned she died; and a few months afterwards he received a letter from her husband, acquainting him with his intention of marrying an Italian lady, and requesting my father to take charge of the infant Elizabeth, the only child of his deceased sister. 'It is my wish,' he said, 'that you should consider her as your own daughter, and educate her thus. Her mother's fortune is secured to her, the documents of which I will commit to your keeping. Reflect upon this proposition; and decide whether you would prefer educating your niece yourself to her being brought up by a stepmother.'

My father did not hesitate, and immediately went to Italy, that he might accompany the little Elizabeth to her future home. I have often heard my mother say, that she was at that time the most beautiful child she had ever seen, and shewed signs even then of a gentle and affectionate disposition. These indications, and a desire to bind as closely as possible the ties of domestic love, determined my mother to consider Elizabeth as my future wife; a design which she never found reason to repent.

From this time Elizabeth Lavenza became my playfellow, and, as we grew older, my friend. She was docile and good tempered, yet gay and playful as a summer insect. Although she was lively and animated, her feelings were strong and deep, and her disposition uncommonly affectionate. No one could better enjoy liberty, yet no one could submit with more grace than she did to constraint and caprice. Her imagination was luxuriant, yet her capability of application was great. Her person was the image of her mind; her hazel eyes, although as lively as a bird's, possessed an attractive softness. Her figure was light and airy; and, though capable of enduring great fatigue, she appeared the most fragile creature in the world. While I admired her understanding and fancy, I loved to tend on her, as I should on a favourite animal; and I never saw so much grace both of person and mind united to so little pretension.

Every one adored Elizabeth. If the servants had any request to make, it was always through her intercession. We were strangers to any species of disunion and dispute; for although there was a great dissimilitude in our characters, there was an harmony in that very dissimilitude. I was more calm and philosophical than my companion; yet my temper was not so yielding. My application was of longer endurance; but it was not so severe whilst it endured. I delighted in investigating the facts relative to the actual world; she busied herself in following the aerial creations of the poets. The world was to me a secret, which I desired to discover; to her it was a vacancy, which she sought to people with imaginations of her own. [*Last two sentences written by Percy Shelley.*]

My brothers were considerably younger than myself; but I had a friend in one of my schoolfellows, who compensated for this deficiency. Henry Clerval was the son of a merchant of Geneva, an intimate friend of my father. He was a boy of singular talent and fancy. I remember, when he was nine years old, he wrote a fairy tale, which was the delight and amazement of all his companions. His favourite study consisted in books of chivalry and romance; and when very young, I can remember, that we used to act plays composed by him out of these favourite books, the principal characters of which were Orlando, Robin Hood, Amadis, and St George.

No youth could have passed more happily than mine. My parents were indulgent, and my companions amiable. Our studies were never forced; and by some means we always had an end placed in view, which excited us to ardour in the prosecution of them. It was by this method, and not by emulation, that we were urged to application. Elizabeth was not incited to apply herself to drawing, that her companions might not outstrip her; but through the desire of pleasing her aunt, by the representation of some favourite scene done by her own hand. We learned Latin and English, that we might read the writings in those languages; and so far from study being made odious to us through punishment, we loved application, and our amusements would have been the labours of other children. Perhaps we did not read so many books, or learn languages so quickly, as those who are disciplined according to the ordinary methods; but what we learned was impressed the more deeply on our memories.

In this description of our domestic circle I include Henry Clerval; for he was constantly with us. He went to school with me, and generally passed the afternoon at our house; for being an only child, and destitute of companions at home, his father was well pleased that he should find associates at our house; and we were never completely happy when Clerval was absent.

38.26 ... *to my father.* [*The sentence following this was cancelled in*

1831]: I cannot help remarking here the many opportunities in-structors possess of directing the attention of their pupils to useful knowledge, which they utterly neglect.

38.35–37 *have contented my . . . my former studies.*, with my imagination warmed as it was, should probably have applied myself to the more rational theory of chemistry which has resulted from modern discoveries.

39.8–35 *myself. I have . . . my new preceptors* myself; and although I often wished to communicate these secret stores of knowledge to my father, yet his indefinite censure of my favourite Agrippa always withheld me. I disclosed my discoveries to Elizabeth, there-fore, under a promise of strict secrecy; but she did not interest herself in the subject, and I was left by her to pursue my studies alone.

It may appear very strange, that a disciple of Albertus Magnus should arise in the eighteenth century; but our family was not scientifical, and I had not attended any of the lectures given at the schools of Geneva. My dreams were therefore undisturbed by reality; and

40.8–12 *And thus for . . . of my ideas.* The natural phenomena that take place every day before our eyes did not escape my examinations. Distillation, and wonderful effects of steam, processes of which my favourite authors were ignorant, excited my astonishment; but my utmost wonder was engaged by some experiments on an air pump, which I saw employed by a gentleman whom we were in the habit of visiting.

The ignorance of the early philosophers on these and several other points served to decrease their credit with me: but I could not entirely throw them aside, before some other system should occupy their place in my mind.

40.27–41 *Before this I . . . and terrible destruction.* The catastrophe of this tree excited my extreme astonishment; and I eagerly inquired of my father the nature and origin of thunder and lightning. He replied, 'Electricity;' describing at the same time the various effects of that power. He constructed a small electrical machine, and exhibited a few experiments; he made also a kite, with a wire and string, which drew down that fluid from the clouds.

This last stroke completed the overthrow of Cornelius Agrippa, Albertus Magnus, and Paracelsus, who had so long reigned the lords of my imagination. But by some fatality I did not feel inclined to commence the study of any modern system; and this disinclination was influenced by the following circumstance. My father expressed a wish that I should attend a course of lectures upon natural philosophy, to which I cheerfully consented. Some accident prevented my attending these lectures until the course was nearly finished. The lecture, being therefore one of the last, was entirely incomprehensible to me. The professor discoursed with the greatest fluency of potassium and boron, of sulphates and oxyds, terms to which I could affix no idea; and I became disgusted with the science of natural philosophy, although I still read Pliny and Buffon with delight, authors, in my estimation, of nearly equal interest and utility.

My occupations at this age were principally the mathematics, and most of the branches of study appertaining to that science. I was busily employed in learning languages; Latin was already familiar to me, and I began to read some of the easiest Greek authors without the help of a lexicon. I also perfectly understood English and German. This is the list of my accomplishments at the age of seventeen; and you may conceive that my hours were fully employed in acquiring and maintaining a knowledge of this various literature.

Another task also devolved upon me, when I became the instructor of my brothers. Ernest was six years younger than myself, and was my principal pupil. He had been afflicted with ill health from his infancy, through which Elizabeth and I had been his constant nurses: his disposition was gentle, but he was incapable of any severe application. William, the youngest of our family, was yet an infant, and the most beautiful little fellow in the world; his lively blue eyes, dimpled cheeks, and endearing manners, inspired the tenderest affection.

Such was our domestic circle, from which care and pain seemed for ever banished. My father directed our studies, and my mother partook of our enjoyments. Neither of us possessed the slightest pre-eminence over the other; the voice of command was never heard amongst us; but mutual affection engaged us all to comply with and obey the slightest desire of each other.

46.6 *power* wealth [*MS substitution by Percy Shelley.*]

47.9–26 *Such were the . . . Waldman a visit.* I departed highly pleased with the professor and his lecture, and paid him a visit the same evening.

47.34–48 *He said that . . . without any presumption* [*Written by Percy Shelley.*]

51.3–4 *All the minutiae . . . death to life* [*Written by Percy Shelley.*]

51.6–8 *I became dizzy . . . which it illustrated* [*Written by Percy Shelley.*]

55.5–10 *the fall of . . . away incipient disease* a disease that I regretted the more because I had hitherto enjoyed most excellent health, and had always boasted of the firmness of my nerves. But I believed that exercise and amusement would soon drive away such symptoms

56.13 *beautiful* handsome [*MS substitution by Percy Shelley.*]

63.18–28 *The republican institutions . . . a human being.* [*Written by Percy Shelley.*]

71.25–26 *we must reserve . . . his miserable survivors.'* the survivors are the greatest sufferers, and for them time is the only consolation. Those maxims of the Stoics, that death was no evil, and that the mind of man ought to be superior to despair on the eternal absence of a beloved object, ought not to be urged. Even Cato wept over the dead body of his brother.'

77.17–21 *altered her since . . . sensibility and intellect.* made great alterations in her form since I had last beheld her. Six years before she had been a pretty, good-humoured girl, whom everyone loved and caressed. She was now a woman in stature and expression of countenance, which was uncommonly lovely. An open and capacious forehead gave indications of a good understanding, joined to great frankness of disposition. Her eyes were hazel, and expressive of mildness, now through recent affliction allied to sadness. Her hair was of a rich dark auburn, her complexion fair, and her figure slight and graceful.

83.18 *goodness* benevolence

84.32–37 *Justine shook her . . . will of heaven!'* 'Dear sweet Elizabeth, do not weep. You ought to raise me with thoughts of a better life, and elevate from the petty cares of this world of injustice and strife. Do not you, excellent friend, drive me to despair.'

'I will try to comfort you; but this, I fear, is an evil too deep and poignant to admit of consolation, for there is no hope. Yet heaven bless thee, my dearest Justine, with resignation, and a confidence elevated beyond this world. Oh! how I hate its shews and mockeries! when one creature is murdered, another is immediately deprived of life in a slow torturing manner; then the executioners, their hands yet reeking with the blood of innocence, believe that they have done a great deed. They call this *retribution*. Hateful name! When that word is pronounced, I know greater and more horrid punishments are going to be inflicted than the gloomiest tyrant has ever invented to satiate his utmost revenge. Yet this is not consolation for you, my Justine, unless indeed that you may glory in escaping so miserable a den. Alas! I would I were in peace with my aunt and my lovely William, escaped from a world which is hateful to me, and the visages of men which I abhor.'

Justine smiled languidly. 'This, dear lady, is despair, and not resignation. I must not learn the lesson that you would teach me. Talk of something else, something that will bring peace, and not increase of misery.'

VOLUME TWO

92.8–21 *A tingling lost-lost . . . space of time* During this journey, I sometimes joined Elizabeth, and exerted myself to point out to her the various beauties of the scene. I often suffered my mule to lag behind, and indulged in the misery of reflection. At other times I spurred in the animal before my companions, that I might equally forget them, the world, and, more than all, myself. When at a distance, I alighted, and threw myself on the grass, weighed down by horror and despair. At eight in the evening I arrived in Chamounix. My father and Elizabeth were very much fatigued; Ernest, who accompanied us, was delighted, and in high spirits: the only circumstance that detracted from his pleasure was the south wind, and the rain it seemed to promise for the next day.

We retired to our apartments, but not to sleep; at least I did not.

93.1–12 *I spent the . . . in their hands.* The next day, contrary to the prognostications of our guides, was fine, although clouded. We visited the source of the Arveiron, and rode about the valley until evening.

93.18–27 *I retired to . . . rain was pouring* I returned in the evening, fatigued, but less unhappy, and conversed with my family with more cheerfulness than had been my custom for some time. My father was pleased, and Elizabeth overjoyed. 'My dear cousin,' she said, 'you see what happiness you diffuse when you are happy; do not relapse again!'

The following morning the rain poured down.

VOLUME THREE

149.3–11 *again quitted my . . . tearful, silent farewell.* departed, to pass two years of exile. Elizabeth approved of the reasons of my departure, and only regretted that she had not the same opportunities of enlarging her experience, and cultivating her understanding. She wept, however, as she bade me farewell, and entreated me to return happy and tranquil. 'We all,' she said, 'depend upon you; and if you are miserable, what must be our feelings?'

153.25–31 *He was also . . . of his plan.* [*Not in 1818.*]

176.34–177.11 *Yet one duty . . . the Irish shores.* I remember, as I quitted the prison, I heard one of the men say, 'He may be innocent of the murder, but he has certainly a bad conscience.' These words struck me. A bad conscience! yes, surely I had one. William, Justine, and Clerval, had died through my infernal machinations; 'And whose death,' cried I, 'is to finish the tragedy? Ah! my father, do not remain in this wretched country; take me where I may forget myself, my existence, and all the world.'

My father easily acceded to my desire; and, after having taken leave of Mr Kirwin, we hastened to Dublin. I felt as if I was relieved from a heavy weight, when the packet sailed with a fair wind from Ireland, and I had quitted for ever the country which had been to me the scene of so much misery.

185.29–34 *Through my father's . . . which it stood.* A house was purchased for us near Cologny, by which we should enjoy the pleasures of the country, and yet be so near Geneva as to see my father every day; who would still reside within the walls, for the benefit of Ernest, that he might follow his studies at the schools.

205.24–27 *Yet it is . . . the cause. And* We may survive; and if we do not, I will repeat the lessons of my Seneca, and die with a good heart.

209.25–26 *the beings of my own species* my fellow-creatures.

213.13 *crime* vice.

213.14 *guilt* crime.

213.16 *sins* deeds.

APPENDIX B:

'A FRAGMENT'*

BY LORD BYRON

―――――

June 17, 1816.

In the year 17—, having for some time determined on a journey through countries not hitherto much frequented by travellers, I set out, accompanied by a friend, whom I shall designate by the name of Augustus Darvell. He was a few years my elder, and a man of considerable fortune and ancient family – advantages which an extensive capacity prevented him alike from undervaluing or overrating. Some peculiar circumstances in his private history had rendered him to me an object of attention, of interest, and even of regard, which neither the reserve of his manners, nor occasional indications of an inquietude at times nearly approaching to alienation of mind, could extinguish.

I was yet young in life, which I had begun early; but my intimacy with him was of a recent date: we had been educated at the same schools and university; but his progress through these had preceded mine, and he had been deeply initiated into what is called the world, while I was yet in my noviciate. While thus engaged, I had heard much both of his past and present life; and although in these accounts there were many and irreconcileable contradictions, I could still gather from the whole that he was a being of no common order, and one who, whatever pains he might take to avoid remark, would still be remarkable. I had cultivated his acquaintance subsequently, and endeavoured to obtain his friendship, but this last appeared to be unattainable; whatever affections he might have possessed seemed now, some to

---

* The text follows that printed at the end of the first edition of *Mazeppa, a Poem* (John Murray, London, 1819), pp. 59–69.

have been extinguished, and others to be concentred: that his feelings were acute, I had sufficient opportunities of observing; for, although he could control, he could not altogether disguise them: still he had a power of giving to one passion the appearance of another in such a manner that it was difficult to define the nature of what was working within him; and the expression of his features would vary so rapidly, though slightly, that it was useless to trace them to their sources. It was evident that he was a prey to some cureless disquiet; but whether it arose from ambition, love, remorse, grief, from one or all of these, or merely from a morbid temperament akin to disease, I could not discover: there were circumstances alleged, which might have justified the application to each of these causes; but, as I have before said, these were so contradictory and contradicted, that none could be fixed upon with accuracy. Where there is mystery, it is generally supposed that there must also be evil: I know not how this may be, but in him there certainly was the one, though I could not ascertain the extent of the other – and felt loth, as far as regarded himself, to believe in its existence. My advances were received with sufficient coldness; but I was young, and not easily discouraged, and at length succeeded in obtaining, to a certain degree, that common-place intercourse and moderate confidence of common and every day concerns, created and cemented by similarity of pursuit and frequency of meeting, which is called intimacy, or friendship, according to the ideas of him who uses those words to express them.

Darvell had already travelled extensively; and to him I had applied for information with regard to the conduct of my intended journey. It was my secret wish that he might be prevailed on to accompany me: it was also a probable hope, founded upon the shadowy restlessness which I had observed in him, and to which the animation which he appeared to feel on such subjects, and his apparent indifference to all by which he was more immediately surrounded, gave fresh strength. This wish I first hinted, and then expressed: his answer, though I had partly expected it, gave me all the pleasure of surprise – he consented; and, after the requisite arrangements, we commenced our voyages. After journeying through various countries of the south of Europe, our attention was turned towards the East, according to our original destination; and it was in my progress through those regions that the incident occurred upon which will turn what I may have to relate.

The constitution of Darvell, which must from his appearance have been in early life more than usually robust, had been for some time gradually giving way, without the intervention of any apparent disease: he had neither cough nor hectic,[1] yet he became daily more enfeebled: his habits were temperate, and he neither declined nor complained of fatigue, yet he was evidently wasting away: he became more and more silent and sleepless, and at length so seriously altered, that my alarm grew proportionate to what I conceived to be his danger.

We had determined, on our arrival at Smyrna, on an excursion to the ruins of Ephesus and Sardis, from which I endeavoured to dissuade him in his present state of indisposition – but in vain: there appeared to be an oppression on his mind, and a solemnity in his manner, which ill corresponded with his eagerness to proceed on what I regarded as a mere party of pleasure, little suited to a valetudinarian; but I opposed him no longer – and in a few days we set off together, accompanied only by a *serrugee* and a single *janizary*.[2]

We had passed halfway towards the remains of Ephesus, leaving behind us the more fertile environs of Smyrna, and were entering upon that wild and tenantless track through marshes and defiles which lead to the few huts yet lingering over the broken columns of Diana – the roofless walls of expelled Christianity, and the still more recent but complete desolation of abandoned mosques – when the sudden and rapid illness of my companion obliged us to halt at a Turkish cemetery, the turbaned tombstones of which were the sole indication that human life had ever been a sojourner in this wilderness. The only *caravansera*[3] we had seen was left some hours behind us, not a vestige of a town or even cottage was within sight or hope, and this 'city of the dead' appeared to be the sole refuge for my unfortunate friend, who seemed on the verge of becoming the last of its inhabitants.

In this situation, I looked round for a place where he might most conveniently repose: – contrary to the usual aspect of

Mohometan burial-grounds, the cypresses were in this few in number, and these thinly scattered over its extent: the tombstones were mostly fallen, and worn with age: – upon one of the most considerable of these, and beneath one of the most spreading trees, Darvell supported himself, in a half-reclining posture, with great difficulty. He asked for water. I had some doubts of our being able to find any, and prepared to go in search of it with hesitating despondency – but he desired me to remain; and turning to Suleiman, our *janizary*, who stood by us smoking with great tranquillity, he said, 'Suleiman, *verbana su*,' (i.e. bring some water,) and went on describing the spot where it was to be found with great minuteness, at a small well for camels, a few hundred yards to the right: the *janizary* obeyed. I said to Darvell, 'How did you know this?' – He replied, 'From our situation; you must perceive that this place was once inhabited, and could not have been so without springs: I have also been here before.'

'You have been here before! – How came you never to mention this to me? and what could you be doing in a place where no one would remain a moment longer than they could help it?'

To this question I received no answer. In the mean time Suleiman returned with the water, leaving the *serrugee* and the horses at the fountain. The quenching of his thirst had the appearance of reviving him for a moment; and I conceived hopes of his being able to proceed, or at least to return, and I urged the attempt. He was silent – and appeared to be collecting his spirits for an effort to speak. He began.

'This is the end of my journey, and of my life – I came here to die: but I have a request to make, a command – for such my last words be – You will observe it?'

'Most certainly; but have better hopes.'

'I have no hopes, nor wishes, but this – conceal my death from every human being.'

'I hope there will be no occasion; that you will recover, and –'

'Peace! – it must be so: promise this.'

'I do.'

'Swear it, by all that' – He here dictated an oath of great solemnity.

'There is no occasion for this – I will observe your request; and to doubt me is –'

'It cannot be helped, – you must swear.'

I took the oath: it appeared to relieve him. He removed a seal ring from his finger, on which were some Arabic characters, and presented it to me. He proceeded –

'On the ninth day of the month, at noon precisely (what month you please, but this must be the day), you must fling this ring into the salt springs which run into the Bay of Eleusis: the day after, at the same hour, you must repair to the ruins of the temple of Ceres, and wait one hour.'

'Why?'

'You will see.'

'The ninth day of the month, you say?'

'The ninth.'

As I observed that the present was the ninth day of the month, his countenance changed, and he paused. As he sate, evidently becoming more feeble, a stork, with a snake in her beak, perched upon a tombstone near us; and, without devouring her prey, appeared to be stedfastly regarding us. I know not what impelled me to drive it away, but the attempt was useless; she made a few circles in the air, and returned exactly to the same spot. Darvell pointed to it, and smiled: he spoke – I know not whether to himself or to me – but the words were only, ' 'Tis well!'

'What is well? what do you mean?'

'No matter: you must bury me here this evening, and exactly where that bird is now perched. You know the rest of my injunctions.'

He then proceeded to give me several directions as to the manner in which his death might be best concealed. After these were finished, he exclaimed, 'You perceive that bird?'

'Certainly.'

'And the serpent writhing in her beak?'

'Doubtless: there is nothing uncommon in it; it is her natural prey. But it is odd that she does not devour it.'

He smiled in a ghastly manner, and said, faintly, 'It is not yet time!' As he spoke, the stork flew away. My eyes followed it for a moment, it could hardly be longer than ten might be counted. I felt Darvell's weight, as it were, increase upon my shoulder, and, turning to look upon his face, perceived that he was dead!

I was shocked with the sudden certainty which could not be mistaken – his countenance in a few minutes became nearly black. I should have attributed so rapid a change to poison, had I not been aware that he had no opportunity of receiving it unperceived. The day was declining, the body was rapidly altering, and nothing remained but to fulfil his request. With the aid of Suleiman's *ataghan*[4] and my own sabre, we scooped a shallow grave upon the spot which Darvell had indicated: the earth easily gave way, having already received some Mahometan tenant. We dug as deeply as the time permitted us, and throwing the dry earth upon all that remained of the singular being so lately departed, we cut a few sods of greener turf from the less withered soil around us, and laid them upon his sepulchre.

Between astonishment and grief, I was tearless.

THE END

APPENDIX C

'THE VAMPYRE: A TALE'

BY DR JOHN WILLIAM POLIDORI

———

John William Polidori was born on 7 September 1795, son of Gaetano Polidori, who had left his native Italy to settle in London after serving as secretary to the poet and dramatist Vittorio Alfieri. Polidori *père* married an English woman, Miss Pierce, and, after being brought up by them in the expatriate surroundings of Soho, young Polidori was sent to Ampleforth, a Roman Catholic college in Yorkshire. From there he attended Edinburgh University, leaving with a doctoral degree in medicine in 1815 at the unprecedented age of nineteen. (The comparison with the precocious Frankenstein is here striking).

Early in 1816 Lord Byron was laying plans for his final departure from England for the Continent and sought a travelling companion. Sir Henry Halford recommended the young doctor. Initially impressed by Polidori's learning both in sciences and the humanities, and pleased with his literary aspirations, he engaged him as his personal physician and travelling companion. They travelled together on the Continent for five months before Byron, unable any longer to endure the squabbles which his vain and jealous companion regularly initiated, dismissed him. Byron later judged Polidori to be 'not a bad fellow, but young and hot-headed, and more likely to incur diseases than to cure them'. The young doctor continued travelling on alone after his quarrel with Byron, eventually visiting relations in Italy before returning to England. He began praticising medicine in Norwich, where it is said that the fifteen-year-old Harriet Martineau became infatuated with him. Unable to settle into his medical career, he began studying for the Bar, which in turn he also abandoned.

Polidori died in August 1821 under unhappy circumstances, whichever version of events one accepts. One account has him committing suicide with prussic acid because of massive gambling debts. The other says he died after an illness caused by internal head injuries sustained in a carriage accident. The coroner's jury who deliberated on the untimely death of the 26-year-old literary doctor was strangely content to pronounce that he had 'died by the visitation of God'. His sister Frances Polidori married Gabriele Rossetti and was the mother of poet Christina, the poet and painter Dante Gabriel, and William Michael Rossetti, who produced an edition of Polidori's 1816 Journal in 1911. (See *Further Reading* for publication details.)

Polidori's *The Vampyre: a Tale* was first published in the *New Monthly Magazine* on 1 April 1819, and the text printed here reproduces this. It seems that Polidori gave an ambiguous account of the story's origin, such that the journal's publisher Henry Colburn felt able to publish it as 'A Tale by Lord Byron', so as to capitalize on the fame of the poet's name. Byron's friend Hobhouse stepped in and insisted that Polidori offer a public explanation of the novella's genesis. Accordingly, Polidori wrote to the editor of the *New Monthly* a letter which appeared on 5 May 1819 in *The Courier*:

Sir,

As the person referred to in the letter from Geneva prefixed to the Tale of 'The Vampyre', in your last number, I beg leave to state, that your correspondent has been mistaken in attributing that tale, in its present form, to Lord Byron. The fact is, that though the ground-work is certainly Lord Byron's, its development is mine, produced at the request of a lady, who denied the possibility of any thing being drawn from the materials which Lord Byron had said he intended to have employed in the formation of his Ghost Story.

I am, etc
J. W. Polidori

Despite this explanation, *The Vampyre* continued to be attributed to Byron for many years, a fact which gave Polidori's story great celebrity, especially on the Continent, where popular melodramas and operas were based on it. The novella also had a direct influence on the other two foremost nineteenth-century vampire stories, Sheridan Le Fanu's *Carmilla* (1872) and Bram Stoker's *Dracula* (1897).

If Byron in his *Fragment* had thought of himself as a model for the aristocratic Darvell, Polidori almost certainly drew on Byron's character and his own relationship to the poet for the 'development' of *The Vampyre*. Lord Byron is the model for Lord Ruthven, named after Ruthven Glenarvon, haughty and cynical hero of Lady Caroline Lamb's romantic *Glenarvon* (1816). This was a vengeful *roman à clef* written after the poet had grown bored with her obsessive pursuit of him. Polidori's Lady Mercer appears to be based on Lady Caroline. Some features of the Byron–Polidori relationship find several echoes in that of Ruthven and Aubrey. Like Polidori, Aubrey is a young, talented gentleman, full of admiration for his aristocratic and wordly mentor (Ruthven/Byron), who leaves a sister in England for the Continental tour and becomes disgusted when the older man abuses the honour of women. Polidori was warned by his parents about linking himself with someone of Byron's reputation, as Aubrey's guardians warn him of Ruthven's. Like Polidori too, Aubrey is an amateur antiquarian and artist.

Apart from *The Vampyre*, Polidori produced two collections of mediocre verse, one of which contained a drama, *Ximenes*, some essays, and a novel whose sub-title seems influenced by that of *Frankenstein*: *Ernestus Berchtold, or, The modern Oedipus* (1819). Polidori tells us in the Introduction that this was the story 'began at Coligny [*sic*], when *Frankenstein* was planned, and when a noble author having determined to descend from his lofty range, gave up a few hours to a tale of terror, and wrote the fragment published at the end of *Mazeppa*'. *Ernestus Berchtold* contains no trace of the 'skull-headed lady' that Mary Shelley claims was the central idea for Polidori's ghost story attempt in 1816.

'THE VAMPYRE: A TALE'

It happened that in the midst of the dissipations attendant upon a London winter, there appeared at the various parties of the leaders of the *ton*[1] a nobleman, more remarkable for his singularities, than his rank. He gazed upon the mirth around him, as if he could not participate therein. Apparently, the light laughter of the fair only attracted his attention, that he might by a look quell it, and throw fear into those breasts where thoughtlessness reigned. Those who felt this sensation of awe, could not explain whence it arose: some attributed it to the dead grey eye, which, fixing upon the object's face, did not seem to penetrate, and at one glance to pierce through to the inward workings of the heart;

but fell upon the cheek with a leaden ray that weighed upon the skin it could not pass. His peculiarities caused him to be invited to every house; all wished to see him, and those who had been accustomed to violent excitement, and now felt the weight of *ennui*, were pleased at having something in their presence capable of engaging their attention. In spite of the deadly hue of his face, which never gained a warmer tint, either from the blush of modesty, or from the strong emotion of passion, though its form and outline were beautiful, many of the female hunters after notoriety attempted to win his attentions, and gain, at least, some marks of what they might term affection; Lady Mercer, who had been the mockery of every monster shewn in drawing-rooms[2] since her marriage, threw herself in his way, and did all but put on the dress of a mountebank,[3] to attract his notice – though in vain – when she stood before him, though his eyes were apparently fixed upon hers, still it seemed as if they were un-perceived – even her unappalled impudence was baffled, and she left the field. But though the common adultress could not influ-ence even the guidance of his eyes, it was not that the female sex was indifferent to him: yet such was the apparent caution with which he spoke to the virtuous wife and innocent daughter, that few knew he ever addressed himself to females. He had, however, the reputation of a winning tongue; and whether it was that it even overcame the dread of his singular character, or that they were moved by his apparent hatred of vice, he was as often among those females who form the boast of their sex from their domestic virtues, as among those who sully it by their vices.

About the same time, there came to London a young gentleman of the name of Aubrey: he was an orphan left with an only sister in the possession of great wealth, by parents who died while he was yet in childhood. Left also to himself by guardians, who thought it their duty merely to take care of his fortune, while they relinquished the more important charge of his mind to the care of mercenary subalterns, he cultivated more his imagination than his judgment. He had, hence, that high romantic feeling of honour and candour, which daily ruins so many milliners' ap-prentices. He believed all to sympathise with virtue, and thought that vice was thrown in by Providence merely for the picturesque effect of the scene, as we see in romances; he thought that the misery of a cottage merely consisted in the vesting of clothes, which were as warm, but which were better adapted to the painter's eye by their irregular folds and various coloured patches. He thought, in fine, that the dreams of poets were the realities of life. He was handsome, frank, and rich: for these reasons, upon his entering into the gay circles, many mothers surrounded him, striving which should describe with least truth their languishing or romping favourites: the daughters at the same time, by their brightening countenances when he approached, and by their sparkling eyes, when he opened his lips, soon led him into false notions of his talents and his merit. Attached as he was to the romance of his solitary hours, he was startled at finding, that, except in the tallow and wax candles, that flickered not from the presence of a ghost, but from want of snuffing, there was no foundation in real life for any of that congeries of pleasing pictures and descriptions contained in those volumes, from which he had formed his study. Finding, however, some compensation in his gratified vanity, he was about to relinquish his dreams, when the extraordinary being we have above described, crossed him in his career.

He watched him; and the very impossibility of forming an idea of the character of a man entirely absorbed in himself, who gave few other signs of his observation of external objects, than the tacit assent to their existence, implied by the avoidance of their contact; allowing his imagination to picture every thing that flattered its propensity to extravagant ideas, he soon formed this object into the hero of a romance, and determined to observe the offspring of his fancy, rather than the person before him. He became acquainted with him, paid him attentions, and so far advanced upon his notice, that his presence was always recognised. He gradually learnt that Lord Ruthven's affairs were embarrassed, and soon found, from the notes of preparation in — Street, that he was about to travel. Desirous of gaining some information respecting this singular character, who, till now, had only whetted his curiosity, he hinted to his guardians, that it was time for him to perform the tour, which for many generations has been thought necessary to enable the young to take some rapid steps in the career of vice towards putting themselves upon an equality with the aged, and not allowing them to appear as if fallen from the skies, whenever scandalous intrigues are mentioned as the subjects of pleasantry or of praise, according to the degree of skill shewn in carrying them on. They consented: and Aubrey immediately mentioning his intentions to Lord Ruthven, was surprised to receive from him a proposal to join him. Flattered by such a mark of esteem from him, who, apparently, had nothing in common with other men, he gladly accepted it, and in a few days they had passed the circling waters.

Hitherto, Aubrey had had no opportunity of studying Lord Ruthven's character, and now he found, that, though many more of his actions were exposed to his view, the results offered different conclusions from the apparent motives to his conduct. His companion was profuse in his liberality – the idle, the vagabond, and the beggar, received from his hand more than enough to relieve their immediate wants. But Aubrey could not avoid remarking, that it was not upon the virtuous, reduced to indigence by the misfortunes attendant even upon virtue, that he bestowed his alms; these were sent from the door with hardly suppressed sneers, but when the profligate came to ask something, not to relieve his wants, but to allow him to wallow in his lust, or to sink him still deeper in his iniquity, he was sent away with rich charity. This was, however, attributed by him to the greater importunity of the vicious, which generally prevails over the retiring bashfulness of the virtuous indigent. There was one circumstance about the charity of his Lordship, which was still more impressed upon his mind: all those upon whom it was bestowed, inevitably found that there was a curse upon it, for they were all either led to the scaffold, or sunk to the lowest and the most abject misery. At Brussels and other towns through which they passed, Aubrey was surprised at the apparent eagerness with which his companion sought for the centres of all fashionable vice; there he entered into all the spirit of the faro[4] table: he betted, and always gambled with success, except where the known sharper was his antagonist, and then he lost even more than he gained; but it was always with the same unchanging face, with which he generally watched the society around: it was not, however, so when he encountered

the rash youthful novice, or the luckless father of a numerous
family; then his very wish seemed fortune's law – this apparent
abstractedness of mind was laid aside, and his eyes sparkled with
more fire than that of the cat whilst dallying with the half dead
mouse. In every town, he left the formerly affluent youth, torn
from the circle he adorned, cursing, in the solitude of a dungeon,
the fate that had drawn him within the reach of this fiend; whilst
many a father sat frantic, amidst the speaking looks of mute
hungry children, without a single farthing of his late immense
wealth, wherewith to buy even sufficient to satisfy their present
craving. Yet he took no money from the gambling table; but
immediately lost, to the ruiner of many, the last gilder he had just
snatched from the conclusive grasp of the innocent: this might
but be the result of a certain degree of knowledge, which was not,
however, capable of combating the cunning of the more experienced. Aubrey often wished to represent this to his friend, and
beg him to resign that charity and pleasure which proved the
ruin of all, and did not tend to his own profit; – but he delayed it
– for each day he hoped his friend would give him some opportunity of speaking frankly and openly to him; however, this
never occurred. Lord Ruthven in his carriage, and amidst the
various wild and rich scenes of nature, was always the same: his
eye spoke less than his lip; and though Aubrey was near the
object of his curiosity, he obtained no greater gratification from it
than the constant excitement of vainly wishing to break that
mystery, which to his exalted imagination began to assume the
appearance of something supernatural.

They soon arrived at Rome, and Aubrey for a time lost sight of
his companion; he left him in daily attendance upon the morning
circle of an Italian countess, whilst he went in search of the
memorials of another almost deserted city. Whilst he was thus
engaged, letters arrived from England which he opened with
eager impatience; the first was from his sister, breathing nothing
but affection: the others were from his guardians, the latter astonished him; if it had before entered into his imagination that there
was an evil power resident in his companion, these seemed to give
him almost sufficient reason for the belief. His guardians insisted
upon his immediately leaving his friend, and urged, that his

character was dreadfully vicious, for that the possession of irresistible powers of seduction, rendered his licentious habits more dangerous to society. It had been discovered, that his contempt for the adultress had not originated in hatred of her character; but that he had required, to enhance his gratification, that his victim, the partner of his guilt, should be hurled from the pinnacle of unsullied virtue, down to the lowest abyss of infamy and degradation: in fine, that all those females whom he had sought, apparently on account of their virtue, had, since his departure, thrown even the mask aside, and had not scrupled to expose the whole deformity of their vices to the public gaze.

Aubrey determined upon leaving one, whose character had not yet shown a single bright point on which to rest the eye. He resolved to invent some plausible pretext for abandoning him altogether, purposing, in the mean while, to watch him more closely, and to let no slight circumstance pass by unnoticed. He entered into the same circle, and soon perceived, that his Lordship was endeavouring to work upon the inexperience of the daughter of the lady whose house he chiefly frequented. In Italy, it is seldom that an unmarried female is met with in society; he was therefore obliged to carry on his plans in secret; but Aubrey's eye followed him in all his windings, and soon discovered that an assignation had been appointed, which would most likely end in the ruin of an innocent, though thoughtless girl. Losing no time, he entered the apartment of Lord Ruthven, and abruptly asked him his intentions with respect to the lady, informing him at the same time that he was aware of his being about to meet her that very night. Lord Ruthven answered, that his intentions were such as he supposed all would have upon such an occasion; and upon being pressed whether he intended to marry her, merely laughed. Aubrey retired; and, immediately writing a note, to say that from that moment he must decline accompanying his Lordship in the remainder of their proposed tour, he ordered his servants to seek other apartments, and calling upon the mother of the lady, informed her of all he knew, not only with regard to her daughter, but also concerning the character of his Lordship. The assignation was prevented. Lord Ruthven next day merely sent his servant to notify his complete assent to a separation; but did not hint any suspicion of his plans having been foiled by Aubrey's interposition.

Having left Rome, Aubrey directed his steps towards Greece, and crossing the Peninsula, soon found himself at Athens. He then fixed his residence in the house of a Greek; and soon occupied himself in tracing the faded records of ancient glory upon monuments that apparently, ashamed of chronicling the deeds of freemen only before slaves, had hidden themselves beneath the sheltering soil or many coloured lichen. Under the same roof as himself, existed a being, so beautiful and delicate, that she might have formed the model for a painter wishing to pourtray on canvass the promised hope of the faithful in Mahomet's paradise, save that her eyes spoke too much mind for any one to think she could belong to those who had no souls. As she danced upon the plain, or tripped along the mountain's side, one would have thought the gazelle a poor type of her beauties for who would have exchanged her eye, apparently the eye of animated nature, for that sleepy luxurious look of the animal suited but to the taste of an epicure. The light step of Ianthe often accompanied Aubrey in his search after antiquities, and often would the unconscious girl, engaged in the pursuit of a Kashmere butterfly, show the whole beauty of her form, floating as it were upon the wind, to the eager gaze of him, who forgot the letters he had just decyphered upon an almost effaced tablet, in the contemplation of her sylph-like figure. Often would her tresses falling, as she flitted around, exhibit in the sun's ray such delicately brilliant and swiftly fading hues, as might well excuse the forgetfulness of the antiquary, who let escape from his mind the very object he had before thought of vital importance to the proper interpretation of a passage in Pausanias. But why attempt to describe charms which all feel, but none can appreciate? – It was innocence, youth, and beauty, unaffected by crowded drawing-rooms and stifling balls. Whilst he drew those remains of which he wished to preserve a memorial for his future hours, she would stand by, and watch the magic effects of his pencil, in tracing the scenes of her native place; she would then describe to him the circling dance upon the open plain, would paint to him in all the glowing colours of youthful memory, the marriage pomp she remembered viewing in her infancy; and then, turning to subjects that had evidently made a greater impression upon her mind, would tell him all the supernatural tales of her nurse. Her earnestness and apparent belief of what she narrated, excited the interest even of Aubrey; and often, as she told him the tale of the living vampyre, who had passed years amidst his friends, and dearest ties, forced every year, by feeding upon the life of a lovely female to prolong his existence for the ensuing months, his blood would run cold, whilst he attempted to laugh her out of such idle and horrible fantasies; but Ianthe cited to him the names of old men, who had at last detected one living among themselves, after several of their near relatives and children had been found marked with the stamp of the fiend's appetite: and when she found him so incredulous, she begged of him to believe her, for it had been remarked, that those who had dared to question their existence, always had some proof given, which obliged them, with grief and heartbreaking, to confess it was true. She detailed to him the traditional appearance of these monsters, and his horror was increased, by hearing a pretty accurate description of Lord Ruthven; he, however, still persisted in persuading her, that there could be no truth in her fears, though at the same time he wondered at the many coincidences which had all tended to excite a belief in the supernatural power of Lord Ruthven.

Aubrey began to attach himself more and more to Ianthe; her innocence, so contrasted with all the affected virtues of the women among whom he had sought for his vision of romance, won his heart; and while he ridiculed the idea of a young man of English habits, marrying an uneducated Greek girl, still he found himself more and more attached to the almost fairy form before him. He would tear himself at times from her, and, forming a plan for some antiquarian research, he would depart, determined not to return until his object was attained; but he always found it impossible to fix his attention upon the ruins around him, whilst in his mind he retained an image that seemed alone the rightful possessor of his thoughts. Ianthe was unconscious of his love, and was ever the same frank infantile being he had first known. She always seemed to part from him with reluctance; but it was because she had no longer any one with whom she could visit her favourite haunts, while her guardian was occupied in sketching or uncovering some fragment which had yet escaped the destructive hand of time. She had appealed to her parents on the subject of Vampyres, and they both, with several present, affirmed their existence, pale with horror at the very name. Soon after, Aubrey determined to proceed upon one of his excursions, which was to detain him for a few hours; when they heard the name of the place, they all at once begged of him not to return at night, as he must necessarily pass through a wood, where no Greek would ever remain after the day had closed, upon any consideration. They described it as the resort of the vampyres in their nocturnal orgies, and denounced the most heavy evils as impending upon him who dared to cross their path. Aubrey made light of their representations, and tried to laugh them out of the idea; but when he saw them shudder at his daring thus to mock a superior, infernal power, the very name of which apparently made their blood freeze, he was silent.

Next morning Aubrey set off upon his excursion unattended; he was surprised to observe the melancholy face of his host, and was concerned to find that his words, mocking the belief of those horrible fiends, had inspired them with such terror. – When he was about to depart, Ianthe came to the side of his horse, and earnestly begged of him to return, ere night allowed the power of these beings to be put in action – he promised. He was, however, so occupied in his research, that he did not perceive that daylight would soon end, and that in the horizon there was one of those specks which in the warmer climates, so rapidly gather into a tremendous mass, and pour all their rage upon the devoted country. – He at last, however, mounted his horse, determined to make up by speed for his delay: but it was too late. Twilight, in these southern climates, is almost unknown; immediately the sun sets, night begins: and ere he had advanced far, the power of the storm was above – its echoing thunders had scarcely an interval of rest – its thick heavy rain forced its way through the canopying foliage, whilst the blue forked lightning seemed to fall and radiate at his very feet. Suddenly his horse took fright, and he was carried with dreadful rapidity through the entangled forest. The animal at last, through fatigue, stopped, and he found, by the glare of lightning, that he was in the neighbourhood of a hovel that hardly lifted itself up from the masses of dead leaves and brushwood which surrounded it. Dismounting, he approached, hoping to find some one to guide him to the town, or at least trusting to obtain shelter from the pelting of the storm. As he approached, the thunders, for a moment silent, allowed him to hear the dreadful shrieks of a woman mingling with the stifled, exultant mockery of a laugh, continued in one almost unbroken sound; – he was startled: but, roused by the thunder which again rolled over his head, he with a sudden effort forced open the door of the hut. He found himself in utter darkness; the sound, however, guided him. He was apparently unperceived; for, though he called, still the sounds continued, and no notice was taken of him. He found himself in contact with some one, whom he immediately seized, when a voice cried, 'Again baffled!' to which a loud laugh succeeded, and he felt himself grappled by one whose strength seemed superhuman: determined to sell his life as dearly as he could, he struggled; but it was in vain: he was lifted from his feet and hurled with enormous force against the ground: – his enemy threw himself upon him, and kneeling upon his breast, had placed his hands upon his throat when the glare of many torches penetrating through the hole that gave light in the day, disturbed him – he instantly rose, and, leaving his prey, rushed through the door, and in a moment the crashing of the branches, as he broke through the wood, was no longer heard. – The storm was now still; and Aubrey, incapable of moving, was soon heard by those without. – They entered; the light of their torches fell upon the mud walls, and the thatch loaded on every individual straw with heavy flakes of soot. At the desire of Aubrey they searched for her who had attracted him by her cries; he was again left in darkness; but what was his horror, when the light of the torches once more burst upon him, to perceive the airy form of his fair conductress brought in a lifeless corse. He shut his eyes, hoping that it was but a vision arising from his disturbed imagination; but he again saw the same form, when he unclosed them, stretched by his side. There was no colour upon her cheek, not even upon her lip; yet there was a stillness about her face that seemed almost as attaching as the life that once dwelt there: – upon her neck and breast was blood, and upon her throat were the marks of teeth having opened the vein: – to this the men pointed, crying, simultaneously struck with horror, 'A Vampyre a Vampyre!' A litter was quickly formed, and Aubrey was laid by the side of her who had lately been to him the object of so many bright and fairy visions, now fallen with the flower of life that had died within her. He knew not what his thoughts were – his mind was benumbed and seemed to shun reflection, and take refuge in vacancy – he held almost unconsciously in his hand a naked dagger of a particular construction, which had been found in the hut. They were soon met by different parties who had been engaged in the search of her whom a mother had missed. Their lamentable cries, as they approached the city, forewarned the parents of some dreadful catastrophe. – To describe their grief would be impossible; but when they ascertained the cause of their child's death, they looked at Aubrey, and pointed to the corse. They were inconsolable; both died broken-hearted.

Aubrey being put to bed was seized with a most violent fever, and was often delirious; in these intervals he would call upon Lord Ruthven and upon Ianthe – by some unaccountable combination he seemed to beg of his former companion to spare the being he loved. – At other times he would imprecate maledictions upon his head, and curse him as her destroyer. Lord Ruthven chanced at this time to arrive at Athens, and, from whatever motive, upon hearing of the state of Aubrey, immediately placed himself in the same house, and became his constant attendant. When the latter recovered from his delirium, he was horrified and startled at the sight of him whose image he had now combined with that of a Vampyre; but Lord Ruthven by his kind words, implying almost repentance for the fault that had caused their separation, and still more by the attention, anxiety, and care which he showed, soon reconciled him to his presence. His Lordship seemed quite changed; he no longer appeared that apathetic being who had so astonished Aubrey; but as soon as his convalescence began to be rapid, he again gradually retired into the same state of mind, and Aubrey perceived no difference from the former man, except, that at times he was surprised to meet his gaze fixed intently upon him, with a smile of malicious exultation playing upon his lips; he knew not why, but this smile haunted him. During the last stage of the invalid's recovery, Lord Ruthven was apparently engaged in watching the tideless waves raised by the cooling breeze, or in marking the progress of those orbs, circling, like our world, the moveless sun; – indeed he appeared to wish to avoid the eyes of all.

Aubrey's mind, by this shock, was much weakened, and that elasticity of spirit which had once so distinguished him now seemed to have fled for ever. – He was now as much a lover of solitude and silence as Lord Ruthven; but much as he wished for solitude, his mind could not find it in the neighbourhood of Athens; if he sought it amidst the ruins he had formerly frequented, Ianthe's form stood by his side – if he sought it in the woods, her light step would appear wandering amidst the underwood, in quest of the modest violet; then suddenly turning round, would show, to his wild imagination, her pale face and wounded throat with a meek smile upon her lips. He determined to fly scenes, every feature of which created such bitter associations in his mind. He proposed to Lord Ruthven, to whom he held himself bound by the tender care he had taken of him during his illness, that they should visit those parts of Greece neither had yet seen. They travelled in every direction, and sought every spot to which a recollection could be attached; but though they thus hastened from place to place yet they seemed not to heed what they gazed upon. – They heard much of robbers, but they gradually began to slight these reports, which they imagined were only the invention of individuals, whose interest it was to excite the generosity of those whom they defended from pretended dangers. In consequence of thus neglecting the advice of the inhabitants, on one occasion they travelled with only a few guards, more to serve as guides than as a defence. – Upon entering, however, a narrow defile,[5] at the bottom of which was the bed of a torrent, with large masses of rock brought down from the neighbouring precipices, they had reason to repent their negligence – for scarcely were the whole of the party engaged in the narrow pass, when they were startled by the whistling of bullets close to their heads, and by the echoed report of several guns. In an instant their guards had left them, and placing themselves behind rocks, had begun to fire in the direction whence the report came. Lord Ruthven and Aubrey, imitating their example, retired for a moment behind the sheltering turn of the defile; but ashamed of being thus detained by a foe, who with insulting shouts bade them advance, and being exposed to unresisting slaughter, if any of the robbers should climb above and take them in the rear, they determined at once to rush forward in search of the enemy. – Hardly had they lost the shelter of the rock, when Lord Ruthven received a shot in the shoulder, which brought him to the ground. – Aubrey hastened to his assistance and no longer heeding the contest or his own peril, was soon surprised by seeing the robbers' faces around him – his guards having, upon Lord Ruthven's being wounded, immediately thrown up their arms and surrendered.

By promises of great reward, Aubrey soon induced them to convey his wounded friend to a neighbouring cabin and having agreed upon a ransom he was no more disturbed by their presence, they being content merely to guard the entrance till their comrade should return with the promised sum for which he had an order. – Lord Ruthven's strength rapidly decreased, in two days mortification ensued, and death seemed advancing with hasty steps. – His conduct and appearance had not changed; he seemed as unconscious of pain as he had been of the objects about him; but towards the close of the last evening, his mind became apparently uneasy, and his eye often fixed upon Aubrey, who was induced to offer his assistance with more than usual earnestness – 'Assist me! you may save me – you may do more than that – I mean not my life, I heed the death of my existence as little as that of the passing day; but you may save my honour, your friend's honour.' – 'How, tell me how? I would do any thing,' replied Aubrey. – 'I need but little – my life ebbs apace – I cannot explain the whole – but if you would conceal all you know of me, my honour were free from stain in the world's mouth – and if my death were unknown for some time in England – I – I – but life.' – 'It shall not be known.' – 'Swear!' cried the dying man, raising himself with exultant violence, 'Swear by all your soul reveres, by all your nature fears, swear that for a year and a day you will not impart your knowledge of my crimes or death to any living being in any way, whatever may happen, or whatever you may see.' – His eyes seemed bursting from their sockets; 'I swear!' said Aubrey; he sunk laughing upon his pillow, and breathed no more.

Aubrey retired to rest, but did not sleep; the many circumstances attending his acquaintance with this man rose upon his mind, and he knew not why; when he remembered his oath a cold shivering came over him, as if from the presentiment of something horrible awaiting him. Rising early in the morning he was about to enter the hovel in which he had left the corpse, when a robber met him, and informed him that it was no longer there, having been conveyed by himself and comrades, upon his retiring, to the pinnacle of a neighbouring mount, according to a promise they had given his lordship, that it should be exposed to the first cold ray of the moon that rose after his death. Aubrey astonished, and taking several of the men, determined to go and bury it upon the spot where it lay. But, when he had mounted to the summit he found no trace of either the corpse or the clothes, though the robbers swore they pointed out the identical rock on which they had laid the body. For a time his mind was bewildered in conjectures, but he at last returned, convinced that they had buried the corpse for the sake of the clothes.

Weary of a country in which he had met with such terrible misfortunes, and in which all apparently conspired to heighten that superstitious melancholy that had seized upon his mind, he resolved to leave it, and soon arrived at Smyrna. While waiting for a vessel to convey him to Otranto, or to Naples, he occupied himself in arranging those effects he had with him belonging to Lord Ruthven. Amongst other things there was a case containing several weapons of offence, more or less adapted to ensure the death of the victim. There were several daggers and *ataghans*.[6] Whilst turning them over, and examining their curious forms, what was his surprise at finding a sheath apparently ornamented in the same style as the dagger discovered in the fatal hut; he shuddered; hastening to gain further proof, he found the weapon, and his horror may be imagined when he discovered that it fitted, though peculiarly shaped, the sheath he held in his hand.

His eyes seemed to need no further certainty – they seemed gazing to be bound to the dagger; yet still he wished to disbelieve; but the particular form, the same varying tints upon the haft and sheath were alike in splendour on both, and left no room for doubt; there were also drops of blood on each.

He left Smyrna, and on his way home, at Rome, his first inquiries were concerning the lady he had attempted to snatch from Lord Ruthven's seductive arts. Her parents were in distress, their fortune ruined, and she had not been heard of since the departure of his lordship. Aubrey's mind became almost broken under so many repeated horrors; he was afraid that this lady had fallen a victim to the destroyer of Ianthe. He became morose and silent and his only occupation consisted in urging the speed of the postilions, as if he were going to save the life of some one he held dear. He arrived at Calais; a breeze, which seemed obedient to his will, soon wafted him to the English shores; and he hastened to the mansion of his fathers, and there, for a moment, appeared to lose, in the embraces and caresses of his sister, all memory of the past. If she before, by her infantine caresses, had gained his affection, now that the woman began to appear, she was still more attaching as a companion.

Miss Aubrey had not that winning grace which gains the gaze and applause of the drawing-room assemblies. There was none of that light brilliancy which only exists in the heated atmosphere of a crowded apartment. Her blue eye was never lit up by the levity of the mind beneath. There was a melancholy charm about it which did not seem to arise from misfortune, but from some feeling within, that appeared to indicate a soul conscious of a brighter realm. Her step was not that light footing, which strays where'er a butterfly or a colour may attract – it was sedate and pensive. When alone, her face was never brightened by the smile of joy; but when her brother breathed to her his affection, and would in her presence forget those griefs she knew destroyed his rest, who would have exchanged her smile for that of the voluptuary? It seemed as if those eyes – that face were then playing in the light of their own native sphere. She was yet only eighteen, and had not been presented to the world; it having been thought by her guardians more fit that her presentation should be delayed

until her brother's return from the continent, when he might be
her protector. It was now, therefore, resolved that the next
drawing-room, which was fast approaching, should be the epoch
of her entry into the 'busy scene'. Aubrey would rather have
remained in the mansion of his fathers, and fed upon the melancholy which overpowered him. He could not feel interest about
the frivolities of fashionable strangers, when his mind had been so
torn by the events he had witnessed; but he determined to sacrifice
his own comfort to the protection of his sister. They soon arrived
in town, and prepared for the next day, which had been announced as a drawing-room.

The crowd was excessive – a drawing-room had not been held
for a long time, and all who were anxious to bask in the smile of
royalty, hastened thither. Aubrey was there with his sister. While
he was standing in a corner by himself, heedless of all around
him, engaged in the remembrance that the first time he had seen
Lord Ruthven was in that very place – he felt himself suddenly
seized by the arm, and a voice he recognized too well, sounded in
his ear – 'Remember your oath.' He had hardly courage to turn,
fearful of seeing a spectre that would blast him, when he perceived, at a little distance, the same figure which had attracted
his notice on this spot upon his first entry into society. He gazed
till his limbs almost refusing to bear their weight, he was obliged
to take the arm of a friend, and forcing a passage through the
crowd, he threw himself into his carriage, and was driven home.
He paced the room with hurried steps, and fixed his hands upon
his head, as if he were afraid his thoughts were bursting from his
brain. Lord Ruthven again before him – circumstances started
up in dreadful array – the dagger – his oath. – He roused himself,
he could not believe it possible – the dead rise again! – He
thought his imagination had conjured up the image his mind was
resting upon. It was impossible that it could be real – he determined, therefore, to go again into society; for though he attempted to ask concerning Lord Ruthven, the name hung upon
his lips, and he could not succeed in gaining information. He
went a few nights after with his sister to the assembly of a near
relation. Leaving her under the protection of a matron, he retired
into a recess, and there gave himself up to his own devouring

thoughts. Perceiving, at last, that many were leaving, he roused himself, and entering another room, found his sister surrounded by several, apparently in earnest conversation; he attempted to pass and get near her, when one, whom he requested to move, turned round, and revealed to him those features he most abhorred. He sprang forward, seized his sister's arm, and, with hurried step, forced her towards the street: at the door he found himself impeded by the crowd of servants who were waiting for their lords; and while he was engaged in passing them, he again heard that voice whisper close to him – 'Remember your oath!' – He did not dare to turn, but, hurrying his sister, soon reached home.

Aubrey became almost distracted. If before his mind had been absorbed by one subject, how much more completely was it engrossed, now that the certainty of the monster's living again pressed upon his thoughts. His sister's attentions were now unheeded, and it was in vain that she intreated him to explain to her what had caused his abrupt conduct. He only uttered a few words, and those terrified her. The more he thought, the more he was bewildered. His oath startled him; – was he then to allow this monster to roam, bearing ruin upon his breath, amidst all he held dear, and not avert its progress? His very sister might have been touched by him. But even if he were to break his oath, and disclose his suspicions, who would believe him? He thought of employing his own hand to free the world from such a wretch; but death, he remembered, had been already mocked. For days he remained in this state; shut up in his room, he saw no one, and ate only when his sister came, who, with eyes streaming with tears, besought him, for her sake, to support nature. At last, no longer capable of bearing stillness and solitude, he left his house, roamed from street to street, anxious to fly that image which haunted him. His dress became neglected, and he wandered, as often exposed to the noon-day sun as to the midnight damps. He was no longer to be recognized; at first he returned with the evening to the house; but at last he laid him down to rest wherever fatigue overtook him. His sister, anxious for his safety, employed people to follow him; but they were soon distanced by him who fled from a pursuer swifter than any – from thought. His conduct, however, suddenly changed. Struck with the idea that he left by his absence the whole of his friends, with a fiend amongst them, of whose presence they were unconscious, he determined to enter again into society, and watch him closely, anxious to forewarn, in spite of his oath, all whom Lord Ruthven approached with intimacy. But when he entered into a room, his haggard and suspicious looks were so striking, his inward shudderings so visible, that his sister was at last obliged to beg of him to abstain from seeking, for her sake, a society which affected him so strongly. When, however, remonstrance proved unavailing, the guardians thought proper to interpose, and, fearing that his mind was becoming alienated, they thought it high time to resume again that trust which had been before imposed upon them by Aubrey's parents.

Desirous of saving him from the injuries and sufferings he had daily encountered in his wanderings, and of preventing him from exposing to the general eye those marks of what they considered folly, they engaged a physician to reside in the house, and take constant care of him. He hardly appeared to notice it, so completely was his mind absorbed by one terrible subject. His incoherence became at last so great, that he was confined to his chamber. There he would often lie for days, incapable of being roused. He had become emaciated, his eyes had attained a glassy lustre; – the only sign of affection and recollection remaining displayed itself upon the entry of his sister: then he would sometimes start, and, seizing her hands, with looks that severely afflicted her, he would desire her not to touch him. 'Oh, do not touch him – if your love for me is aught, do not go near him!' When, however, she inquired to whom he referred, his only answer was, 'True! true!' and again he sank into a state, whence not even she could rouse him. This lasted many months: gradually, however, as the year was passing, his incoherences became less frequent, and his mind threw off a portion of its gloom, whilst his guardians observed, that several times in the day he would count upon his fingers a definite number, and then smile.

The time had nearly elapsed, when, upon the last day of the year, one of his guardians entering his room, began to converse with his physician upon the melancholy circumstance of Aubrey's being in so awful a situation, when his sister was going next day to be married. Instantly Aubrey's attention was attracted; he asked anxiously to whom. Glad of this mark of returning intellect, of which they feared he had been deprived, they mentioned the name of the Earl of Marsden. Thinking this was a young Earl whom he had met with in society, Aubrey seemed pleased, and astonished them still more by his expressing his intention to be present at the nuptials, and desiring to see his sister. They answered not, but in a few minutes his sister was with him. He was apparently again capable of being affected by the influence of her lovely smile; for he pressed her to his breast, and kissed her cheek, wet with tears, flowing at the thought of her brother's being once more alive to the feelings of affection. He began to speak with all his wonted warmth, and to congratulate her upon her marriage with a person so distinguished for rank and every accomplishment; when he suddenly perceived a locket upon her breast; opening it, what was his surprise at beholding the features of the monster who had so long influenced his life. He seized the portrait in a paroxysm of rage, and trampled it under foot. Upon her asking him why he thus destroyed the resemblance of her future husband, he looked as if he did not understand her – then seizing her hands, and gazing on her with a frantic expression of countenance, he bade her swear that she would never wed this monster, for he – But he could not advance – it seemed as if that voice again bade him remember his oath – he turned suddenly round, thinking Lord Ruthven was near him but saw no one. In the meantime the guardians and physician, who had heard the whole, and thought this was but a return of his disorder, entered, and forcing him from Miss Aubrey, desired her to leave him. He fell upon his knees to them, he implored, he begged of them to delay but for one day. They, attributing this to the insanity they imagined had taken possession of his mind, endeavoured to pacify him, and retired.

Lord Ruthven had called the morning after the drawing-room, and had been refused with every one else. When he heard of Aubrey's ill health, he readily understood himself to be the cause of it; but when he learned that he was deemed insane, his exultation and pleasure could hardly be concealed from those among whom he had gained this information. He hastened to the house of his former companion, and, by constant attendance, and the pretence of great affection for the brother and interest in his fate, he gradually won the ear of Miss Aubrey. Who could resist his power? His tongue had dangers and toils to recount – could speak of himself as of an individual having no sympathy with any being on the crowded earth, save with her to whom he addressed himself; – could tell how, since he knew her, his existence had begun to seem worthy of preservation, if it were merely that he might listen to her soothing accents; – in fine, he knew so well how to use the serpent's art, or such was the will of fate, that he gained her affections. The title of the elder branch falling at length to him, he obtained an important embassy, which served as an excuse for hastening the marriage, (in spite of her brother's deranged state,) which was to take place the very day before his departure for the continent.

Aubrey, when he was left by the physician and his guardians, attempted to bribe the servants, but in vain. He asked for pen and paper; it was given him; he wrote a letter to his sister, conjuring her, as she valued her own happiness, her own honour, and the honour of those now in the grave, who once held her in their arms as their hope and the hope of their house, to delay but for a few hours that marriage, on which he denounced the most heavy curses. The servants promised they would deliver it; but giving it to the physician, he thought it better not to harass any more the mind of Miss Aubrey by, what he considered, the ravings of a maniac. Night passed on without rest to the busy inmates of the house; and Aubrey heard, with a horror that may more easily be conceived than described, the notes of busy preparation. Morning came, and the sound of carriages broke upon his ear. Aubrey grew almost frantic. The curiosity of the servants at last overcame their vigilance, they gradually stole away, leaving him in the custody of an helpless old woman. He seized the opportunity, with one bound was out of the room, and in a moment found himself in the apartment where all were nearly assembled. Lord Ruthven was the first to perceive him: he immediately approached, and, taking his arm by force, hurried him from the room, speechless with rage. When on the staircase, Lord Ruthven whispered in his ear – 'Remember your oath, and know, if not my bride to day, your sister is dishonoured. Women are frail!' So saying, he pushed him towards his attendants, who roused by the old woman, had come in search of him. Aubrey could no longer support himself; his rage not finding vent, had broken a blood-vessel, and he was conveyed to bed. This was not mentioned to his sister, who was not present when he entered, as the physician was afraid of agitating her. The marriage was solemnized, and the bride and bridegroom left London.

Aubrey's weakness increased; the effusion of blood produced symptoms of the near approach of death. He desired his sister's guardians might be called, and when the midnight hour had struck, he related composedly what the reader has perused – he died immediately after.

The guardians hastened to protect Miss Aubrey; but when they arrived, it was too late. Lord Ruthven had disappeared, and Aubrey's sister had glutted the thirst of a VAMPYRE!

THE END

NOTES

1 (p. 5). *two persons of distinguished literary celebrity*: Mary Wollstonecraft and William Godwin.

2 (p. 6). *eyry*: or, aery, aerie, eyrie: the nest of any bird of prey,
especially of an eagle, which builds high in the air; here used
figuratively to convey the sense of a high-perched human retreat.

3 (p. 7). *the Capulets*: the family of Juliet in Shakespeare's *Romeo
and Juliet*.

4 (p. 8). *to speak in Sanchean phrase*: i.e. as Sancho Panza speaks
in Cervantes' *Don Quixote*: 'in this matter of government every-
thing depends upon the beginning ...' (Book II, xxxiii).
Mary and Percy Shelley were both reading *Don Quixote* during
1816.

5 (p. 8). *the story of Columbus and his egg*: a famous story, related
in Washington Irving's *Christopher Columbus* (1828). When told
by a courtier that others beside himself had the ability to
discover the Indies, he challenged those around him to stand
an egg on one of its ends: 'Everyone attempted it, but in vain;
whereupon he struck it upon the table so as to break the end,
and left it standing on the broken part; illustrating in this
simple manner, that when he had once shown the way to the
New World, nothing was easier than to follow it.'

6 (p. 8). *Dr Darwin*: Erasmus Darwin (1731–1802), physician,
poet and free-thinking radical. By his first wife he was grand-
father of Charles Darwin, discoverer of 'natural selection', and
by his second of Francis Galton, the famous explorer, scientist
and psychologist. Percy Shelley was a great admirer of the
poet–doctor, who embodied his own theory of evolution into the
epic poem *The Temple of Nature* (1803). The following (Canto
IV, ll. 397–402) is very suggestive as one of the possible sources
for *Frankenstein*:

> While Nature sinks in Time's destructive Storms,
> The Wrecks of Death are but a change of forms;
> Emerging matter from the grave returns,
> Feels new desires, with new sensations burns;
> With youth's first bloom a finer sense acquires,
> And Loves and Pleasures fan the rising fires.

7 (p. 8). *galvanism*: after Luigi Galvani (1737–98), the Italian physiologist and experimenter whose experiments with frogs led him to believe that an 'animal electricity' resided in the nerves and muscles of animals. Observing that the convulsions of a frog placed in a circuit containing a piece of metal were accompanied by motions in its nerve juices, he assumed the convulsions to be the work of a subtle but vital electrical fluid 'animating' the animal's enclosed nerves and muscle fibres. His notion that this fluid was analogous to ordinary electricity may have inspired Mary Shelley's idea that 'perhaps a corpse would be reanimated', no doubt through the agency of an enormous voltaic electricity-producing Galvanic battery (the 'powerful engine' mentioned in her Introduction).

8 (p. 18). *keeping*: 'The maintenance of the proper relation between the representations of nearer and more distant objects in a picture; hence the maintenance of harmony of composition.' (SOED)

9 (p. 24). *ground sea*: 'a heavy sea in which large waves rise and dash upon the coast without apparent cause'. (OED)

10 (p. 31). *syndics*: government magistrates of Geneva.

11 (p. 34). *schiavi ognor frementi*: in context, the phrase refers to the 'trembling' of the Italian population while under Austrian rule during the eighteenth and nineteenth centuries.

12 (p. 36). *campagne*: a country cottage or house.

13 (p. 36). *a league*: 'An itinerary measure of distance, varying in different countries, but usually estimated at about three miles.' (SOED) In English use the word was often employed poetically or rhetorically, but the application here is fairly accurate.

14 (p. 37). *temperature*: temperament.

15 (p. 38). *Natural philosophy*: the old term for physical science, especially physics.

16 (p. 38). *Cornelius Agrippa*: magician and cabbalist (1486–1535).

17 (p. 39). *Paracelsus and Albertus Magnus*: Paracelsus (1493–1541), real name Theophrastus Bombastus von Hohenheim, a Swiss alchemist and physician who pioneered the treatment of certain diseases based on empirical observation; he also stated that human beings could be produced without mother and father by alchemical procedures. Albertus Magnus (1193–1280), Dominican theologian and Aristotelian teacher of St Thomas Aquinas who thought magic essential to the pursuit of knowledge. As a natural scientist he studied plant life and the human brain; the making of a brazen head that could answer questions, probably some kind of automaton, has been ascribed to him.

18 (p. 44). *'old familiar faces'*: a reference to Charles Lamb's poem 'The Old Familiar Faces' (1798), which begins, 'Where are they gone, the old familiar faces?'

19 (p. 51). *I was like the Arabian who had been buried with the dead*: from *The Thousand and One Nights*; Sinbad the Sailor's Fourth Voyage.

20 (p. 59). *the Dutch schoolmaster in 'The Vicar of Wakefield'*: the passage continues: '"and, in short," continued he, "as I don't know Greek, I do not believe there is any good in it"' (Oliver Goldsmith, *The Vicar of Wakefield*, Chapter 20).

21 (p. 63). *the beauty of Angelica*: heroine of Ariosto's *Orlando Furioso* (1516).

22 (p. 72). *'the palaces of nature'*: from Byron's *Childe Harold's Pilgrimage*, Canto III, lxii.

23 (p. 77). *presumption*: Richard Brinsley Peake's *Presumption; or The Fate of Frankenstein* was the first stage melodrama based on Mary Shelley's story. She saw the Peake production at the Royal Opera House in 1823.

24 (p. 90). *brake*: an area of dense undergrowth, a thicket.

25 (p. 91). *access*: a sudden attack or outburst, of illness, rage, etc.

26 (p. 92). *aiguilles*: peaks.

27 (p. 94). *necessary beings*: William Godwin's Doctrine of Necessity maintained that 'In the life of every human being there is

a chain of events, generated in the lapse of ages which preceded his birth, and going on in regular procession through the whole period of his existence, in consequence of which it was impossible for him to act in any instance otherwise than he has acted' (*Enquiry Concerning Political Justice*, Book IV, Chapter VIII).

28 (p. 95). *We rest ... mutability*: last part of P. B. Shelley's 'Mutability' (1816).

29 (p. 102). *as Pandaemonium appeared to the daemons of hell*: cf. Milton, *Paradise Lost* I, ll. 670 ff.

30 (p. 110). *discover myself*: here meaning 'reveal myself'.

31 (p. 112). *the ass and the lap-dog*: from La Fontaine's 'L'Âne et le petit chien', in *Fables* IV, 5. When the ass sees the lap-dog's master petting it as a reward for its friendly fawning, it tries the same thing, but gets beaten for its pains.

32 (p. 115). *Volney's 'Ruins of Empires'*: the Comte de Volney's *Les Ruines, ou Méditations sur les révolutions des empires* (1791) was a popular essay in the philosophy of history that impressed both Mary and Percy Shelley.

33 (p. 124). *'Paradise Lost', a volume of Plutarch's 'Lives', and the 'Sorrows of Werter'*: John Milton's *Paradise Lost* (1667 and 1674), Plutarch's *Parallel Lives* (c. AD 100) and Johann von Goethe's *Sorrows of Young Werther* (1774) are considered by Yale scholar Peter Brooks to 'constitute a possible Romantic *cyclopedia universalis*'.

34 (p. 125). *'The path of my departure was free'*: cf. l. 14 in P. B. Shelley's 'Mutability': 'The path of its departure still is free.'

35 (p. 144). *siroc*: or sirocco, a hot, oppressive wind blowing from North Africa across the Mediterranean to parts of southern Europe.

36 (p. 151). *'very poetry of nature'*: from Leigh Hunt's *The Story of Rimini* (1816).

37 (p. 155). *the amiable Falkland, the insolent Goring*: *Falkland*: Lucius Cary, second Viscount Falkland (1610?–43). A humanist and scholar who served as Secretary of State to Charles I in the last two years of his life. 'His claim to our reverence lies in the fact that his mind was as thoroughly saturated as Milton's was with the love of freedom as the nurse of high thought and

high morality, while his gentle nature made him incapable of the harsh austerities of Milton's combative career.' (*Dictionary of National Biography*) The character of Falkland in William Godwin's *Caleb Williams* is partly modelled on Lucius Cary.

Goring: Lord George Goring (1608–57). Astute courtier and general who initially alternated his support between King and Parliament in the Civil War before siding with the Cavaliers. 'The disputes between King and Parliament afforded an opportunity which he resolved to use for his own advancement . . . of all his qualifications dissimulation was his masterpiece.' (Clarendon's *History of the Rebellion*, VIII, p. 169)

38 (p. 155). *the illustrious Hampden*: John Hampden (1594–1643). English statesman and prominent amongst the leaders of the Parliamentary opposition to Charles I.

39 (p. 176). *maladie du pays*: homesickness.

40 (p. 177). *laudanum*: New Latin name chosen by Paracelsus for a costly medicament in which opium was the active ingredient: the soothing preparation Frankenstein uses is the simple alcoholic tincture of opium.

41 (p. 202). *manes*: shades or spirits of the dead.

42 (p. 212). *Evil thenceforth became my good*: cf. Milton, *Paradise Lost* 4, l. 110, 'Evil be thou my good.'

'A FRAGMENT'

1 (p. 229). *hectic*: 'that kind of fever which accompanies consumption or other wasting diseases, and is attended with flushed cheeks and a hot dry skin.' (SOED)

2 (p. 229). *a* serrugee *and a single* janizary*: serrugee*: or, sometimes, *suridgee*: Turkish word for a man who looks after the pack-horses.

janizary: a Turkish infantryman of the Sultan's personal guard, established in the fourteenth century, and disbanded in 1826.

3 (p. 229). *caravansera*: 'A kind of inn in the East where caravans put up, being a large quadrangular building enclosing a spacious court.' (SOED)

4 (p. 232). *ataghan*: or *yataghan*: a Turkish sword with a curved, single-edged blade.

THE VAMPYRE

1 (p. 235). *ton*: fashionable world.

2 (p. 236). *drawing-rooms*: originally, a drawing-room was a room to withdraw to; here it refers to a 'reception at which ladies are presented at court' (SOED), a mixed assembly where royalty, aristocracy and the *beau monde* can display themselves to each other, intrigue, and exchange polite gossip.

3 (p. 236). *mountebank*: a clownish charlatan or fake.

4 (p. 238). *faro*: 'a gambling game at cards, in which the players bet on the order in which certain cards will appear when taken singly from the top of the pack'. (SOED)

5 (p. 246). *defile*: military term for 'a narrow way along which troops can march only by files or with a narrow front; a narrow mountain gorge or pass': (SOED)

6 (p. 248). See note 4, p. 260.

READ MORE IN PENGUIN

In every corner of the world, on every subject under the sun, Penguin represents quality and variety – the very best in publishing today.

For complete information about books available from Penguin – including Puffins, Penguin Classics and Arkana – and how to order them, write to us at the appropriate address below. Please note that for copyright reasons the selection of books varies from country to country.

In the United Kingdom: Please write to *Dept. EP, Penguin Books Ltd, Bath Road, Harmondsworth, West Drayton, Middlesex UB7 0DA*

In the United States: Please write to *Consumer Sales, Penguin Putnam Inc., P.O. Box 12289 Dept. B, Newark, New Jersey 07101-5289.* VISA and MasterCard holders call 1-800-788-6262 to order Penguin titles

In Canada: Please write to *Penguin Books Canada Ltd, 10 Alcorn Avenue, Suite 300, Toronto, Ontario M4V 3B2*

In Australia: Please write to *Penguin Books Australia Ltd, P.O. Box 257, Ringwood, Victoria 3134*

In New Zealand: Please write to *Penguin Books (NZ) Ltd, Private Bag 102902, North Shore Mail Centre, Auckland 10*

In India: Please write to *Penguin Books India Pvt Ltd, 11 Community Centre, Panchsheel Park, New Delhi 110017*

In the Netherlands: Please write to *Penguin Books Netherlands bv, Postbus 3507, NL-1001 AH Amsterdam*

In Germany: Please write to *Penguin Books Deutschland GmbH, Metzlerstrasse 26, 60594 Frankfurt am Main*

In Spain: Please write to *Penguin Books S. A., Bravo Murillo 19, 1° B, 28015 Madrid*

In Italy: Please write to *Penguin Italia s.r.l., Via Benedetto Croce 2, 20094 Corsico, Milano*

In France: Please write to *Penguin France, Le Carré Wilson, 62 rue Benjamin Baillaud, 31500 Toulouse*

In Japan: Please write to *Penguin Books Japan Ltd, Kaneko Building, 2-3-25 Koraku, Bunkyo-Ku, Tokyo 112*

In South Africa: Please write to *Penguin Books South Africa (Pty) Ltd, Private Bag X14, Parkview, 2122 Johannesburg*

BY THE SAME AUTHOR

Mary Wollstonecraft: **Mary** *and* **Maria**
Mary Shelley: **Matilda**

Edited with an Introduction by Janet Todd

This book brings together three extraordinary novels by an extra-ordinary pair, Mary Wollstonecraft, radical feminist and author of *A Vindication of the Rights of Woman*, and Mary Shelley, her daughter, author of *Frankenstein*.

Mary Shelley wrote *Matilda* in 1819, while in mourning for her first son. William Godwin, her father, found its subject of father–daughter incest so 'disgusting and detestable' that he refused to publish it and the work remained suppressed for over a century.

In her illuminating introduction to this edition Janet Todd explores how these novels are linked, not only through the mother–daughter relationship of their authors, but in their perceptions of feminism and female sexuality and in their autobiographical richness.

Frankenstein by Mary Shelley is also available as a Penguin Audio-book, read by Richard Pasco.